Saving Amy

by Nicola Haken

Saving Amy

Copyright © 2013 Nicola Wall

This book is a work of fiction. All names, characters, events and places are created from the author's imagination or are used fictitiously. Any resemblance to actual events or people, living or dead, is entirely coincidental.

All rights reserved. No part of this book may be reproduced without written permission from the author, except in the case of critics or reviewers who may quote brief passages in their review.

ISBN-13: 978-1490911915

ISBN-10: 149091191X

Dedicated to Michael. He knows why.
xxx

Contents

Chapter One	1
Chapter Two	25
Chapter Three	47
Chapter Four	70
Chapter Five	94
Chapter Six	113
Chapter Seven	128
Chapter Eight	143
Chapter Nine	167
Chapter Ten	189
Chapter Eleven	210
Chapter Twelve	231
Chapter Thirteen	248
Chapter Fourteen	271

Chapter Fifteen	288
Chapter Sixteen	302
Chapter Seventeen	323
Chapter Eighteen	336
Chapter Nineteen	354
Chapter Twenty	373
Chapter Twenty-One	391
Chapter Twenty-Two	409
Epilogue	434
Acknowledgements	443
About The Author	445

Chapter One

I was awoken by the silence. The lack of raised voices told me it must be morning and my dad must have left for work. He is a lawyer for one of Seattle's most prestigious law firms so that means to the outside world he is an upstanding, respected member of the community.

I know different.

Grudgingly, I swung my legs out of bed and headed to the window. I twisted the cord for the purple blackout blind and let the beams of early morning sunlight flood the room, startling my eyes. Then I glanced towards the small, black travel alarm on my nightstand and realized I was late. *Shit.* I had thirty minutes before homeroom and Mrs. Clarke had already threatened to call my parents if I turned in late again. *Good luck with that*, I remember thinking.

Thankfully there is only four months left until graduation and then I'll never have to lay eyes on her sour face again.

After stepping out of the shower and running a towel over my damp body I quickly threw on the first clothes I came to – some black boot-cut pants and a cream vest top – before inhaling a deep, preparing breath at the top of the stairs, wondering what state I would find my mom in today.

I found her wallowing in the kitchen, slumped over the round pine table and staring unseeingly into her mug. At first glance it looked like regular black coffee but I could smell the gin from across the room. As usual I threw a brief 'morning' her way and also as usual she didn't bother to look up. It was when I grabbed my satchel off the back of the kitchen door she flipped her unruly black hair from her face, revealing a fresh, marbled bruise on her jaw. Rightly or wrongly, this was such a frequent occurrence I classed it as the norm. She took another sip of her gin disguised as coffee and I grabbed my black jacket from the back of her chair and left without looking back.

The school parking lot was bursting at the seams and I circled it for nearly ten minutes before giving up and parking at the tire shop across the way. After a quick will-I-do glance in my visor mirror I noticed I still had a faint scar-like indentation down my right cheek from falling asleep on Love Conquers All – a soppy (sickeningly so) book about a girl called Penny whose life only seemed worth living when she was with Neil. He was just a regular guy but the way she droned on about him you'd think he was some kind of superhero.

Still, I have this thing about books – a disease almost – that won't let me give up until I've read to the end. Plus, you never know – Penny might grow herself a set of balls along the way.

My ears pricked up at the low hum of the homeroom bell across the street so I threw my satchel over my shoulder and ran towards the noise. My feet finally skidded to a halt as I reached classroom A1 and I breathed an exhausted sigh of relief when I noticed Mrs. Clarke wasn't at her desk yet. My best friend Julie waved me over to our table and I hurriedly scuttled in beside her. Julie is stunning; petite, brunette, electric-blue eyes and the kind of body that belongs on a hot beach somewhere – my completely opposite. Don't get me wrong I'm no howler – just a 'pass in a crowd' type.

We met in sixth grade. Julie was the new girl – just moved here from West Virginia. People didn't exactly flock to be her friend. She might be beautiful now but back then she was the spotty kid with out of control hair and braces on her teeth. Kids are cruel and I guess I pitied her so I let her latch onto me. It was kind of refreshing to feel sorry for someone other than myself.

It was the other way round now of course. Julie has made a ton of friends along the way but she still sticks by me. Whether that's out of pity, gratitude or genuine friendship I'm not really sure.

"Jeez, Amy you're cutting it fine," Julie said, stating the damn obvious.

"She been in yet?" I asked, pointing towards the empty teacher's desk.

"Nope. Think you got away with it this time." In that exact moment Mrs. Clarke appeared in the doorway, her stern, wrinkle-framed eyes boring into mine.

"Just in time, Amelia," she stated, her dull eyes bursting with warning.

Damn.

I looked down to my desk and rolled my eyes when she turned away. After a run through of everyone's names the second bell rang and the sound of thirty screeching chairs pulling out from under their desks deafened my ears.

"Ugh, Biology," Julie muttered as she remembered our first class of the day.

"Screw it. I'm getting out of here," I replied defiantly, unwilling to spend yet another day being told what to do by the usual mix of patronizing teachers on a power trip or the interfering ones who pretend to care.

"You want company?" Julie winked. I nodded eagerly and we hurried towards my car (Julie takes the bus to school) knowing the swarm of other students making their way to class would conceal our getaway.

After yanking the passenger door open on my rusty, red Ford Fiesta I dashed round to my side to do the same. My car is possibly older than me. The driver door is a more faded shade of a red than the rest, the bumper clings for dear life by the license plate screws and there is a huge dent spanning the entire width of the trunk at the back. But I love it nonetheless. I spent a whole year working every hour the weekend sent washing cars for a guy called Fat Phil at his second-hand dealership last summer. My car was there when I started right through to the day I drove it away as my own.

It was like we were destined to be together.

Julie giggled as I hit the ignition – amused at yet another unseen escape. I had no laughter in me today so I pretended I hadn't heard her, grabbed two cigarettes from the stash under my seat, lit one for Julie then one for me and headed straight for the highway.

Saving Amy

I pulled up ten minutes later at Lake View Cemetery – our usual ditching hideout. It's quiet and peaceful and we can talk for hours on the benches beneath the trees without being disturbed. We walked through the maze of moss covered gravestones and flowers, and for a moment I found myself admiring the earth, unable to suppress the pang of jealousy I felt towards the bodies underneath.

How peaceful they must be…

We settled down on the familiar wooden bench, under the shade of the vast green canopy of trees and grabbed two more cigarettes. I slumped myself backwards as I looked out onto the shimmering lake that was rippling softly in the spring breeze, the wooden slats boring into my back as I welcomed the calming nicotine into my lungs.

"Another bad night?" Julie asked, noticing my subdued disposition.

"Yeah. You know, the usual – shouting, cups throwing…" I replied, not wanting to go into too much detail and relive it all over again.

Julie knows my mom drinks too much, my dad has a short fuse and they argue relentlessly but she has no idea just how bad things can get. Nobody does; I wouldn't want them to. I don't exactly have the kind of upbringing to be proud of. Besides, I'll be getting the hell out of there after graduation and then they can enjoy their fucked-up relationship in peace. I just need to work out how and where and I'm gone.

I doubt they'll even notice.

"It's been so long since I saw you smile. You can talk to me you know?" Here was me thinking I was putting on a good act.

"I know. I'm fine though… honest," I lied. I couldn't talk to Julie. I couldn't talk to anyone. I was too ashamed. If I was honest with myself, I was probably afraid too.

"I know just what you need," Julie said with a mischievous grin. "Romy's throwing a party tomorrow night; her parents have booked a last minute weekend away. Should have everything you need to put that spring back in your step. Cute guys, alcohol…" The one good thing about having parents who are too busy hating each other to care about me is that I don't have to ask for permission to go out – or stay out. I can come and go as I please.

Julie winked and breathed her childlike giggle again. It was infectious and my lips seemed to regain the ability to smile.

"Count me in. Text me the details later," I replied enthusiastically, welcoming the thought of a night out of earshot from the screaming match – even though I can't stand Romy. She is a typical cheerleader – blonde, immature and shamefully dumb. I'm pretty sure she doesn't like me either – not many people do. But that suits me just fine.

Glancing at my watch I noticed the time had flown straight into the afternoon and I needed to get Julie home before the school bus arrived. Unlike mine, her parents give a damn and insisted one of them drove her to and from school for a month last time she was caught skipping school.

We headed back to the car and once inside Julie doused herself in perfume from her purse to mask the smell of stale tobacco and I dropped her off at the bus stop near the end of her street before heading home myself. I huffed into my shoulder when I noticed my dad's car on the drive and then walked reluctantly down the concrete path.

I hate this house. I hate the white walls, the arched russet door, the overgrown lawn… they all lead inside. Animosity consumed me as I turned my key in the brass lock and my heart plummeted into the depths of my stomach when I saw my dad stood before me. He was dressed impeccably as usual - ever the professional in his grey, pinstripe suit with a crisp white shirt. His slick black hair was combed neatly to the side and his thick black moustache was groomed to perfection.

"And where the hell do you think you've been?" he yelled in my face. I shrugged my shoulders, unsure of the answer he wanted from me. "I've had some condescending teacher on the phone today, reading me the riot act about you skipping school. You think I need that while I'm at work?" I was stunned into silence. "Well DO YOU?" he roared, more force with each word.

His face was just inches from mine and the vile stench of Old Spice aftershave burned my nose, making my stomach churn. I shook my head at him and then my mom appeared from the kitchen door across the hall. She didn't intervene. She never does. She simply bowed her head, hiding her face with her greasy black hair while she listened to him yell at me.

"You fucking stink. Have you been smoking?" he shouted and I wanted to scream 'and what if I have?' but I couldn't seem to summon the courage for fear of where this was heading. Instead, I nodded once.

"Yes, sir," I muttered, fixing my eyes onto the marble floor. I'm forbidden from addressing him as 'Dad'. It took only a handful of slaps across the face to learn that. It's a power thing, I assume.

And then it came… a harsh, smarting slap to the side of my cheek – swinging my head to the side and making me stumble. *Enough!* A brave voice buried deep in my subconscious bellowed and suddenly I refused to be afraid of him any longer. I breathed a defiant laugh.

"Is that all you've got?" I goaded him, feeling bold and rebellious. His blue eyes widened and for a moment he was paralyzed with disbelief. Then I saw the veins in his neck begin to bulge under the pressure of blood rushing to his cheeks and I knew what was coming but for the first time I didn't care.

I watched as his hand clenched into a fist and transformed into a blur as he rammed it into my side with excessive speed, thrusting me into the wall. I slid to the floor against it and watched vacantly as his fist retracted and flew back again, then again… but I couldn't feel it. My eyes locked onto the bottom stair and I completely tuned out of my body. I couldn't feel anything. I couldn't hear anything. I could see hazes of movement in the corner of my eye but my mind was firmly focused on the plum carpet hugging the stairs.

"Don't ever talk to me like that again," he said sternly, forcing his boot into my thigh and snapping me back into consciousness.

I stared after him, feeling physically sick with revulsion as he retreated to the magnolia living room. My mom was still stood in the doorway and her eyes met mine for a brief second. Part of me wanted her to rush to my side and hold me, but the rational part of me knew she was too selfish to bother. I was proved right when she turned away and headed back into the kitchen – to pour another glass of gin no doubt.

I used to love her… I *think*. Or at least I used to believe she loved *me*. I was only a young girl – five, six maybe – when she first witnessed me scream as my dad jabbed his fist into my ribs and yet she did nothing to stop him. Too young to know any better, children love their mothers instinctively and so I used to believe she was too afraid to help me. It was only as I grew older I began to see her for what she really is – a selfish drunk who blames my entrance into the world for my dad turning into a violent monster.

I ran to the bathroom taking two stairs at a time and slammed the door closed behind me before bolting it and sliding to the floor against it. I hugged my knees and thoughts of razor blades slicing into my flesh overwhelmed my mind. I tried to ignore it, rocking back and forth, closing my eyes and fighting desperately against the urge, swearing I wouldn't visit that dark place again.

But the craving was too intense. It always is.

I opened my eyes and found my hands picking apart the plastic casing on a razor from my vanity case and not remembering how I got there. Perching myself on the edge of the bath I rolled my pant leg up to the top of my thigh. A faint voice in the back of my mind was telling me to stop but I defied it, craving the relief I knew it would bring.

I glided the blade through the skin of my thigh slowly, meticulously. I needed to see it. I needed to physically *see* the excruciating pain I felt reverberating throughout my insides. Again, I tuned out of the pain as I focused on the rich, red blood spiraling down my pale leg. I sighed contentedly and repeated the process, trying desperately to carve away *his* touch. It was deeper this time and I felt an even greater sense of release. And pride. I felt fulfilled and I smiled inwardly at the knowledge that my dad couldn't hurt me as much as I could hurt myself.

I noticed spots of blood dripping onto the white marble floor tiles, which stunned me back into reality and I realized I needed to clean myself up. After cleaning the floor, wrapping the blade in tissue and flushing it down the toilet, I took a steaming shower – feeling similar relief as the hot water stung my thigh. Then I took myself to bed, applying pressure to my cuts with a hand-towel. The house was eerily silent but I savored the still and drifted into a heavy sleep.

****

When I arrived home from school I was relieved to see my dad's car wasn't there. I hurried inside and headed straight upstairs without bothering to look for my mom. I knew she was in the house somewhere – she hadn't ventured farther than the mailbox in years.

I emptied my school satchel and placed the textbooks in a neat pile on my dressing table, making room for my clothes for the party tonight. I'd arranged to get changed at Julie's so we could go together, and the fact that meant being away from this godforsaken house for even longer was an added bonus.

Next, I placed my journal and notebook under my mattress. I had to either carry them with me or hide them since my dad burnt the others. They are the only way I can share my thoughts before my mind explodes under the pressure. I write for hours some days. Mostly stories – immersing myself in a hope-filled fantasy world to escape from the harrowing one I actually exist in for a while.

I headed to the en-suite and ran a bath overflowing with lavender bubbles. I gasped as I tentatively lowered my thigh into the stinging foam and delicately trickled the steaming water over the dried blood. The seeping scars were a welcome distraction from my life and my thoughts, but running my finger over them caused the urge to build once again so I quickly dismissed it and clambered out of the tub before I succumbed and prized open the healing wounds.

After toweling myself dry I patched up my leg with a dressing from the drawer under my bed, threw on my most unflattering pair of grey sweats and gathered my things for Julie's.

****

Romy's porch was alive with fairy lights of at least nine different colors and a swarm of people were spilling out of the house. Julie breathed one last tut of disapproval as she eyed up my formal black pants then she hitched her already too short ivory skirt up a little further before dragging me towards the blaring music coming from inside.

We were plied with alcohol the second we stepped through the door and I glugged it down eagerly without knowing what it was. It tasted like vodka mixed with some kind of tropical fruit juice. Julie went off to find Adam Berry – the guy she's been lusting after forever – while I drained my glass and then followed my fellow partygoers towards a large bowl filled with emotion-numbing liquid on a high-gloss eggplant-purple island in the kitchen.

"Amelia Hope right?" a boy who I thought I recognized from my History class asked as I topped up my glass.

"Amy, " I corrected. My birth name reminds me of my parents.

"We have Chemistry together," he said with a suggestive wink.

I knew he was in one of my classes.

That annoying voice in the back of my mind was screaming 'back off, loser' and I was pretty sure my expression was saying the same.

"Let's spice this up a little," he said, producing a bottle of vodka from inside his jacket like a magician and emptying the lot into the punch bowl. I raised an impressed eyebrow and found myself warming to him immediately.

We knocked back a couple – maybe even seven – glasses of now tropical vodka with a hint of juice and I lost all sense of time and purpose. I couldn't remember why I was here or who I came with and I didn't care. The boy from chemistry was entertaining me and I suddenly noticed just how attractive he was. His tight-fitting white shirt hugged the muscles of his chest and my eyes kept wandering back to them. His eyes – popping out from under the wisps of his jet-black fringe – were a dazzling blue and sparkled under the halogens.

My pulse quickened as his face neared mine.

"Fancy something a little stronger?" he whispered into my ear and then pulled away, keeping his eyes just inches from mine as he gauged my reaction. The people around me were moving blurs and I was sure if I stood up I would fall straight back down.

"I think it's strong enough," I replied, angling my head towards the nearly drained punch bowl and feeling sure just one more sip would floor me.

"That's not what I mean. Come with me…" He took my hand and pulled me from the breakfast stools we'd been perched on for I don't know how long. The room swirled and I stumbled but the strong grip of Chemistry Boy's hand steadied me. I looked up at his amused face and followed his lead to the stairs.

We weaved our way through a mass of drunk and amorous teenagers hogging the stairs and after peering into a series of rooms he pulled me into an empty bedroom, tossed me onto the bed and kissed me… hard. Instantly it felt wrong and I didn't think I wanted to be there anymore. I knew I was intoxicated, my thigh was throbbing and I would only be doing it to feel close to someone for a few minutes.

I pushed him away and he raised a mischievous eyebrow as he reached into his denim pocket and pulled out a small, clear bag that looked to be half filled with something white. My mind's voiced yelled 'oh shit' as I realized what his idea of something stronger was and I was both afraid and excited.

"Wanna forget your troubles for a couple of hours?" he asked and the thought was overwhelmingly tempting. A tiny part of me knew I should leave but a greater part knew where I'd be going. *Home.*

"Sure," I agreed, feeling intrigued… and hopeful that it really would erase my problems for a while.

I had no idea what to do so I just watched him and followed his lead. He sprinkled some of the mysterious powder onto the dresser by the window and I perched on the edge of the bed to watch him, fascinated as he separated it into two perfectly straight lines with a credit card from his wallet. Next, he removed a ten-dollar bill and rolled it until it resembled a straw.

"Wanna go first?" he asked as he offered me the rolled up bill. I shook my head and hoped I didn't look as nervous as I felt.

He shrugged and I stared at him as he slipped the ten-dollar straw into his right nostril and pressed his left one closed with his finger as he bent towards the neat lines and snorted one from bottom to top in one fluid motion. Then he tipped his head back and rubbed his nose. His face looked instantly relaxed. He looked so calm, content. I was eager to experience what he was feeling so I quickly took the rolled up bill from him and copied what I'd just seen.

The powder burned the back of my nose and I now knew why he rubbed his afterwards. I did the same before flopping back onto the bed laughing.

Saving Amy

Minutes later I jolted back up, bursting with energy. I felt so alive. My veins were physically buzzing with vigor. It didn't last long before I started to feel flushed and my heart started to race. The boy from Chemistry pulled me backwards onto the bed and started kissing me again; slowly at first, pulling back every few seconds as if to test the water. I gripped his face with both my hands, fixed my mouth firmly onto his and searched his eyes – they never met mine. His touch electrified my overly sensitized skin and he was on top of me before I could undress fully. I felt incredibly brave and rebellious – completely lost in the moment. His breathing accelerated. His skin felt clammy. He was excited.

He wanted me.

Me.

But then, without warning, my eyes sprang open and it was as if I'd abruptly been pulled out of a dream. *What the fuck am I doing?* I mentally chastised myself.

My stomach felt nauseous and the boy's every thrust pushed the threatening vomit a little further towards my throat. I could feel his lips slobbering all over my bare skin and the stench of his stale vodka breath repulsed me. I tried to focus on the ceiling rose above me, breathing steadily in an effort not to throw up before he'd finished. But then he wrapped his arms underneath me and lifted me up so I was straddling his lap.

Oh shit.

The sudden movement gave my stomach ammunition and it violently spilled its contents. Chemistry Boy was stood at the foot of the bed, shaking himself down and cussing before I'd even finished hurling. I'd never felt so utterly disgusted with myself.

After wiping my mouth on the corner of the bed sheet I flopped backwards onto the bed. *Ugh...*

I didn't remember falling asleep (or passing out) but when I woke up I was alone and naked. I didn't know where Chemistry Boy had gone or if he was coming back so I gathered my wrinkled clothes from the floor and threw them on quickly. My head started to pound as I bent to slip my shoes on and every throb of my pulse thudded violently in my ears. My vomit infused sandy-blonde hair flicked my face as I stood upright and after feeling my wrist I noticed my hair-tie was missing.

I decided to rummage through the dresser drawers in search of one after looking around the fairly neutral bedroom, noticing a pink vase in the corner and assuming it must belong to a girl. There was a small plastic box in the second drawer down crammed with every color and style of hair-tie you could dream of. I picked up the first one I came to – a black band with red plastic cherries – and scraped my hair into a ponytail with my fingers.

After rubbing the smudges of mascara from under my eyes with the pads of my fingers I picked up my clutch bag and headed for the stairs. Mocking stares bored into my back as I hesitantly made my way down them. Giggles and whispers burned my ears and I knew immediately that Chemistry Boy had filled them in. Flushing

redder than a prostitute's lipstick, I bowed my head and picked up my pace towards the front door.

Saving Amy

The icy air whipped my face and instantly erased the last traces of nausea from my delicate stomach. Desperate to escape, I started to sprint. I didn't know where I was running to but my speed increased until the houses alongside me merged into a blur. My legs began to slow when I noticed a flashing blue sign emerging in the distance. I focused on it, trying to read what it said as it became closer and closer.

The Blue Hog.

I'd found my destination. I was in a part of Capitol Hill I was unfamiliar with but I was pretty sure if I headed west I'd end up somewhere near my high school. Dark, run-down buildings surrounded me but I didn't pay any more attention to them than that, walking instead into the entrance of the seedy looking Blue Hog.

Three vodka-Coke's later I could feel my tense body start to relax again. If only my mind would do the same. Each sip of alcohol intensified the shame I felt and brought me one step closer to my next inevitable destination… *home*.

I ordered another vodka - again without the need to produce my fake I.D. – and decided to wallow on the tatty brown corner bench a little longer. There was a long, walnut bar in front of me – concealed by a layer of bikers and whores who looked as miserable as I felt.

Engrossed in 'people watching' my eyes were drawn to a suspicious looking man. He wasn't much older than me at a guess and he was loitering outside the men's-room by the entrance. His foot tapped impatiently against the dirty floor, only pausing every few seconds while he glanced at his watch. Seconds later he was joined by another equally suspicious man and my eyes shifted focus to their unsuccessful slight-of-hand attempt.

There was an exchange of some sort and then I noticed the tip of a small transparent pouch sticking out from Suspicious Man Number Two's pocket. I recognized it instantly. It was the same as the bag Chemistry Boy had earlier. Suddenly my heart was quickening and I longed to be back in that thoughtless paradise I was in just a few hours ago.

****

I did it. I plucked up the courage to approach Suspicious Man Number One with the line 'you got any more?' and hoping he wouldn't guess I had no idea what I was doing or what I was asking for. I was now the owner of a tiny pouch of 'blow', which I was almost certain was slang for cocaine. Even saying it my head sounded stupid. Reckless. Ridiculous. Shameful.

Exciting.

Soon enough I was back there again and it felt fantastic. I danced my way out of the ladies room and high-fived a biker who winked at me as I passed him. I had too much energy to sit back down so I quickstepped my way outside to light a cigarette from my purse. I giggled like a naughty child when I noticed my cell resting on my packet of smokes and remembered I hadn't told Julie where I was going. I pressed 'Call' instinctively without checking for missed calls or texts.

"Amy! Where the hell are you?" she roared down the line.

"Julie-e-e-e-e! What's up, girlfriend?" I teased playfully. Turned out Julie wasn't in the mood for playing.

"Amy, seriously... I've been calling you all freakin' night. *Everyone's* talking about you and Ed Stevens."

So that's his name? For a fleeting moment the shame returned but it was soon quashed by another immature giggle.

"What happened between you? Are you okay?"

"He fucked me. I threw up on him. I'm over it," I blurted, a little too flippantly for her liking.

"You're wasted!"

No flies on her.

"Where are you? Are you alone? I'll come and meet you," she rushed out in a fluster. No way in hell could I be bothered with Julie fussing over me. I needed to sober up. Fast.

"Sorry, Jules. I'm fine I swear. I'm going home now. I'll catch you tomorrow," I replied, trying desperately to sound sober and praying I sounded convincing.

"Promise?"

"Promise. Just had too much to drink that's all. I've made an ass of myself and now I'm going home to sleep it off. I'll call you in the morning."

I hung up the call before I heard a reply. My mood was slipping already. The nausea was returning with a vengeance and I felt a slight twinge deep in the back of my head, threatening to explode at any moment.

I headed west with the hope of finding my school and my bearings. Nothing looked familiar. There was a cluster of tall, swanky looking buildings cordoned off with immense steel gates ahead of me – apartments I assumed. I concentrated on the myriad of yellow lights escaping through the mass of windows and dragged myself forwards, hoping to find someone with a sense of direction.

Suddenly I felt worse. I paused to lean against an ostentatious looking car, dragging in deep breaths of the cold, cleansing air and praying it would ease the stomach-twisting queasiness. Beads of sweat started to drip relentlessly down the back of my neck, despite the icy wind. I wiped it away with flattened fingers and noticed that my hands were shaking. My legs felt weak. The sidewalk began to move. The swanky buildings rippled in the wind.

The ground was coming towards my face...

****

I woke up in a bed. Double if not king-sized, covered by cream satin sheets and surrounded by cream feather pillows. As I sat up the satin glided against my bare skin and I realized I was only wearing my bra and panties. More shame flooded my veins as I tried in vain to remember whose bed I was in. My mind was blank. I vaguely remembered making a drunken phone-call to Julie but after that all I could see was darkness. I didn't know where I was, who I'd been with (most likely *slept* with) or why I could feel a band aid on the back of my head.

A light tap on the bedroom door startled me and I pulled the satin sheets up beneath my chin.

Saving Amy

"Good morning. How's the head?" a tall man – late twenties at a guess - dressed only in a pair of jeans, asked me in a deliciously deep voice.

Fuck me he was beautiful. His dark auburn, naturally copper highlighted hair was messy yet perfect – ruffled with no obvious direction but in a precisely-styled-with-fancy-hair-product-for-the-just-got-out-of-bed-look way. He had the most glorious set of abs I'd ever seen in my life and that perfect 'V' coming off his sculpted hips that you only ever see on underwear models.

He looked far too respectable to bring a drunken slut that stank of vomit home to bed with him…

"Um…" was all I could muster, too embarrassed to admit that I didn't know who he was or why I was lying in his bed.

"Your ribs have taken a fair thump too. Do you remember what happened last night?"

"Of course I do," I lied curtly. He raised an unconvinced eyebrow at me. "A little," I claimed. "No," I finally admitted, dropping my head.

I felt the mattress dip beside me and I looked up to find the eye-wateringly hot man sitting there.

"I found you on the sidewalk outside. From the knock to your head I think you fainted. You weren't making much sense when I brought you inside."

Why the fuck didn't he just call an ambulance like normal people would? Oh my god he's a freakin' weirdo. I need to get out of here…

"I had a little to much to drink last night," I mumbled, ashamed.

"Is that all?" he quizzed dubiously.

"Yes!" I protested. *Who the hell does he think he is?* "Did we…" I nodded my head towards the space next to me on the bed and hoped I didn't need to actually say the words.

"No. We didn't. Not only am I not that kind of man, you were in no fit state and you're far too young."

How would you know how old I am?

Suddenly I started to wonder if he'd been snooping through my purse and then convinced myself he had and was basing his mini interrogation on the empty polythene pouch inside. What a jackass.

"Did you do this to yourself?" I followed his gaze and found it resting on my thigh. Immediately I yanked the sheet over it and wondered why my dressing was missing.

"I fell." Shrugging, I watched his eyebrow shoot up again. He was starting to annoy me. "What's it to you anyway?" I snapped. "Where are my clothes?"

He stood effortlessly from the bed and as he walked towards a wicker chair in the corner of the room my eyes refused to shift focus from the delectably defined muscles hugging his hips just above the waistband of his black, low-hung jeans. Forcing my eyes away I noticed my clothes (clean and pressed by the look of them) folded neatly on the back of the chair, causing my frustration to raise a notch.

"I can clean my own clothes," I barked ungratefully.

"They were covered in vomit."

Oh…

Saving Amy

"I was just trying to help," he said as he draped my clothes over his forearm and moved towards me. I ignored him because I was mad... and embarrassed... and more than a tiny bit attracted to him. Sighing, he laid my clothes next to me on the bed and left without another word. The second I heard the door close behind him I threw my head into my hands and sobbed violently into my palms.

What is happening to me?

It took me a good half an hour to calm myself down before I attempted to find the bathroom. After peering into three ridiculously spacious rooms I eventually found it. I headed straight towards the basin to splash my face and spray myself with some deodorant I found in his cabinet. I would shower at home. I was ready, *desperate*, to leave.

I successfully managed to navigate my way back to the overly long hallway and found my clutch purse resting neatly between two empty, white ceramic bowls on a half-moon glass table by the entrance. I planned on grabbing it and running for the hills but as I reached for it... *he* appeared from a room across the hall.

"My name is Richard by the way..." he stated, now dressed in a cream turtleneck, allowing my brain to focus more clearly. I nodded and attempted to smile but I couldn't seem to find the right muscles in my face.

Turning away from him, I pulled on the door handle. Thankfully, it was unlocked and I stepped out into a long, white and stainless steel filled corridor. There was tension on the door as I attempted to close it and I then saw it was because he was holding it open.

"Look after yourself, Miss Hope," he called after me.

I knew it! He *must* have rifled through my things. *Who the fuck does he think he is?* I was too angry to acknowledge him – with him *and* myself – so I kept on walking towards the elevator at the far end, grateful for the fact I'd never have to see him again.

Chapter Two

Two months later…

The sound of the bedroom door slamming stirred me. I noted the time on my alarm clock – 6:30 AM. Next came the sound of the power shower and I knew it was my dad getting ready for work. Seizing my opportunity, I swung my legs out of bed and stepped into my pink bunny slippers before tiptoeing down the stairs and into the kitchen. I peered around the doorjamb first, making sure there was no sign of life, and then moved swiftly towards the kitchen counter in between the kettle and the toaster. His wallet was in its usual spot, beside an empty coffee mug and his car keys.

One more fleeting glance over my shoulder and I was in, out and back in my bedroom within one minute. Fifty dollars should see me through a couple of days and I smiled smugly as I counted it under my quilt. He'd never notice a mere fifty dollars missing from the hundreds he usually had stuffed in there. God knew what he did with it all. I didn't really care.

His heavy feet made the stairs creak on his way down and I knew the slam of the front door would follow shortly which would mean I could get up for the day. While I waited for the slam of the door I rifled through my closet for something to wear. A bleep from my cell disturbed me and I sighed heavily, *guiltily*, knowing it was probably another text from Julie. I was right.

```
Julie: Call me. PLEASE. I'm
worried about U, J. xoxo
```

I threw the phone down on the bed and tore at my hair as I choked back the tears. Julie was my best friend – my *only* friend – and I hadn't spoken to her in almost three weeks or seen her in just over nine. In fact, the last time I saw her was the night of Romy's party. I wanted to see her. I *needed* to see her. But I couldn't. I just couldn't let her see how fucked-up I was right now.

I'm a mess. Leon – the guy from The Blue Hog – is programmed into my speed-dial, I've lost a shit load of weight and my legs are shredded to the point where I look like I've been caught in an explosion in a glass factory. Mrs. Clarke took great pleasure I'm sure in questioning my dad about my lack of attendance at school last week, which resulted in three fresh bruises and a cracked rib – or a fall down the stairs to the outside world – and I spend my days either getting high or coming down and wishing I had the balls to slice into the flesh over my wrist rather than my legs.

In a moment of madness I decided to text Julie. After all I didn't necessarily have to see her to put her mind at ease.

```
Me: I'm so sorry, J. I'm fine I
promise. Things at home r just a
little rough right now. I miss u.
xoxo
```

Saving Amy

I found myself crying as I hit send. I really did miss her. Life had always seemed that little bit more... *normal* when we were together. But I would only bring her down now. I'm better off alone, with nobody able to hurt me but myself. I'm counting down the days until my eighteenth birthday – two months, six days – and then I'm out of here. Leon says he can help me get set up somewhere. I don't know how and I don't know where but I don't care. Anything has to be better than living here between my mother's drunken wails and my father's fists.

My cell bleeped again – startling me from my reverie.

```
Julie: Meet me later? After school
at the cemetery. Please? Xo
```

Pangs of guilt twisted in my stomach as I read it, causing the tears to flow even faster. I typed my response quickly before I had chance to change my mind.

```
Me: Ok. 3:30. Usual bench.
```

I regretted sending it almost instantly. I stared myself down in the mirrored closets and I looked a mess. A thin – disgustingly so – girl stared back at me. Her eyes were dark and sunken. Her body was torn and bruised. I didn't recognize her. I didn't want to look at *that* girl anymore so I quickly turned away and got dressed into my indigo skinny-jeans and a thick black sweater – wincing from the pain in my ribs as I bent down.

There was no sign of my mom downstairs and I didn't bother to look for her before grabbing my car keys from the hook behind the front door and heading outside. I felt edgy, anxious. My fingers were fidgeting with each other and my legs felt restless. I drove for over an hour – maybe longer – down to Beacon Hill and back again, hoping to regain some kind of composure.

It didn't work. If anything I felt worse. I was beginning to sweat and the tips of my fingers were trembling. It was sheer nerves about seeing Julie – seeing *anyone*. It wasn't withdrawal or anything. I don't have an addiction as such – yet at least. I can go days at a time if I have to – if I can't get my hands on any of my dad's cash for example. I suppose the problem is, I don't actually care about my new habit *becoming* an addiction. The reality is, being high – and even coming down – hurts a hell of a lot less than being sober. I guess I'm more than willing to risk becoming addicted to 'forgetting'.

Eventually I pulled up outside the local Mini-Mart and soon enough my index finger was hovering over Leon's number on my cell. A stern voice deep in my subconscious warned me not to be so stupid so close to meeting Julie but my newfound selfishness thought 'fuck it' and I hit the call button. I'd arranged a time to meet him in less than thirty seconds and my twitchy fingers were already starting to calm.

An hour later I found myself parked in the small lot behind The Blue Hog. It never occurred to me to meet Leon elsewhere. He was already waiting for me - leaning casually against a large brown dumpster, dressed as usual in ripped jeans and a tan leather jacket.

"Usual?" he asked as he reached into the pocket tucked away inside his jacket. I shrugged. I felt like utter shit and I wanted something that would see me through my time with Julie but had no idea what to ask for.

"Something a little stronger perhaps?" he suggested, noticing my dejection. I shrugged again. "I got just what you need. Lasts a *lot* longer. Here…"

He passed me a pouch similar to the ones I was used to but the powder was slightly darker – brown almost. I eyed it up curiously. That annoying warning voice banged away in the back of my head but I locked it away. I thought I might as well give whatever it was a whirl – I had nothing to lose after all.

"Dope…" Leon interrupted, answering my unspoken question.

Holy fuck.

"*Heroin*… right?" I questioned naively.

"Don't believe all the hype. It gets a lot of bad press but it's cool if you manage it properly. Trust me."

I stared unseeingly at the small pouch as I tried to focus on slowing my racing heart, which was on the verge of bursting through my already delicate rib cage.

"Of course, if you want to sniff it you'll need this one…"

What else was I expected to do with it?

My breathing accelerated to an astronomical level when the realization hit that I was supposed to *inject* it. Holy shit. What the hell was I messing with here? What in God's name had happened to me? I was both disgusted and intrigued by the new pouch of brilliant-white powder.

Fuck it.

I wrapped up the exchange quickly, suddenly feeling overwhelmed and maybe even a little scared. After handing over the cash – almost twice as much as usual – with the discreet slight-of-hand manoeuver I had become so good at, I turned and left without a destination in mind.

I ended up at the cemetery. I still had an hour before Julie was supposed to meet me but I relished the silence I found there. After settling myself down on the familiar wooden bench that was rotting around the edges, I pulled out my latest purchase. I fiddled with it for a while – curling it, folding it and tipping the powder from side to side. I contemplated taking it but pulled a cigarette out instead.

The nicotine wasn't having its usual effect and my legs were beginning to ache from constantly scraping the earth back and forth beneath my feet. Restless, I stood up and paced the length of the bench. Then I walked around it until I was back where I started. I continued until I'd completed fourteen laps – I counted – and then I sat back down and lit another smoke.

I repeated the whole process – fiddling with the pouch of… I don't even want to say the word, smoking, pacing and kicking the earth several more times until I saw Julie approaching in the distance. The decision was finally out of my hands. I didn't have time to take anything now.

"Jesus Christ, Amy, you look terrible," Julie fussed as she ran towards me and flung her arms over my shoulders. I flinched and used my arm as a barrier between her body and my ribs. She pulled back immediately. "What is it? What's wrong?"

"I'm fine, don't worry. I took a bit of a tumble down the stairs last week that's all. It's still a little sore."

"Jeez, I'm sorry. No more hugging…"

We settled down on *our* bench surrounded by an uncomfortable, deafening silence. I tried to make idle chitchat about school but she wasn't convinced and just kept staring at me – her expression doleful and oozing concern.

"Oh, Amy, I'm here for you… you know that right?"

"Sure I do," I replied, nodding. "I'm fine, really. Or at least I will be when I'm old enough to leave that goddamn house."

"Things still rough?"

I wish I could tell you just how rough.

"You could say that. It's just a little… *intense*, at the minute."

"And you're sure that's all it is? I mean, you've missed so much school. You've been ignoring my calls. You've lost weight. You look-"

"I promise, Jules" I interrupted, placing my hand on her knee. "I'm not gonna lie and say everything's peachy 'cause it's not. Things have been getting on top of me and I've been kind of down but I'm coming out of it now," I lied. "That's why I came here today. I'm feeling better and it's because I realized once I move out of that fucked-up house in a few months time I can start planning my future again. Please don't worry about me. I'm on the up… I *promise*."

"Hmm. Well, you definitely sound better than last time I spoke to you…"

Wow, I'm a better liar than I thought.

"So I guess I'll take your word for it. No more disappearing acts though okay?"

"'Kay," I answered sheepishly.

Selfishly, I didn't want to deal with any more guilt right now so I gave Julie a one-armed hug and a dodgy excuse about a dental appointment and left.

****

Back in my bedroom I could hear the vile sound of my mom hurling into the toilet. This was standard protocol when she hadn't had a drink in a few hours. No doubt my dad would pick her some up on his way home from work – his way of shutting her up.

I lay back on top of my bed and gingerly rolled onto my side. Then I pulled a pillow over my face and clamped it down around my ears to drown out the noise coming from the bathroom.

A noise startled me – a smash I think. I looked at my watch. It was 9:30 PM and dark outside; I must have fallen asleep. Next I heard the thud of my dad's feet pounding the stairs. I was thirsty but decided to wait until he was in bed before heading downstairs. Instead, I rolled onto my other side, grabbed my latest book and planned to read away another hour or so.

I didn't hear the door open but seconds later I was pulled abruptly upright by my arm.

"I've just had a visitor," my dad uttered before releasing my arm and making his way to the foot of my bed. His voice was unnervingly calm and I knew he was about to lose it. I didn't know what he wanted me to say. "Your friend Julie popped by. She's just left."

Oh shit.

"Why didn't you wake me?" I mumbled nervously. He tucked one hand in his pocket and ambled eerily slowly towards me.

"She wasn't here to see *you*," he stated in a threateningly composed tone. I shifted my body slightly as he perched next to me on the bed. I didn't ask what Julie wanted. I didn't say anything. I kept my arid mouth closed and fixed my eyes onto my floral quilt. "It seems she's rather worried about you."

"Really?" I asked, my voice cracking as I tried to sound nonchalant. "I don't know why," I explained, hoping he'd accept that I hadn't told her anything that could implicate him and leave.

"She doesn't seem to believe that you had that unfortunate accident down the stairs last week, among other things. Why do you think that could be?" he grilled calmly, but I knew he was threatening me. I stayed quiet. There was no point in talking – he wouldn't believe me anyway.

"You see, *I* think you've been saying a little too much to your friend."

"I haven't said anything. I swear it. I've barely even seen her the last couple of months. Maybe that's why she's worried? She can't accept that I'm moving on with my life."

I knew he wasn't listening and part of me wished he'd just get whatever he had planned over with.

"Moving on huh? Moving on where?" He couldn't keep the amusement from filtering into his voice. He knew damn well I had nowhere to go and no one to go to.

"I graduate next month. I guess I'm just growing out of my childhood friends, that's all." I sounded weak and pathetic.

"Well let's hope that's all it is. I should've known you wouldn't be so silly." He rose from the bed and hovered his body over mine. I closed my eyes in anticipation. "Good night, Amelia," he whispered, and then as he rose he laid his flattened palm over my fractured rib and forced his entire body weight into me. I cried out and he insulted me further by planting a gentle, stomach-churning kiss – filled with promise – on my forehead.

My breathing was labored as I watched him leave the room. Then I rolled back onto my side, gasping and choking on the tears that clogged my throat.

****

Holy hell it felt good. The effects were immediate. A beautiful warmth passed through every single vein in turn, tickling them as it went. My limbs felt heavy so I flopped backwards and closed my eyes. I felt sated, relaxed and so, so happy. Even though my eyes were closed I could see so much brightness. And color... colors of every shade and depth. My breathing slowed and the delicate thrum of my heart slowly sent me into a wonderful, serene slumber...

I didn't know how long I'd been bathing in paradise but I could feel my body begin to wake. I sat up fluently – my legs no longer weighing me down. My bedroom was brighter… more peaceful. Everything appeared new – as if I were there for the first time. I had never felt so alive, so positive, so happy.

It was 10:45 PM but I didn't have an ounce of tiredness left inside. It would have been sinful to waste the rush of sensational energy I was experiencing stuck inside those four walls so I glammed myself up, applying sparkly blue shadow to my eyelids and slipping on my sexiest black dress – making sure it rested below my shredded thighs; it did.

Despite being a lawyer's daughter I wasn't sure what the law would make of me driving under the influence of heroin. It would object I assumed and so I walked to the main road to hail a taxi.

"Where to, lovely?" the round, British sounding driver asked me. I hadn't planned that far ahead and his question took me by surprise, leaving me grinning like an idiot while I decided.

"The city. I don't care where… Somewhere bright – somewhere lively," I finally responded. Then I rested my head sideways against the window and admired the beauty of the buildings lit up like Christmas trees in the dark of the night. I'd never truly noticed how beautiful Seattle was before. The streets were so busy – so alive. It was so easy to walk around here completely unnoticed. That suited me most of the time. But sometimes, when I was just a single breath away from breaking completely, I

wanted someone to notice me – to know I existed…
To *save* me.

"Will here do?" the driver asked, snapping me from my trance. I decided then that he was definitely British. I looked ahead and we were surrounded by clubs, bars, novelty pubs and swarms of people dressed to impress and having a blast.

"This is perfect. Thank you." I handed over my fare, opened my door and swung my legs from the cab in a very ladylike fashion.

There was so much to see. So many people. So many colors. So many bright lights.

I walked eagerly into the buzz of the crowd. The hum of laughter encompassing me was infectious and I found myself giggling as I swayed into the first bar I came to. My fake I.D. worked like a charm and soon I was dancing along to Rihanna - alone in the middle of a vast, crowded dance-floor with my purse in one hand and a vodka-Coke in the other.

Four drinks in and I was getting a little bored. Things didn't look so beautiful anymore. I considered going home but then remembered I still had half a pouch of magical powder left. I recalled Leon's words in my mind – 'it's cool if you manage it properly'. I assumed he meant not to overdo it. What the hell, I decided. It wasn't like I *needed* it. I just *wanted* it. When I started to feel like I *needed* it, I'd stop. Simple.

After I'd finished up rationalizing with my subconscious I headed to the ladies room. I was soon back in that thoughtless paradise and it felt easily as good as before – if not better. The warmth, the calm, the delightful tingle dancing through my veins like sweet music…

Back on the dance-floor I was startled by someone wrapping their arms around my waist. Instinctively I prized them off and spun around. It was a man with short brown hair spiked into a quiff at the front, light-green eyes which sparkled under the fluorescents and dressed in a muscle-hugging fitted black shirt and jeans which hung low – exposing the neon pink waistband of his boxer shorts. Like everything else tonight, he was beautiful.

We didn't speak. We simply danced – grinding our hips together and flirting with our eyes. Or at least *I* was – he seemed too preoccupied staring at my boobs to look into my eyes. I felt sexy as hell right now and so I didn't hesitate when he asked me to join him somewhere a little quieter.

He led me by the hand to an abandoned parking lot outside around the back of the bar. Then he pushed me lustfully up against a wall, the cool brick sending divine shivers down my spine. I used my arm as a barrier between him and my fragile ribs and threw my head back exposing the throbbing, wanton vein in my neck as he kissed hungrily along it.

I closed my eyes and focused on the sound of our ragged breathing. I felt so alive. So wanted. He hitched my dress up and in one lithe movement he was holding me up. Using the wall for support against my back I wrapped my legs around his waist and he grabbed the underside of my thighs.

My subconscious – that irritating voice which seemed intent on ruining all traces of fun in my life – mumbled something about protection but I dismissed it immediately. I felt so powerful – nothing could hurt me now. I was living for that very moment and that was all I allowed myself to focus on.

It was over too quickly and he lowered me down. I noticed immediately that his eyes had changed. They were darker without the bright lights and suddenly I felt intimidated by them. Swiftly, he pulled up his zipper and started to walk away without so much as breathing a single word. But then he paused and looked back at me – making eye contact for the first time since I'd met him. I watched inquisitively as he reached into his pocket and removed a five-dollar bill. Then he threw it at my feet before walking off into a crowd of other men who were laughing and cheering him on.

I slid down onto the damp, stone floor. I felt empty. Worthless. Utterly humiliated.

I couldn't feel my heart beating anymore.

I laid down on the cold concrete and made patterns in the dirt with my fingers. I wanted to cry but I couldn't. I couldn't do anything. I was numb. Frozen. Ashamed…

I rolled backwards and my head knocked into something cold and hard. Looking up, I noticed it was a fire escape. It was only two stories high but for some unknown reason I felt compelled to climb it.

It stopped alongside a heavy duty, metal door. I rested my body against the safety rail and looked out onto the city. The buildings ahead parted in front of me and I could see out onto the brightly lit streets. The colors were still there. So were the people and the lights. Everywhere was so full of life. Yet no matter how hard I tried I couldn't seem to find the beauty.

I felt so alone. I was standing there in this massive city and nobody knew. Nobody cared. There were swarms of people below me and I meant nothing to a single one of them. I meant nothing to anybody.

Tentatively I hitched myself up onto the rail and swung my legs over the edge. I was only two stories high but the ground seemed so far away. It looked so inviting. For a fleeting moment I wondered if letting go would end it all. After all, I died inside a long time ago – maybe it was time for my body to catch up? The thought was painfully tempting. Would I feel it? Would I feel anything ever again? *That would show him*, my subconscious piped up and suddenly I felt powerful. This was something *he* couldn't control. The idea of nothing… of darkness - no pain, no worry, no anything overwhelmed me and I let go.

I was flying into the icy breeze… into paradise. I was free.

****

"She also has a fractured wrist and some swelling to the brain. That is likely to be the cause of her unconsciousness. Going off her CT scan this morning it appears to be settling down and so we're hoping she'll come round fairly soon. Your daughter has been extremely lucky, Mr. Hope," I heard a man say in a voice I was almost certain I'd heard before.

I didn't know where I was but I knew my father was with me. I felt a warm hand grasp mine, making me feel physically sick at the thought it might be his.

"Thank you, Doctor. I'll call my wife and let her know. She is simply too upset to visit just now." I thought it was safe to assume I was in a hospital and I found myself wondering if the doctor was falling for my dad's bullshit.

The hand disappeared and I heard the sound of a door closing shortly after. I still wasn't alone – I could hear the sound of papers rustling. Footsteps re-entered the room and I could hear a man and a woman talking incomprehensible jargon. I latched on to certain words – contusions, systolic, hypertension, thoracic… my ears gave up eventually.

I told my eyes to open but they wouldn't. My whole body was paralyzed. The feeling was overpoweringly frustrating and my subconscious was screaming at me to move so forcefully it deafened my ears. I sensed someone next to me – I could hear breathing that was out of sync with my own. Then came the sound of beeping and keys being tapped before the footsteps moved away from me, getting fainter and fainter until eventually they disappeared.

I think I was alone now. The silence was peaceful. I reveled in it, trying not to disturb it with thoughts. It was no use. I didn't know why I was there and I had an inexplicable feeling that I was supposed to be somewhere else.

Then it hit me…

I was supposed to be free. I was supposed to fall and it was all supposed to end. If only I'd climbed higher. I didn't want this. I didn't want to be here but I was trapped in every sense of the word. I thought I was crying but I couldn't feel the tears on my face. Then the footsteps returned, getting louder and heavier until they paused by my bed.

I could feel someone's warm breath on my face before my eyelids were forced open and a piercing light was shone in to them one at a time. My body writhed with frustration inside. I wanted to push them away. I wanted to shout and scream and tell whoever it was to leave me the fuck alone. But I couldn't. I couldn't do *anything*.

It wasn't right. I wasn't supposed to be here...

"I'm leaving now, Doctor. Please call me as soon as there's any change," I heard my dad say. His voice churned my stomach.

"Of course, Mr. Hope," was the doctor's reply. I *definitely* knew his voice and my head ached as I frantically tried to wrack my memory. Seconds later the door slammed closed and immediately I felt my heartbeat begin to slow, knowing my dad had left the building.

"Come on, Sleeping Beauty. Time to wake up now," the familiar voice said as he continued to make papers rustle and machines sing around me.

Pessimistically I told my eyes to open once more and my heart began to race in anticipation when I felt a flicker. I couldn't see yet but there was definitely movement. I thrust all the energy my body held into my eyes, focusing solely on getting them open and blocking every other thought or sound from my mind. Gradually light began to flood my pupils, startling them as my eyelids peeled open at an exasperatingly slow speed.

The doctor was facing away from me. If I squinted I could see his ruffled auburn/copper hair and long white overcoat. I tried to speak to gain his attention but something was choking me and I gagged - coughing and spluttering and certain I was dying. I couldn't breathe and it scared the hell out of me. I started to panic and the white overcoat flung round and towards me at lightning speed.

"Try and relax for me, Amelia," he soothed as he pulled something long and obtrusive from my throat. I heaved and wheezed as I fought desperately to fill my lungs with air. "Amelia, I need you to focus for me. Deep breaths," the familiar man ordered and as much as I wanted to tell him where to go I knew I needed to listen to him.

I drew in long, deep breaths – counting as I went. I'd taken six when slowly each one was becoming easier. I was calming down and my tense muscles started to relax. I regained the ability to breath without thinking and my efforts shifted to my sense of sight. The auburn/copper-haired doctor was scribbling away on a clipboard with his head down. Then his thumb clicked his pen closed and his eyes met mine.

Oh fuck...

"Nice to see you again, Miss Hope," the patronizing bastard said to me. It was *him*. The dodgy guy whose swanky, over-the-top apartment I woke up in after the nightmare that was Romy's party.

"You're a doctor?" I mumbled but suspected I was barely audible under the sound of my rasping breath. He moved to sit beside me on the bed and I felt deeply ashamed that this was the second time I'd woken up in such a desperate mess in front of this hot as hell stranger.

Saving Amy

What must he think of me?

"Last time I checked. You've been very lucky, Miss Hope." I smirked inwardly at the irony of my name. *Hope* – something I'd never been fortunate enough to experience.

"Please, call me Amy," I interjected, noticing how well his baby-blue shirt and silver tie went together under his coat. My eyes landed on a navy-blue lanyard around his neck with an official I.D. badge attached showing his name – Dr. Richard Lewis – and a passport style photo that didn't do his fine face justice.

"*Amy*... do you remember what happened last night? *Truthfully* this time," he asked while raising that irritatingly gorgeous suspicious eyebrow – just like the last time we met. I considered saying no but soon realized there was no point. He might be a condescending son-of-a-bitch but he wasn't stupid.

I decided to suss out what he already knew before I worked out how much I was prepared to divulge.

"I might need you to jog my memory a little. *You* tell *me* what happened first?" He puckered his eyebrows together in frustration and I knew he thought I was being petulant.

"Well, you were brought in at 01:54 this morning after a suspected fall from a fire escape. You presented with a GCS of nine, head trauma, carpal fracture, possible spinal damage and an elevated BP of 140/98. You should also know your blood results have shown traces of narcotics in your system," he answered, very matter of fact.

"Spinal damage?" My heart shuddered to a near stop and I couldn't tell if my legs wouldn't move because I was so afraid or because they physically couldn't.

"An MRI scan has revealed some swelling around the thoracic nerves in your spinal cord, although we expect this to subside within a few days leaving no permanent damage. In the meantime however you may experience some muscle weakness in your legs, possibly even paralysis but this should be temporary and now you're back with us we can begin the relevant tests to show us what we're dealing with."

'Should' be temporary...

I nodded as if I understood what the hell he was saying to me. But then suddenly my body was paralyzed with an even greater fear... the blood results.

"The blood results... does my father know?"

"No. We have a duty to respect patient confidentiality. He knows you have experienced a fall and the immediate danger you suffered as a result. We won't disclose anything else without your consent. Although, maybe that is something you should talk through with your parents yourself. I think you need their support right now."

"No! No please, you can't tell them anything. Please..."

"Miss Ho- *Amy*, I've told you I have to respect your wishes. But I really do think you need to talk with somebody. How would you feel about having a chat with a colleague of mine – Joanna Spencer?"

"What, like a shrink? No way."

"No, not a shrink. She's our young person's drug and alcohol counselor. She deals with a range of issues from addiction to depression. She's simply there to listen. I really believe it would be of benefit to you."

I couldn't think of anything worse than spilling my guts to a complete stranger – to anyone for that matter – but I felt like I owed the doctor somehow. He had saved me twice now for no other reason than compassion that I could think of. Besides, meeting the shrink didn't mean I actually had to tell her anything.

"Okay." I shrugged in defeat.

"Good girl." There he went again… patronizing bastard. Good girl? Seriously? "I'm just going to call your father and let him know you've come around." He rose from the bed so fluidly I didn't feel the mattress move and then started to walk away.

"No. Please don't call him," I called after him once his words has sunken in.

"Amy, I've assured you I won't breach your patient confidentiality. I just need to let him know you're awake, that's all. He's very worried about you."

Like hell he is.

"Please? Not yet. I-I know you'll have to do it eventually but please just give me some time. I beg you, *please*," I pleaded, turning into a stuttering mess.

"Is there something you need to tell me, Amy?"

My heart sank into the depths of my stomach. I wanted to tell him. I wanted to scream and shout what a sadistic bastard my father was so he would keep him away from me. I attempted to speak but my mouth was so dry the words stuck to my lips. Then a rogue tear escaped and trailed miserably down my cheek when I realized no one could keep him away from me. He was my father…

"No, I just don't want to see him yet." I watched the doctor's face intently. He was doing the questioning eyebrow thing and I knew he didn't believe me.

"Okay. Well, I need you to rest for me now. I'm going to bleep Joanna and arrange a visit from her this afternoon. I'll be back shortly to check on you, but for now… *sleep.*" He was so bossy. If he wasn't so goddamn good looking I was pretty sure I'd hate him.

I stared after him as he left the room and closed the heavy yellow door behind him. I was insatiably tired so I closed my eyes. For some incomprehensible reason I seemed to trust the dishy doctor and I drifted into a peaceful sleep in the knowledge I wouldn't wake up to the sight – or *force* – of my dad.

Chapter Three

"Amy?" I felt a gentle nudge on my right shoulder. It stirred me and slowly, my eyes peeled open. It was the ridiculously handsome doctor and a tall blonde woman – late twenties, early thirties maybe – with flawless porcelain skin and a figure that belonged on the red carpet. This sure as hell wasn't the place for someone with self-esteem issues.

"This is Joanna Spencer; the lady we talked about this morning." He proffered his hand towards the movie-star woman as he introduced her. I nodded but I couldn't find the right muscles in my face to smile. Thrusting my clenched fists into the too-firm mattress I tried to heave myself up into a sitting position but an engulfing shooting pain radiated from my lower back, making me cry out as I was sent crashing back down. A strong, protective arm was beneath me, holding me up before I hit the mattress.

The shock – or the pain – made me dizzy and when I'd composed myself I was in the doctor's arms, our faces just inches apart. The proximity sent an unnerving, delicious current through my veins; not dissimilar to the effects of heroin and I wondered if perhaps there was some lingering in my system. Too soon, the woman was against my other side and between them they hitched me a little higher up the bed, creating a makeshift hoist with the crook of their elbows under my armpits.

"I'll leave you two alone," Richard — or should it be Doctor Lewis now I was in the hospital — said with a reassuring hand on my shoulder. That inexplicable charge resurfaced at his touch and I wondered if it was the after effects of the come down.

His words disappointed me more than they should. I nodded in response but I didn't want him to leave. I only felt safe when he was with me and that in itself made me feel stupid.

"My name is Joanna. I believe Richard has told you a little bit about me," she introduced as she pulled the green plastic visitor's chair by my bed a little closer and lowered herself onto it. I nodded in acknowledgement, but the uncomfortable silence that followed made me think she was expecting me to say something.

"Would you like to start?" she asked me, finally breaking the deafening silence. I shook my head. Seemingly I had turned into an utter imbecile and couldn't find two words to string together. "Well, do you mind if I ask you some questions? You don't have to answer anything you feel uncomfortable with."

I nodded, *again*. She must have thought I was completely backwards. The whole atmosphere felt very unnatural and I couldn't decide if she genuinely wanted to help or if she was just an interfering do-gooder. It didn't matter either way — nobody *could* help.

"Do you remember what happened before you were admitted to us?" And so it began…

"A little. I assume you've been told I'd taken something. I guess I just overdid it and lost my

Saving Amy

balance." At last I had regained the ability to speak – even if not truthfully.

"You say you took something... was that the first time?" I shook my head and found myself staring unseeingly at the metal guardrail at the foot of my bed. I was too ashamed to make eye contact and my fingers were starting to ache from knotting themselves together so tightly. "Can I ask what it is you've been taking?"

Like you don't know... I felt like she was trying to humiliate me by forcing me to say it aloud.

"Heroin," I muttered under my breath as I stared down at my knees.

"So, you've been taking it for a while?" she assumed ever so calmly, without a hint of judgment in her voice.

"No, that was the first time. I thought you just meant in general. I've dabbled with cocaine before." Holy shit, the shame was crushing me. My cheeks were on the verge of setting alight and I could feel beads of sweat dripping furiously down the back of my neck.

"So what do you think made you want to take the step up to heroin?"

Um... I'd had enough of my dad beating seven shades of shit out of me. I'd had enough of ripping my thighs to pieces in an effort to distract myself from a greater pain that I have no control over. I'd had enough of looking into my mom's eyes and seeing the pitch-black pool of regret bubbling behind them. I'd had enough of being treated, and acting, like a cheap slut just to feel wanted for a few brief minutes... I fell silent.

"Peer pressure perhaps?" she continued. "If it's something your circle of friends are into, then it can be all too easy to feel like you need to follow suit." I shook my head.

"No. Nobody else even knows. I don't have a lot of friends. I didn't do it to 'fit in', or for attention if that's what you think."

"I don't think anything. I'm here to find out what *you* think. You can trust me, Amelia." But I didn't.

I'm almost nineteen years old. I've had doctors appointments before, teacher conferences, hospital admissions, home-visits from a healthcare worker over my hip-dysplasia as a small child… no one else has ever been able to help me. Nobody has ever even noticed I might *need* help. No one else has ever been able to see through my seemingly pillar of the community, doting father.

Why would this shrink be any different?

"Maybe we should talk about something else. The scars on your legs… did you do those to yourself?" I wondered idly if it was compulsory to have a degree in patronization in order to work here. There was no denying her question. It was blatantly fucking obvious. I was embarrassed and frustrated and I wanted her to leave. "Is there something that triggers you to do that?"

"I'm really tired. I'd like to go to sleep now," I lied, still refusing eye contact. She sighed and I could tell she was disappointed that she didn't manage to drag more dirt of me.

"Okay. I'd like to come and see you again tomorrow. Are you okay with that?"

No.

Saving Amy

I nodded passively. I doubted she'd give up on me without a condescending lecture and I was too drained to listen to her anymore.

****

I woke up to the sound of more beeps and rustling papers.

"Good morning, Amy. Did you manage to get some sleep?" It was *him* - the deliciously annoying doctor.

"Guess I must've done if you're back already." I wondered if he'd even been home. I had no idea what time it was – or even what day it was – but I eventually decided he must have been because he was wearing a white shirt and purple pinstripe tie today.

"I should let you know I called your father last night before I left."

"What! You said you wouldn't. You said you couldn't without my consent. You said-" He cut me off and started talking over me.

"I have only told him that you're awake and that your vitals are picking up. I said you were still very groggy and that we needed to carry out some observations before you could accept visitors. He asked me to call him again this morning," he said in a sorrowful tone – guilty almost. "He is going to expect to see you at some point."

My heart plummeted and tears burned the back of my eyes. It was starting. I had almost forgotten that I wasn't supposed to be here but the ache to escape was now tearing through me with vigorous speed once again. I simply nodded. He was right. I *would* have to see him.

I'm not supposed to be here…

"How did your chat with Joanna go yesterday?" He was calling it a *chat*. Interrogation more like.

"I don't like her." I shrugged sulkily and I knew I was behaving like a child. I swear I caught a glimpse of a smirk on his face.

"Do you think she can help you with your habit?"

"I don't need help," I protested. "I'm not addicted to anything. I was just dabbling; being stupid," I tacked on, assuming by 'habit' he meant drugs. There went the eyebrow again, but he let it go… for now. His eyes seemed strained – heavy… like he had something more pressing on his mind.

"What about your father? Did you talk about him?"

I shook my head and refused eye contact. I knew he thought the shrink could help me and I felt like I'd let him down by not even trying.

"Amy, can I ask why you don't want to see your father?"

Shit, a direct question. I wasn't expecting it and my heart began to race and my throat felt swollen. Instinctively I wanted to run – run far away and never look back… but my legs were still unwilling to move.

"He's not a good man," I admitted out loud for the first time in my life. Remarkably he didn't raise a doubtful eyebrow. Could he *actually* believe me?

"Not good, how?" he asked cautiously as he lowered himself down onto the edge of my bed – much less formal than the visitor's chair. I opened my mouth but the words were lodged in my throat. "You can trust me," he said as he rested a gentle palm on my forearm. It sent that bewildering current coursing through my veins and I idly wondered if he had some kind of supernatural power. Either that or I was going crazy. Well... crazy-*er*.

I didn't know why but I believed him. I *did* trust him.

"I'm not sure where to start," I admitted, deflated.

"How about the beginning..."

I drew in a deep, shaky breath and rubbed my sweaty palms on the bed sheets.

"Well, my earliest memory is watching him beat the living shit out of my mom." He scooched a little nearer and arched his back slightly towards me. He was listening. Actually *hearing* me. The honesty was unsettling yet ever so liberating. "He beats me too. He always has. When I was young it was if I didn't tidy my toys away. As I got older maybe I'd forget to clean the dishes or take the trash out, or even just look at him in the wrong way. Now, he doesn't need an excuse. If he's had a bad day... I have to pay for it."

Christ this felt good. It felt like I could go on forever.

"I note from your records you were admitted to us a couple of weeks ago with severe bruising and a fracture to your ribs. Was your father responsible for those injuries?" he asked a little too formally for my liking. Then he gently squeezed my trembling hand – encouraging me to continue. I simply nodded and without warning a stream of tears washed over my face. "Have you told anyone else about this?"

I shook my head and snorted in my tears.

"No. Never. Nobody would believe me anyway. I mean look at him – he's a rich, high-flying lawyer with friends and contacts in all the right places. He sets a very good impression as I'm sure you saw last night." His face twisted into that serious, pursed-eyebrows look. I still thought he believed me. The feeling was overwhelming and only succeeded in making my tears fall faster.

"That's not true. I believe you for one. There are so many people that can help you, Amy. You don't need to suffer this alone anymore."

"No. I'm not telling anybody else. You mustn't either. Promise me? *Please…*"

"You have to understand what kind of position this puts me in. If I suspect you're in danger…"

"Please, Richard," I begged, grabbing hold of his arm. His name just fell out of my mouth and I hoped I hadn't overstepped the mark. His eyes momentarily widened as if taken aback by my informality. I decided pleading ignorance was the best policy and carried on as if nothing had happened. "*Please…*"

He sighed heavily.

"You have my word. Like I said, you can trust me. I *want* you to trust me. I would like you to consider it though. What about your mother? Maybe you could confide in her, and she in you?" he suggested obliviously.

"She already knows. She's too wasted to care most of the time." Something vibrated in the pocket of his black suit-pants, interrupting me. It was his pager. He looked at it and sighed, running his now tense fingers through his just-got-out-of-bed hair. He seemed frustrated and I knew he had to go. My heart sank. How ridiculous was that?

"Look, I need to leave for a little while but I'll be back as soon as I can. Thank you for opening up to me, Amy." I had to mentally fight with my arm to stop it reaching out for him and pulling him back. I didn't want to be alone. For the first time in my life I wanted somebody – I *needed* somebody. I needed *him*. "And I'll make sure you have no visitors until I get back okay?"

I nodded gratefully. For the first time in my miserable existence I felt like someone had my back. Whether it was born out of professionalism or genuine compassion didn't really matter – someone cared.

After giving me a courteous nod he picked up his pace into a sprint and was out the door in a flash, making me assume he had been called to some sort of emergency.

There was a white foldout TV by my bed. I swung it around and hovered my index finger above the numerous buttons along the right hand side until I found the power switch. Once it was on, I left it on the first channel I came to. I didn't particularly want to watch anything - I was simply hoping some background noise would drown out my thoughts. Maury Povich managed to do just that and I drifted off listening to the why's and woes of a woman whose husband had been sleeping with her sister.

****

"Miss Hope, your father is here to see you, dear," a round, elderly receptionist with snow-white hair and thick-rimmed glasses informed me in a heavy southern accent. My body froze and all traces of moisture evaporated from my mouth.

I thought I could trust him.

"Amelia, thank god. Your mother and I have been so worried about you," my dad said, bursting into the room and looking every bit the loving father. The receptionist turned to leave and instinctively I closed my eyes and held my breath because I didn't know what was coming.

"I thought I said no visitors!" My eyes were startled open. It was Richard and he was chastising the old lady with his eyes.

"But it's just her father…"

"That'll be all, Mrs. Andrews." He was back in Bossy Doctor mode and he gestured his hand for her to leave. She did as she was told and I was rather impressed with his obvious authority.

I was sat just inches away from my dad and he had so many reasons to want to punish me right now… but I didn't have an ounce of fear inside me. I was also just inches away from Richard, and for some inexplicable reason I felt completely protected in his company.

"I'm glad you're here, Doctor. How's my little girl doing?" His voice nauseated my stomach.

"She's doing well, sir. Though she's not out of the woods yet. We still have observations to make and she needs further MRI scans on her spine to ensure the swelling is subsiding. In fact I have some tests to carry out just now so maybe you would like to come back later?"

"That's quite alright. I will stay with her while you carry out whatever you need to do."

No. Please...

"I'm sorry, Mr. Hope but I really can't allow that. You will need to wait outside at the very least."

"That's ridiculous. I am her father!"

"Mr. Hope," Richard addressed sternly and I was intrigued to see how he was going to get rid of him. Because I knew he would. I trusted him. "Your daughter has sustained significant injuries to her spine and to put it bluntly, she is in a state of undress under that gown. Now, I'm sure you wouldn't wish her the embarrassment of having her father watch while I examine her, would you?"

Ooo he's good.

My dad's face crumpled in irritation. He'd been backed into a corner and had no reasonable justification for putting up a fight unless he wanted to come across as a complete pervert.

"Of course. But I would like a moment alone with her before you get started."

Shit.

"I'm sorry, sir, but I really need to start now. I have a lot of patients to see today. I'm sure you understand. I suggest you go home and I will call you later on with her progress."

My dad's cheeks were visibly burning with frustration as he smoothed his moustache with his tense fingers. He was angry. I would have to pay for that soon...

"Fine," he snapped. "Although I think this is totally unnecessary and if I don't get some time alone with my daughter today I will be taking this further. Have you any idea how worried I have been?"

Richard straightened his back and shoved his hands in his pockets looking altogether... bored. He wasn't going to back down and both he and my dad knew it.

"Do you have children, Doctor Lewis?"

"No, sir," Richard replied, his voice becoming exasperated.

"No. Exactly. You're clearly not a parent, otherwise you wouldn't deny me this precious time with her."

I couldn't bear to look at him until he'd finished his little show. Though credit where it's due – he had definitely honed his acting skills. For a fleeting moment I almost believed he cared. Okay, I didn't – but jeez he put on a good performance.

Before he left my dad bent down and kissed my forehead with his slimy lips, and the razor-sharp hairs of his thick black moustache felt like they were trying to pierce my flesh. My heart ceased to beat and my skin felt like it was frantically trying to crawl away from my body. When he pulled away his eyes were wide – promising. He was warning me.

Seconds later he was gone and I could breathe again. My gasping lungs relished every gulp of air and I clamped my plastered arm to my chest, cherishing the thrum of my heart beating again. I knew I couldn't avoid him forever – but it felt like the only way I was managing to stay alive was to focus on the present. And for now… he was gone.

****

Nine days passed too quickly and apart from the cast on my wrist I was all healed – physically at least. My dad had visited several times, keeping up the pretense that he gave a shit. Thankfully Richard had never ventured further than the opposite side of my side-room door in his presence – something that my dad was quite clearly aware of given the fact I had no fresh injuries. I didn't quite understand why he was looking out for me. The feeling was overwhelming and undoubtedly undeserved.

Still, his reasons were irrelevant. I was just so tremendously grateful to him.

Julie came by yesterday with a bag of grapes and a box full of guilt. I knew it wasn't intentional and I should be flattered by how worried she was, but people (well... *person*) feeling bad for me is just too much to deal with right now; I'm doing a good enough job of that myself.

She asked what had been going on with me lately, cried a little, waffled on about being such a bad friend to me for not noticing, cried a little more... To be honest it was just frustrating. As far as Julie's concerned I got drunk and fell, yet she babbled on like I'd been struggling alone to come to terms with a terminal cancer diagnosis.

Maybe that would be easier...

It was almost lunchtime and yet my bowl of untouched cereal and curdled milk was still sitting on the wheeled table at the foot of my bed, churning my stomach. My heart was rapidly gaining weight, crushing my insides a little more each day – knowing that each hour that passed was one step closer to going home.

At least that meant no more daily visits from Joanna Interfering Shrink Lady. I was getting sick to my stomach with her. She suggested I was depressed and tried several times to get me to agree to a course of antidepressants. What a load of bullshit. I'm not depressed. It's not a simple little chemical imbalance temporarily distorting my view of the world. A box of pills isn't going to calm my dad's twitchy fists. They aren't going to heal the scars on my legs and they're not going to repair the damage done to my mind.

Still, I eventually agreed just to get her off my case. Though I have no intentions of taking them.

A knock on the door snatched me out of my episode of self-pity and I sat up sharply, swinging my legs over the edge of the bed. My anxious face instantly melted into a smile when I saw Richard coming towards me. Pulling up the visitor's chair, he sat down beside me.

"You didn't get these from me," he whispered, winking and slipping a pack of cigarettes under my pillow.

Yesterday was a *bad* day. I felt physically crushed by unyielding feelings of frustration... anger, fear, guilt... and I threw quite a spectacular tantrum about having not smoked for almost two weeks.

I smiled bashfully as he slid his hand from under my pillow.

"Look, Amy... I really am going to have to discharge you soon. I'm running out of reasons to keep you here." His serious face erased my smile and despite knowing his words were inevitable they still managed to tie a knot around my heart. "Please reconsider accepting some form of support," he continued, almost pleaded – his voice dripping with what sounded like concern.

I shook my head defiantly.

I had coped for this long and I could do it again. Besides, with nothing better to do than stare at these drab walls for nine days I had occupied myself by making plans. I'm going to keep my head down at home and find a job. I don't care what or how much it pays – I will do anything and live anywhere. I crashed straight through the stone at rock bottom the night I ended up in here so surely the only is was up?

"I'll be fine, Richard." I was comfortable saying his name now. "I've got plans."

I looked up to study his delectable face and his brow was furrowed. He was vigorously rubbing his left forearm with his tense right hand and he looked like he was frustrated. With me? Why? His reaction puzzled me and I snapped.

"Look, you've done your bit now. You've fixed me up – made me better. Why are you so bothered what happens to me?"

His emerald eyes widened. He looked surprised – maybe even a little pissed. After pausing for a few long seconds he dragged in a deep, preparing breath and opened his mouth to speak. His eyes burrowed intently into mine. My heart began to stutter as if I was expecting to hear something magical.

"I'm your doctor. It's my duty to care," he finally responded. The words twisted around my heart, crushing it. I think it would have hurt less if he'd kicked me in the stomach.

What did you want him to say? That he loves you? Stupid bitch, my sarcastic, pain in the ass subconscious piped up.

I had foolishly conceived some kind of bond between us and reality had just punched me in the face. He was my doctor and I was his patient… period. My cheeks burnt with embarrassment and suddenly I was eager to escape – desperate to leave this dreary room and desperate to leave *him* and the nonsensical fascination I'd developed behind.

****

It was early evening and I could hear my dad's voice outside my room – he was here to pick me up. I refused to succumb to the fear beginning to simmer deep in my belly so I stretched my neck, defiantly held my head up high and reached for the door.

He was standing in front of me flattering a receptionist.

"Let's get you home," he said tenderly, under the glare of his sadistic eyes.

The timid red-haired clerk thrust some papers in front of me and I signed them without bothering to read what they were. I hadn't seen Richard since this morning and despite telling myself that was a good thing, I still found my eyes wondering the corridor in search of him.

As we exited the hospital I scanned the grounds of the building one last time. I sighed disappointedly. He may well only be my doctor but surely a goodbye wasn't beyond his code of *duty*? We'd had some intense conversations while I'd been here as well as some lighthearted ones. He even managed to make me laugh a few times. It'd been so long since I'd even smiled, I had forgotten how good it felt.

"Get in," my dad ordered, snapping my eyes from their unsuccessful search. Reluctantly, I clambered in to the back seat of his silver Jag, stuffed the bag of meds I had no plans to take into my belongings bag and then rested my head against the window, closing my eyes.

The engine vibrated through the glass, tickling my cheek and momentarily making me forget where I was and who I was with. Too soon, I was pulled back into reality when the car halted with a jolt. We were here. I was... *home*.

My dad got out first and marched straight to the house without so much as a glance in my direction. I climbed out hesitantly – my back still a little tender – and trailed tautly behind him.

Walking into the regrettably familiar atmosphere slammed into my body like a brick wall the second I crossed the threshold. My mom was stood timidly in the doorway of the living room, knotting her trembling fingers. I could tell she was about an hour away from the vomiting stage. My dad shoved past her, making his way to the kitchen.

"Amelia," she greeted in a foreign tone. Bizarrely she sounded like she was actually pleased to see me. "Are you okay?"

I was stunned into silence by the sound of her voice and I realized it was the first time she'd spoken to me in what must be years.

"I'm fine," I eventually managed to mutter. My dad re-emerged and clicked his fingers at her before pointing into the living room like a master over his dog, to which she dutifully obeyed. He followed after her and I began the process of dragging my heavy legs up the stairs to seek solace in my bedroom. When I reached it I threw my clear 'Patient

Belongings' bag to the floor and climbed into bed, pulling the covers straight over my head.

Tears began to sting as they leaked from the corners of my eyes. Soon enough they were flowing freely and settling into a pool in the crook of my neck. The pain in my chest was excruciating. I could feel my heart begin to swell. My lungs felt crushed by the weight of it – struggling to fill with air. It was so painful – as if it was about to burst. I needed to get it out. Release the pressure. I needed to *see* it.

Just one.

Of course once I started I couldn't seem to stop at just one. Perched on the edge of the bath I ran the blood-stained blade through my soft flesh for the fourth time... but I wanted more. The painful balloon that'd formed in my chest deflated a little more with each cut. Each time was deeper and I watched intently as the pain drained from my body, making pretty red patterns as it spiraled down my leg.

I could breathe again after the sixth cut. My heart felt lighter and my lungs were freed. I sighed contentedly as I cleaned myself up and sprayed the evidence of my anguish with antiseptic before grabbing my dressings from under my bed and covering them up. That always disappointed me somewhat. I liked to see them. I *needed* to see them. They were a reminder that my pain was real.

Regret consumed me as I curled myself up into a tight ball on top of my comforter. I didn't think I'd ever have to lie here again. I didn't *want* to ever have to lie here again. Once again I sobbed heavily into my pillow, crying until my eyes were too sore and swollen to produce fresh tears.

Saving Amy

****

My ears pricked up at the sound of the doorbell and automatically I noted the time – 07:45 PM. No one ever visited this house and it was surely too late for a salesman. Gently easing myself out of bed I crept across the landing to the top of the stairs, making sure I avoided the loose floorboard outside my bedroom door.

"Well you can't. She's sleeping. Surely this can wait until morning?" I heard my dad say. He sounded angry and it ignited fear in my bones. Whoever it was would be my fault.

"I'm afraid it can't. This medication was missed off her prescription and it's vital I explain the dosage and instructions to her," replied the most soothing voice in the world.

I was already half way down the stairs. When I reached the bottom my dad turned and glared at me. His sinister eyes were bursting with promise and I knew he was annoyed with me. Possibly foolishly - with Richard just feet away from me – I didn't care.

"Amy," Richard said and his velvety voiced melted into my ears. "I'm sorry to bother you so late but I just need to run through a couple of things with you. Is that okay?" I nodded overenthusiastically and I heard my dad's breathing becoming jagged beside me. Bravely – or stupidly – I stepped past him and out onto the front yard, closing the door behind me.

Richard was wearing tight blue jeans and a white v-neck sweater. He looked like he'd just jumped off the cover of Vogue magazine and my ridiculous heart did that stupid fluttering thing. He looked nervous as he handed me a white paper bag containing a small box of pills. *Surely a late night home visit to drop off meds is above and beyond his precious duties,* my smartass subconscious bellowed. I mentally slapped the invisible face behind the unwelcome voice and embraced the few minutes of feeling safe that were about to follow.

"What are these?" I asked, peering into the paper bag.

"Aspirin," he answered in a confessional tone, leaving me bewildered. "I was called into the E.R. this afternoon on my way to see you. When I'd finished you were gone. I had to know you were okay."

Why?

"I'm fine. I told you I would be fine."

"And would you tell me if you weren't?" I thought about it for a moment and decided I probably wouldn't. What would be the point?

"Yes, I would," I lied. "But let's face it, you're not around for me to tell now. I'm not your patient anymore," I answered a little more acerbically than I'd intended. The realization sent my heart diving into my stomach.

"I'm here now."

Again, why?

What did he want from me? Was I really just his patient? I had no reason to believe he was anything more than my doctor but I could just *feel* some kind of invisible, inexplicable force between us. Magnetic almost – as if I was physically being pulled towards him. I studied his face intently for signs that he felt it too. His brow was furrowed – was he confused, like me? His breathing was strained – was his heart aching, like mine? His fingers were fidgeting by his sides – was it stop them reaching out and touching me, like mine with him?

Of course it isn't. Stop being so fucking dumb.

Struggling to believe he felt it too I convinced myself I was just seeing what I wanted to and the sheer perplexity of it all rapidly grew into frustration.

"Look, Richard… I've told you I don't want support from any shrink, counselor or whoever else you've got up your sleeve," I snapped.

"What about me? What about support from *me?*"

Why!

"I really do understand some of what you're going through."

Like hell you do.

"You've been great – everyone at the hospital has. But I've been discharged now. I'm not your responsibility anymore." Richard's brow dropped and he started rubbing his forearm. I couldn't tell if he was disappointed or frustrated but he was most definitely not what he should've been – indifferent.

My mind and my heart were bursting at the seams.

"Of course." He nodded crisply – back in doctor mode. "My apologies again for disturbing you so late. If you need anything or have any concerns, please don't hesitate to contact the hospital," he responded so frustratingly formally. I decided there and then he definitely had two sides. Richard and Doctor Lewis were like two completely different people – like Jekyll and Hyde.

Nodding equally formally, I turned to go back inside.

"Amy?" He gently grabbed my arm just above my cast and pulled me back a step. "Take care of yourself."

I nodded once again and smiled warmly at him. When he released his hold of my arm my heart struck a painfully fast rhythm and I knew this was probably the last time I'd ever see him. Swallowing back a choking lump in my throat I headed back inside, closing the door without looking back.

I was taking my first step on the stairs when I was abruptly pulled back down.

"What have you been telling him?" my dad roared. Before my brain had time to process his words I found myself pinned up against the wall by the strong, smarting grip of his hand around the base of my throat.

"Nothing. I've said nothing," I wheezed.

"Don't bullshit me, girl. Doctor's don't just turn up like that. I'm sure he has enough monkeys to do his dirty work for him. I hope for your sake you're telling the goddamn truth."

"I am. I swear it," I choked out.

"Get upstairs," he demanded after giving my neck one last shove into the wall. I breathed a sigh of relief. I was expecting worse.

I was back hibernating under my quilt – which was still damp from my earlier tears – when every bad thought that led me down the path to the hospital returned with vigorous speed. I tried to remember the plans I made but now I was here, back in reality, I couldn't see them actually materializing.

Saving Amy

Graduation was one week away and I'd missed all but one final. Who would employ me now?

There was no way out. I would never escape my father – he'd make sure of it. Trying to resign myself to the life I'd been given, I sank my face into my tearstained pillow and sobbed violently into it – *again.*

Chapter Four

```
Me: Good luck 2day. Sorry I'm not
with U. I'm sure you'll do
amazing! xoxo
```

I tapped Julie's name into the recipient bar and hit 'send'. Today was graduation and Julie had been asked to give a short speech as a sort of consolation prize for missing out on being valedictorian by just two credits. Today was the start of her future and I just knew she'd go on to do amazing things with her life. She had everything I used to wish for and nobody deserved it more than she did.

I started to wonder if school had bothered to contact my dad over the fact I'd just stopped attending one day, and what excuse he gave them if they had. Eventually I decided they couldn't have done – I'd be a few bruises worse off if they had. They mustn't give a rat's ass about me either.

My cell vibrated against the wood of my dresser.

```
Julie: Cheers Amy. Wish u were
here. I'll fill u in tomoz! Love u
xo
```

Shit. I'd forgotten we were meeting tomorrow. If graduating was about passing the world's shittiest friend final I'd have been the first to get my diploma.

Saving Amy

I was both relieved and grateful that she'd reminded me. I didn't know when I would see her again now she'd been accepted into the University of Florida.

I could've quite easily gotten depressed about that today so I decided to jump in the shower before it took over my mind. By the time I'd finished it was time to trawl the city in search of a job. Someone must have to something to offer. I was prepared to do *anything*. Selling, waitressing, scrubbing toilets…

I got in my car feeling unusually upbeat - *positive* – and headed out towards the city.

****

When I got back in my car I slammed the door closed and slumped my head over the wheel. I was all rejected out. I couldn't take another 'no', 'sorry no vacancies' or 'what qualifications do you hold?' for today. It was 05:15 PM but I couldn't face going home yet – my dad was due home shortly so I planned to hold out until I knew he'd be in bed.

My only friend was busy graduating and I had no money so it looked like I was in for a few hours sat in my car with the stereo blaring to drown out my thoughts. I scanned through the stations until I came across a half-decent song, threw my head back and closed my eyes – letting Adele distract me for what wouldn't be long enough.

Startled by a knock on my window, my eyes jolted towards the glass. Then my heart sank. It was Leon. Hesitantly, I rolled down the window.

"Long time no see," he chatted as if we were friends but I knew he was only here to make money.

"What do you want, Leon?"

"That's no way to greet an old friend now is it? You seem tense. I can help you with that."

Here we go.

"No thanks. I'm done with that shit," I declared and hoped it was enough to send him packing. Oddly, I hadn't given the stuff a single thought since ending up in the hospital and I'd had more than enough reasons to. Bizarrely, somewhere entrenched in the back of my mind, I wondered if it was because of Richard and some kind of deep desire not to let him down – even though the rational part of me knew I'd probably never see him again.

"*Really?*" The arrogant fucker sounded surprised. "Well it's always best to have something handy for when things get too much. Here…" He passed me a familiar pouch through the window. Immediately I pushed it away.

"Seriously, I'm not interested. I've no cash on me even if I was," I declared, positive the fact I had nothing to offer him would definitely send him on his merry way.

"Call it a favor. You'll thank me in the end." Leon dropped the pouch onto my knee and then winked and walked away before I could pass it back to him. I huffed into my shoulder and stuffed the packet into a rip in the lining of my purse before anyone saw it. I would dispose of it later.

It was 06:45 PM already. The time had passed quicker than expected but I didn't think I could hold out much longer. My neck was stiff and I was getting cramp in my legs. I gave in and started the engine to head home. If I was fast enough I could probably make it to my bedroom without seeing my dad on the way.

His car was missing from the drive when I arrived home and my veins were saturated with relief. After killing the engine I grabbed my purse and scuttled hurriedly down the path to the front door. As usual I planned to run straight upstairs but I froze when I stepped inside and saw my mom crumpled on the floor, rocking back and forth.

"Amelia," she gasped and held out her hand for me to help her stand. Selfishly I wanted to ignore her and get to my room but deep down I knew that would make me as sadistic as my father. Taking her shaking hand, I pulled her upright. Her lips were swollen to double their size and a trail of dried blood was stuck to her chin.

"Are you alright?" I felt obliged to ask. She nodded and sniffed in her tears. She looked a mess and as much as I wanted to think she deserved it, I didn't. I looked into her empty eyes and saw my future. The thought ripped through my heart and suddenly I was terrified.

"Go sit down. I'll get you some water," I offered. That was probably the longest interaction we'd ever had. She smiled as gratefully as she could manage and went into the living room. When I stepped past her to get to the kitchen she stopped me, pulling me back by the arm.

"Maybe something a little stronger," she suggested – erasing all traces of my sympathy. My eyes scanned her up and down in disgust then I reached for the half-empty gin bottle on the walnut bookshelf and threw it onto the couch where she was heading. Immediately I left the room and I could hear her screwing the cap off before I'd even reached the stairs.

That was another day over and nothing had changed. I was back here – alone under my flowery quilt – with no job, soon to be no friends, no education and no escape.

I was scared…

****

Sitting in The Daily Grind coffee house waiting for Julie I'd almost finished my iced-tea. Leaning back into the dark green couch, which housed a squared-off lightwood table, I was surrounded by businessmen and students. I found myself staring at the passers-by – watching and admiring them going about their business. Watching them *live*…

Julie inadvertently pulled me out of my self-pitying episode by flailing her arms in the air like a lunatic when she caught my eye across the floor.

"Amy!" she greeted vociferously as she bent down to my seated level to throw her arms around me. She looked different – more mature. She only graduated yesterday but she already seemed too old for high school. She exuded a confidence I'd never noticed before and suddenly looked all intellectual. Not that she looked dumb before or anything…

"How are you, Miss University of Florida Student?" I quipped. She giggled and was so obviously proud of herself. And so she should be.

"Oh, Amy, I'm just so happy. There's so much to look forward to. A whole new world is waiting for me." Her words panged in my heart and I wanted to cry. I mentally chastised myself for being so goddamn selfish when I should've just been happy for her.

"That's fantastic, Jules. I'm so proud of you." She smiled bashfully and then reached across the table to take hold of my hand.

"What about you?" she asked empathically. "Are things getting better at home? I know you've had a rough couple of months."

I wish I could tell you the half of it.

"Yeah, things are picking up. I'm looking for a job and hoping to get my own place pretty soon." I tried my utmost to sound upbeat. I didn't want to send her away on a downer.

"That's great!"

"Don't get me wrong, I know I've blown my chances of a decent career just now. But hopefully if I can find a job that pays me enough to get set up somewhere I can concentrate on re-taking my finals later or something. We'll see…" I was trying desperately to sound hopeful about my future but I wasn't sure how convincing I sounded.

"I'm sure you'll do just great. I'm going to miss you so much." My eyes fought with every breath against the urge to cry as she squeezed my hand.

"I'll miss you too. We've had some fun together haven't we?" The thought, and the memories, were heart-warming and mournful at the same time. It felt almost like I was grieving for her.

We spent the afternoon ordering coffees, laughing and reminiscing about our high school years together. We promised to keep in touch but I knew in reality that would eventually fade. She had a life bursting with new experiences and opportunities ahead of her and I knew I would soon become a distant memory.

Julie is my very best friend. My *only* friend. My only distraction from the fucked-up world in which I live. Now she's leaving and I'll have nobody.

I'll have nothing…

****

Life was bleak. It was my birthday yesterday. I celebrated another year of this miserable existence tucked under my quilt, using the light from my cell to read The Only Way Is Up – a true story about a boy who was locked in his grandfather's basement for the first fifteen years of his life – and listening to the arguments radiating up the stairs.

I sat on the edge of the bed staring myself up and down in the arched mirror on my dresser. I looked so old. So tired. Why was I here? What was my purpose? I could see no viable reason for my existence other than to suffer. Maybe I was a murderer in a previous life. Maybe I was being tested by some higher being.

Maybe I was just bad…

I remained completely unsuccessful in my search for work so decided to change direction. Instead of walking in and asking for vacancies I now had a tidy pile of written applications stacked up on my bedside table waiting to be mailed. I planned to mail them today but first I needed money for postage. As usual, I waited for the sound of the power shower so I could head downstairs and find my dad's wallet.

Saving Amy

I didn't have to wait long before I heard the jet of water and my dad's morning coughing ritual so I knew it was him. I quickly threw on my baby-blue sweats and tiptoed over the loose floorboard and down the stairs. His wallet was resting in its customary spot on the kitchen counter and I slipped my fingers in and grabbed three notes without checking what they were.

"What the fuck are you doing? YOU THIEVING LITTLE BITCH!"

I screamed as I was spun around and my back slammed into the stove behind me. I refused to feel afraid. Fear had been slowly killing me for nineteen years and I'd had enough.

"Get your hands off me," I said firmly, sending waves of hot, rage-fuelled blood into his cheeks. His breathing accelerated and I watched his hand as he balled it into a fist. "Get it over with already," I snapped, utterly emotionless, trying not to retch as the stench of Old Spice flooded my nose. I was pushing him and I didn't care. In fact, I think I wanted him to lose it.

"Go on... DO IT!" I yelled and within half a second the first punch momentarily blinded me.

He lost all control and I took blow after blow to my face. He was usually so clever but he'd lost himself completely. I smelt a hint of whiskey coming from his sickening breath and I wondered if that was why he'd become so careless.

A couple of strikes later and I couldn't feel it anymore. I threw my head back to steady my neck and prevent it jolting too far. My body felt lifeless and I didn't know how I was managing to stay upright. I willingly accepted each blow and then it dawned on me that this could all be over so quickly. The one person I was so desperate to escape from could set me free with one hard, precise blow.

I needed to antagonize him.

"Surely you can do better than that?" I spluttered, my mouth filled with hot blood.

My eyes closed in preparation but were forced open immediately when I felt myself being dragged across the floor.

"Get the fuck out of my sight," he slurred when he eventually let go of my sweater, sending me flying into the gravel on the front yard. I was hurt and disorientated and so had no choice but to lie in the dirt for a few long minutes while I gathered my bearings.

I looked around hoping to see someone – anyone. But there was nobody in sight. The street and all its houses seemed lifeless. *Figures.* The one time the lucky bastard lost it outside the confines of the house and there wasn't a soul to witness it. He couldn't have planned it better if he'd tried.

After a few minutes I managed to crawl into a kneeling position and pull myself up on the drainpipe. My battered face was starting to ache. I touched my lip and gasped when it stung, noticing blood on my fingers when I pulled them away. What in hell was I supposed to do now?

I had no money, no purse, no car keys, no cell… I didn't even have any shoes. Tears scratched at the back of my eyes but they were too swollen to let them escape. Dazed, I began to walk down the path but had no idea where I was going. The coarse asphalt scraped at the soles of my bare feet when I reached the sidewalk, burning them the farther I went. In an effort to hide my face I pulled the hood of my sweater up over my head and walked gingerly past the house and down the street.

I'd managed only a few yards when a fancy black car screeched to a sudden halt beside me. I picked up my pace – the last thing I wanted was someone asking for directions when I looked like God knows what. When I heard the slam of a car door and footsteps hastening towards me from behind my body went rigid. Should I run? Ask what they wanted without turning around and showing my face? Collapse and beg for help?

I flinched when a hand landed on my shoulder. I didn't notice that was sore until now. Every self-defense move I'd ever seen in a movie flashed through my head as I prepared to scream. I'd never believed in God but I found myself begging him for help in my head.

He answered.

"Amy?" Immediately I flung myself around.

"Richard!" I wailed, throwing myself onto him and clutching his open military-style grey jacket into my fists.

"Shh, shh," he whispered into my hair. "It's okay. You're okay. What's happened, Amy?" I couldn't respond. My head was buried in his chest and my fingers were aching from clawing at him so hard but they refused to let go. The tears found their way out then, and began spilling rapidly onto his shirt.

"Amy, please. Look at me." I raised my head slowly, peering out through the tight slits of my swollen eyes. "Jesus Christ! Is that bastard still in there? I'm calling the police…" he trailed off, easing away from me, and then started pounding towards the house while reaching into his pocket for his cell.

"Richard no! Please don't leave me. Please!" I whimpered. Suddenly I was overwhelmed with exhaustion and I collapsed to my knees. He was by my side in seconds, supporting me with his body weight.

"He can't be allowed to get away with this," he said quietly but firmly. I could feel the frustration – the *anger* – writhing through his tense body but I just wanted to get away from here. I just wasn't strong or courageous enough to take on my father again.

"Just get me out of here. *Please…*" I begged him.

"Okay," he murmured, sighing heavily in defeat. "Okay."

I clung to his arm to pull myself up but before I could even try I was scooped in his arms like a baby. Wrapping my weak arms around his neck I held on as tightly as I could, burying my face in his shoulder. The feeling was so alien to me – I had never felt so secure. He held me effortlessly with one arm as he used his other to open the passenger door of his car and then slowly, cautiously, he lowered me into the seat.

"Where are you taking me?" I asked as he slid in beside me and assisted my fumbling fingers on their mission to fasten my seatbelt. The thought of more time in the hospital filled my veins with dread – more questions, more interrogations, more interfering nurses trying to help…

"I'm taking you back to my place while I examine your injuries," he replied very matter of fact.

Saving Amy

Doctor Lewis was back but I didn't mind. I was just relieved he was here... and that I was safe.

Richard had to use a small black key fob and punch three different sets of numbers into various keypads to gain us entry but finally we were in his apartment. It seemed bigger than the last time I was here. He gestured for me to sit on an ostentatiously large, black-leather corner suite in a vast open-plan living area – every wall painted a brilliant white. There was a *huge* kitchen at the far end which was glossy white and stainless steel and right in front of me, built into the wall, was a white, open coal fire – although I was pretty sure it was electric.

He couldn't be more than twenty-eight years old, which meant he couldn't be so high up in the world of medicine. So where did all this extravagance come from?

"Let me take a look," Richard said softly as he settled down next to me on the couch. He gently raised my chin with his forefinger and set about assessing me. I studied his eyes intently as they wandered over my face. They were a vivid green – sparkling like emeralds under the ceiling halogens – and heavy with what looked like concern.

He was... beautiful.

"Son of a..." I gasped when the slight pressure of his tender finger brushed my lips.

"I'm sorry. I think this needs stitches." His expression was painful, worried. I felt guilty that it was *me* making him feel like that. *Stitches*. I sighed heavily and dropped my head.

"What is it?" he asked.

"I was just hoping I wouldn't need the hospital again."

"Don't worry," he assured, smiling softly. "I can do it here. Wait there."

Phew...

Richard disappeared into another room and my eyes wandered my surroundings. They were drawn to a photograph in a silver, embellished frame sitting proudly in the center of a set of three floating glass shelves. It was an old man – the image of Richard but with snow-white hair and deep lines framing his eyes – with his arm around a lady with a short, honey-blonde bob and Richard's smile. It was his parents without a doubt.

Upon his return Richard set a steel tray down on the coffee table in front of our knees. Then he picked up a sterile blister pack and carefully peeled it open, exposing a pre-filled needle.

"This is just a local anesthetic. It might sting a little." Slowly, he brought the sharp point towards my lips.

Holy fuck that hurts...

"Good girl," he said when it was over and I couldn't help but giggle.

"What?" he asked curiously.

"You know, you can be a condescending son of a bitch at times," I admitted playfully – and honestly. A small smirk crawled across his lips.

"Funnily enough you're not the first person to say that," he conceded with a mischievous expression.

The left side of my face felt like it had doubled in size and I could no longer feel my lips or my tongue – or my nose for that matter. Richard tested the area with the prod of a different kind of needle.

"Can you feel that?" I shook my head. I didn't think I could speak with a numb tongue. "Good," he said with a slight nod before getting to work on my busted face. He didn't talk while he was patching me up. His eyebrows were set firmly down and I decided that must be his concentrating face.

"All done," he said proudly, assessing his handiwork. Then he sat up straight and stretched his back.

"That was quick," I noted, sounding like I had a mouth full of Jell-O. I must have lost all sense of time immersed in studying his perfect face.

"I'm a fast worker." He winked at me, sending tickling ripples through my stomach, and then he left the room with the tray. He returned less than a minute later and handed me two pills and a glass of water.

"Advil," he stated, answering my unspoken question. "For the swelling." I popped them in my numb mouth but couldn't feel them on my tongue so I just kept glugging the water until I assumed they must be gone. "You can't keep living like this, Amy." His voice turned abruptly serious, instantly turning the air heavy.

What other choice do I have?

I stayed quiet. I had no answer that he would want to hear.

"What were you doing at my house tonight?" I asked curiously, even though I didn't actually care. I was just glad he was there.

"I noticed you didn't turn up for your appointment with Kevin – sorry, Doctor Carroll. I needed to see you were okay."

He needed *to?*

"Why, Richard? Why did you need to?"

His eyes refused contact with mine and his eyebrows knitted together. He looked… embarrassed? Then he shook his head.

"I wish I had an answer for that. But the truth is…" His face contorted into an unreadable expression – almost as if he was having some kind of internal debate with himself. Then he paused and drew in a deep breath. "The truth is I have absolutely no fucking idea."

Um… okay.

"Look, you need to rest. You can stay here while we figure something out." He changed the subject abruptly – *too* abruptly.

The sheer relief I felt from his words was overpowering and once again I started blubbering like a baby. His protective arms were around me in seconds, which only succeeded in making me cry harder.

"You're safe here," he whispered into my hair. "Come on…" Slowly releasing me, he took hold of my hand and pulled me gently from the couch.

He led me to the familiar bedroom. It looked exactly as my mind remembered it except the bedding was different. This time the mattress rested under a rich purple quilt, patterned with embroidered silver butterflies – very feminine. My heart sank a little as I pondered whether someone else – a woman – lived here too.

"My mother bought it," Richard admitted as he followed my gaze towards the bed. I smiled inwardly and my ridiculous jealousy faded. "The bathroom is two doors down the hall – it should have everything you need. Oh, and there's some of my t-shirts in those drawers if you want to get changed," he said, gesturing his hand towards a set of beech drawers at the foot of the bed.

"Thank you. For everything…" I smiled gratefully at him. Or at least I thought I did – my face was still too numb to know for sure.

"I'll leave you alone. *Sleep*," he ordered in his Bossy Doctor voice. It was starting to grow on me.

I took a moment to absorb my surroundings once he left the room. This bedroom was easily three times the size of mine. The wall to my right was lined with fitted beech closets – the doors concealed by full-length mirrors. The wall on my left housed an enormous flat screen which looked like it was floating – no signs of wires or brackets – and straight ahead on the far wall was a large, gleaming window comprising of three separate panes which spread across the full width of the room; an idyllic frame to the picturesque view of Seattle's tallest and finest buildings.

This place must have cost a small fortune.

Venturing out into the hall I counted two doors along as instructed to find the bathroom. I knew I'd been here before but I didn't remember it being so big. I was faced with a mammoth white oval bath – easily big enough for three – standing freely in the center of the limestone room. In the far right corner there was a floor to ceiling shower cubicle and next to it stood a huge – *naturally* – mirrored unit, home to a double sink set and what looked like fancy faucets; two stainless steel channels protruding from the wall which I assumed water flowed through like a river.

Above the basins hung an elaborate mirror, embellished with frosted swirls around the edges. I walked tentatively towards it – refusing to look directly into it because I was nervous about the image that would greet me. Once I was positioned in front of it I closed my eyes for a short while, dragging in deep breaths and preparing myself.

Eventually I summoned the courage and peeled my eyes open slowly. I was stunned backwards a step or two when my eyes met those of the swollen, battered face in the mirror. I didn't recognize myself. My left eye was a blue/purple color – engorged to the point of being almost closed. My lips were virtually black and so bloated they nearly touched my nose. Richard was right. How long could I go on like this? Painful knots began to coil in my stomach because I knew the answer was forever. I wasn't brave or clever enough to escape.

If I hadn't been so drained I would've cried. I was physically and mentally exhausted. I was too tired to wait for the bath to fill – it was so big it would probably take days – so I opted for a shower. It took me a good five minutes to work out how to get into it and then a further five to switch the damn thing on.

At last, a powerful stream of cathartic water fell from the stainless steel jets burrowed into the ceiling above me –cleansing my body and my mind. There was a suspended glass shelf unit in front of me stocked with every kind of men's toiletries you could think of. My swollen eyes struggled to read the labels so I picked up each one in turn to examine them closer. Shave gel, expensive-looking moisturizer, exfoliator and finally shower crème – enriched with aloe apparently. I squirted the white, marbled foam generously into my palms and tentatively lathered it over my bruised body, washing any traces of *his* vile touch away.

Next I found a bottle of tea-tree shampoo and smoothed it liberally through my hair. It smelt divine – fresh and masculine; it smelt like Richard. The residue bit into the stitches in my bottom lip as I rinsed the lather away and it stung like hell. I made a mental note to tip my head backwards next time.

I impressed myself by managing to turn off the ridiculously complicated shower in under a minute and cautiously stepped out onto the slatted wooden slip board. My hair was saturated and dripping down my back and I realized I didn't have a towel. I scanned the room but there was none on show. *Damn.*

Luckily I found them in the first place I looked – piled neatly in size ascending order inside the mirrored closets under the basins. I briefly wondered who would design cupboards with mirrors so low down? Who needed to see their feet and calves?

I took two towels – both exceptionally white and fluffy – wrapped one around my hair and one around my body, then I headed out to find my bedroom again. *It's not* your *bedroom,* I was reminded by my wide-awake, smartass subconscious. I told it to fuck off.

Back in the bedroom I rummaged through Richard's t-shirt drawer. Every single one was designer label and I decided this drawer alone must be worth thousands of dollars. I settled on a plain white v-neck with the Ralph Lauren polo logo sewn into the breast and before I slipped it on I found myself clutching it to my nose and inhaling Richard's scent. It calmed me but I had no idea why. Maybe the blow to the head was making me lose my mind.

After throwing the shirt on quickly, I climbed into bed. Like everything else it was bigger than I remembered – and comfier. The plump feather pillows molded to my head and before I had chance to torture myself with thoughts, I drifted into a deep, dreamless sleep.

I woke to pain radiating from my entire face. My heart sank as reality punched me once more. When my eyes first opened, for a few brief seconds, I had forgotten…

Despite the pain I felt rested. I think I must have slept straight through for the first night in years – if ever. A gentle tap on the door pulled me from my musing.

"Come in," I said in a high-pitched tone, knowing it would be Richard. He popped his head around the doorjamb and I felt an irrational disappointment that I couldn't see more of him.

"Good morning," he greeted with a delicious smile. "I've made you some breakfast. It's in the kitchen when you're ready."

Wow.

"Thank you. I'll be out in just a minute."

He was gone as fast as he came and I found myself rushing around to get ready. It was only after I'd been to the bathroom, changed into another one of Richard's t-shirts – black with silver stitching – and fussed around with my hair to make it look half way to presentable, I realized I was in such a hurry because I was so eager to be in Richard's presence again.

I didn't understand myself at all.

Separating the kitchen from the living room was a large rectangular, glass dining table surrounded by eight iron chairs with elaborate swirled backs and plump, cream padded seats. It was adorned with white square plates, flowers and at least ten different varieties of breakfast foods. As I moved closer I could see a collection of cereals, toast, croissants, fruit salad, freshly ground coffee…

"I didn't know what you liked to eat in the mornings so I figured I couldn't go wrong with a bit of everything." That delectable smile of his was back. I could stare at it all day.

"You really didn't need to go to all this trouble," I said, feeling slightly embarrassed and unworthy of his generosity.

"You've been through an awful lot, Amy. You need energy inside of you if you have any hope of getting better," he replied in his Bossy Doctor voice. Then he proffered his hand towards the iron chair at the head of the table before pulling it out for me to sit on. I did, and as he pushed me towards the table I noticed the sweet, sunny music swirling around my ears.

It was coming from his iPod dock on the kitchen counter. The librettos were slow and expressive – uplifting… comforting. I opened my mouth to ask who she was but Richard got in there first.

"I've got to leave for work soon." The words squeezed my heart so tightly I feared it might burst. *He's leaving me.* "But don't worry, I'm only doing a half shift. I'll be back around lunchtime." His smile reassured me and my heart began to accept the flow of blood once more. I nodded and attempted to smile before he turned to leave the room without sitting down for breakfast. Had he really gone to all this effort *just* for *me*?

"Feel free to take a look around while I'm gone. And don't even *think* about clearing these dishes away – I'll do it when I get back," he ordered, eyeing up the lavish table as he paused in the doorway and briefly popped his head back into the room.

I stared after him as he left and I wished I were brave enough to ask why he was being so nice to me. I was getting attached to him – reliant even – and it frightened the hell out of me. Deep down I knew his support wouldn't be around forever. It was only a matter of time before it got too much for him and he passed me on to one of his shrink friends. The thought of facing life without him ignited a fire of panic inside my belly and I started blubbing pathetically into my cornflakes.

I can't do this alone…

After a few long minutes my tears turned to snuffles and suddenly I was ravenous. I was faced with a table packed with mouth-watering food and the delicious smell made my stomach rumble. Pushing my tear-drenched cornflakes aside, I reached across the table for a croissant. It was still warm and smelt heavenly – fresh and buttery. I made the most of being alone and devoured it in just three bites. Then I worked my way through two of the four slices of toast sitting gracefully in a porcelain toast rack before finishing off with a generous dollop of fruit salad.

I had eaten to the point of feeling sick but jeez it felt good. I couldn't remember the last time I ate so well. I felt satisfied – ready for the day. There was no way I would allow Richard to return to such a mess though so I stood up, gathered as many plates as I could with one arm hindered in a cast and took them through to the kitchen. I returned and repeated the process until the table was clear. Well... almost. It was only when I moved the percolator, I noticed two Advil, a glass of freshly squeezed orange juice and a little note hiding behind it.

Take these and REST!

My mouth melted into a smile before my interfering subconscious knocked it straight back off again. *Why is he doing this?*

Seeing the painkillers reminded my lips to throb so I gulped them down quickly before cracking on with the clearing up. I must've opened at least five different glossy white cupboards before I found the one hiding the dishwasher. Then I scraped the plates into the trashcan I found in the first cupboard before loading them onto the racks. Surprise, surprise, it was huge and overly complicated. It had so many rows of buttons and switches it could've easily been misconstrued as a jet-plane cockpit. Afraid of breaking it, I decided to leave that job for Richard and set about wiping the surfaces down.

I was finished all too quickly and the place looked as neat and showy as it did before. I remembered Richard telling me to look around but it felt cheeky of me so decided against it. Until the potent mix of boredom and curiosity got the better of me that is…

Exiting the main living space I entered the vast hallway and worked my way through the doors one by one. I came across two more bedrooms – neutrally decorated like the one I'm staying in – and a study. Inside was a sizeable walnut desk, home to an impressive laptop, strip lamp and dozens of papers. Behind it stood an extensive bookcase housing hundreds of books and my eyes couldn't even begin to read the vast array of titles. It reminded me of one of those great libraries inside an old English country mansion like you see on TV.

Finally, at the end of the hallway I wandered into another bedroom. It was easily the biggest room in the whole apartment and I knew straight away this was Richard's room. I stepped in onto the glossy black, tiled floor, adorned with a massive snow-white shaggy rug and was faced with a mammoth bed complete with black leather headboard and silver satin bedding. It was all very masculine. Bizarrely I started picturing myself in his bed… with *him,* and I had to mentally slap myself out of it.

What is wrong with you? He's trying to help you not fuck you…

Annoyed with myself, I retreated back to the living room before my errant mind could wander any further down the wrong path. Then I paced up and down the great room a few times, absorbing my surroundings. Nestled between the leather corner suite and the equally large matching couch I noticed a glass side table. On it was a tall, coiled lamp with a dangly crystal shade and an ornate silver frame holding a photo of a young girl. She looked a similar age to me at a guess, with the same auburn hair and vivid green eyes as Richard. Just like him, she was beautiful.

I wonder who she is?

The twinge of a headache was threatening to explode in the back of my head so I lay down on the couch to rest my eyes. Time passed relatively quickly, snooping around the apartment, and it was almost lunchtime. Richard would be home soon. The thought warmed my veins. *How ridiculous.*

Tucking one of the cream feather cushions under my head, I closed my eyes and let my weary body relax into the leather – although I didn't intend to fall asleep.

Chapter Five

I was awoken by a clatter and I abruptly bolted upright.

"I'm so sorry," Richard uttered while picking up two empty saucepans from the kitchen floor. I rubbed my weary eyes and then gasped at the pain – once again, sleeping had made me forget.

"How long have you been home?" I asked through a yawn when I noticed the time – 04:30 PM.

"A couple of hours. I'm just making a start on dinner."

So much for not falling asleep.

"I didn't mean to fall asleep. You should've woken me," I mumbled awkwardly.

"You needed it. Your body recuperates a lot faster with plenty of rest. Besides, you looked pretty cute. Did you know you suck your thumb?"

"I do not!" I protested as playfully as he was being – although in reality, how would I know for sure? He flashed me a wicked grin before turning his back on me to carry on with dinner. I couldn't help staring after him for a few long minutes. He mesmerized me and I couldn't even begin to understand it.

"You don't need to keep doing this you know. I can feed myself," I said nervously, feeling guilty from all the special treatment.

"I'd be doing it for myself anyway. Now go sit down. It'll be about an hour."

"Let me help you." I knew I would feel better if I could at least contribute. His eyes automatically narrowed and I could tell Bossy Doctor was about to make an appearance – telling me I needed to rest no doubt. "Please?" I said with a pathetic flutter of my eyelashes before he had a chance to respond.

"Here… slice these." He reluctantly passed me a punnet of closed-cup mushrooms and I took a knife from the array of utensils he'd already set out and started chopping. My task was complete in less than a minute and I could see that I wasn't needed – he had everything under control.

Not wanting to get in the way, I perched myself on one of the glossy black stools by the breakfast bar and watched him glide effortlessly around the kitchen. He chopped, he stirred, he mixed… pausing only to flash me the odd hypnotic smile which turned my insides to a puddle of goo.

Bossy Doctor ordered me to the table when our appetizer was ready and I waited impatiently for him to join me. Soon enough Richard placed a small china plate with two lumps of something that looked like raw tofu stacked precariously on top of some wilted green leaves.

"Foie gras," he elucidated, noticing my curiosity. "Also known as fattened ducks liver."

Eww.

Richard tucked eagerly into the lump of fat and after giving it a wary prod with my fork I tentatively did the same. It tasted sickening – like pure butter. If I'd chewed it any longer I was almost sure I'd vomit so I forced it down with a large glug of iced-water from the table.

"Not a fan?" Richard probed through a stifled laugh – clearly amused.

"Yes, it's, um…" I racked my brain for polite words that wouldn't make me sound ungrateful. I failed – the sight of it on my plate made me want to retch. "It tastes like feet." Thankfully, Richard didn't take offense as he tipped his head back and laughed.

"*Feet?* Well, I hope whoevers feet you've been licking takes a shower once in a while." Straight away, after blinking a tear of laughter from his eye, he took his empty and my barely touched plate away.

Next I was served with baby lamb steaks on a bed of carrots and new potatoes with a creamy mushroom sauce. My mouth watered before I even tasted the food and it didn't disappoint. It was truly delicious and I discovered that lamb and mushrooms make for an unexpectedly tasty marriage.

I found myself staring at him as he ate. He was wearing a ribbed, white v-neck sweater that teased my eyes – allowing them a tiny glimpse of his toned chest and smattering of chest hair, which was the same rich auburn as that on his head. He sat so eloquently – back straight, head forward… So graceful.

Beautiful.

Richard cleared the dishes, after refusing my offer to help, before returning with dessert – steamed lemon sponge and vanilla cream. Of course, it was exquisite. I doubted I'd find its rival even in a fancy five star restaurant.

"Where did you learn to cook like this?" I asked inquisitively.

"My sister Kate and I used to do *everything* together. Then when we were ten, eleven maybe, she got it in her head she wanted to be a chef, so she followed the kitchen staff around everywhere they went. Like I said, where she went – I went. Guess I was so bored of standing around at the back of the kitchen I thought taking an actual interest would pass the time until she grew out of it."

Kitchen staff? Who the hell is he… fucking royalty?

Suddenly everything made perfect sense. The size of his apartment, his articulateness, the flashy car… he was brought up like this.

"What about you? Do you cook?"

"I've been known to make a mean bacon sandwich in my time," I replied, winking at him. "But besides that, my culinary talents pretty much end at Pop Tarts and Cheerios."

"Well the art of preparing cereal is harder than it looks. I believe it's all about the milk-cereal ratio. Screw that baby up and you risk getting a bowl full of tasteless mush. You'll have to teach me sometime?" He was being playful, smirking as he picked up his glass of white wine and then hiding his beaming grin behind it.

"Maybe. But I'm not sure you're quite ready. Best to start with Pop Tarts and work your way up."

He laughed at me as I picked up my own glass of wine and took a sip. It had some fancy name that I couldn't remember and no doubt cost a ridiculous amount of money but it tasted good. I was no connoisseur of course, but I could tell it was crisp, light and slightly fruity.

"Leave them until tomorrow." I grabbed his arm when he reached for the dessert dishes. It was the first time I'd ever purposely touched him and I could feel it all the way through my body. There was a charge, a *warmth* radiating from him that passed through my hand and into my veins. His eyes widened and he looked… stunned. *Shit*. I'd clearly overstepped some kind of mark

"It won't take long. I like things tidy," he said as he assessed the table. His voice was uneven, nervous. I felt waves of heat rush straight to my cheeks, certain I'd pissed him off somehow.

Deciding feigning ignorance was the best approach, I ignored his attempts to stop me helping and together we cleared the table in half the time. He showed me how to work the unnecessarily complicated dishwasher and by the time we were finished everything was back to normal. All polite smiles and nervous energy.

Later in the evening we sat at opposite ends of the corner-suite talking about irrelevant nonsense – movies, music, favorite colors… He had such mature, eclectic tastes in everything; classical music, sixties music, old-fashioned films, modern day thrillers – he fascinated me. Though, it also made me realize how boring I am in comparison. I'm so inexperienced with everything. I can't remember ever sitting down through a full movie, my favorite color has always been black to match my mood and I wouldn't know an aria if it hit me in the face.

I did however, manage to impress him with my best joke.

'How do lion's like their steak? ROAR!'

I say impress… Well, he laughed, put it that way. Whether that was *with* me or *at* me, I wasn't entirely sure.

"Who is that?" I asked, pointing towards the photo of the girl that looked like him. There was a

noticeable change in the atmosphere.
Instantaneously the air became so dense it was almost choking and I became more intrigued than ever to know who she was.

"That's my twin sister – Kate." From what he said during dinner it sounded like Kate was his best friend as well as his sister. So I didn't understand why he looked so sad. His brow furrowed as he stared longingly at the photo – his eyes bulging with what looked like guilt.

"She's beautiful," I said, breaking the deafening silence.

"Yes. She was."

Was?

"She passed away almost ten years ago. She was just nineteen."

"Shit I'm- I mean, fuck I'm so-"
For Christ's sake stop swearing you idiot!
"I'm sorry," I finally managed to splutter. Forcing a grateful smile he pulled his gaze away from the photo – the corners of his eyes had reddened as if they were being burnt by unshed tears. My whole body ached to hold him… but I knew I couldn't.

"I'm going to bed soon – early start tomorrow. You should too. You're still recovering. You need to rest." Bossy Doctor was back and I started to wish I hadn't mentioned the photo. He'd been so playful all evening and me and my big mouth had gone and ruined it.

On the flip side however I felt privileged to know something so personal about him. Though I couldn't stop thinking about the pain he'd been – and was clearly still going – through. It brought mysterious little stabbing pains to my chest.

I stood up first to go to bed, but then Richard gently tugged on my arm bringing me back down to the couch.

"Before you go, I just want you to know that I'm here for you while you're staying with me. You know that right?"

"Um, sure?" What was he getting at?

"What I mean is – I'm no expert in the field of course… but if you're struggling with anything…" he stuttered, staring intently at me as if I should know what the hell he was on about. "Amy, if you ever feel like things are too much to deal with – if you feel like… *hurting* yourself in any way. Come and tell me. Okay?"

Wow. I swear you could have fried eggs on my cheeks just then. I'd never felt so ashamed, so embarrassed… so cared about.

"Okay," I resolved. I'd never had someone to talk to before and the only place *that* landed me was in the hospital. I guessed it wouldn't hurt to give this talking thing a shot.

"Promise me, Amy? I won't ever judge you, and it won't ever go further than me. So will you do that? Will you promise me?"

"I- I promise," I choked out, suddenly overcome with emotion. I knew the second I reached my bedroom I would burst into a fit of tears. I wasn't sure why… Gratitude? Relief? Hope? Lov-

Stop right there.

"Good girl." I couldn't stop the corners of my lips turning up into a soft smile. Not so long ago that comment would have annoyed the hell out of me, yet now I found it almost adorable. Why? I had absolutely no frigging idea. "Now bed," he ordered.

"Yes, Doctor Lewis." Saluting him, I did as I was told and retired to bed. The anguish I witnessed on his beautiful face when talking about his sister earlier tonight was etched onto my eyelids when I tried to sleep, making my heart ache as it slid down into the pit of my stomach.

****

"Good morning," I said cheerily to Richard, who by the look of his bed-hair had only just got up – it was his day off.

I had been staying in his apartment for nine days now and this was the first opportunity I'd had to make breakfast for him. It was also the first time I had two free hands which made the whole effort a hell of a lot easier. My cast was finally removed yesterday and I'd been left with a pale, dry and itchy cast-shaped impression in its wake. It was annoying the crap out of me.

"Good morning yourself." His bright green eyes widened in surprise and his now familiar wicked grin tugged at the corners of his mouth. I looked away from him, knowing his face – and the fact he was wearing nothing but his black, low-hung jeans – would distract me and I'd end up burning everything. He had a white t-shirt draped over his arm and I was both wishing he would put it on and keep it off in equal measure.

He held such confidence as he strode his gloriously half-naked body over to me. And why wouldn't he? He is gorgeous… and the vain bastard knows it. I swear he spent over an hour in the bathroom getting ready for work every morning.

When his body was in touching distance of mine I heard him sniff exaggeratedly – trying to suss out what I was cooking.

"Bacon and eggs," I informed him – answering his unspoken question and looking at him just long enough to wink. He peered into the sizzling pan over my shoulder and the bare flesh of his muscular arm brushed mine. That had happened six times in the past week – yep, I was pathetic enough to count – and each time injected my body with that mystifying charge, tingling as it spread through my veins like wildfire.

"Smells good." He nodded his head in approval. *What? No lecture? No telling me to rest?* "I'll wait in here shall I?" He grabbed the newspaper from the counter and tucked it under his arm as he gestured his head towards the dining suite.

I ogled him as he slid into his seat, humming along to The Turtles' 'Happy Together', which was playing in the background from his 'Sixties' iPod playlist. His eyes were mischievous. He was letting me play housewife and I was reveling in being able to repay some of his kindness. *You owe him a lot more than breakfast,* my subconscious sneered. I wondered where it'd been hiding lately.

I don't know how to say it without sounding like a breathing cliché, but I'd noticed this warm and fuzzy – almost ticklish – sensation bouncing around my insides over the last few days. I had no idea what it was. I wondered if that was what happiness felt like. Or maybe the knowledge that I was safe.

Saving Amy

Perhaps this was what ordinary non-fucked-up people felt like all the time?

All I knew was that it felt pretty nice – refreshing even. I'd been sleeping straight through which gave me bountiful amounts of energy during the day. I'd stopped crying myself to sleep for the first night in... well forever. I hadn't thought about cutting once – not *once*. Something was different about me – something had changed. Hell if I knew what. I wasn't foolish enough to believe it would last forever - I just hoped it stayed around a *little* longer.

Breakfast was ready a few minutes later and although everything was cooked pretty well, my thrown-together-in-a-big-heap plate of food looked shameful compared to the works of art Richard had been serving me for the past week. When he saw me approaching, Richard folded up his newspaper and pulled his t-shirt on. I stared a little too fervently at his perfectly defined chest muscles, watching them flex as he raised his toned arms above his head.

Wow, I think I *actually* drooled a little.

He eyed up the plate expectantly. When he saw the food he raised an incredulous eyebrow at my cooking abilities. At least I *hoped* he was faking.

"It's all in the taste," I teased. He laughed softly – such an adorable sound. After setting my own plate down I sat on the chair next to him - I had been moving progressively closer during my time here – and tucked into the perfectly cooked bacon. *Mmm*. It was delicious – the perfect crisp. I was quite impressed and more than a little proud of myself. I'd never cooked for anyone before.

"Will you take me home after breakfast?" I hadn't heard from my mom or dad since the night that brought me here – not that I expected to of course.

"Why the hell would I do that?" he demanded and a flash of what looked like rage caused his eyes to shoot open.

"I need some of my things," I replied, shrugging.

"I can buy you anything you need. You don't have to go back there."

I appreciated the gesture but I couldn't take any more from him. He had issued me with a full wardrobe of clothes and enough toiletries to last me an entire year this past week. There was no point in telling him as much – *again*. As usual he would no doubt wave me off and tell me to do as I was told.

"I want to go," I protested. "I'll feel better when they know I've left for good." And hopefully it would put an end to the fear of waking up in the middle of the night to my dad banging Richard's door down. There was no denying I was dreading going home – shitting it would perhaps be more fitting – but I needed to face it… *end* it.

"Although I know I can't stay here forever. I will find somewhere soon. I promise," I felt obliged to add. He shook his head, dismissing me. He did that a lot. In theory it should've pissed me off, but in some bizarre way it made me feel… protected.

"Well I'm coming with you," he insisted and once again I was having breakfast with Bossy Doctor Guy.

"You're not," I argued, equally bossy. He was risking enough for me as it was. I wasn't prepared to put him in the firing line of my father. "You can wait right outside," I tacked on when I sensed the unease radiating from his body. "If I'm not out within fifteen minutes feel free to don your cape and break in to rescue me." I winked at him, hoping to lighten the suddenly dense atmosphere. It didn't work. His eyebrows were pursed so tightly together his forehead must surely have ached.

"Fine," he grudgingly agreed.

We were silent throughout the rest of breakfast and again through clearing the dishes. I felt like he was annoyed with me and I didn't like it. I *hated* disappointing him. Was that a bad thing? Had I become weak and needy?

Yes. Yes I had.

****

I could feel Richard's eyes boring into my back as I made my way down the graveled drive. My dad's car was missing and relief washed through my veins. My pissed-up mother I could deal with. When I reached the door I realized I didn't have my keys – I didn't have anything anymore – and I knew if I had to knock she wouldn't answer. I sighed, frustrated. I'd wasted my time. Still, I decided to give the handle a tug before I left and to my great surprise, it was unlocked.

She always *locks it.*

I walked inside even more apprehensively now, wondering what state she must be in to leave the house unsecure.

"Jim?" I heard my mom mumble from the living room. She must've been expecting my dad home soon. I needed to be quick.

"It's me," I declared, walking towards the sound of her voice.

"Amelia," she gasped, seeming surprised to see me. "Your father will be home soon," she said but it sounded like a warning – as if she was helping me by telling me to leave. For a brief second it sounded like she gave a damn. How ridiculous.

I shrugged emotionlessly at her.

"I've moved in with a friend. I've just come for my things." Turning sharply on my heels I headed – *ran* – to my bedroom. Despite trying my best to act nonchalant my stomach had twisted into a thousand knots at the prospect of seeing my dad, so I hurriedly threw as much as would fit into my old black rucksack from under the bed. I was back downstairs in under five minutes and I dashed straight for the front door.

"Amelia?" my mom called after me without bothering to get up.

"What?" I barked.

"Be safe, baby girl." Her words burrowed into my tear ducts causing a small river to flow over my face.

What the hell was that?

I felt stunned and confused and I hated her more than ever. Of all the times to show me the slightest hint of affection she chose now – when I'd finally escaped. I'd at long last found the courage to discard any kind of fucked-up relationship we ever had and she did *that* to me.

My heart was pounding, my mind was reeling and my cheeks were flooded with tears. I ran desperately back to Richard's car and was met with an expression of stark alarm when he saw the state I was in.

"What is it? What happened?" he pressed anxiously.

"Nothing. I'm fine I promise. My dad wasn't even there. I guess it was just overwhelming being back in that house," I lied and hoped he believed me. I think he did. He patted my knee reassuringly and his touch resonated throughout my entire body.

"Good. Let's get you home."

Home? I wondered if he realized what he'd just said or if it was a simple slip of the tongue. I could've quite easily obsessed over it so I made myself let it go before I gave my subconscious a chance to make me feel like shit.

Turning away from me, Richard brought his impressive Mercedes engine to life and sped off before I'd even put my seatbelt on.

I walked back into Richard's apartment without feeling so much as a flicker of awe. I must've finally been getting used to the magnificence of the place. Nothing seemed too *big* anymore. Turning to the hall after closing the front door behind me I smacked straight into Richard – our chests touching, his warm breath blanketing my face.

"Sorry," I muttered, feeling a little breathless. He stared at me for what felt like minutes, but was really only a couple of seconds longer than necessary – neither of us moving an inch.

"Don't be," he said, his voice low, raspy as he made no attempt to move. His harsh breathing mirrored mine and for a few long seconds our eyes seemed incapable of leaving one another.

"I, um… better get this to my room," I said croakily, stumbling back a step and wondering what the hell had just happened. Why was my chest suddenly throbbing like it was about to detonate? Richard nodded and one side of lips turned up into what looked like a nervous smile. Then I practically ran to my bedroom with my rucksack in one hand, clutching my aching chest with the other.

Setting my bag on the bed, I rummaged through it to see what I'd manage to salvage. I pulled out my favorite grey sweats – threadbare and full of holes but oh so comfy – a few t-shirts, some underwear, my make-up case and what I called my shoebox of memories… but really it was just a box full of birthday cards from Julie.

Next I pulled out my purse, my cell, my notebook and my black travel alarm from my bedside table. Bizarrely, despite this whole apartment being kitted out with an endless array of impressive and baffling gadgets, my bedroom didn't have a clock. I knew my subconscious would have something to say about me referring to it as *my* bedroom so I threw my things back in my bag and left the room before it had a chance to pipe up.

"I've made you some coffee," Richard said warmly, handing me a tall white mug when I entered the living room. I smiled gratefully and as I opened my mouth to thank him I was interrupted by the sound of his apartment buzzer.

"Come on up," I heard him say from the hallway before hanging up the receiver. I was suddenly nervous. It'd only ever been the two of us here. "I won't be long," he muttered to me without saying who it was. Then he left the room and headed

Saving Amy

for the front door. Being the nosey bitch that I am, I crept towards the hallway and paused behind the door, my hand cupping my ear.

"It could've waited until work tomorrow. You didn't need to go out of your way," I overheard him say. He sounded... *nervous*. It didn't suit him.

"It's no trouble - I was passing anyway. So? Aren't you going to invite me in?" a woman's voice teased. I was sure I recognized it.

"Um, I'm a little busy just now," Richard answered as if trying to get rid of her. Was he ashamed of me? *Of course he is...* My heart sank a little.

"Oh, Richard... just let me in," she demanded playfully and then I heard her push past him. I bolted from the doorway before I was caught eavesdropping red-handed.

Ugh. It's her, my subconscious snarled as Joanna Interfering Shrink Lady sauntered into the room. She stopped in her tracks when she saw me. Richard stood behind her, rubbing his forearm. I'd noticed he only did that when he was mad or frustrated.

"*Amelia?*" she noted in surprise, offering me a tight-lipped smile.

"She prefers Amy," Richard interrupted and she glowered at him with a what-the-hell-is-going-on face.

"Amy could you leave us alone for a while?" Richard asked me. I nodded once and immediately left the room, but I planned to hear every word the officious bitch had to say so I headed to my bedroom opposite the great living room, leaving my door ajar. I wasn't quite sure *why* I hated her already – I just knew that I did.

"What is she doing here?" she asked disapprovingly, almost scolding him. She was trying to whisper but I could hear every word.

"She's staying here for a while. She's been having some trouble at home."

"And that's your problem... *why?*"

That right there. *That* is why I hate her.

"She's been through so much. She has no one else, Joanna. What was I supposed to do? Leave her to fend for herself and probably end up dead somewhere?" Just then the reality of my situation slapped me in the face. It was too easy to forget while I was with him.

"Everyone who comes into the hospital has problems, Richard. You can't take your work home with you. You know this... I don't get what you're playing at."

"Like I said, she has no one else." He was getting irritated and even though I couldn't see him, I just knew he would be rubbing his forearm.

"You're making no sense! We have systems in place for girls like her. There are plenty of people to help. Your job was to fix up her spine and send her home – not invite her to live with you!" All efforts to whisper had disappeared. I waited anxiously for Richard's reply but it turned out she hadn't finished her little tirade. "You could get fired if this gets out. Is she really worth risking your career for?" My ears pricked up, eager to hear his response.

"That won't happen. I've done nothing wrong."

"Have you completely lost your mind? You're screwing a patient! You've abused your position of trust, of course there'll be consequences."

Whoa...

Saving Amy

"Hold on a second... I'm not *screwing* her, Joanna. She needed a friend and that's exactly what I'm being. Besides, she's not my patient anymore." My heart couldn't seem to stop itself from doing a little dance. I wasn't his patient. Did that mean something *could*... I shook the thought away quickly. It would only lead to disappointment.

"I know what's going on here..." An eerily long silence followed and I wondered if Richard was as intrigued as I was to hear her theory. "She's not Kate."

What's his dead sister got to do with anything, my subconscious hissed.

"Trying to save this girl because you couldn't save your sister? It's just not right."

"DON'T YOU DARE bring her name into this!" Richard roared – and I mean *really* roared. It was the first time I'd ever heard him angry. I didn't like it.

"I'm sorry. I didn't mean- look all I meant was, I know you blame yourself for not noticing Kate's problems, and maybe you're seeing this as an opportunity to put things right?"

Problems? I was suddenly eager to know how she died but it wasn't the kind of thing I could just blurt out over the breakfast table.

"I want you to leave now," Richard said curtly.

"There's no need for that. I can't lie, I still don't understand what's gotten into you – but I *am* sorry I've upset you."

"Please, Joanna... just go." He sounded so dispirited. I'd grown so attached - *too* attached - to his velvety voice (even his Bossy Doctor version), and hearing him sound so sad panged in my heart.

This was all because of me. As much as I'd decided I hated *Joanna* – ugh, even *thinking* her name goes through me – I knew deep down that she was right. Richard was putting so much at stake for me… and for what?

My mind began to ache as I frantically ransacked it for answers. I found nothing. I couldn't think of one single reason for Richard being so good to me. I was nothing special. As far as Richard was concerned I was just a depressed young girl with a screwed-up home life and drug problems.

Problems…

Realization swiped me across the face and suddenly Joanna's little rant about his sister started to make sense. The more I thought about it the more I convinced myself that drugs were responsible for her death and now Richard was using me to ease his conscience out of some warped notion that he didn't save her – but he could save *me*.

My insides were reeling and I didn't know if I felt angry, hurt or guilty. Whatever it was didn't feel good. It was a nice notion that someone wanted to save me I supposed – or even thought I was capable of saving. A nice one – but an unrealistic one. I was too fucked-up – too far gone.

Hopeless.

Chapter Six

"Sorry about that. It took longer than I thought," Richard apologized, appearing at the doorway and abruptly dragging me out of my musing. He was rubbing his arm and I decided he must do that when he's nervous too.

"She's right. You're risking too much for me."

"You were listening?" he asked but he didn't sound annoyed. He sounded... *remorseful.*

"I'll leave tomorrow," I said, ignoring his assumption. My heart struggled to beat through the crushing pressure weighing down on it, but I knew it was the right thing to do.

"There's no need for that. If you were listening you'd have heard me say I'm not risking anything. I've told you, you are welcome to stay here as long as you need. Nothing's changed." But it had. I shook my head – words eluded me. "Where will you go?" he asked somberly and I was both relieved and heartbroken that he'd accepted my decision.

"I'll stay with a friend," I lied, shrugging. I didn't know where I would go yet. A cheap motel? A hostel perhaps? There must be somewhere...

"What friend?" he questioned suspiciously, doing that censorious eyebrow thing he does so well – and often.

Is it that obvious I have no friends?

"It doesn't matter which friend. Look, Richard... I can't begin to tell you how much I appreciate everything you've done for me – but you've done too much already. This was only ever supposed to be temporary. I had to leave sometime," I replied and I couldn't be sure if I was trying to convince *him* or myself.

Suddenly – maybe because I was leaving so it didn't matter if I overstepped the mark - I couldn't stop thinking about his sister and I was trapped in a fierce battle with my subconscious about whether to mention it or not.

I lost.

"Can I ask how your sister died?" The abrupt subject change caused an unwelcome decline in the atmosphere. Sadness flooded the air and my lungs struggled to breathe it in. Richard straightened his crumpled brow and dragged in a deep, striving breath.

"Kate died of a heroin overdose," he revealed reluctantly, staring down at his feet. *I knew it.* "But that has *nothing* to do with this. Ignore anything you heard Joanna say. She knows shit about our situation."

'Our' situation?

Even after everything I'd ever experienced in my life I didn't think my mind had ever been so full. It was painful just to think. I wanted to stay but I *needed* to go. I thought I loved him – if that was an emotion I was even capable of – but I knew he didn't love me; he just wanted to *save* me. Most of all I was afraid – petrified of falling into my old life when I left. Let's face it, I hadn't done a very good job of tackling life alone the last nineteen years.

"It's still best that I leave," I said as I stood up to make my way to the bathroom to gather my things. I couldn't prolong this… whatever *this* was, any longer. I was growing more attached to him every day and the longer I stayed, the higher the drop would be when I inevitably fell.

"Where are you going?"

"To get some things from the bathroom. I'll pack now and then I can leave first thing in the morning." Tears threatened to burst their banks but I blinked them away. I was upset, overwhelmed and unbearably confused. A thousand different thoughts and emotions were shooting through my mind at one hundred miles per hour and the pain exceeded any blow I'd ever taken to my body.

"Please… don't rush into anything. Think about it for a few days – plan where you're going first." For a brief moment I allowed myself to believe that he actually *wanted* me to stay. *Don't be so ridiculous. He feels sorry for you, that's all,* my annoying as hell subconscious bellowed and it pained me that this time I was forced to agree.

I felt physically weighed down with the overpowering urge to run away. Away from Richard and all the bewildering and damn right painful emotions that accompanied him. It was fight or flight time, and any ounce of fight I ever held was knocked out of me years ago.

Brushing past Richard, I continued on my way to the bathroom.

"Amy, please…" he called after me. His words darted straight into my heart, momentarily stopping me from breathing. Ignoring him, I carried on walking, but then he grabbed me by the elbow and pulled me to a standstill. "Please don't go." There was such desperation in his voice – like he was begging. Or maybe I was just hearing what I wanted to.

"Joanna's right. This just isn't right. Nothing makes sense anymore and I don't know how much more I can take!" Wow, it was all spilling out now. I'd quickly turned into a desperate, emotional wreck – crying pathetically into my hands. Pulling out of Richard's gentle grip, I tried to walk away.

"Stay. *Please*. Please don't leave."

"Why the hell not?" I turned and yelled at him – my overloaded mind finally exploding.

"BECAUSE I DON'T WANT YOU TO!" he shouted – *actually* screamed. Suddenly nervous, I turned to face him and he was knotting his fingers in his hair. His expression was pained – crumpled. My mouth dropped open, rendering me speechless.

What is he saying?

I watched him open his mouth to speak but all that came out was a sigh. Then, before my eyes had chance to register his movement, his hands were cupping my face and he was just inches away from me. Instinctively I rose onto my tiptoes, bringing my tiny five feet two inch frame a little (*very* little) more level with his six plus feet.

"Please, stay with me," he pleaded.

Before I could reply I felt him on my lips. My breathing hitched to an almost painful level and all of my senses sprang to life. I inhaled his scent – tea-tree shampoo and expensive cologne. I tasted the sweetness of his breath mixed with the saltiness of my tears. I twisted the hair on the back of his head – which felt rough from whatever styling product he used – with my eager fingers. I listened to his harsh, wanton breath against my throat and I intermittently peeled my eyes open to absorb every inch of his beauty.

Holy fuck…

"Come with me," he whispered, releasing me from his embrace and taking my hand. He led me down the hall, past the bathroom and to the room at the far end – his bedroom. Every nerve ending in my body stood to attention.

Is this really happening?

The window blinds were partially closed and soft beams of light filtered through the gaps, shimmering onto him like a spotlight. We stood unnaturally still – our chests rising and falling exaggeratedly, gazing at each other. My eyes soaked up the delicious sight of him as I watched him undo the buttons of his white linen shirt tantalizingly slowly before throwing it on the floor beside him.

This was the third time I'd ever seen him that way and unbelievably he seemed more stunning each time. His pale skin, his perfectly toned muscles… Tentatively I reached out and stroked his smattering of auburn chest hair – something I'd been dreaming about for what seemed like forever.

Could I actually be asleep?

Staring intently into my eyes he pulled me in at the waist. His hands travelled slowly, teasingly down my quivering body until he reached the hem of my blouse. My arms instinctively raised themselves in the air as he pulled it upwards and lifted it over my head. I closed my eyes when I felt his silky lips on my throat and let out an involuntary moan. My heart was throbbing – if it beat any harder I was sure it would escape through the walls of my chest.

I wanted to touch him back but I was frozen – completely lost in the sensation. As his chaste kisses travelled along my neck to my shoulder, I felt him unclasp my bra and then slide it painstakingly slowly down my arms, following its path with soft little licks.

"You are so beautiful," he whispered, his thumbs grazing my nipples while he kissed me all the way down to my bellybutton.

I opened my eyes and he was gazing up at me – his intense green eyes blazing with desire and I struggled to breathe. Gently, he tucked his thumbs into the waistband of my jeans and slowly peeled them down, taking my panties with them. I clumsily stepped out of them and flushed beetroot-red when I almost fell on top of him. A hint of a smile teased his lips and straightening himself up, he backed away a step – staring at me.

I was completely naked – exposed. He was still wearing his pants and I felt awfully self-conscious. His body was beautiful – defined and cared for. Whereas mine was thin, neglected and covered in hideous scars. I felt completely unworthy being stood before him like this. Ashamed, I bowed my head.

"What's wrong? Do you want me to stop?" he asked, concern washing over his delectable face. Then he positioned his finger under my chin and raised my head so I had no choice but to look at him. After studying my eyes for a few brief seconds he dropped his head and I watched, bemused as he lifted my hands which were covering the scars on my legs; I didn't even realize I was doing it.

"Don't hide from me, Amy," he murmured and I gaped, captivated and slightly confused as he dropped down to his knees. Slowly, tenderly, he ran his fingers over my scars and then, unexpectedly, he softly kissed each one in turn. As he did, his face crumpled in anguish as if he were trying to draw out my pain with his lips.

Holy shit. It felt like my insides were about to explode. My breathing was loud and rapid and my heart pounded so hard it physically ached.

"Each and every one of these should be a reminder of how strong you are. You should look at them and remember what you've been through, and feel proud that you're still here – still fighting."

That was it. I couldn't resist any longer and I fell to my knees – desperate to touch him. Wrapping my arms around his back I pulled him closer. I clutched his hair and drew his face towards mine, kissing him hard and wanting on the lips. His tongue brushed mine and I couldn't seem to prevent the whimper that followed. It was incredible – the feel, the touch, the taste of him… It had never been like this before – the lust, the eye contact… the pure sensuality of it all. At that moment I idly, and shamefully, realized this was probably the first time I'd ever been sober too.

Breathing harshly against my ear, Richard ran his fingers across my back – his touch igniting every nerve in my body. My skin had become so sensitive it was only just not painful to touch. That inexplicable charge I'd felt radiating from him since our first accidental touch was between us and it was stronger than ever. I was being pulled towards him and I was powerless to stop it.

While tenderly kissing my lips he gently pushed me backwards with his bodyweight until I was lying flat on my back with the tufts of the shaggy white rug tickling my bare skin. Then he raised himself slightly, his lips barely leaving mine as he slid lithely from his pants. I closed my eyes again and tipped my head back. My hips involuntarily began to thrust as I became desperate to feel him on top of me.

The sound of a packet being torn forced my ears to prick up and impossibly my breathing accelerated even further when I realized just how close I was to feeling him inside me. Goosebumps appeared in the wake of his warm lips as he trailed them upwards from my stomach, over my breasts and finally settling on my mouth.

"I've wanted to do this to you for so long," he moaned into my mouth before letting his tongue dance with mine. Then he glided into me excruciating slowly, filling me, teasing me, and making me whimper his name.

His hungry eyes bored into mine, burning brightly with passion and need. This was unlike anything I'd ever experienced before and the feeling was intoxicating. The warmth, the desire, that delicious inexplicable charge spreading through my veins faster than heroin… This was more than just sex – more than just physical. We were bearing our souls through our eyes and it was an exquisite sensation that I couldn't even begin to understand.

My ears relished the sound of his ragged breathing as he gripped my hips and began pumping faster – deeper. He wanted me and the feeling was so alien. I could feel the doubts, the insecurities and the feeling of worthlessness setting in but I forced myself to push them aside before I ruined this beautiful moment. Instead, I focused on the fact that *I* wanted *him*. I *needed* him. And for now, I had him.

"You feel even better than I imagined you would," he managed to say through gritted teeth before wrapping his strong, protective arms around my waist and pulling me upwards until I was straddling his legs. "And by Christ have I imagined it."

"Me too," I croaked out - because I had… repeatedly. To know that Richard had been imagining us together too felt too amazing to be real.

He held me so close, his fingers kneading into my back. My whole body responded to his touch and the faster he worked his fingers into my back the faster I found myself grinding against him. The pleasure was becoming unbearable – building to the point of almost agony. It was a completely foreign feeling and I didn't know what the hell was going on inside my molten body but all I could think about was releasing the delicious pressure.

"Ah fuck, Amy. I need this, baby. I need you."

His skin was so hot - glistening with beads of sweat bubbling on the surface – and his eyes were burning brighter than I'd ever seen before. Our bodies worked together rhythmically, thrusting together harder and faster until we both reached our pinnacle and the universe and all the shit it had ever thrown at me shattered around us.

Wow. I was pretty sure I had just experienced my very first orgasm and holy hell what an incredible feeling. I could finally see what all the hype was about and it was all down to the beautiful creature gazing up at me.

"That was amazing," Richard breathed – his words tipping me over the edge and stealing any last traces of strength. I collapsed onto him, pushing him backwards as I inhaled the delicious scent of his overly warm, moist skin. Even his sweat smelled sweet. We lay in complete silence for an immeasurable length of time. Five minutes… ten… an hour perhaps. Time had dissipated into insignificance.

Nestling into his chest, Richard held me. *Held* me. Like actually wrapped his arms around my naked body and pulled me close. Not because I was upset, or hurt, or falling… but because he wanted to. No one had ever wanted to hold me before. I savored the feeling. The thrum of his heart beneath my ear, the tickle of his chest hair against my cheek, the warmth of his breath settling on my face as he looked down on me…

If I was never going to be held again… I wanted to remember it.

And then they came. The doubts. The insecurities. The feelings of worthlessness… hitting me like a freight truck driving straight into my stomach.

"Why are you doing this?" The words were out of my mouth before I could stop them.

"What do you mean?" he asked, his voice dripping with confusion as he straightened himself up a little to gain a better view of my face as I stared nervously up at him.

"I mean why are you being so good to me? There's so much wrong with me. I'm nothing. I've *got* nothing. I just-"

"Baby stop. I won't listen to you talk like that. Everything you consider to be *wrong* with you are just the results of you trying to be strong for too long – trying to cope *alone* for too long. Don't you think it's amazing that after everything you've been through – the violence, the fear, the isolation… you can still do *this?*" He motioned his hands over our entangled bodies. "That you can still *feel?* Still trust? Because I sure as hell think it's a miracle. I think *you're* a miracle."

I was rendered speechless – overcome with an emotion I couldn't place. Silent, leisurely tears began to trickle down my cheeks as I tried to absorb his words – and more importantly *why* he said them.

"Truth is, I've never felt like this in all my twenty-seven years. I wouldn't be able to pinpoint what it was about you, I just no that no matter how I tried to shake you out of my mind… you just wouldn't leave."

So he *tried* to forget me. He knew he shouldn't touch me with a fifty-foot pole and he *tried* to stay away.

"Don't do that, baby," he said solemnly, interrupting my silent moment of self-pity as he curled loose tendrils of my blonde hair around his fingers.

"Do what?"

"Assume. Don't ever assume you know what I'm thinking – always *ask*."

Huh?

"You're wondering why I tried to stay away and you're assuming its because you're more trouble than you're worth. Am I wrong?"

What the… How did he…

Wordless, and slightly embarrassed, I shook my head.

"Well if you'd asked instead of assumed, you'd know that the only reason I tried to stay away from you was because what I was feeling scared the living shit out of me. I'm used to controlling everything in my life. I control people at work, I control who I spend my time with, what I spend my money on… but I couldn't control what you were doing to me.

"It started the first night we met. When I saw you lying on the sidewalk I was already dialing for the ambulance when I ran over to you, because that's what I *should* have done. I'm a doctor – I should have happily packed you off to get patched up by my colleagues and never thought about you again. What I *shouldn't* have done that night… is look into your eyes.

"You came round and begged me not to call an ambulance. I took zero notice of you until I looked into those rich caramel eyes. I could see the pain in them… the fear. They looked straight into mine and it was like they were pleading for somebody to help you… to *save* you… to love you, Amy. And I guess I was just too weak to walk away."

Wow.

"I'm glad you didn't," I managed to choke out as that bewildering emotion clawed at my throat. "That night, or rather the next morning, you said I was far too young for you. What's changed?" I asked curiously after a few minutes of contemplative silence. Thought I might as well give this 'asking' thing a shot.

"Yeah. Let's just say my mom helped me out with that one. Something along the lines of 'the heart isn't powered by mathematics, darling… it's powered by chemistry'."

"Your mom?" I asked disbelievingly. "You've told her about me?"

"Of course. She's my mom," he answered, shrugging like it was completely insignificant. "What's wrong?" he asked. Clearly I wasn't doing a very good job of hiding my sudden anxiety.

"Nothing," I tried to lie – until that famous eyebrow of his shot up. "I guess I just didn't think you'd want people to know I was in your life. I don't want anyone to judge you. Least of all your family."

"First of all, my mom is the most gracious and accepting person you're ever likely to meet. She loves you already, if for no other reason than you make me happy. Second, I know we don't know each other all that well yet – something which I hope to change very soon – but trust me when I say I didn't *have* a life before you came into it, and I'm certain that is something my mom won't be able to help filling you in on when you meet her."

Meet her? Meet his parents? Shit.

"And third, you need to stop thinking like this, Amy. You are a strong and courageous young woman. You're a survivor. I am both privileged and proud to have met you. I wish you could see what I do when I look at you," he said with pure admiration saturating his husky voice.

"Sorry," was all I could think of to say. For what, I wasn't sure.

"*Sorry?* Damn you know how to frustrate the hell out of me, baby," he said in mock anger before rolling me onto my back and pinning me down with his body. "You *will* learn to see how magnificent you are. I'll make sure of it."

Before I could reply I felt his silky tongue teasing my lips. I gladly parted them and eagerly explored the taste of his mouth. It didn't make sense to me how he made me feel so wanted… so alive. I didn't want to dwell on the if's and but's so for now, I vowed to just enjoy him.

I barely had time to break free for air before he was inside me once again. How was it possible that it felt even better than the last time? It was rougher this time – hungrier. More similar to what I was used to yet so unbelievably different. His eyes never left mine as he worked himself in and out of me like he needed me in order to survive. Every time his lips caressed my name, every time he groaned, every time his breathing grew harsher… my body feel like it was melting. My limbs ached and the blood in my veins had turned to molten lava – it was the most beautiful kind of discomfort.

"Thank you," I breathed, my body tingling as I came down from the intense euphoria. My eyes met his, and up shot his eyebrow. It made me smile.

"You're thanking me for having sex with you?" Richard asked, bemused. I giggled like a little girl.

"No," I replied, playfully slapping his chest. "For everything… for *helping* me." He pulled me closer into his chest and I nuzzled his naked body contentedly. "Although the sex was pretty darn amazing. So yes, thank you for that too." I winked up at him and he laughed his adorable laugh before leaning his head towards mine and kissing my numb lips.

Saving Amy

Within seconds he was on top of me once more – smothering every inch of my nakedness with lustful kisses.

"I'll help you a thousand times over just to keep you by my side."

It was in that very moment I knew for sure... that I was in love with him.

Chapter Seven

```
Julie: Good luck! Not that you'll
need it - they'll love u!
```

We were in Richard's car – well *one* of them – travelling up the 1-5 N heading to Medina to meet his parents. I was trying not to think about it too much for fear I might literally crap my pants and ruin Richard's cream leather interiors. As we drove, I fidgeted with the hem of my black lace dress that rested just below my knees with one hand, and twisted strands of my hair that I'd curled specially for the occasion around the other. Every muscle in my belly had wound into painful knots and the closer we became to our destination the queasier I felt.

I was sure I'd read somewhere that Bill Gates lived in Medina and I found myself wondering just how wealthy Richard actually was. We'd talked about anything and everything since officially getting together but money never really came up. Why would it? He knew I had nothing and as far as I was concerned, he gave me everything just by breathing. I knew he'd worked his way up to being a senior physician at such a young age through hard work, determination and the finest tuition America had to offer. But still, he was far from the top in his field and besides, how much can an ER physician *actually* make in a year?

Granted he had three ridiculously flashy cars, a humongous apartment and a closet bursting at the hinges with designer clothes… but Bill Gates style wealthy? Surely not.

```
Me: Thanks. Nearly there now. I am
CRAPPING myself! Xo
```

I replied to Julie because I wouldn't have time soon. Though I planned to send her regular updates whenever I nipped to the bathroom. I craved speaking to Julie more than ever now I actually had a life to share with her. Now I had happy thoughts and dare I say it… plans for the future. It was a shame she was so far away now. I missed her.

As Richard pulled off the interchange he flashed me a mischievous wink and I knew that meant we were nearly there. My stomach was in the process of chewing into my heart and I was about three deep breaths away from hurling all over my best dress. I was meeting his parents. The thing that scared me the most however, was that his parents were meeting *me*.

They couldn't possibly approve of me – despite what Richard had told me. I assumed he was just pacifying me. I was too young. I had no career, no decent education. Christ, never mind his parents, what the hell did Richard see in me? I was starting to depress myself so I shook my head in an effort to scatter my unruly thoughts. Richard noticed and glanced over at me, looking concerned.

"Something wrong, baby?"

"I'm just a little nervous," I replied, although it was a *serious* understatement. He smiled and rested his spare hand on my knee, squeezing it reassuringly.

"Amy, they will *love* you. How could they not?"

You want me to give you a list?

I dismissed his optimism and leaned my head against the window, admiring the leafy green scenery as some of Richard's classical crap flooded the air.

In an effort to distract myself I switched my thoughts to the last three weeks. Just thinking about it seemed like a dream. It was twenty-four days since I knew that I loved him and twenty-three days since I told him so. He'd told me repeatedly since that he loved me too and even though I couldn't figure out why, I chose to believe him. I'd never known the meaning of happiness but if this was it I would give up my life just to hang onto it for one extra minute.

It had been twenty-four days of the most blissful pleasure. Twenty-four days of making love, talking, laughing, learning to slow dance in Richard's living room. Twenty-four days without pain, without arguments, without (too many) tormenting thoughts. Quite simply, it had been the best twenty-four days of my existence.

"We're here," Richard said, cutting the engine and dragging me from my delightful pondering.

We'd driven up a long (*really* long) secluded road that wound around a forest of the most dense and luscious green trees. My mouth involuntarily dropped open as I gaped in utter awe out of the windshield. I was staring at a gigantic, eye-twitchingly exquisite mansion. It was so big I couldn't see both ends without moving my head and Richard's apartment suddenly seemed miniscule in comparison.

I was so engrossed in my surroundings I didn't notice Richard had left the car until he was by my side and holding my door open. He flashed me the wicked grin I'd grown to adore and I knew my nerves were amusing him. *Bastard.* Sliding up his sunglasses onto the top of his head he proffered his hand and I nervously took it before sliding gracefully out of the car.

He led me down the grand, graveled path (which didn't mix well with four inch heels) and up to the white sandstone, half-moon steps leading up to the impressive glass front door. The whole house was white stone and surrounded by a myriad of vivid green shrubs and flowers of all varieties and colors. Above me was a black metal balcony guardrail – swirled and molded into elaborate flower and leaf patterns – which spread across the full width of the great house.

Completely overwhelmed, it dawned on me that I had fallen in love with a man who came from an obscenely, incomprehensibly rich family. *Lucky bitch,* my subconscious sneered. I mentally slapped the face behind the silent voice, feeling utterly ashamed with my thoughts.

"Ready?" Richard asked eagerly but I could tell by his playful wink that he was reveling in my suffering.

"No," I spat, pouting like an impish child.

"Come on," he said, dismissing my qualms and tugging gently on my reluctant hand as he dragged me into the unknown.

"Good to see you, Dicky Boy!" a tall, pretty fine looking, auburn-haired man – a few years younger than Richard at a guess – greeted while giving Richard a very masculine one-armed hug. I figured with the same rich auburn hair as Richard, he must surely be a relative.

"Amy, this is my brother David. David, meet Amy," Richard said, addressing us both and gesturing his hand to each of us in turn. I didn't even know he had a brother and it hit me that there was still so much left to learn about him. The thought excited me – I doubted I would ever tire of discovering new things about him.

But then, the more I thought about it... *why* didn't he tell me? It dawned on me then, that we only ever really spoke about *me*.

"Nice to meet you, Amy," David muttered politely with an infectious 'cheeky boy' grin. I offered my hand but he bypassed it and leaned in for a peck on the cheek. It was unexpected and I felt my face burn instantly. "Damn, brother, you landed well with this one. She's a stunner!"

"Fuck off, David," Richard replied flatly. Maybe I should've been offended but I couldn't help but giggle. It felt like they were both thirteen years old. In the brief moment I'd spent with him I'd noticed such a youthful, carefree charm exuding from David. I liked him immediately.

The couple from the photo on Richard's floating shelves appeared next from one of the many doors lining the grandiose hallway. After a quick welcoming glance in Richard's direction they skirted straight past him and headed towards me. Suddenly I felt awfully overwhelmed and terribly self-conscious.

Saving Amy

"You must be Amy," Richard's mother greeted warmly. She was so elegant – the same honey-blonde bob as in the photograph with bright red lipstick and flawless skin. "It's such a pleasure to finally meet you," she continued before pulling me into a full-on embrace, making me blush… again. She smelt lovely. In fact she smelt just like Julie's mom and so I knew she was wearing Chanel no.5 without a doubt. I wasn't used to such familiarity and I patted her back awkwardly as I tried to return her affection.

Richard's dad opted for a subtler peck on the cheek followed by a formal handshake.

"Lovely to meet you, dear," he said, equally welcoming but in a slightly more reserved tone. "Son." He nodded towards Richard.

"Amy this is my mother Vivienne, and Alexander, my father." Richard officially introduced us and the mere sound of his comforting voice dissipated some of the burning nerves pulsing through my veins. Vivienne's attention turned to Richard and she pulled him into a loving hug – a little more fervently than she did with me.

"Well, darling, this is quite the little beauty you have here…"

Me? I felt like I should turn around. Surely she must be referring to someone behind me? She smiled teasingly at Richard and then turned it onto me.

"*Mom…*" Richard mock scolded her and I could see from the glint in their eyes that they adored one another. It was fascinating to witness and I felt a twitch in my heart as I wondered what that must feel like.

Formalities over, we followed Richard's parents and David down the extravagant hallway and through a set of arched, frosted glass double doors. We were in the living room – or *a* living room at least. I suspected in a house this size there were probably several more similar rooms dotted around the place. The room was unexpectedly modern in contrast to the traditional pale cream and dark wood hall.

There were two plump, white leather corner suites, a matching four-seater and two matching recliners. They were all angled towards a tremendous, real log fire surrounded by a white stone fireplace which mirrored the exterior of the house. I noticed four different pictures of Richard's sister Kate speckled around the place and my mind began to wander as I tried to imagine the pain this family had been through. I guessed money couldn't buy you everything.

"Bethany?" Vivienne called, using her hand as a makeshift megaphone and making me jump. Bethany? Another new name... Moments later a girl – fifteen-ish at a guess – burst into the room and I could tell by how beautiful she was that she was part of this fine-looking family.

Like everyone else she flew straight over to me without so much as a glance in Richard's direction. So this was what the new toy in kindergarten felt like? I was winded when without warning, she lunged herself onto me – almost knocking me over.

"Oops, sorry!" she apologized when I stumbled. "I'm just so excited to meet you!"

Seriously, what the hell has he been telling these people?

Saving Amy

I smiled clumsily. I was in a room full of strangers who seemed to know all about me and it felt unnerving that I knew *nothing* about them. I didn't even know some of them existed until a few minutes ago and I couldn't seem to prevent myself throwing a chastising glance in Richard's direction. His brow furrowed at my reaction – clearly not comprehending why I was feeling a little pissed.

"Dinner is almost ready, Mom," Bethany said, finally removing herself from my personal space. *So he has a sister too?* Rightly or wrongly I was feeling pretty put out – did he not think I was important enough to tell me about his family?

We made our way to a large dining room with dark walls that were humbly lit by a handful of subtle wall lanterns and a lavish chandelier that spanned the full width of the twelve-seater mahogany table. The table was festooned with fine china, silver cutlery, crystal glasses and a plethora of freshly cut white lilies. It looked like a royal banquet and I was suddenly feeling very out of my depth.

Alexander sat at the head of the table on one of the ornately carved, mahogany chairs with plush, red velvet seats. Richard sat beside him - looking awfully suave in his grey suit with the top three buttons of his crisp white shirt undone – and I beside Richard. David stood opposite me topping up our glasses with white wine and I assumed Vivienne and Bethany were preparing dinner in the kitchen. They joined us moments later and took up their seats adjacent to David. In all honesty I was grateful for the empty space beside me… until I started to wonder if there would be any more new faces joining us.

I watched curiously as Vivienne and Bethany relaxed into their seats, engaging in idle chitchat. They showed no signs of moving and so I decided someone else must have been preparing dinner. Another new face? Seconds later a woman – late forties maybe, dressed in a long black pencil skirt and fitted white blouse – entered the room with four plates balanced effortlessly along her outstretched forearms.

"Amy this is Gracie. My parents' housekeeper," Richard clarified. I nodded, smiling timidly.

They have staff. Of course they do, my subconscious snickered – making me feel stupid.

It surely went with the territory when you were so obscenely rich. I shuddered at the realization and I had never felt so overwhelmingly… *ordinary.* The heat from my disloyal cheeks radiated through my face as they began to burn, followed by a gentle squeeze of reassurance on my knee under the table. I looked up to meet Richard's eyes and he flashed me a playful wink that instantaneously melted any traces of nervousness from my system.

Staring down at my appetizer I now realized why Richard's food was always so pretentious – he'd been raised with it. I was faced with an array of elaborate silver cutlery in size descending order on either side of my plate and it was only because I'd seen snippets of Pretty Woman I knew to work from the outside-in. I caught Richard doing his incredulous eyebrow thingy as he watched me pick up my fork. He seemed unexpectedly impressed that I knew what I was doing.

I'm not a complete imbecile, I thought – inwardly rebuking him.

Saving Amy

I poked around the showy plate of food and although I was sure it probably had some posh-sounding name, to me it was shredded pancetta on an open flat mushroom with some kind of green herb sprinkled on top for effect. It tasted delicious and I flushed when I noticed I'd finished before anyone else.

"So, Amy... I trust my boy is treating you well?" Vivienne asked with her warm smile. She was so easy to like.

"I couldn't ask for anything more from him. You have a wonderful son, Mrs. Lewis," I replied honestly – my heart beating noticeably faster as I thought of everything he'd done for me. She smiled at me and then Richard and I could tell she already knew.

"Richard tells us you'd like to go into real estate someday," Alexander interjected.

Did he?

"Well, you have definitely chosen the right family," he continued without waiting for my response. Then he winked as if I should understand his little quip. I forced a giggle out of politeness – or maybe nervousness – but I had no idea what he was talking about.

While chatter continued around me I ransacked my brain for clues as to where the hell Richard got the idea I dreamt of being a realtor from. I briefly remembered making a joke about the insane amount of money they legally steal from people while I was still absorbing the enormity – therefore expensiveness – of his super-sized apartment. Maybe he took me too literally. Or maybe he just had to tell them *something*... anything that made me sound more enriching than I actually was.

I was abruptly pulled back into feeling out of place and itchy heat began to crawl up my neck and settle in my cheeks when I realized I didn't belong here with all these rich, focused, intellectually stimulating people. I had never been so painfully aware of just how little I had to offer the magnificent man sitting next to me. I had nothing.

I was nothing...

I was grateful when Gracie re-entered the room, snatching me out of my self-pitying episode and interrupting Alexander before he had chance to press me further about my non-existent aspirations.

"There's a phone call for you, Mr. Lewis," she formally informed Richard's father. Excusing himself, he stood up and left the room.

"More wine, Amy?" Vivienne asked while already topping up my glass.

"Is she even old enough?" David piped up, displaying an impish yet loveable grin. Naturally I blushed tomato-red and decided there and then he must be the joker of the family.

"That's enough, David," Vivienne admonished and I caught sight of Richard shielding one hand with the other as he flipped David the bird with a satisfied smile on his face. Their immaturity was just too adorable.

David had a point of course. Eight years is quite a significant age gap that I'd always expected to be frowned upon, and I found myself wondering why his parents were being so gracious, so accepting of me. I couldn't even begin to work it out so I decided not to try, knowing it would only spiral into another episode of self-pity. I'd have plenty of time for that later.

Silently, I willed Richard to say something and take the attention away from me but he remained frustratingly quiet. Assessing the wicked grin splayed across his face I was almost sure he enjoyed watching me squirm. *Jackass.*

"I've not seen Richard this happy in such a long time. You're clearly doing something right," Vivienne praised. My boggled mind was so busy mulling over her words that my cheeks forgot to blush.

Richard unhappy? Why?

"That's awfully nice of you," I muttered nervously and by now my cheeks were blazing a full on inferno.

"Well, it's true. I was beginning to think he'd never get over Joanna."

What the actual fuck? Joanna! Joanna *Joanna? Joanna Interfering Shrink Lady Joanna?* Just when I thought I couldn't despise her any more.

"*Mom!*" Richard finally broke the silence. He looked at me warily and I turned away, wrestling with a thousand different emotions yet trying to remain calm and polite.

The atmosphere between Richard and me was dense and uncomfortable throughout the main course of wild salmon, rocket and baby potatoes. My stomach churned with irrational jealousy and I didn't enjoy the meal one bit.

Alexander returned halfway through the course. His face was unyielding and serious – even more so than before. My nosey subconscious wondered who the call was from but then I decided it was probably something wholly uninteresting and business related.

Dessert followed – homemade profiteroles bursting with salted caramel cream and melted dark chocolate – and the Lewis clan continued their endless ream of irrelevant questions and cheek-burning compliments.

"Amy would you like a tour of the rest of the house?" Richard asked while Gracie cleared away our dishes. I nodded passively. I was annoyed with him even though I knew I had no right or reason to be. The rational part of my mind knew he was entitled to a past, but my subconscious was livid – full-blown jealous with its masked eyes blazing greener than the hulks.

Richard guided me by the hand up the impressive, open spiral staircase which led to a vast landing with lightwood floors and rich red walls, lined with an assortment of spectacular framed pieces of art. It was stunning; like a high-end gallery – or at least how I imagined one to be. My eyes wanted to pause and admire the paintings but I could still feel the gentle pull of Richard's hand, encouraging me to follow him.

He slowed to a stop at the end of the landing by a gleaming window that spanned the full width of the first floor, allowing the most dazzling, panoramic view of the world below us. I stared in awe through the glass, absorbing the beauty of the perfectly manicured lawn of at least ten acres that was lined with four or five different varieties of trees, evergreen shrubs and meadow-like flowers. It backed onto a glittering lake with the scene of the forest silhouetted onto the still water like a flawless canvas.

Saving Amy

"Are you annoyed with me?" Richard asked, genuinely confounded and snapping my eyes back into the room.

"Yes," I answered honestly. "But I know I have no right to be."

"Can I ask *why* you're mad at me?" He truly had no idea and my anger faded into guilt. *I* didn't even know why I was mad anymore and I shrugged my shoulders like a sulking child. Then he raised my chin with his finger, forcing me to look at him. "Talk to me, baby."

I couldn't ignore him when he was like this – his intense green eyes blazing with concern, his brow furrowed, his voice soft and encouraging…

"I don't really know anymore. I think I'm just a little overwhelmed." Yep, there went the eyebrow. I'm sure it's a reflex as natural as breathing for him. "I know so little about you, Richard and it's all been thrust upon me in under two hours." His jaw dropped open and his expression morphed from confused to nervous in a nanosecond.

"And you don't like it? The things you've learned today…" His brow crumpled, narrowing his beautiful eyes and I'd say he looked scared though I couldn't fathom why.

"No. I mean yes, of course I do." Holy crap I was a stuttering mess.

Pull yourself together, my subconscious scolded.

"If I'm honest, I just feel a little out of my depth. Your parents have *so* much money. *You* probably have so much money, but I wouldn't know because I don't really know you. I didn't even know you had a brother and sister till a few hours ago." He definitely looked scared now. And so was I.

"Right, we're leaving," he said sternly and I didn't know if I was relieved or afraid.

"Why? *Where?*"

"We're going home and we're going to talk. You want to know about me? Then get your ears ready, baby, 'cause I'm going to talk into them till they start to burn." He winked an adorable wink and my whole body tingled with excitement – and maybe a little apprehension.

Chapter Eight

Back in Richard's apartment I kicked off my heels and flexed my squished toes. I didn't realize they were too tight until I took them off and the feeling was exquisite – like sinking into soft leather. With that in mind, I headed to the corner-suite and slumped myself into it. Suddenly I was exhausted, but then Richard joined me, pulling my feet onto his lap and rubbing them gently, causing the tiredness to leave me as fast as it came.

"So, what do you want to know?" I sat up sharply. He'd taken me off-guard with such a direct question. Being so close to him, absorbing the warmth of his fingers kneading the soles of my aching feet, I had almost forgotten why we were here.

Right, where to start?

"Your parents… am I right in thinking they're ridiculously wealthy?" I asked in a playful tone. He grinned, amused.

"My father owns the largest real-estate company in Washington State. It is the second largest in the U.S. and the fourth largest in the world." Real estate, *of course!* Alexander's remark suddenly made sense now. "He ranks at fifty-three on the Forbes 400."

Holy fuck!

My heart picked up its pace as I realized I had just had dinner with one of the wealthiest men in

America… and I was in a relationship with his son. *Eek!*

"What about your mom? She's so lovely," I felt obliged to add – because she really was.

"Yes, she is. And she seems quite taken with you." I smiled bashfully even though I wasn't quite convinced. I was sure if she *really* knew me, she'd realize I wasn't good enough for her son. "She's the chief founder of the Finding Hope charity. She set it up shortly after Kate's death. It's an organization dedicated to the support and rehabilitation of young addicts. They do such amazing work."

Abruptly, I began to feel awfully embarrassed and burning shame bored into my cheeks. I wondered idly if Vivienne was the 'support' Richard was always trying to push on me in the hospital. Maybe one way or another, I was always destined to meet his mother.

"Have you told her about me?" I asked because a niggling voice in the back of my head wanted to know if Vivienne just wanted to *save* me too. His reflexive eyebrow sprang into action. He clearly didn't understand my question and I sighed dejectedly when I realized I was going to have to spell it out for him. "About my… *problems?*" Holy hell I was embarrassed.

"Not everything," he admitted and I didn't think I wanted him to elaborate any further if I was ever going to be able to look her in the eye again. "Is that why you're mad at me?" he asked regretfully.

"I'm not mad at you."

"But you *were*." Crap, there was no getting out of it. I was going to have to let him know what a crazy, jealous bitch I was.

Saving Amy

"I wasn't mad, Richard. I was… jealous." I stared at my knees and tried to conceal my blazing cheeks with my hand.

"Jealous?" The son of a bitch grinned at me!

"Glad I amuse you," I muttered under my breath.

"I'm sorry. I should be flattered." He winked at me and amazingly it didn't shift the foul mood I was drowning in. "This is about Joanna isn't it?" *Ugh.* The mere sound of her name made my stomach churn.

"You had a relationship with her?" I questioned and I knew I sounded pathetic and possessive but I just couldn't help it. My subconscious would undoubtedly continue to torture me until it knew all the gory details.

"Yes. But it was a long time ago."

"How long?" Christ, I sounded desperate. If I'd been him, I would've told me to fuck the hell off.

"We met in college, became friends and it went from there. The rest is history."

"How long were you seeing each other?"

"Four years," he answered, very matter of fact. I thought I was finally starting to piss him off. But four years? He must have loved her. The thought pounded into my heart.

"Did you love her?"

What are you playing at, Amy? Let it go.

"I used to think I did." *What's that supposed to mean?* I felt my brow furrow like his often did. "It was only when I met you I realized I had no idea what love was before." My jaw dropped open and even though he'd said it before, I think it might have been actually sinking in.

He loves me.
Me!

"Oh, Richard, I'm sorry," I said guiltily before nestling into his chest. He tightened his arm around me and kissed my hair.

"Don't be. Just know that you have *nothing* to worry about. Joanna is my past, baby. *You* are my future." My heart danced a quickstep – he had just said out-loud that we had a future.

"She's still crushing on you, you know," I said because I knew damn well that she was. I'd seen the way she gaped at him with her puppy-dog eyes. Plus I couldn't think of another reason for her to hate me as much as she does.

"I know she does."

What!

"I'm not blind, Amy. But I can assure you the feelings are most definitely not reciprocated." My pulse quickened and I felt rather proud of myself. I'd won. Take that, Interfering Shrink Lady. I planned to reply with a light-hearted, possibly sarcastic comment but before I had chance his face was in front of mine and I felt him on my lips.

****

I woke up in an empty bed and my tired half-open eyes scanned the bedroom in search of clues to Richard's whereabouts. His pointy black work shoes were still paired neatly on the floor by the fitted closets so I knew he had to be in the apartment somewhere. Heaving my weary legs out of bed, I stretched my arms above my head. It revived me a little and I threw on Richard's stripy blue shirt from the previous night and set off to find him.

I could hear his voice filtering through into the hallway and I knew straight away he was on the phone. His 'phone voice' was louder than his 'real life' one and a little more eloquent and authoritative. Following the sound, I found him shirtless and edible in his study. He had his concentrating, pursed eyebrows face on but it smoothed out immediately when he spotted me in the doorway.

"Yes… 7:15… And the private departure lounge is reserved? Yes… Thank you."

My heart sank. Was he going somewhere? How long would he be away? After hanging up the call he sauntered towards me with his arms outstretched. I fell eagerly into them and held him close, savoring the feel of his warm skin against my cheek and the scent of tea-tree mixed with Armani cologne.

"Are you going somewhere?" I asked dejectedly. Releasing me, he cupped my face in his hands.

"*We* are going to Florida for a few days."

What the… My sunken heart leapt straight back up into its rightful place.

"I have a conference at Gainesville Medical Center Thursday morning. We leave tonight."

Tonight! Internally I was battling against a full-on panic. I wasn't ready. What would I pack? What would the weather be like over there this time of year? It's early September – did that mean it was still summer or had fall began? Was it hot or cold in the fall? Was I going on an airplane? Of course I was going on an airplane…*duh*. Would I need sunglasses? Shit I didn't own any sunglasses. Would I…

"I have to leave soon. I'll be back around lunch," Richard said, snapping me back into the room. I nodded in slow motion and realized I still hadn't said anything. Then he smiled his deliciously wicked grin at me like he knew just what a fantastic bastard he was, kissed my forehead and left.

I stood alone in Richard's study feeling altogether dazed for a few minutes before it hit me. Florida. Julie was in Florida! The thought injected my mind with a rush of pure excitement and I found myself wondering (and hoping) that I would get a chance to see her. I had no idea how big the state of Florida was but surely it was small enough for us to be relatively near her wherever we were staying?

With Julie in my head I felt spurred on to pack my things and I rushed straight to the bedroom to rifle through my clothes. I considered texting her but eventually decided against it, not wanting to get her (or my) hopes up until I knew what Richard had planned for us. His conference was three days away after all and so I pondered why we were leaving so early, feeling flutters of nervous excitement as I tried to imagine what he could have in store for us.

After laying out a selection of clothes on the bed – something for all weathers and eventualities – I eyed them up expectantly. Most of them were ridiculously over-priced and an emotion I couldn't quite place flooded the pit of my stomach. Did I feel lucky? Guilty? Unworthy? All three? Whatever it was unsettled me but I didn't have the time or patience to get into an argument with my subconscious so I quickly folded the first clothes I came to and stuffed them into a small grey suitcase from under the bed.

Saving Amy

Next, I headed to the bathroom armed with an empty vanity case. I froze as I reached into the shower to pick out toiletries from the notably stocked shelves after being interrupted by the sound of the apartment buzzer. I briefly remembered Richard saying something about a delivery so I picked up the receiver in the hall and hit the button to unlock the entrance without checking who it was.

The knock came faster than expected and I was starting to feel intrigued. Richard didn't mention what his delivery actually was and my nosey subconscious was eager to find out. But then it could be in a plain, unrevealing box and I would be none the wiser. I couldn't open it – it wasn't for me. Or could I? How would I have felt if he'd opened *my* mail? I was pretty sure I wouldn't care – there was nothing I couldn't share with him.

Another knock came – fervent and impatient this time, snapping me out of my pathetic pondering and sending me dashing down the long hallway.

Oh shit.

Instinctively I stumbled back a step when I saw Joanna standing tall, smug and completely unwelcome opposite me.

"Richard isn't here," I said a little snappier than intended – though in hindsight not snappy enough. She hadn't even spoken yet and I was fully riled.

"I know. It was you I came to see." My breath stuttered and I couldn't begin to fathom what she could possibly want with *me* but I suspected I wasn't going to like it. "Can I come in?" she asked instead of barging straight through like she would if Richard was here.

If you must.

Stepping to one side, I gestured her through with my hand. She sauntered past me in her ivory pantsuit and slut-red heels and headed straight into the living room where she flopped down onto the corner-suite as if she owned the place.

"Can I get you a drink?" I felt obliged to ask. As much as I wanted to slap that haughty, caked-in-too-much-make-up face, I endeavored to remain civil for Richard's sake. For some absurd reason that I couldn't even begin to comprehend… he liked her.

"Let's cut the crap, Amelia. We both know you wish I wasn't here."

Whoa…

It was the first time the narcissistic bitch had talked to me like that and looking into her spiteful eyes it was difficult to believe this was the same supposedly caring counselor who was first introduced to me as an offer of support. Jaw open, I simply stood there – stunned.

"But that's the problem isn't it? I *am* here… And I'm not going anywhere," she continued. My fist was clenched so tightly by my side my nails felt like they were trying to draw blood from my fleshy palm. Trying to remain calm (outwardly at least) I hid it behind my back to stop me flinging it straight into her face. What in hell was her problem?

"Look, Joanna, I know you don't approve of me and Richard…" She forced out an exaggerated laugh. I let it go. "But I really don't understand why you've taken such a dislike to me. I've done *nothing* to you." I was trying out the nicey-nice approach and I was secretly rather proud of the restraint I managed to hold.

"You really can't see it can you?" I shrugged at her. She was confusing the hell out of me and I wished she'd just get to the point. "You know Richard and I had a relationship?" she asked and I could tell by the smug tone in her voice that she thought it was a revelation.

"Yes. He's told me all about his past," I replied feeling rather superior – it sent that conceited grin flying straight off her face.

"Well then you will know how much he means to me. I don't want him to get hurt, Amelia. And you *will* hurt him, sooner or later." I was shocked into silence. How could I possibly respond to that? My heart was racing, my blood simmering into a slow boil and my tears felt like acid as they stung the back of my eyes.

"Look, you have so many issues, so many problems. I imagine you think they've all gone away now you've been given a bit of attention and flashed a bit of cash…" *What the fuck!* "But believe me they haven't. I see tens of young girls like you every day in my profession and I can assure you, one man can't erase your past and you're extremely naïve if you think he can."

Holy shit, this was all so unexpected and I was lost in the violent thud of my heartbeat. It pounded so hard against my ribs it physically weakened me and I lowered myself down onto the four-seater before I collapsed. Words failed me and I sat in an overwhelmed silence, staring unseeingly around the vast room.

"What you have now can't last. You must know that. This isn't who you are. This isn't where you're from. And next time you need a 'quick fix' or Daddy comes knocking to take his anger out on you, who do you think will suffer? *Richard*... that's who."

After what seemed like an hour – though in reality it was probably two minutes – I breathed a sigh of relief, assuming her tirade was over. Turned out she was just catching her breath.

"You're allowing him to develop these, quite frankly, insane feelings for you and the longer this goes on the harder it's going to be for him when you let him down."

She was still talking but I couldn't hear her. My subconscious seemed fixated on the fact that Richard had told her about my father. I felt betrayed. And angry. And... guilty. Deep down in the depths of my unsettled heart I knew everything she had to say was the truth. But I also knew I was too selfish to let Richard go. I needed him.

"I want you to leave," I muttered solemnly as I rose from the couch, pointing towards the door. Surrendering her hands, she stood up to leave – but not before issuing me with one final blow.

"I know you think you love him, but if you did you'd let him go. You'd let him be with someone he deserves – someone who can give him something back." Then, with one last penetrating glare, she turned sharply on her heels and left.

What the fuck just happened?

****

Hibernating under the thick, satin covered duvet I relived my unexpected encounter over and over again. The bitch made sense and I didn't know who I hated more – *her*, or myself. Emotions from every corner of my heart were tearing through my body. It hurt so badly and I wanted it out. I *needed* it out before I imploded.

Since the second the door slammed behind Joanna my subconscious had been torturing me with images of sharp blades and gaping flesh. I craved the feeling I knew such destruction would bring – distraction, forgetfulness, numbness…

But I couldn't. Not now. I would have to keep it locked away and let it shred me to pieces on the inside instead. The saddest – or sickest – part of it is I was almost disappointed I wasn't patching up a wound right now and the simple fact was, if I thought I could do it without Richard noticing, my legs would have been in ribbons.

The sanctimonious bitch said I was naïve – right again it would seem. I had genuinely and foolishly started to believe I could leave my past precisely there. Before I met Richard I didn't think I was capable of love, or being loved. But now I knew I was and the feeling was so powerful I'd convinced myself I could tackle anything with love as my armor.

That theory had been blown straight out of the window now though. The first whiff of an uncomfortable emotion and I had to truss myself so tightly in my quilt just to stop my twitching fingers reaching for the first sharp object I came to. In fact, all that was missing right now was the sound of my mom's piercing cries.

Realization hit me unbearably hard. I was the same fucked-up girl I always was only now I was dragging Richard down with me. The thought made me sob violently into my pillow – the plump feathers masking the wails that came with so much force I struggled to breathe.

He deserved so much more…

"Amy? *Amy?*" Richard nudged my shoulder and I began to stir. "Baby what are you doing, we have to leave for the airport in an hour!" he mock scolded as I rubbed my puffy eyes with my knuckles. "What is it? What's wrong?" His playful mood shifted abruptly into panic when he saw I'd been crying.

"That's what's wrong," I muttered, my voice hoarse. "You're always so worried about me. I mean, I could've just stubbed my toe, watched a sad movie, or got my period which has turned me into a hormonal monster… But you always assume something terrible has happened. I can see the fire of panic spark up behind your eyes if you ever catch me post-tears." I watched, guilt-ridden as his face crumpled in front of me. I was hurting him already. How did I not see this coming? More to the point, how did *she?*

"Of course I worry about you. I love you!"

"It's more than that," I replied sorrowfully, shaking my head. He joined me on the bed, sitting on the edge and clutching my hand so tightly it almost stung. "You panic in case I've seen my dad, or cut myself, or taken something… And I can't blame you for thinking any of those things. That's who I am. I'm fucked up – screwed in the head… and you shouldn't have to waste your life second guessing my every emotion to try and stop me hurting myself."

Saving Amy

The tears were flowing freely now and I suspected it was because I was about to give up the most wonderful thing that'd ever happened to me.

"Where the hell has all this come from? Have you no idea what you mean to me at all? You can't if you can spout shit like this," he said almost angrily, vigorously rubbing his forearm. I was frustrating him and I hated it. "Something's happened. You were fine when I left this morning. What aren't you telling me, Amy?" he demanded. Bossy Doctor had taken over and my mouth felt compelled to answer him before my brain had chance to think about it.

"*Joanna* came by earlier." Richard sighed heavily and rolled his eyes, seeming utterly exasperated – yet *not* altogether surprised.

"Look here," he ordered gently, using his taught finger to raise my quivering chin and forcing my gaze to meet his. "You take no notice of *anything* she said to you. I'll deal with her later." In that moment I knew they had already exchanged some not-so-friendly words about me, and I was damn sure he knew exactly what she had to say to me earlier too.

But now *I* was frustrated. I didn't want him to *deal* with her later. I didn't want him to deal with her at all. I'd rather he just forgot all about her – forever.

"She knows nothing about us or what we have. She had no right to confront you," he continued and I knew he was trying to reassure me. It didn't work…

"She knows plenty," I snapped, causing his eyebrow to shoot up like he had no idea what I was talking about. "You told her about my dad. I didn't think you'd tell *anyone* about that… you promised me." A surge of sickening guilt pulsed through my veins as I watched him drop his head into his hands, and then drag his palms down his face as if he was smoothing out a Play-Doh model. I detested myself for putting such pressure on him, but of all the people in the world he could confide in – he chose *her*.

"You're right, and I'm so, *so* sorry. Joanna is my oldest friend, she knew something was bothering me and I guess she just caught me at a weak moment. Though I trust her implicitly – you can be sure it will go no further." I didn't believe that for a second. I could see through the scheming bitch even if he couldn't.

I wanted to be so angry with him – how selfish was that? I wanted to hate him for not hating *her*. But when he wrapped his protective arms around me and pulled me into his chest, I melted. The warmth of his body absorbed all traces of unstable emotion and injected my veins with pure need – sheer desire to have him hold me and never let me go. I love him. I love him too much to let him go. Like I said – selfish.

"I wanted to cut before," I whispered so faintly I hoped he would and wouldn't hear me in equal measure. Despite feeling physically ill with shame, I wanted to give the talking thing a try. Not only did I want to be able to share every part of me with Richard, I would give anything a try in the hope that one day I could be 'normal'. He released his hold of me and rested his hands on my shoulders. He'd definitely heard me. "I thought that part of me had… I don't know… gone."

"It won't ever be 'gone', baby." Okay, so that wasn't what I either wanted or expected to hear. I felt my eyebrows knit together and my lips start to tremble. "A part of you will probably always want to do it and you have to accept the fact that one day you probably *will* do it. But that's not because you're weak, or selfish or 'fucked-up' as you put it. It's because the release that you feel when you harm yourself has become your instinctive coping mechanism.

"Craving wise, it's really no different from someone who would automatically reach for a shot of whiskey, or smoke five cigarettes in a row. But of course the reality is, the relief that *you* seek could easily cause you serious damage if you weren't careful. You know it's not healthy and you *want* to get better. And you will, I *promise* you.

"I can't say you'll never think about it again, or even never *do* it again because it was your only escape for so long. Those scars are part of you, they always will be. But you're not alone anymore, Amy, and you will find new ways to cope – to adapt. We'll find them together, you hear me?"

"You're so good to me," was all I could think of to say. "You always seem to know how to handle me." He expelled a soft laugh.

"Seriously, Amy…" His voice turned low, determined. "I need you to remember that anything that's ever happened to you – anything or *anyone* that's ever hurt you – won't ever hurt you again while you're with me. I *will* protect you. I will *never* give up on you. I love you… *and* all your fucked-up-ness." He winked and then smiled his breath-taking hypnotic smile.

Seconds later his lips were on mine and my heart roared back to life with a noticeable thump.

Fervently, I returned the kiss as I gripped and twisted my fingers in his hair, clutching him close to me. My heartbeat was furious, my breathing erratic… It felt like I was drowning in the depths of my love for him. I knew I should come up for air but an unprecedented weight, tied firmly around my heart was pulling me deeper.

An involuntarily whimper escaped from my throat as I started un-popping the buttons of Richard's light-blue shirt, leaving me confused and a little embarrassed when he choked back a laugh and broke away from me.

"As much as I'd love to spend the afternoon in bed with you, we have a plane to catch." After throwing me the delicious wink I'd developed such a weakness for he leapt off the bed, dragging me with him.

I stopped giggling when we reached the door and pulled him back a step.

"Can we just forget today ever happened?" I asked, shamefaced and unable to look him in the eyes. Richard spun around to face me, taking my face in his hands.

"No, baby, we can't. But we can learn from it and move on… together, right?"

"Right," I agreed, smiling weakly.

"Never forget how much you mean to me," he whispered against my forehead before kissing it chastely and leaving the room.

Suddenly I was flustered. My little relapse into an unstable, emotional wreck made our trip completely disappear from my mind and it hit me that I still hadn't finished packing or done my hair. I checked out my reflection in the mirrored closets – *ugh* – and then headed to the bathroom to carry on where I left off before my unwelcome visitor this morning.

Again, I caught sight of my face in the mirror and I tried to splash some life back into it with cold, crisp water from the estuary-like faucets. It revived me instantly and I set about harvesting my favorite items of makeup.

"You've no time for that now. Our cab is outside!" Richard said, startling me as he burst into the room carrying our suitcases.

"But I'm not ready! I've not finished packing and my hair is-"

"They have shops in Florida you know," he interjected, winking at me and cocking his head for me to follow him. Sighing, I did as I was told but I looked and felt like an utter mess. How could I go out in public like this? Grudgingly, I trailed behind Richard as we left the apartment, grabbing my bag and jacket along the way and double-checking the door was locked behind me.

A man was waiting for us by the elevator. He was tall and stocky with a shaved head, dressed unfittingly in a smart black suit like some high-end gangster. He was no run-of-the-mill taxi driver and I imagined he would be awfully intimidating to a passing stranger on a dark night. After taking our luggage from Richard we travelled together in awkward silence to the ground floor.

The car that awaited us didn't resemble a cab at all. It was sleek, black and like everything else that surrounded Richard – expensive looking. It obviously belonged to some kind of private company only fancy rich people knew about. Our driver set down our luggage while he opened our doors for us and I felt incredibly important – like a movie star being chauffeured to some place glitzy and glamorous. Shame that in reality I looked like a hobo who'd just been dragged from underneath the bushes.

"You look beautiful," Richard flattered as if he could read my mind, pausing for a brief moment before he climbed in the car.

As Richard patted the seat beside him I smiled gratefully even though I didn't believe him, and then slid in to the back seat next to him. When the driver slammed the door closed a thousand butterflies hatched inside my stomach. I'd never flown before and I found myself succumbing to the fear of the unknown.

There must be a reason why so many people are afraid to fly.

Great, while driving to the airport all I could think about was how many different, lingering ways there were to die in the air. Unless we drowned after crashing into the sea of course… or the plane blew up before we'd even left the runway… or a terrorist decided to gas us all while we were still in the airport…

Shit.

****

I was lying – yes *lying* – in a very large, gray-leather recliner. It was easily as comfortable as Richard's couch and if I closed my eyes it was hard to believe I was actually on a plane. Pulling the lever that rested beside my seat a little too firmly, I flung back up to Richard's level.

"Finished?" he teased after witnessing me fidget, all wide-eyed and excited with all the fancy features and gadgets that surrounded me. My cheeks pinked with embarrassment and I had to purposely stop myself reaching forward to mess with our own private flat screen. I felt like a kid in a toyshop and I had the most inappropriate urge to touch *everything!*

"Drinks, sir?" a petite blonde with skin so orange it would make an Oompa Loompa jealous, asked Richard.

"Yes, we'll take a bottle of your finest pinot noir please." I'd noticed my age never got questioned when I was with Richard. I suspected it was because people were too busy drooling over his too-perfect face to notice the nobody sitting beside him.

The orange woman set two tall glasses on the table that separated our seats and topped them up with the rich red wine before placing the bottle next to them. Then she smiled – a little too flirtatiously for my liking – at Richard and continued her journey down the aisle, ignoring me completely. I couldn't help but notice no cash was exchanged. Wow, we really must've been flying first class if Richard's favorite wine was free. Richard doesn't *do* cheap wine. In fact, Richard doesn't do cheap anything.

"Are we okay," Richard asked tentatively after taking a sip of his drink.

Are we? Would I ever push him too far one day? In all honesty I just didn't know. But for now I refused to look that far ahead and risk losing the most precious thing that'd ever happened to me. So, for now, yes… we were okay.

I nodded sweetly at him and gently squeezed his knee beneath my fingers. I resented the distance this darn table was putting between us and I just wanted to fling myself onto him and never let him go. For now, I'd just have to make do with holding his hand.

Weary from my exhausting morning of tears and tantrums, Richard caught me trying to stifle a yawn. Then I watched curiously as he stood from his seat to reach into the overhead lockers, and smiled gratefully when he re-emerged with a pillow and blanket. Still smiling as I closed my eyes, I reclined my seat and rested my heavy head on the plump pillow. Then after kissing my forehead, Richard draped the fleecy blanket over my legs and tucked me in at the side.

"Rest," he ordered gently and my heart danced as I was taken back to the first time I encountered Bossy Doctor. God, I love him.

****

In the cab en route to our hotel it was too dark to take in the scenery so I focused my weary eyes on something beautiful instead – Richard. He was slumped back in his seat with his head tilted towards the window next to him, smoothing his hand over his tight-fitting jeans. I wondered what he was thinking behind those hypnotic eyes of his.

I slept away the majority of the six-hour flight and yawned my way through baggage control yet amazingly I was still tired. Though it was 2:30 in the morning. Or was it? I didn't know if my cell had adjusted itself or not while I was comatose.

Saving Amy

The car slowed to a halt outside The Diamond Plaza. It was a mammoth white building with endless windows and a huge canopied porch supported by great stone pillars. My pulse raced as my eyes tried to absorb the magnificence of it all. Would I ever get used to this? I hoped not.

Stepping out of the car we were greeted by a tall man in a dark blue suit complete with tailcoat and pershing hat. I didn't thinking people like that actually existed outside of old-fashioned movies! He took our luggage without needing to be asked – *I'm sure my case has grown* – and led us inside through an immense sandstone lobby and up to an impressive reception desk that spanned the full width of the far wall.

I remained quiet while Richard checked us in with a flame-haired lovesick receptionist. Despite being the middle of the night I was surrounded by beautiful people, impeccably dressed guests and staff alike going about their business. Feeling awfully self-conscious, I dragged out my hair-tie and shook out my hair in an effort to conceal my face. Naturally, Richard fitted in perfectly.

"Would you like the newspaper delivered with your breakfast in the morning, sir?" Red Head asked, her infatuated eyes never leaving Richard's. I wondered if I waved my arms in the air she'd notice that he was with someone.

He nodded curtly – rudely even – like she'd just asked him a ridiculous question. *What's up with Mr. Cranky Pants?* Her eyes fell to the ground as heat rushed to her cheeks. I almost felt a little sorry for her as I started to question whether I had just met 'Tired Richard' for the first time.

Delivered... the word bounced around my brain and it reminded me I didn't sign for Richard's delivery this morning – *yesterday* morning. I hoped it wasn't important.

Next, we were introduced to our concierge – Michael – and he took our baggage before leading us to the top floor in an elevator easily big enough for twenty people. Unbelievably the elevator was manned by yet another finely suited man. Were rich people incapable of pushing a button all by themselves?

Upon reaching the twenty-first floor we followed the blue-suited man known as Michael to the far end of the landing that was all cream and gold with plush red carpet. He guided us to a suite – not a room – that was possibly larger than my old house. *Wowzers.* Yep, still wasn't used to this. Michael settled our luggage beside a rich-red chaise longue in the corner of the room before turning to leave. Then he paused by the open door with an expectant look in his eyes. I was momentarily confused until I saw Richard stride towards him with his open wallet.

Cheeky bastard! He only carried a couple of suitcases... Richard slipped him some money (even though I was secretly hoping he'd do a Kevin McAllister and drop him some gum) then he nodded courteously and left us alone.

"Your delivery didn't arrive today," I said as Richard strolled towards me with outstretched arms. I gladly fell into them.

"Not to worry. I had the courier inform me of any issues and had it redirected to the hospital. I have it right here."

Saving Amy

"Where?" My eyes instinctively scanned the room in a full circle before settling back on his face. Then I followed his gaze as he proffered his hand towards the corner of the room. *The suitcases?* Was he inviting me to take a look? Was it for me?

"Your suitcase," he stated, as if that should quash my confusion. It didn't. "You know, it's times like this your blond hair really suits you," he teased and I playfully punched his arm.

Striding over to the luggage I heaved my suitcase up onto the chaise longue. I was sure it seemed heavier than when I left it. Or perhaps the jetlag had just made me weaker.

"Here," Richard hollered, throwing something small and shiny into the air. It was too late – or too *early* – for hand-eye coordination and I missed, letting it drop to my feet. It was a key. Again, I was baffled, until I noticed the small brass lock fixing the zipper closed. Hmm, I didn't remember it having a lock when I packed it.

Clumsily, I removed the lock and flipped open the grey case.

"This isn't mine." Fantastic, we'd picked up the wrong luggage. That explained why it was so darn heavy. What the hell would I wear now?

"Yes it is. I figured you wouldn't know what to pack at such short notice, so I had someone do it for you." My eyes widened in shock. Was the extravagant bastard for real? I slowly rifled through the contents and found it fully stocked with clothes – tags still intact and designer, naturally – makeup, toiletries, and lingerie *ooo*. He'd had a whole department store smuggled into there.

"Richard, this is absurd!" His eyebrow sprung to life quicker than he could take in a breath. "Don't get me wrong, everything in here is perfect… but you have to admit, it's a little extreme," I said as politely as I could manage because I worried I'd offended him.

"You need clothes, Amy." He sounded disappointed.

"Not designer ones I don't. I don't even want to guess how much this lot is worth."

"Not as much as you," he flattered and I could hear the smile in his voice. I didn't hear him walk towards me and it momentarily startled me to feel his arms snake around my waist.

"I don't mean to sound ungrateful," I admitted as he spun me around to face him. "It's just you have given me so much – *too* much – already. I just wish I had something to give back to you, that's all," I declared because I felt like a money-grabbing freeloader.

"You give me the world just by being here. You have given me more than I ever knew existed. You've changed me, baby. I wish you could see how much." Before I could respond he was kissing me – my cheeks, my neck, my lips… The taste of him expelled any residual tiredness and soon enough the suitcase had been tossed to the floor with Richard taking its place, and I was naked and on top of him – working off some of that sleep.

Chapter Nine

4:00 AM and I was still wide awake. I was curled up into Richard's arms, inhaling his skin as I twiddled the hairs on his chest between my fingers, in a four-poster, super king-sized bed that, wait for it… was *upstairs!* What kind of hotel room had *two* floors?

"I'm not tired," I muttered sulkily, staring into his emerald eyes.

"Me neither." He winked and we both knew *why* he wasn't tired. Lying in blissful silence, the only interruption was the calming sound of his heart thrumming beneath my ear.

"Tell me what you're thinking," he asked and I was taken unawares. God knows why but I was actually thinking of his sister, Kate. Should I be honest with him and risk bursting this serene bubble we were floating in? Or should I talk about the weather…

"Tell me about Kate," I murmured because it was on my mind and it was a part of him – a huge part – that I knew nothing about. The muscles in his chest constricted under my cheek and his breathing accelerated a little. Tightening the arm I had draped across his waist, I pulled him closer to me.

"She was beautiful. And fun… *so* much fun. She had the most infectious laugh." His body began to relax as he described her. "What about *your* family? You've never mentioned anyone besides your parents." He changed the subject abruptly – *too* abruptly. I sighed, disappointed. Why couldn't he open up to me?

I bet he's opened up to her, my interfering, pain-in-the-ass subconscious narked. I mentally slapped the face behind the infuriating voice. Richard loved me – I didn't need anything else from him.

For now.

"There is no one else. As far as I know my parents are both only children and my maternal grandparents died before I was born. I did have a grandma though – my dad's mom." My insides began to ache as I reminisced. "She was the sweetest lady. My dad would take me to see her once a month and she would *always* have ingredients set out in little glass bowls on the kitchen counter for us to bake cakes for afternoon tea together."

A rogue tear escaped at the memory. Richard caressed it away with the edge of his thumb before it had chance to fall very far.

"I remember, I had this little pink notebook with a calendar inside and I would cross off the days until our monthly visit. It was the only thing I ever remember looking forward to." Richard tightened his grip around my shoulders and kissed my hair. "And my dad, well he was the doting father in her presence. When I was *very* young, I was fooled every single time. He'd sit me on his lap and I'd think 'at last, I'm being a good girl', then we'd get back in the car and... Well, I'm just glad she died without knowing what a monster he is."

I could literally feel a physical, fuzzy warmth radiating from my heart and tickling its way through my veins as I thought about my grandma. She was such a kind, loving person. I'd never be able to understand how my dad ended up like he is. It certainly wasn't passed down from Grandma.

"How old were you when she passed away?"

"Nine, ten maybe. We hadn't been to see her in a few months - though it felt like years to such a young kid – and my dad was bawling in my face over something one day and I cried out for her. 'You're grandmother's dead. Now get up those stairs before you make me *really* angry', he said so calmly – so… matter of fact," I told him, mirroring the stern, unnerving tone of my dad's voice. "To this day I don't know how or when she died. The worst part is I don't even remember the last time I saw her. I hope I told her I loved her."

"I'm sure she knew, baby," Richard consoled as he clutched me tighter. I'd never spoken about my grandma before – not even to Julie. I'd forgotten how much I missed her. I was getting used to this 'talking' business – enjoyed it even. In some ways it felt very cathartic, therapeutic.

"Why don't you like to talk about Kate?" I pressed, willing him to unload his deepest emotions onto me as I had just done to him.

"Guilt," he confessed solemnly after a long pause. I knew from eavesdropping that he blamed himself for Kate's death and I'd always struggled to understand why. Was I about to find out?

"Richard it wasn't your fault. She must have had problems far beyond your control. You weren't responsible." Releasing his hold of me, he hitched his way up the bed so he was sitting against the ornately carved headboard.

"But I was. I was responsible for all of it." After hiding his troubled face away in his hands I tentatively reached up and pulled one away, exposing his red eyes that were burning with unshed tears. "I was the person who offered her her first bag of heroin."

Fuck.

"I was such an asshole back then. I was young and rebellious. I came from this perfect, wealthy, upstanding family and I resented it. We'd go to church every Sunday, a different charity event every Saturday... I was expected to follow suit – do something great with my life, give something back. Studying medicine ticked all the criteria I guess. But I just wanted to be like my friends. I wanted to go to college because I'd chosen to, not because I was expected to. I wanted to party, get wrecked, sleep around... do everything a teenage guy was supposed to do and not be some role model for the community's messed up kids."

He paused briefly and I struggled to understand where this was heading. So, he didn't want to be a doctor so he got his sister hooked on crack instead? He was making no sense, but I didn't push him. I was too afraid of what I might hear.

"Basically, I was just a typical selfish, egotistical teenager. I soon learned the art of working hard through the week and partying even harder at the weekend. Like I said, I was young – I had all this money and it made me feel powerful, superior even. I enjoyed impressing people, showing off. I'd think nothing of buying a round of drinks for a bar full of complete strangers while other students were taking out crippling loans just to feed themselves." He shook his head in slow motion and his words cracked as they struggled to leave his throat.

Saving Amy

"Naturally people were soon queuing up to be my friend... and I loved every second of it." His tone was oozing remorse and it was clear he was struggling deeply. I could also tell this was heading somewhere dark and my anxious heart was pounding.

"I know you know how easy it is to get something 'that bit stronger' pushed upon you and I was more than willing to accept. I knew exactly what I was doing." My heart slowed to a near stop as I watched him hide his face behind his trembling hands. My mouth dropped open and I couldn't seem to find the right muscles close it again. "Like I said, I was a selfish bastard."

"No more selfish than me," I interrupted.

"Amy, you can't possibly compare. You suffered a *harrowing* childhood. No one could blame you for trying to seek solace the way you did. Whereas me? I had *everything*... Loving parents, money, everything handed to me on a silver fucking platter. I chose that path out of some kind of pathetic rebellion."

"Why get Kate involved?" I asked and instantly regretted it. He drew his knees into his chest and I knew he thought I was judging him.

"Kate was my best friend. We grew up doing *everything* together. We were even studying medicine together. Saying that, I knew she looked up to me. I was her older brother – she'd have done anything I told her to." I felt my eyebrows furrow.

I thought you were twins?

"Older by twelve minutes," he clarified, attempting but failing to smile. "I took advantage of that. You see, for me... the drugs, getting smashed... it was all just a bit of fun – a bit of escapism. I reveled in the confidence, the power, that odd wrap gave me and I wanted to share it with her. But... she took it too far."

He was firing so many revelations at me and I struggled to assimilate the intensity of it all. My mind was bursting. My body was frozen solid and my arid mouth was rendered speechless. Yet impossibly, seeing him struggle, I was falling in love with him all over again. Ironically, *I* wanted to save *him*.

"I was always pretty confident though, so although I enjoyed the amplified version of that I could take it or leave it depending on what mood I was in. It was more than that for Kate though. She was a follower – my shadow – and I think the confidence part of it was her downfall. It became addictive to her. By then it was too late. That shit'd claimed her and I hadn't even noticed."

I raised my hand towards his agonized face that was shrouded in tears and tried to wipe them away as they fell... but they were falling too fast and I couldn't keep up.

"I *should have* known! I could've helped her. She did anything I said... she would've stopped I *know* she would. But the first I knew about just how bad she had it, was when the police came knocking at my mom's door at three AM one Tuesday morning." A painfully long silence followed and I hitched myself up to his level and curled myself up against his trembling shoulder. I stayed silent. I doubted there were any words in the world that could've comforted him.

"A friend of hers approached me at the funeral. We went for coffee and she informed me just how out of control Kate had gotten. Even now I feel sick knowing she confided in her and not me – her brother. Her best friend. I killed her, Amy."

"Jesus, Richard," I muttered under my breath as his whole body crumbled and fell into me. He was shaking and sobbing uncontrollably and I ached to comfort him but I was lost. Words just wouldn't cut it – not that I could even find any. As he buried his face in my chest my fingers instinctively clutched the back of his auburn hair, squeezing him so tightly to me my knuckles turned white.

"I obviously never knew her but I know it would destroy her to see you like this. I know that because it's destroying *me*. She was in charge of her own decisions, Richard, and I'm sure the reason she didn't tell you is because she loved you too much to want to worry you."

I knew from experience that guilt worked its way into your veins faster than any brand of heroin. And once it's there it spreads like wildfire until it consumes you – *destroys* you. I feared that he would always carry this guilt, this gut-wrenching pain, with him for the rest of his life. The thought ripped through my heart until I was crying along with him.

"I've never told anybody that before," he confessed as our entangled, naked bodies swayed back and forth together.

Not even her… The voice deep in my subconscious was feeling extremely smug but I ignored it, realizing what a selfish bitch that thought made me. This whole situation was nothing to feel any kind of pride or victory about.

"Is that why you tried to help *me?* Because you saw me heading down the same path as Kate?" I asked, possibly insensitively, because the question had been burning a hole in the back of my mind since I first eavesdropped on his conversation with Jealous Evil Shrink Lady.

"I don't know," he admitted, shrugging slightly. "I've met countless patients in your position before but none of them have ever affected me the way you did. I can't lie, your situation *did* remind me of her… but then so have a thousand other patients. So no, I don't think that's why. I can't explain it – I just felt… *drawn* to you, if that makes sense?"

It really does… because I feel it too.

"I kept telling myself to ignore it. Christ knows I tried, but the more time I spent with you… the more times I saw that tiny flicker of life ignite in your eyes whenever you saw me…" he trailed off, smiling contentedly as if reliving a fond memory. "And the first time I made you smile – do you remember?"

"Um…" I shook my head.

"I do. I always will. It wasn't intentional, if I remember correctly I banged my head on your guardrail after I dropped my pen. It stung like a mother but your twisted inner bitch seemed to find it very amusing!"

"Oh yeah," I remembered, laughing all over again. "You looked so pissed!"

"That's because it hurt! But before that moment, I'd only ever seen fear…*hopelessness* in your eyes. Then that day, for a few brief moments… I saw *you*. You caught me, Amy… and no matter how hard I tried, I just wasn't strong enough to pull away."

I smiled warmly, gratefully… utterly beguiled.

"Thank you." His eyebrow responded, letting me know he was confused. "For trusting me... for *loving* me."

"No, baby, thank *you*. For staying."

"Richard, know that anything you've just told me doesn't change how I feel about you. I can't change how you feel about yourself, but I *know* you are a good, honest man. People fuck up – granted sometimes with disastrous consequences, but it doesn't have to define who we are."

Christ, when did I swallow a therapist's textbook? As much as I hoped my insightful words offered Richard some sense of comfort I was sure my own subconscious would take a little more convincing.

"I want to tell you something too," I said after a few long minutes of contemplative calm.

"Anything," he replied as he leaned in to inhale the scent of my hair.

"The night I was admitted to hospital? I didn't fall…" I admitted for the very first time. I couldn't bear to look at him as I spoke, overcome with crushing feelings of guilt and shame. But I *needed* him to know. Now, he was the only person in the whole world who knew me absolutely.

When I eventually summoned enough courage to lift my head and face him he opened his mouth, inhaling sharply as if he were about to speak. I silenced him by placing a finger over his perfectly soft lips.

"Please, you don't have to say anything. I just wanted you to know." He held onto me with his whole body, pulling me in at the waist with his strong, protective arms and twisting his legs around mine.

"You don't ever have to feel like that again," he assured, his voice gruff and shaky.

We lay together for what could've been forever. Two guilt-ridden souls, laid bare in every sense of the word – both silently begging to be saved.

My mind woke up but my exhausted eyes were welded shut. When I eventually managed to prize them open they flipped their focus to the dark wood pendulum clock on the wall opposite. It was 8:15 in the morning. *Ugh.* I must've had about two hours sleep.

When I felt the mattress beside me Richard's side of the bed was empty and cold – the only sign of him being a head shaped impression in his pillow. I turned straight to the nightstand and took one of the contraceptive pills I'd started taking a couple of weeks ago. This was my new morning ritual. I had to do it the second I woke up because I was sure if I didn't I would forget.

Feeling lonely all by myself in such a mammoth bed I reluctantly clambered to my feet, grabbed one of the fluffy white complementary gowns from the en-suite and set off in search of him.

I still couldn't acclimatize to the sheer size of the place. It was a whole apartment in its own right, minus a kitchen. Though it wouldn't have surprised me if I found one hiding somewhere. I casually started to wonder just how much access Richard had to his parents' finances. I wasn't sure how much his own salary was worth but I was almost certain he lived beyond an average doctor's means.

Saving Amy

After making my way down the spiral staircase I found Richard in the larger part of the living room, sitting at the large oak dining suite and helping himself to food from a silver cart which definitely wasn't there when we went to bed. I stopped in my tracks for a moment, admiring him from afar. He looked completely edible, even with bed-hair, morning stubble peppered across his chin and a hotel gown that was gaping open at the top, exposing his defined chest. *Yum.*

He stopped humming along to the music trickling from the speakers behind him when he caught my eye and motioned me to join him with a wave of his hand.

"Croissant?" he asked, taking two from a silver salver and placing them on separate gold-rimmed porcelain plates.

"I'd rather go back to bed." He raised an eyebrow and flashed me a deliciously suggestive grin. "I meant to sleep," I clarified through a yawn before becoming unable to stop myself from giggling.

"Well you can't. You have a busy day ahead."

I' have a busy day ahead?

"You need to eat, shower and be ready for ten-thirty."

Yes sir! I mentally saluted him.

"Where are we going?" I asked inquisitively as I joined him at the table, peeling open my croissant ready to smother it with jam.

"That'd be telling," he said craftily, throwing a salacious wink my way and leaving me more intrigued than ever.

Eager to get ready for my surprise I rushed breakfast and headed to the wet room to take a shower. It was a fairly small – yes, *small* – room in comparison to the rest of the suite, tiled floor to ceiling in shimmering white granite. I stood, weary and naked in the center of the room, absorbing the powerful spray of steaming water which rained from the ceiling above me.

Closing my eyes I let the reviving water wash over my tired face. Then my entire body stiffened, momentarily startled, when I felt two strong muscular arms wrap around my waist. Richard pulled me into him, my back to his front, and swept the damp hair from my neck before kissing along the vein that was now very awake and throbbing with desire.

My eyes still closed, I felt him bend down to the freestanding shelf unit beside us and select a complimentary shower soap. He squeezed it liberally into his palm and worked it into a warm, foamy later between his fingers before smothering the full length of my naked body with it – massaging the citrus fragranced crème into my skin and following the trace of his touch with kisses.

I spun myself round to face him, needing to see him. The sight of him - his deliciously wet, naked body smothered in thousands of tiny, reflective drops of water, his vibrant green eyes blazing with need… it charged my veins with hunger. Hunger for *him*. Automatically I reached up and cupped his face in my hands, my eyes absorbing every visible inch of him. Then I splayed my fingers into his dripping, auburn hair and pulled him into me.

My heart was pounding, thrashing against the walls of my chest. My breathing was ragged. Every inch over my over-sensitized skin was tingling with that mysterious charge that never failed to invade the atmosphere between us. My body never seemed to tire of him. The more I got to touch him, to taste him, inhale him… the more I wanted him. The more I *needed* him.

Teasing entry into his mouth with my tongue I kissed him hard – bursting with passion and longing. Then in one lithe movement he lifted me, hitching my legs up and around his waist. I wrapped my arms around his neck for support and I could feel the veins in his neck throbbing as hard and fast as mine. Taking us away from the cascade of water lashing over us, he carried me to the edge of the room and forced my back into the smooth, wet tiles – the ice-cold granite sending delicious shivers down my spine.

My head threw itself backwards, exposing the pulsing, desirous vein in my neck. I clutched Richard close to me with all my strength, my fingernails boring into the flesh on the back of his neck as he buried his face in my chest. Within seconds he thrust himself deep inside me, warming the tiles along my spine as he glided my hot, moist skin up and down against them.

"I love you so much, baby," he whispered through gritted teeth. My breathing was too erratic to respond with words. Instead, I moved faster against him, supporting my weight with my arms across his strapping shoulders. "So. Fucking. Much."

That beautiful sensation – the sensation only Richard has ever given to me – started to build, growing desperate and heavy between my legs until it was almost unbearable.

"Come on, baby," he muttered harshly straight into my ear… and it undid me completely. My whole body shuddered violently, the vice grip my legs had around him becoming too weak to support me. "Fuck, Amy," Richard cried as he pounded impossibly hard into me for the very last time. Then he lowered me to the floor with trembling arms, my sweltering skin welcoming the coolness that the lower down tiles still possessed as I slid gently against them.

"I love you too," I finally murmured. Suddenly, nestling into Richard's damp chest without the steaming water or the heat of passion warming my veins, I was freezing.

"You're shivering. Let's get you dressed." Richard stood and offered his hand for me to take. He pulled me upright, shut the water off and then wrapped my cold, exposed body in a soft white towel from the heated rail. It felt heavenly – almost as comforting as Richard's arms… but not quite.

After throwing a towel a little less meticulously around his own waist he led me to the bedroom by the hand before opening the set of fitted, cherry-wood closets. Inside all the new unnecessary clothes from my suitcase were hanging neatly. I wondered when he'd found time to do this as I stepped closer to choose an outfit. The vast array of strappy tees and vests seemingly answered my question about the Florida climate. Judging this closet, the weather must be hot even at this time of year – though our suite's air-con gave nothing away.

I eventually settled on a pair of ivory boot-cut pants, cerise spaghetti-strap top and flat black sandals. Noticing the time – 10:10 AM – I threw them on quickly. There was only twenty minute to spare before the big reveal and I still had to do my hair. *Where is he taking me?*

After running the compact travel dryer over my damp hair I swiftly scraped the blonde mess into a loose ponytail. Then I applied the bare minimum of makeup required to make me look presentable and skipped to the living room to join Richard. I found him standing by the window, dressed impeccably in smart black slacks and a lilac pinstripe shirt with a rich purple tie. Following his gaze I noticed he was staring wistfully towards a picturesque lake ahead. Is that where we were going?

"You look perfect," he complimented when he turned and noticed me loitering in the doorway. I felt anything but. I wasn't used to wearing such bright colors – *any* colors for that matter. My wardrobe had always tended to color coordinate with my mood; black, grey… brown if I felt like mixing things up a little.

"So, where are we going?" I asked curiously, feeling a little underdressed next to his full-on business attire.

"*I'm* going to the medical center. I've been asked to head a meeting there this morning." *What about me?* My brow dropped along with my heart. "Ready for your surprise?" he asked eagerly with a wicked glint in his eyes.

No, my disenchanted subconscious piped up. Some surprise if he wasn't even going to be with me.

"Come with me," Bossy Doctor said before striding forwards to take my hand. He led me to the door and then paused, rummaging through his pockets. "Here's the room key." He passed me a little blue card. "And here's some money. If you need any more the safe combination is nine two six three." Grudgingly I swept the cash from his hand. *Any more?* There was easily five hundred dollars here. I couldn't help the pout that suddenly took over my face. I felt like a prostitute.

I need my own money...

"Oops, almost forgot this," he tacked on. *Forgot what?* His hands were empty. But then, cupping my face in his warm hands he planted a soft, lingering kiss on my lips. *Wow.* In that moment, all my frustration melted away.

Richard led me down to the lobby and it appeared we were heading in the direction of the hotel bar. I glanced up at his face, searching for clues in his expression and I was met with that beautifully irritating wicked grin of his. He was so obviously pleased with himself about something. *But what?*

We hovered outside the arched glass doors that led inside the bar. Richard glanced at his watch then pulled his cell from his pants pocket before tapping away at the screen. My feet drummed impatiently against the marble floor. I was getting increasingly frustrated. And nervous. And sad that I wouldn't be spending the day with him.

"We're all set," he said, looking up from his cell. "Go meet your surprise," he said with a mischievous wink, extending his hand into the bar as he opened the heavy glass door. My eyes wandered eagerly into the bar. My body followed shortly after. I scanned the room starting from the far left and when I reached the center I spotted my surprise.

Saving Amy

"Julie!" I screamed, catapulting myself across the room and throwing myself onto her with outstretched arms.

"Jeez, Louise!" she said when I almost knocked her over. "Steady, girl!"

"Sorry! I'm just so happy to see you! What are you even doing here?" My arms were still wrapped around her. I didn't want to let her go.

"I was invited," she said, nodding her head towards something behind me. Releasing her, I followed her gaze – landing on Richard. For the first time, I had completely forgotten his existence. How did he contact her? How did he know where she lived? I must've told him, though I didn't remember. Eventually I dismissed all my questions, deciding I didn't care. Julie was here. *I* was here. Everything else was irrelevant.

"I'll leave you two ladies alone." Richard winked and flashed me that familiar hypnotic smile. I turned and hugged him… hard.

"Thank you," I whispered meaningfully into his ear.

"I love you," he whispered back.

"I love you more."

"Impossible."

"Sweet Jesus, enough already!" Julie interrupted, grabbing my arm and pulling me away from him. Naturally, I flushed beet-red. Richard just snickered – clearly harder to embarrass than I was.

"Goodbye, ladies," Richard said with a cheeky glint sparkling in his green eyes. I stared after him as he turned and disappeared, then – in an instant – forgot all about him as I turned my attention to Julie.

I'd missed her incredibly. I didn't realize just how much until now.

"You look amazing," she enthused.

Me? Was my instinctive reaction. But then I remembered just this morning, eyeing myself up in the mirror, I barely recognized myself. My cheeks were a little fuller, my skin brighter – less gray.

"I feel it," I replied honestly.

"Good looking son of a bitch isn't he?" Julie winked at me and of course, she meant Richard. I nodded proudly.

"You need to tell me *everything*. How did it happen? Do you love him? Does he love you? Is he treating you right?"

Whoa, slow down! She fired questions at me faster than a bullet and my overwhelmed mind struggled to keep up.

"Steady on, Jules! We've got all day. Let's get the drinks in first."

"Good idea. Though, I think we should go somewhere else. I'm sure even breathing the air in this place costs money," she muttered while her blue eyes – wide with awe – scanned the room.

"Don't worry, I'll get them."

"Of course you will," she said with a smirk and I knew she was accusing me of being a kept woman. I immediately resented the thought… until I realized that's exactly what I was.

We headed over to the burnished white bar and I ordered two caramel lattes. After Julie's innocent quip I suddenly felt ashamed pulling Richard's money from my purse. I let it go – for now – refusing to allow it to dampen my day. However I

Saving Amy

knew my subconscious would have a field day when I was alone later.

I led Julie over to a glossy black table surrounded by four curvy white leather chairs at the end of the far room beside a floor to ceiling window.

"I still can't believe you're here," I declared as we settled into our seats.

"Well, when Mr. Gorgeous Pants called there was no way I'd have said no! I've missed you, Amy."

He called her? How? When?

"You look so different… so happy. Is he good to you?"

"Oh, Julie, like you wouldn't believe. He is *so* good to me… *too* good."

"Bullshit! Don't you dare sell yourself short like that. You deserve happiness, and it's about time too." I smiled bashfully at her and idly wondered if I'd ever believe that was true.

"How's things with your mom and dad? You haven't mentioned them in a while."

Can't it stay that way?

"I haven't seen or heard from them since I moved in with Richard."

"Seriously? Things that bad huh?" I shrugged nonchalantly. "So they don't approve of you and Dishy Doctor then I take it?" I smiled inwardly at her blissful naivety. I was glad she never discovered the half of it. I didn't think I could bear the shame.

"Something like that." I nodded impassively, hoping to wrap up that particular topic. "So, how's college life?" I asked, turning the attention onto her and knowing it would easily distract her. Once Julie got going, it was almost impossible to stop her.

"I'm loving it. New opportunities, friends, independence... what's not to like?" I was sure my golden eyes must've been exuding some not-so-subtle hues of green right now. I blinked it away, my subconscious reminding me this conversation wasn't about me or my failures. "And as of last week I have a job too!"

Ooo this is news. I blinked the now blazing green away a little more forcefully.

"I thought your parents helped out?"

"Don't get me wrong they've been amazing. They pay for my apartment and transfer two hundred dollars a week into my account, but with food and bills it's just not enough. There's nothing left for a social life, and I've been thinking it's about time I get a car."

"Well then I'm real pleased for you. Where is it?" I asked, wondering how she even found the time.

"I am now officially a waitress at The Olive Branch," she announced with a proud, beaming grin. "It's a little family-run Italian a few blocks from here and I work Monday through Thursday evenings after college and all day Sundays. It's nothing exciting but it brings in some cash."

"Sounds great. But how do you find the time? Doesn't studying take up most of it?"

"It *should*, I suppose. I try and work it around lectures and on Saturdays," she admitted with a defiant shrug. "If I'm not too hung over that is." Julie threw a familiar mischievous wink my way – the kind that used to mean 'let's ditch this place after homeroom. I'd missed it and I couldn't help but giggle.

Saving Amy

Julie continued to fill me on everything that'd happened in her life since leaving Seattle over two more lattes. After just over an hour my ears were starting to ache a little and I now felt like I knew Julie's new friends personally. I was also pretty confident that I knew my way around The Olive Branch well enough to carry out a full shift there with ease.

"Fancy coming back to mine? I'll give you a tour of my palace," Julie asked and the enthusiasm in her voice was hard to resist.

"Sure. I'll go ask reception to call us a cab."

"We need a smoke first. Let's head outside," she said while reaching into her purse for her cigarettes.

Hold on a minute... I didn't smoke anymore. How did that happen? It hadn't even crossed my mind while living with Richard. How the hell do you give up something that was once as instinctive as breathing without even realizing?

"What's up?" Julie asked upon noticing my furrowed brow.

"I, um... don't smoke anymore." Her eyebrow shot up and I couldn't work out if she was surprised or amused.

"Wow. Mr. Mega Wallet really has changed you," she said dryly and it felt like she was mocking him.

"It's got nothing to do with Richard. He's never had a problem with anything I do," I blurted, feeling compelled to defend myself – and Richard. Julie surrendered her hands, playfully it seemed, and on reflection I realized I answered a little too snappily.

"Sorry. Maybe I *do* need a smoke," I teased with an apologetic smile before heading off to arrange a cab.

Chapter Ten

What a day. Jesus, Julie knew how to talk. I'd missed that about her – just having to listen without thinking of a reply. I was exhausted. My limbs were so heavy it felt like I'd gained 100lbs. Raiding the mini-bar – though I struggled to actually find anything 'mini' about it – I settled for an ice-cold bottle of freshly squeezed OJ and two candy bars for a much needed energy boost.

Slumping back into the soft brown leather recliner, I kicked off my shoes, unwrapped the first bar of orgasmic smelling fruit and nut and laid myself back. I noticed the time on the overstated grandfather clock in the corner of the room. It was 5:45 in the evening. Where the hell was Richard?

I didn't know whether to laugh, cry or sleep. Today had been an overwhelming rollercoaster of emotions and I was physically and mentally drained. Excitement followed by disappointment, superseded by sheer elation, regrets, jealousy…

Julie and I had shared, reminisced and laughed till we cried. She was doing really well for herself and I was so proud of her. Her apartment was small but homely. Though maybe on reflection it was a *normal* sized place and I was just used to everything being so over proportionate these days. Still, it was fully furnished, modern – decorated in neutral colors – and had all the amenities required by one person. With the occasional guest she was keen to point out.

It seems her head has been well and truly turned by a guy named Paul from her sociology class. After babbling on about him for ninety minutes straight I'd say she's pretty fixated with him. I couldn't help sensing a juvenile quality to her feelings however. Hearing her talk of Paul – the giggles, the blushing, the whispers… it all felt very 'school-crush'. There was no mention of her heart swelling to bursting point, or her blood pulsing through her veins agonizingly fast, her heart being eaten alive by her stomach whenever she watched him leave, the feeling that she wouldn't be able to breathe without him…

I started to wonder if my feelings for Richard were normal. Were they supposed to be so intense, so overpowering? Was love like that for everyone, or was it just another element of my fucked-up-ness?

Still, she was bursting with a carefree vivaciousness and it was impossible not to be infected by it. It was only today I realized how little I appreciated Julie's friendship back home. I guess absence really does make the heart grow fonder. Thinking of absence, where was Richard?

In that very instant Richard burst into the room as if he'd heard my thoughts.

"I'm sorry I'm so late. One meeting led to another, then another… I was going to call but my battery died and I don't know your number by heart," he rambled in a fluster. I stood up immediately to greet him. I was pretty sure it was the longest we'd ever been apart and my whole, weary body ached to be held by him. His arms widened at my approach and I eagerly fell into them, burrowing my face into his shirt and breathing him in.

"I've missed you," I whispered into his chest. He raised my chin with his forefinger so our faces were just inches apart, then he twisted his fingers into my hair and set his firm, premeditated lips on mine.

****

After devouring our room service order of steak and vegetables, we finally made it to bed. We lay side by side, facing each other – he was so near I could feel his warm, sweet breath brush my cheeks like a feather. He was so wonderfully beautiful this close up. I could've stared at him forever.

"Thank you so much for today," I breathed and he flashed me the most captivating 'you're welcome' smile.

"Did you have fun?"

"It was perfect. I've missed her so badly."

I continued to ramble on about my day for almost half an hour and even though I was sure I was boring him with my incessant girl-talk, he listened intently – never taking his seemingly fascinated eyes off mine.

"I told Julie I'd go out with her tomorrow night. But of course I'll cancel if you have anything planned?" I felt guiltier than I thought I would. It would be our last night here. On reflection, I should've been spending it with him.

"No, you go," he assured. "*We* have the rest of our lives together. Who knows when you might see Julie again."

Rest of our lives… wow.

"What?" he asked, bemused as I gaped at him in utter awe.

"You're just so... *perfect*. You completely mesmerize me." He choked back a deliciously playful giggle.

"Glad you noticed," he teased. I grabbed a pillow from behind my back and whacked him with it.

After ten minutes of a full-blown, utterly immature pillow fight, we both flopped back onto the bed, exhausted. My breathing was labored and my ribs were physically throbbing from laughing so hard.

For a few brief minutes I was the child I never got the chance to be.

"I'll be gone early in the morning, so I'll leave you some money by the bed." Wow. My good mood evaporated in a nanosecond.

"About that... I'm just not comfortable taking from you all the time," I finally confessed because it'd been eating away at me for weeks. Richard's eyes widened in genuine surprise. In fact he'd been taken so off guard his eyebrow took a fraction longer to catch up with him.

"That's ridiculous. It's not as if I can't afford it. Besides, what's mine is yours."

"And I love you for that, truly I do," I replied as tactfully as I could manage because I was pretty sure I'd wounded his ego. "I just want some independence I guess. I'm still young. I don't want to have to rely on someone else for the rest of my life." His brow furrowed like I was speaking in some unknown language from outer space.

"Not someone, baby... *me*."

Saving Amy

"I need you to try and understand," I said carefully, stroking the stubble on his face with the back of my hand. "I love you, you know I do. I just need something for myself – something for when you're not there. Something to get me 'out there' you know?"

"I'll try."

"Well, I want to look for a job when we get home." His body jerked slightly away from me like I'd just told him I'd killed his childhood puppy.

"What kind of job?" he asked dubiously. "I don't think you've ever mentioned which career path you're interested in taking before."

Except when I wanted to be a realtor, my subconscious teased, cheering me up. It must have been having an off day. Richard snuggled into me, his eyes wide and eager for my response. It unsettled me. I was certain I was about to disappoint him.

"Anything. Office work, cleaning…"

"Oh, Amy no! You're so much better than that!" he scolded and then pulled back again. "You *must* have a particular interest. You can't have grown up aspiring to mop up other people's piss," he said, a little more relaxed. My lungs dragged in a welcome gulp of air. I didn't realize I had been holding my breath.

"That's irrelevant, Richard. I have no qualifications and no experience. I blew my chances of a high-flying career." He shook his head, frustrated. How could he possibly disagree? I was talking fact.

"Just tell me, what did you dream of when you were younger?"

Escaping.

"It doesn't matter anymore," I answered passively, praying he'd let it go. I shifted in the bed feeling uncomfortable, embarrassed…

"Humor me," he probed and I knew there was no getting out of it. After sighing heavily, I gave in.

"I wanted to be a writer. Publisher maybe. Something in that field…" I blurted before I had chance to change my mind. Why was I so embarrassed? Richard's jaw dropped open slightly and his eyebrow shot open so quickly I feared it might leap straight off his head.

"What? I'm not completely stupid you know!" I teased, though truthfully I was a little offended at the extent of his surprise.

"Amy, you are one of the smartest people I've ever met – there's no question there. I just had no idea. I always find it remarkable learning new things about you," he explained and I retracted my sulky pout.

"So, have you ever written anything?" he asked inquisitively. I nodded diffidently. My cheeks were on fire and I just knew he was going to ask if he could read something. "Do you still do it? Write, I mean."

"Sometimes." I shrugged, awkwardly.

"You're not giving very much away are you?" I shrugged, again. It felt so discomfiting talking about myself. Richard was much more interesting and so I drew a deep, preparing breath, ready to change the subject. Unfortunately, he got in there first.

"What do you write about?"

"Stories mainly. Sometimes diaries, poems… anything really." He smiled warmly and it looked like he might even be impressed. It spurred me on to continue. "I used to write for hours at a time. It was a sort of escapism I suppose - immersing myself in a world I could only dream of living in. It was the only way I ever got to experience a happy ending… before I met you of course."

"I'd love to read something," he said with a proud smile tugging at his lips.

Here we go…

"Well, I only have one notepad left. My dad burned the others," I admitted solemnly, quivering at the memory. "It's in my bag over there. I carry it everywhere since my dad found them."

"Can I see?" he asked eagerly while hitching himself up on his elbows.

"I'd rather you read it when I wasn't here. I'm kind of embarrassed." Another look of genuine confusion washed over his face.

"*Why?*" he pressed.

"Because it's probably just a load of old shit that makes no sense to anyone else. Please, I'd just feel awkward."

"Whatever you say. Though you need to have more faith in yourself. I certainly do. You're a very intelligent young woman, Amy."

He shuffled back down the bed so we were face-to-face once again. His fingers worked their way into my hair, curling and twisting the loose tendrils as I studied how beautiful his face was lit up by the moonlight streaming through the window. Tenderly gripping the back of my head he pulled my face into his - kissing me, charging me, *wanting me.*

No more talking occurred that night.

****

By 7:30 PM I was all set for my big night out with Julie. I felt incredibly nervous but I couldn't fathom why. Maybe it was the dress. After spending the best part of an hour raiding my new designer wardrobe I eventually settled on a plum, chiffon halter-neck that cinched at the waist and fell just below my knees. It was undeniably stunning… on the hanger. On me? I just wasn't sure. Still, it was too late to change again – Julie had already text to say she was on her way.

I reached for my shoes – the only dressy ones I could find. They were black peep-toe with diamante bows and ankle-snapping heels. After slipping them on – naturally a perfect fit – I attempted to walk.

"Ah, fuck!" I screamed out loud when I stumbled and had to save myself on the red chaise longue. There was absolutely no way I would be coming home with all my bones intact tonight. *Good job you're coming home to a doctor then,* my subconscious teased. It'd been in an uncharacteristically good mood lately.

****

"You look fantastic!" Julie practically sang when I met her in the lobby.

"So do you." And she really did. Her rich-brown hair was scraped back into a bun with two loose ringlets framing either side of her face. She was dressed in a vivid red, backless mini-dress which I was sure would expose her panties if she was to bend down. Regardless, her stunningly perfect cheerleader figure pulled it off beautifully.

Saving Amy

After requesting a cab from reception we walked outside to wait for it. Or rather Julie walked – I stumbled.

"For old times sake?" she asked, pulling a pack of smokes from her purse. Shrugging, I took it – out of curiosity more than anything. The first puff burned the back of my throat and I coughed and spluttered like a twelve year old trying to look 'cool'. I gave it a couple more goes anyway, childishly refusing the let the sucker beat me.

Whoa...

"Head rush," I muttered, feeling a little dizzy. Julie laughed and it wasn't long before I caught her infectious giggle.

"Amy Hope?" a smartly dressed, gray-haired man interrupted. I flicked the end of my cigarette behind me, prompting a disparaging look from a fellow guest, and walked *(stumbled)* towards him and the gleaming silver car he was stood against. This hotel must use the same kind of fancy cab company as Richard. After nodding towards the well-dressed driver, Julie and I climbed through the door he was holding open for us and into the back seat.

"Holy crap, this is the smartest cab I've ever been in!" Julie's eyes were wide and amazed as she ran her fingers over the soft, cream leather interior.

"You get used to it," I teased with a wink.

Julie instructed our driver where to take us. We arrived at Bedazzled just over ten minutes later. It was nestled in the center of a road lined with shops, nightclubs and palm trees – an odd yet perfect combination.

"Dammit! I've left my purse back in the hotel room," I said in a fluster as the driver turned to collect his fare. I mentally slapped myself. I knew exactly where I left it and even remember telling myself not to forget it.

"No worries. I can see us through tonight. I'm a career woman now remember?" Julie smiled at me and nudged my shoulder but I still sighed, frustrated. It was hard enough relying on Richard and his gigantic wallet for everything, never mind Julie who had a hard enough time affording to feed herself.

"I'll pay you back before we leave tomorrow."

"Nonsense. Tonight's on me." I smiled gratefully at her and left it that. However, I fully intended to pop by her house on the way to the airport tomorrow with some cash. She would be at college anyway so she couldn't exactly stop me posting it through her mailbox. With that decision in mind, I finally started to relax, vowing to enjoy myself.

Bedazzled was in essence just a giant warehouse - gray brick walls adorned with flashing fairy lights, no windows and a concrete floor with black and white tiles painted on it. When we crossed the entrance I was pulled back a step by a strong grip on my shoulder.

"I.D.?" a burly, grumpy-faced man asked when I turned around.

Shit.

"She's with me," Julie blared over the thumping music as if she were some kind of celebrity. He raised his hand off me instantly and waved me forward. What just happened?

"Let's just say we had a bit of a 'thing'," Julie whispered loudly in my ear, complete with air quotes.

Saving Amy

Eww. I thought she had better taste.

"I was wasted," she confessed with a revolted shudder. Was she reading my mind?

I followed Julie's lead as we made our way through the lively crowd and over to the bar. Like old times she ordered two vodka-Coke's and after passing it to me, I sipped it warily. It'd been quite a while and experience told me that it only usually led to trouble. *Things are different now,* my subconscious rationalized – thinking positively for the first time in its life. I wasn't used to the annoying little voice making sense. It unnerved me and I wondered what torture it must have planned for later.

Julie tugged on my hand, pulling me towards the dance floor. I stumbled in my ridiculous shoes and ended up easing out of her grip while I bent down to take them off. *Oh, yes.* I sighed heavily and fluttered my eyelashes as I came down from the climax my feet had just experienced.

Julie and I danced – drink in one hand, shoes in the other – for what must have been hours, only stopping for bathroom breaks or to replenish our vodka's. I was having such a great time. Fun and alcohol seemed like such a bizarre concept. I was pretty sure I was what people described as buzzed. My muscles were relaxed, the blood in my veins was warm and fuzzy and everything was just that little bit more amusing. I'd never experienced the feeling before and in all honesty it was pretty damn good. In the past I had only ever drunk to get drunk – going from stone cold sober to utterly obliterated in under twenty minutes.

By 2:30 AM the bar was quickly emptying – time to go home. I felt tired, woozy and gloriously happy… until I shamefully remembered this was the first night out I'd had with Julie that didn't end up with me hurling into the street or fucking some stranger up a wall. I shuddered at the thought, utterly disgusted with myself. Could my life really have changed forever? God I hoped so.

"Thank you for the *best* time. I'll miss you," I said to Julie, pulling her into a bear hug before we said our final goodbyes.

"You too. But hey, I'll be home for Thanksgiving – that's not too far away." This was news. *Welcome* news. My lips stretched into a smile so wide my jaw began to ache. "One for the road?" she added, flipping open her cigarettes.

"Why not," I agreed, giggling softly.

The coarse asphalt was starting to grate the soles of my feet so I chanced putting my shoes back on as I followed Julie to the circle of wooden benches around the side of the bar. Unfortunately I didn't see the cluster of pebbles that had overflowed from a nearby plant pot, and as it turned out, the death-defying heels didn't get along too well with uneven surfaces. Before I could yell 'oh fuck' I was flat on my face with my scuffed hands covered in dirt.

"Jesus, Amy, are you okay?" Julie fussed, crouching down in front of me and sweeping the hair out of my face. Instead of replying I snorted. *Actually* snorted. I think I was aiming for a laugh but the disorientation mixed with a dash of humiliation had rendered me speechless. Add in the after effects of more shots of vodka than I could count, and I couldn't even summon the ability to make sounds interpretable by other human beings.

Saving Amy

"What the hell are those?" Julie blared abruptly, bolting upright as I rolled myself over into a sitting position. Confused, I angled my head to look up at her but my eyes took a couple of extra seconds to catch up. When they eventually stopped on her face and she stopped swaying from side to side long enough for me to concentrate, I followed her fretful gaze.

Oh shit.

"N-nothing. They're nothing," I stuttered, yanking the hem of my dress back down over my thighs.

"Well they sure as hell don't look like nothing. Let me see." She reached for the bottom of my dress and I batted her hand away.

"Just leave it!" I unintentionally yelled. "Sorry, I just… I had an accident as a kid. I don't like to talk about it." I was one hundred percent sober now. My heart was racing, working extra hard to pump my entire body's worth of blood to my cheeks it seemed.

"Amy, I've known you since sixth grade. We used to get changed together all the time back then. There were *no* scars," she said, determined.

She was right of course. I made my first cut when I was fourteen after being floored by my dad and landing on the shards of a broken glass he'd thrown minutes earlier. I remember the feeling as it sliced into the back of my arm. It burned like hell – the pain was all I could think about. While I tried to stop the bleeding and the overpowering stinging sensation I briefly forgot how it happened – why it happened… who caused it to happen.

It was the most wonderful distraction… and I wanted more.

"You can tell me anything, Amy. You know that right?" Julie settled down beside me on the floor and wrapped her arm around my shoulders. Some people pointed and stared on their way past us but I can't say I particularly cared.

"I don't know what to say." I shrugged and looked to the floor, too ashamed to make eye contact. "I'm a self-injurer? A cutter? A fucking fruit cake? I don't really know the correct terminology."

"I don't- I mean- well... *why?*" she asked, struggling to summon the million-dollar question.

"To distract myself. To *feel* something. To punish myself... Julie I've kept so much from you and I'm so, so sorry," I admitted, slamming my head into my hands and sobbing violently into them.

We sat huddled together on the stone floor for over an hour while I explained in agonizing detail the true extent of my father's depravity. I'd always expected her to pity me, or judge me, or challenge my reasons for never reporting him. I'd thought often about telling her everything over the years, and every time the look of repugnance I envisioned on her face made me bottle out.

I'd always assumed she'd... fuss – change the way she saw me. I know that sounds selfish but I couldn't have dealt with her feeling sorry for me, or feeling bad for not being there for me, or her too wishing she could've saved me. But, when the time came, when she found out in all holy detail who I really was... she simply listened.

"How did I never see it? How did I never notice my best friend was barely keeping herself alive for all those years? I'm so sorry, Amy."

"No, Julie. Please don't think like that. You didn't see it because I didn't want you too. I'm a good liar when I need to be," I admitted shamefully.

"I'm so glad Richard found you that night, and that he saw what a wonderful girl was hiding away inside of you," Julie said, letting go of my hand just long enough to wipe a tear from her face. I nodded weakly. "Do you love him?" she asked out of the blue, taking me unawares.

"What? Of course I do."

"Then why do you look so sad whenever I mention him?" I stuttered for a few seconds before giving up. Instead I thought about it for a while. She was right. It was only in that moment I realized just how much my chest ached whenever I thought about him. I'd always assumed it was because I missed him when we were apart… but it was more than that.

It was fear.

"I guess I'm just waiting for him to give up on me," I admitted honestly for the first time – both out loud and to myself.

"Amy, he *adores* you. I could tell the second I saw you both together. Stood behind you when you first saw me in the bar yesterday, seeing how happy you were… I swear I thought he was going to cry. He looked so… proud. Has he given you any reason to doubt him?"

"No," I admitted. "But it's not even really about him. He's a good man - I know that. But me… I'm a failure. I've never succeeded in anything I've ever set out to do. I'm insecure. I'm jealous. I feel like I need him so much, like I'm so afraid of what would happen if I lost him… that I feel almost possessive of him. I'll screw it up, Jules, I know I will."

"Look here," she ordered, shuffling round until she was facing me. "You're not a failure, Amy. I don't know how you can even think that after everything you've just told me. You've never been given a chance to succeed before now… but you will. You've got Richard behind you. You've got *me* behind you. I'm so sorry I couldn't help you for all those years, Amy… but I'm here now and Richard or no Richard – you will *never* be alone again. Got it?"

"Thank you, Julie. I'm sorry for not trusting you sooner. I was just… ashamed I guess." I looked her directly in the eyes for the first time since I face-planted the sidewalk. "I love you so much, girl."

"You better. I mean I *am* pretty damn awesome," she agreed with a teasing wink. "And remember, if you screw it up… I'll always be here to help you iron it back out again." I smiled gratefully, awestruck by just how amazing she was. How did I never realize that before now? I vowed in that very moment, to never take Julie for granted again.

"You're safe now, Amy. And you're loved incredibly. Hold on to that for me, yeah?"

"Yeah," I agreed, falling into her open arms and letting her sway me from side to side. "We'd better get going I suppose," I said reluctantly, standing up for the first time since I fell.

"Thank Christ for that. I'm pretty sure my ass died about twenty minutes ago." Julie laughed and then we walked hand in hand to hail two separate cabs. Tears burned the back of my eyes when they pulled up in front of us. I didn't want to say goodbye – I missed her already.

"I'm gonna miss you so much," I whispered in her ear, squeezing her tightly one last time.

"You'll hear from me every day in some form or other. I'm never letting my girl down again."

"Julie you-" *didn't let me down*...

"Shh," she silenced me. "Take care, Amy." She gave me a peck on the cheek and then wiped my tears from her lips. I nodded and watched sorrowfully as she turned and climbed into the back of her cab.

"I'll try," I whispered to nobody when her cab pulled out into the road.

We never did have that smoke...

Shit. As the cab pulled up outside the hotel that was twinkling like a palace in the dark of the night, I remembered I had no purse. Therefore I had no money to pay my fare, no key card to get me inside and get some, and no cell to call Richard. Embarrassed by my predicament, I asked the driver to wait while I scuttled over to the night concierge guarding the grand, glass doors and explained

"That's no problem, ma'am. Leave it with me and I'll get reception to add it to your husband's bill."

Husband? The word rang deliciously in my ears and I didn't correct him. Instead, I picked my heart back up off the floor and headed straight for the elevator.

"Goodnight ma'am," the lift attendant said, courteously removing his cap when we reached the top floor. I felt like royalty. Smiling, I nodded in acknowledgement.

After removing my shoes, *again*, I walked to the end of the long corridor to our suite. Without my key I knocked on the door – possibly a little harder and louder than intended. The door swung open almost immediately and Richard was already walking away from it. He didn't speak a single word.

Confused and a little nervous, I followed him cautiously inside, kicking the door closed behind me.

"Is everything okay?" I asked warily, keeping my distance.

"You tell me…"

What? Was it the fact I'd arrived back so late – or *early*. The smoking perhaps? Could he smell it?

"Good night?" he asked curtly, sounding as if he meant something entirely different.

"Richard what's wrong? What have I done?" I shrank back a little further, dropping my shoes on the floor. My voice quaked and tears were scratching at the corners of my eyes.

"You forgot this." He held out my purse.

So?

"And this…" Then he pulled out a little pouch of white powder.

Holy-mother-fucker-from-hell. I recognized it instantly. It was the gear Leon pushed on me after I left the hospital. Too busy becoming accustomed to my new impossibly wonderful life, I'd forgotten all about hiding it away in the lining of my bag.

Shit. Shit. Shit.

"I can explain," I mumbled, waving him off with my hand. This was a simple misunderstanding and once I explained, everything would be fine.

Saving Amy

Richard trusted me. Didn't he? "It really isn't what it looks like," I added before a nervous chuckle escaped from my throat.

"You think this is fucking funny?" he yelled across the room, startling me. He was mad. *Really* mad. I didn't like it. Shaking my head, I walked tentatively towards his hostile body, *desperate* to feel his arms around me. "What if airport security had found this, huh? We'd have been arrested! My whole career, my whole *life* would've been ruined because of you!"

"Please, I can explain…"

"Don't," he scolded firmly when I reached out to touch him.

"Richard, *please*." The tears had found their escape route and I furiously tried to wipe them from my face but they were falling too fast – I couldn't keep up. "It's been in there for months, I swear it. I would never lie to you… I couldn't."

Richard was risking friction burns to his forearm if he rubbed it any harder. His breathing was harsh, his eyes wide, back stiff… He was so angry with me. I was… frightened.

"Please, Richard," I begged again. "What do you want me to do? I'll do anything. Please!" I'd turned into a pathetic and desperate mess, and when I grabbed onto his shoulders, he pushed me away.

"I thought we were past this. HOW COULD YOU, AMELIA!" he roared, his face just inches from mine. Instinctively I cowered, shielding my face with my forearms.

"Shit. No, Amy, please, no, shit… Amy I would never-" Dropping my purse, he clasped his hands together as if he were praying.

I backed away from him. I was scared, bewildered and unbearably alone. My heart was trying to escape through one of the small gaps between my ribs. My pulse was throbbing, violent and painful in the back of my head. Richard – my constant, the only confidante I'd ever had – was gone. We were in the same room but he couldn't have been further away.

I had no one.

Again.

After snatching my bag from the floor beside his feet I turned sharply towards the door. His firm hand grabbed my shoulder and I automatically flinched at the contact. *Not again.* I was never supposed to feel that kind of fear again. He promised me. He... *saved* me.

And I fucked it up just like I knew I would.

"Amy no... *please.* I'm so sorry, baby. I'm so fucking sorry." He removed his hand from my shoulder and surrendered them both in the air. I heard him choke back a sob but I ignored it. I needed to escape. I couldn't deal with the mass of unruly emotions churning deep inside my stomach. I was stunned, confused and beyond hysterical. I needed out...

I opened the door and ran... Barefoot, I bypassed the elevator and headed hastily for the stairs.

"Amy!" Richard called after me – his voice piercing my tear-ducts... and my heart. But I kept going until his voice was a distant whisper. When I reached the lobby I picked up my pace, ran straight towards the revolving glass doors and out into the darkness.

Saving Amy

Chapter Eleven

I collapsed onto some large ornate rocks hidden between some shrubs at the back of the hotel. It was dark, cold and unfamiliar. Sinking my face into my hands I let my tears flow fast and freely into them.

Why are you so surprised? My malevolent subconscious was back with a vengeance and the worst part was, it was talking sense. Of course Richard was always going to assume the worst. How could he not? He could only judge me by how I'd behaved so far in my pointless life. Maybe, despite what he'd said in the past, *he* was always expecting me to let him down too.

I was lost in every sense of the word. What would I do now? Had I left him? Had he left me? Should I talk to him or arrange my own way home?

Wait… I didn't have a home.

I brought my knees up to my chest and hugged them close, balancing on the rocks and swaying myself back and forth. Within seconds my eyes were drawn to a piece of jagged, sharp-looking stone sticking out from the dirt. Picking it up, I twiddled it between my fingers. I was almost certain it would be sharp enough to bring the relief, the distraction I was so urgently craving.

No!

I threw the shard of rock into a wall behind me and shrank back down onto the cold stones. How could I ever prove myself to Richard if I succumbed

Saving Amy

to such destructive behavior? That was if he even gave me a chance to prove myself. Did I even want that chance? I didn't know what I wanted anymore.

My purse vibrated against my knee. When I flipped it open my ringing cell illuminated the contents as **Richard Calling** flashed intermittently on the screen. I hovered my thumb over the little green telephone. Part of me ached to hear his voice – ached to be comforted, to be told everything would be okay. But a stronger, hurt part of me wouldn't allow it, and so I waited until the vibrations had ceased and the light dimmed down before closing my bag.

The vibrations started up again immediately after. Then again… and again. Guilt invaded my veins and I answered straight away before I had chance to talk myself out of it – or check who it was.

"Amy is that you?" It was Bethany – Richard's little sister. Her sweet, timid voice was instantly recognizable. I bolted from the rocks in a panic. She had *never* called me before and it must be almost 2 AM back in Seattle.

"Yes, it's Amy. What's wrong Bethany? Has something happened?"

"That's what I wanted to ask you. Are you with Richard? I can't get hold of him."

Am *I with Richard?*

"Um, he's sleeping," I lied. "He's okay though. Why shouldn't he be?"

"No particular reason I guess. It's just… he always calls home on Kate's anniversary. Today he didn't," she murmured dejectedly and I could hear the threat of tears invade her voice.

It was the anniversary of Kate's death? I briefly wondered why no one had mentioned it, especially when Vivienne and Bethany came to visit just last week. It explained so much. Or did it? Was it really an excuse for him not to trust me? But then, had I even been with him long enough to earn that privilege?

A sniffle in my ear pulled me out of my untimely musing.

"He's been in bed all day… migraine. I know he's been thinking of you all though." I felt obliged to lie – to comfort her. I wasn't nearly brave enough to admit that he was too busy dealing with his fucked-up girlfriend and her accompanying baggage.

"Oh no. Hope he feels better soon. Maybe you could ask him to call me in the morning?"

"Sure I will. Take care, Bethany."

"Sure. Bye, Amy."

After hanging up a fire fuelled by guilt raged blue and furious in my stomach. He shouldn't have been alone just now. *I* shouldn't have been alone just now. I needed him. I could only pray that he still needed me too.

****

"Everything okay, ma'am?" the elevator attendant pried when he saw I'd been crying.

"Fine. Thank you," I responded as politely as I could manage.

The shutters pinged and slid themselves open not a moment too soon. I scurried out and hurriedly tiptoed towards our suite. As I reached into my purse for the key-card I heard the faint rumblings of

Saving Amy

Richard's voice. Who was he talking to? Bethany perhaps?

I eased the door open slowly, not wanting to disturb him. His voice seemed to be coming from the direction of the stairs so I followed the delicious sound up the spiral staircase and towards the bedroom where I hovered for a moment outside the doorway.

"Don't start that again... Because it's all my fault... No... How can you say that? It is... I should've let her explain..."

He was discussing *me!* Who with? *Not his family,* please.

"Because I called you for help, not another damn lecture. I should've known you'd be like this... I know that... You think so? I'm sorry, I know you're only looking out for me, Joanna."

No freakin' way. How could he? A rush of weakness surged through my every muscle and I stumbled, knocking into a crystal vase behind me.

"Amy, thank Christ!" He sounded relieved to see me. *Phew.* "I have to go," he told the receiver, hanging up immediately.

"Why did you call *her?* You know how she feels about me." Rising swiftly from the bed, Richard walked tentatively across the eggshells towards me. He reached out and this time I was the one doing the pushing. I felt utterly crestfallen... *Angry.*

Why her? My subconscious was screaming in my ears, deafening me, telling me to run again. I fought the urge with every bone in my body. I couldn't run again. I *wouldn't*. I needed to face this. I needed to grow the hell up.

"I know how you feel about one another but she's my friend. She might go about it the wrong way sometimes but deep down she only wants what's best for me."

How are you so blinded by the scheming bitch? How I kept that thought from exploding like vomit out of my mouth I'd never know.

"But that's to be without *me* isn't it?" He rubbed at his forearm. He was going to buff away the hairs at that rate. "ISN'T IT?" I bawled when I got no response.

"Forget about Joanna. She doesn't matter just now."

She shouldn't matter ever.

"You came back. That must mean something?" he said, his voice guarded, his eyes pained and sorrowful.

"Where else could I go?" I answered snappishly. I refused my eyes contact with his, knowing the sight of his beautiful, unsettled face would melt away my frustration when I wanted so badly to be angry with him.

"Amy, please. I'm so sorry I didn't let you explain. It's no excuse, but… I've been preoccupied today. My head is still all over the place." He must have meant Kate. "I *do* trust you. You have to believe me. My mind was elsewhere when I found the gear and I flipped. You *have* to forgive me, Amy. I love you."

He reached out to me again and I made the mistake of looking him in the eyes. Damn. The sight of him turned my insides to mush and I fell straight into his open arms.

"Oh, *Richard...*" I sobbed hysterically into his shirt and he lovingly shushed me like a baby, holding me close and stroking my hair. "I promise you I'd forgot it was in there. I haven't touched the damn stuff since I landed myself in the hospital. I don't need it. I don't *want* it. I could never risk losing you."

"I know. I know and I'm sorry. Like I said, I've had a lot of shit going on today. You're the last person I should've taken it out on."

"You mean Kate?"

"How did you-"

"Bethany called. She was worried about you. I said you had a migraine."

"Fuck," he breathed, dropping his head. "How could I forget to call home? I've been so wrapped up in myself today. Too busy being a selfish dick to take care of the people who mean the most to me."

"Yep," I agreed and hoped he could hear the playfulness in my voice. He didn't seem to hear me at all.

"Before... you cowered from me. I would *never* hurt you, baby. I'm nothing like your father. Please tell me you know that." His face crumpled like he was in physical pain. I shrugged, unsure. I loved him so much. I trusted him so much. But for a fleeting moment... I *was* afraid of him.

"I've never seen you so mad before. My dad is the only experience of anger I have to go off I guess." His brow furrowed, forcing his emerald eyes half closed. "And... you called me Amelia." Sighing deeply, regretfully, he cupped my cheeks with his tender hands and lowered his face to my level.

"Amy, I will never, *ever* hurt you. I promise you, baby. You're safe with me. *Always*. I love you. I love you so fucking much and I'm so, so sorry." He pulled me close, inhaling me. I smiled weakly. I had no choice but to believe him.

"I'm sorry I ran from you."

"You have nothing to be sorry for. You're only just learning to trust and I let you down. It won't happen again, I swear it."

Richard edged me over to the bed, sat down and then gently pulled me with him. I rolled onto my side and curled myself up into the fetal position - then from behind he molded himself around me. I was safe again, wrapped inside his protective, loving arms. Hitching backwards a little, closer to him, so that there wasn't an inch of our bodies that weren't touching, I drifted into a deep, fully-clothed, dreamless sleep.

****

I flopped back into the familiar soft leather of Richard's couch. It was good to be home. I smiled inwardly as I realized this was the first time I'd allowed myself to think of this apartment as *home*. After carrying our suitcases to the bedroom Richard joined me and handed me my bag. I only stared at the way his tight-fitting white t-shirt hugged his glorious muscles a *little* longer than necessary before taking it from him. The first thing I did was remove my cell and switch it back on after the flight, prompting Richard to do the same.

The air was soon flooded with a melody of beeps and pings and I found myself gaping at Mr. Popular. I was snapped back into the real world soon after by the call of my own cell and its single, lonely beep.

```
Julie: What the hell is all this
money for? I'm so mad at u!
Missing u already xoxo
```

She got the three-hundred dollars I posted through then. I could see why she thought it was extravagant but she needed it – I didn't… simple. Besides, Richard wouldn't miss it. I surprised myself with my flippancy about that, deciding it was probably because the money wasn't for me.

```
Me: A thanku will suffice ;-) Miss
u more. Had the BEST time. And
thanku - for everything. Love u J
<3
```

After swiping my screen locked my eyes wandered back to their favorite place – the vision of perfection standing in front of me. He was rubbing his forearm…
"What's wrong?"
"I'm sorry, baby I've been called into work. I shouldn't be long." My heart sank and my lips involuntarily puckered into a pout in full-on childish tantrum style. We'd literally *just* got back. I didn't want him to leave already. "I love you."
He bent to my seated level, kissed my forehead and left without waiting for my response. Slumping back into the leather I petulantly kicked my shoes off into the middle of the room, knowing the untidiness would agitate Richard. I didn't even plan on picking

them back up again. *Grow up,* my subconscious hissed, but I wasn't in the mood to listen to the irritating voice so I told it out loud to fuck the hell off.

Soon enough I was bored and irritable. I'd flicked through a bazillion TV channels, attempted to read one of the fifty million books in Richard's study, picked away at some heavily buttered toast and taken a bath. Nothing seemed capable of puncturing the iron balloon of cantankerousness I was trapped inside so I took myself off to bed and hoped to sleep it off.

Not before tidying my shoes away first though…

****

The mattress sinking beside me stirred my weary mind.

"What time is it?" I mumbled through a yawn.

"Just gone midnight. Go back to sleep," Richard whispered before kissing my hair and settling in next to me. For a brief moment I thought I smelt alcohol on his breath but I was too tired to entertain the idea and fell straight back to sleep.

After rubbing the sticky sleep from my eyes I glanced at the clock. It was 6:30 AM and Richard was missing from the bed already. Grudgingly, I heaved myself out of bed, threw on Richard's black toweling gown and set off to find him. He was loitering in the kitchen, picking out packets of coffee beans.

Saving Amy

"Morning, beautiful," he greeted with a crooked smile when he spotted me.

"It's so early. What are you doing up?"

"Couldn't sleep. Still on Florida time I guess." He winked at me, making my insides quiver. *How does he do that to me?* "Coffee?"

"Please," I croaked out, stifling a yawn. "I had a wonderful time. Well apart from, well… you know. Anyway, thank you," I stuttered like an idiot. Richard shook his head at the memory.

"Good. That was my intention." He flashed me the most captivating smile, set two mugs on the glossy white island that I was now sitting at and filled them with caramel coffee from the percolator. "And I'm glad you confided in Julie. Maybe it'll help you realize that you are loved no matter what – because I know damn well you don't believe me when I tell you. Plus, it's good to have that extra support. Sometimes I worry that I'm just not enough. You *need* that extra safe place… someone you can go to if I'm not here."

I told Richard all about what happened the night I tripped during the flight home.

"Why? You planning on going somewhere?" I asked ominously.

"No, baby. I'm not going anywhere," he assured softly, walking over to me and tucking my loose hair behind both of my ears. "But I can't be with you twenty-four-seven. Besides, sometimes you might just need someone else – someone not too close."

"What like if you decide to go all raging caveman on my ass again?" I teased… but Richard couldn't find the humor.

"Don't, Amy. I can't stop thinking about how I treated you. I'm still new at this. I'm not used to putting other people first. But by Christ I want to. You're the only person I've ever wanted to come first in my life. And you *do* Amy – in everything I do. You didn't deserve that reaction from me. Florida had been… *intense* for me. I've never spoken to anyone about Kate before, not my mom, or Joanna… and it sparked all these feelings inside of me that I'd tried so desperately to bury for so long. Then with the anniversary… The guilt – sometimes it feels like a giant fucking boulder strapped to my chest. It crushes me and I can't breathe. I needed to lash out at something… and you were just… *there*. I'm sorry."

Richard looked down to his bare feet. I pulled his hand away from his forearm and brought it up to my cheek.

"I want to make a deal," I said firmly. Richard looked at me warily, his eyebrow diving off his face. "I'll start believing I'm worth saving, if *you* start believing you weren't responsible for Kate." His Adam's apple bobbed slowly as he swallowed.

"That's one hell of a deal," he said, his voice lacking any trace of confidence.

"An achievable one though, don't you think?" Cupping his face in my hands I continued, "You keep saying how much you love me, how much I mean to you… Do you really mean what you say?"

"Of course I do!" he snapped, looking altogether startled. "What kind of question is that?"

"Well then, if that's true I think I owe it to you to start believing it – believing in *me.*" He nodded in complete agreement, his eyes oozing a 'finally' look.

Saving Amy

"Well *I* love *you*. I believe in *you*. I trust *you*. Don't you think I deserve for you to start believing that too? To start believing that you are a *good* man… and that *you* are important too?"

Yeah, that one shut him up for a while.

"So you want to save me?" he asked with a mischievous grin.

"We can save each other," I replied, deadly seriousness dripping from my voice.

"I love you, Amy," he whispered into my mouth before teasing entry past my lips with his tongue. "Let me show you how much." Then he threw me over his shoulder like a bag of rubble, making me squeal, and carried me to the bedroom, where he showed me in every position imaginable, just how much he loved me.

Wow.

****

"Can I use the MacBook in your study this afternoon please?" I asked, looking up at him in bed as I worked my fingers through the fine auburn hair on his bare chest.

"Of course." *Helloooo bemused eyebrow!* "You know you don't need to ask. What are you planning?" he asked dubiously.

"I'm going to look for a job. I might type up a few applications… maybe a resume too." He sighed heavily, purposely. "Don't start, Richard."

"I wasn't going to," he protested and now I was the one raising an eyebrow.

Liar!

"Just promise me you won't degrade yourself."

Here we go… I rolled my eyes at him.

"I read through your notebook."

Oh. Embarrassment set my cheeks alight and my heart started to pound with nerves.

"You're very talented," he declared with what sounded like genuine admiration in his voice. My eyes dropped down. My stomach followed. Regardless of whether my ability to write was good or not, I'd screwed my chances of a career in that field the minute I decided to fail my senior year.

"There's nothing to say I can't work my way up in whatever job I get," I retorted, shamming optimism.

"But it won't be doing what you love." He raised my chin with his finger and then palmed the side of my face with his hand.

"Well, you can't always get what you want," I muttered with an onerous sigh.

"Yes you can. I'll make sure of it," he stated, steadfast. Just as I was about to ask him what the hell *that* was supposed to mean, we were interrupted by the sound of his cell vibrating against the wooden side table by the bed. Releasing me, he rolled himself over and grabbed his phone.

"I need to take this," he addressed me formally, as if I were one of his colleagues. Then in an instant, he was off the bed, and gone.

Lying alone in the giant bed I dug deep into my subconscious, trying to find just a trace of the optimism I felt when I woke up this morning. It didn't work. I had resigned myself – even managed to feel happy about – becoming something as menial as an office clerk, or a waitress like Julie. But now, after witnessing the disappointment, the *judgment* bursting out of Richard's emerald eyes, I suddenly felt... worthless. I'd let him down. I couldn't be the 'trophy' he deserved to have hanging from his arm... The thought twisted around my heart, squeezing it until it became painful to breathe.

It was late in the afternoon when I snapped Richard's MacBook closed a little too firmly in temper and hoped he didn't hear it from the next room.

"Everything okay?" he asked, appearing from nowhere.

Shit.

"Fine," I lied unconvincingly. He cocked that irresistible eyebrow of his. "It's just a little frustrating. There isn't as much choice as I'd hoped."

"Leave it for today. You need a break." He extended his hand for me to take and then fervently pulled me from the chair and into his arms. I briefly inhaled the intoxicating smell of Armani cologne mixed with pure Richard emanating from his crisp white shirt which he wore with the sleeves rolled to his elbows, before pulling back and putting on my serious face.

"I will, because I'm tired. But don't go thinking you've won."

"I always win, baby" he replied with an unsettling level of seriousness. Then a foreboding grin illuminated his entire face. He was up to something. I was certain of it.

But what?

I figured there was no point in probing him. If whatever it was were something I was supposed to know about he'd have told me. Plus, there was always the possibility it was the workings of my overactive imagination reading too much into things as usual.

"I want to take you somewhere," Richard said nervously, as if he were expecting me to say no.

"Where?" I asked, mirroring his apprehension. Curiosity surged through me, making my heart stutter.

"I'd like you to visit Kate's grave with me. But of course you don't have to. I mean, I'd completely understand if-" I silenced him, tracing the firmness of his stuttering lips with my finger.

"I'd like that." His eyes widened.

"*Really?*" he said, almost in disbelief. "Come with me."

Now?

Richard took hold of my hand and led me to the tall silver coat rack by the half-moon table in the hall. Yep, it seemed we *were* going right now. I selfishly remembered that we hadn't had lunch yet and hunger pangs twisted deep, knotting around my stomach when I bent to pull my white sneakers on. Hopefully, he planned to stop somewhere along the way.

We were heading north towards Medina in Richard's red Lamborghini Merciélago (yeah, I can't pronounce it either) – the smallest, sportiest and most penis-enhancing car in his collection.

I stole a glance at his face. Heavy guilt usually radiated from him – visibly graying his troubled face, pursing his eyebrows together and flushing his cheeks – whenever he talked or thought about Kate. Not now though. Staring out onto the country roads

Saving Amy

approaching in the distance he looked... content, peaceful. I'd possibly even go as far as to say he looked happy.

Beautiful.

The car slowed as we veered onto a long winding road that gave the illusion of night under the dense canopy of trees trimming the outskirts. I counted the colors of fall around us – burnt-orange leaves, yellowing grass, brown shrubs... anything to try and distract my mind from lunch – or lack of it. My attempts proved unsuccessful however and my stomach let rip a fierce, demanding growl.

"There's a burger van not far from here. I'll pull over when we reach it," Richard said, nodding his head towards my angry belly. Maybe I should've been embarrassed but I was too hungry to care.

"Thanks," I said with a grateful smile, my mouth already salivating.

Venturing down a dirt track between the trees, Richard pulled up beside a rusting white van with what I think was supposed to say 'Barbara's Burgers' printed tackily on the side but half the letters had worn away. It was very un-Richard-like and I was surprised he even knew it existed. I was surprised *anyone* knew it existed in fact, hidden amongst the dark trees.

"I'll get these," I offered, putting my hand over his to stop him unclipping his seatbelt. Then I tutted out loud to myself, realizing *I* had nothing to 'get these' with. Richard shifted in his seat and pulled his wallet from his jeans pocket. Removing a twenty-dollar bill, he handed it to me and I took it with a sigh.

Barbara, I assumed, was short and round with coarse red hair scraped back into a bun. She wiped her hands on her grease-stained apron as she took my order and then scuttled towards the back of the van to flip our quarter-pounders with extra cheese. When they were ready she piled them on to huge seeded buns, ladened them with cheese and mayonnaise and then tossed some wilted lettuce on for good measure. If I was honest, they looked pretty disgusting, so I asked for two Cokes to wash them down with.

Back in the car I passed Richard his lunch, almost certain he wouldn't approve.

"They were all out of Pinot Noir I'm afraid," I quipped, handing him his Coke. He choked on a laugh, inadvertently exposing a mouth full of grease-squelching burger.

"Sorry," he muttered when he finally swallowed, wiping the grease from the corners of his glistening lips with his fingers.

The burger tasted as slimy and stodgy as expected, but it did the job and my stomach felt content again. Bringing the car back to life with a purr, Richard carried on down the ever-curving road for just over a mile. Eventually the trees broke and sunlight flooded the car, startling my eyes as he pulled onto a long graveled path. I'd almost forgotten it was the afternoon, trapped under the heavy shelter of the trees for so long.

We were almost there I assumed. Gravestones of every size and shade clouded my vision whichever way I looked and something inside me felt astray. At first I couldn't quite place it, but then I realized it was because, looking down towards the earth,

Saving Amy

imagining the bodies underneath and the people they'd left behind, filled me with sadness.

It was then that it hit me – I felt like I was *supposed* to feel, instead of being consumed by the jealousy that used to tear through my heart as I wished *I* too was buried beneath the moss covered stones. My lips unintentionally turned up into a smile as I inwardly thanked whoever might be listening for my new life. Then I literally rubbed it away with my hand, praying Richard didn't notice and deem me disrespectful.

Richard slowed the car to a graceful halt as he claimed a space on the edge of the dirt track.

"Here we are," he said, killing the engine. He sounded nervous again – as if he was still waiting for me to change my mind.

"Richard…" I leaned across the stick shift and took his hand in mine. "I feel really privileged that you asked me here today. Thank you," I said, hoping to quash the doubts he was so obviously feeling. He squeezed my hand and I physically felt his anxiousness melt away from his body.

After vacating the car I followed him along a stony path and then onto the grass. The earth was sodden and muddy and I quickly started cursing myself for choosing my *white* sneakers today as they squelched their way through it. We weaved our way through a maze of headstones that, to me, all looked the same. Richard ploughed ahead however, appearing to know where he was going so, head down to avoid the puddles, I followed his lead.

My eyes were so focused on the task of puddle spotting I didn't notice Richard had stopped and I stumbled straight into him.

"Here she is," he breathed desolately as he gazed longingly towards a burnished black headstone in the shape of a heart, with two magnificent stone cherubs perched either side. His hand instinctively started to rub at his forearm slowly, achingly… I reached out and took it in mine, squeezing all the love my body held into him.

I eyed up the grave, focusing on the photograph of Kate etched onto the stone – the same picture that resided in Richard's living room – and tried to imagine what she was like.

>Here lies Kate Annabel Lewis.
>Born February 1st 1983
>Died September 6th 2002
>Beloved Daughter, Sister and Friend. Taken too soon.
>Rest in Peace Sweet Angel

My heart panged painfully in my chest and I squeezed Richard's hand a little tighter.

"Do you visit her often?" I asked gently, hoping to discover a glimpse of what was happening behind those troubled eyes.

"Very. At least once a week," he replied solemnly, his eyes never leaving the image of Kate's face which was now shimmering with diamond-like raindrops that had just started to fall. I idly wondered when he found the time and decided he must fit it into his workday – that was the only time we spent apart.

"I clean her stone, bring her flowers…" He nodded his head towards the extravagant bouquet of

Saving Amy

red roses and white lilies arranged charmingly in a silver vase embedded into the ground.

"They're beautiful," I said, acknowledging the fine spray. He half-smiled.

"I come here to talk to her mainly. I like to think she can hear me."

"What about?" I blurted without thinking and then instantly regretted it. Something so personal was none of my business.

"Life, work...*you*." His gaze caught mine and I felt the warmth of his hypnotic smile all the way through my body. Unwelcome heat worked its way into my cheeks and I felt bizarrely nervous about what he may have told her about me. Would she approve? My mood began to slip when I decided she probably wouldn't – not if he'd told her *everything*.

"What's wrong?" Richard asked, cupping my chin between his thumb and forefinger.

"Nothing," I lied, a little too high-pitched to be convincing. Then I mentally slapped myself for being so goddam selfish. He'd brought me here to share such a personal, integral part of himself and I thanked him by getting all self-absorbent and paranoid about whether his *dead* sister thinks I'm worthy of her brother.

"You're lying. I know you too well," he pressed questioningly. "Tell me," he breathed, all Bossy Doctory, and as usual I was rendered unable to ignore him.

"I guess I'm just nervous about you discussing me with her." His inquiring eyes pierced into mine. "Ridiculous, I know."

"Baby, if she was here, she would *love* you." I eyed him up sardonically. "I know that because *I* love you, and we shared very similar tastes." His shoulders literally shuddered at his last words and I suspected his choice of phrasing had made the guilt resurface.

The rain, which had been spitting teasingly for the past ten minutes, started to fall faster. The glistening droplets of water turned heavy and less graceful, bouncing and splattering into giant splodges as it smacked into us.

"We should get going," Richard suggested, removing his grey military jacket and canopying it above us both. I huddled into him, mouthed a silent 'nice to meet you' towards Kate's headstone and matched Richard's sprint – just about – back to the car.

Chapter Twelve

"Dammit!" I yelled out loud, burning my throat when I dropped the pile of resumes I'd just spent fifteen minutes stacking neatly into page order, sending them scattering into disarray across the study floor. I was on the verge of giving up altogether. I'd applied for seven different jobs this past two weeks and received five 'thanks but no thanks' back. I guessed the other two couldn't even be bothered to go that far.

Bending down, I started the arduous task of picking them all up, huffing and cussing when I saw they'd amazingly managed to fly into every corner of the room. I was in a full-blown bad mood. I tried to convince myself it was the unsuccessful job search, the papers falling, or stubbing my toe on the trashcan this morning that had blown up this impenetrable balloon of gloom around me, but my subconscious wouldn't quit reminding me of the *real* reason.

He's up to something, it kept bellowing in my ears.

Richard has been acting... *strange* lately - ever since we got back from Florida. Leaving the room to answer phone-calls, getting called into work at ridiculous o'clock and coming home with traces of alcohol lingering on his breath – apparent even through the minty mask of gum.

Yet when he was home he had also never been more perfect, if that was even possible. More loving, more fun, more talkative... Just last Wednesday we stayed up until 4 AM just chatting, laughing, sharing. So deep down I knew there must be a rational explanation for his behavior. Mustn't there? After all, he wouldn't do anything to hurt me. Would he?

"Let me help you," Richard offered, scaring the living shit out of me.

"Jesus! Where the hell did you come from?" I clutched at my chest, trying to remember how to breathe again.

"No, not Jesus. Richard…" he said slowly and drawn out, as if he were talking to someone who wasn't all there. What a beautiful, sarcastic bastard he was. I wanted to stay angry but it was impossible when he was so close and my lips melted into a smile against their will.

"Thanks," I uttered as we worked to pick up the scattered resumes together.

"Any luck yet?" he asked, trying but failing to sound genuinely interested.

"No," I huffed, pouting like a spoilt child.

"Well maybe you can stop looking now."

What! Rage fuelled heat flooded my cheeks.

"No! It *will* happen, Richard. I'm not giving up so don't bother spouting your crap again," I snapped. He surrendered his hands in front of him.

"I didn't mean- Look, please don't be cross. I only want what's best for you… for you to be happy."

Where's this going?

"I've done something for you."

Uh oh.

"What, exactly?" I asked suspiciously, nervously and possibly even a little snappily.

"I've arranged an interview for you. It's for an internship at Salt House Publishing." My jaw dropped open, smacking into my chest. "I've been for a few business drinks with different companies-" A switch flipped, shining a light on his suspect behavior. "I've shown them your work, and Salt House were quite taken with you."

"You did what!" I roared before my brain or subconscious had time to process what he'd just said. "You showed people my notebook... my *personal* notebook, without asking me? How could you?" Christ I was mad. Blood simmering, stomach churning, fist clenching mad. *And...* embarrassed. Someone else – a complete stranger – had read my most intimate thoughts. Most of which were probably a mix of depression-fuelled, fucked-up-ness induced twaddle.

"I didn't ask you because I knew you'd say no," he stated dryly, irritably rubbing his forearm. The cheeky, lying shit had got the nerve to be frustrated with *me!* Maybe seeing the steam blowing from my ears calmed him, because he rolled his neck from side to side and took in a deep breath, composing himself.

"Amy, everyone I showed your work to was very impressed."

Everyone? I wondered just how many people he thought it acceptable to betray me with exactly.

"That's just it! It's not my 'work'. It's just... thoughts. *My* thoughts. Thoughts I'd never intended anyone else to see!" Maybe if I had, I'd have put more effort in.

"Please, baby, just give it a chance. Isn't this what you've always dreamed of?"

"That's not the point and you know it," I said firmly, glowering at him.

"No actually I don't 'know it'. I genuinely didn't expect this reaction from you. This is everything you've ever wanted but convinced yourself you couldn't have. Well you can have it! I'm giving it to you." He leaned forward and took hold of my hands. I tried to shrug away but he gripped me a little tighter, drawing my hands into his chest.

"Look, I can see I may have gone about this in the wrong way…"

No shit, Sherlock.

"But can't you see what a fantastic opportunity this could be for you? You have a chance to earn a place doing something you love."

"But *I* won't be 'earning' my place anywhere. Like everything else, you've done it for me," I spat ungratefully, my anger melting into self-pity. His deliciously annoying eyebrow shot up and he cocked his head to one side. "I rely on you for everything. I wanted to do this by myself," I hissed – head down, lips pouted and chest pushed out. I was in a full-on sulk.

"I've arranged an interview, that's all. That doesn't guarantee you a placement. If you want to succeed, it's down to *you* to make that happen – nobody else." He relaxed his grip around my hands and began to trace the length of my fingers with his. Then, stroking all the way up my arm and across the base of my neck, he settled his finger beneath my chin, raising it and forcing our gazes to meet.

Damn. There went any hope of staying mad with the obscenely beautiful son of a bitch.

Saving Amy

"And they *really* liked it? You're not just humoring me?" I asked, genuine bewilderment flooding my voice as I decided to give up my fight and try rolling with it. He nodded eagerly.

"I've told you all along not to underestimate yourself. You are *extremely* talented." I flushed hooker-lipstick red. "You're going to have to stop doing that if you want them to take you seriously," he added with a wink, tracing the circles of heat burning brightly in my cheeks with his fingers.

"So when is it?"

"Tomorrow. At one."

Holy shit!

"Tomorrow! Like *tomorrow* tomorrow?" Holy mother of all that is fucking holy… tomorrow! I was pretty sure my heart had stopped beating and I felt the blood drain from my face – my whole body in fact – as it cascaded downwards through my violently throbbing veins and pooled at my feet.

Tomorrow!

****

Richard and I had undertaken a whole new level of trust today – one which I never could've anticipated. He'd loaned me one of his babies – his black Audi TT. It was a pain in the ass to drive and I was glad when I finally pulled over outside My Big Fat Greek Buffet and Restaurant, relieved that the tut-and-cuss fest from reaching for the stick shift and then remembering it was an automatic, was over.

I was ten minutes early to meet Vanessa Heart – senior editor at Salt House Publishing. That gave me ten minutes to figure out how to breathe again, and ten minutes to find a way to keep the crap out of my pants.

I lay awake most, if not all, of the night roleplaying with my subconscious – trying to find ways of making myself sound interesting. I came up with a fair few quotes and ideas that would make me sound smart and enthusiastic... and now I couldn't remember a single one of them. In fact, I was struggling to remember my name.

Still, I looked the part. I'd even go as far as saying I looked pretty sophisticated in a grey pinstripe pencil skirt, fitted white blouse and pointy black heels that were only *just* walkable in. All supplied by Richard of course. I tutted out-loud at the thought, but then smiled in the hope this meeting really could be the start of some much craved autonomy.

Five minutes to go. *Shit*. I pulled down the visor ready for one last fidget with my freshly-tongued hair in the mirror and a piece of folded white paper dropped out onto my lap. Unpeeling it carefully, I was met with Richard's flawless handwriting.

I'm with you

My heart constricted and I clutched a hand to my chest. Those three words filled me with courage, with hope. He was with me – I could do anything with him by my side. God I loved him.

I folded it back up, kissed the crisp paper and tucked it back where I found it. Then, after a few deep, composing breaths I shimmied out of the car. Rather gracefully I might add too. A pencil skirt

Saving Amy

holds the amazing ability to quash any attempts at un-ladylike leg behavior.

My heart was pounding harder and louder than my heels against the sidewalk as I made my way over to the gleaming glass double doors showcasing the house specials in white italic script. Stepping inside onto a black and white check tile floor, there was a thin wooden stand in front of me with a handwritten sign saying 'Please wait here to be seated' hanging from it. I did as it told me, my right foot tapping incessant and nervous against the polished floor while I waited.

Soon enough, a small olive-skinned man with black curly hair and thick-rimmed glasses appeared.

"Do you have a reservation?" he asked with a warm grandfatherly smile in a thick Greek accent.

Oh. I don't know!

"Um, I have a meeting with a Vanessa Heart," I said clumsily.

"Ah, I see. Ms. Heart is right this way," he said with familiarity as if he knew her personally.

Damn. She was already here. I wanted to be the first to arrive – prove I was punctual. But then maybe that would've appeared too eager. Though maybe now I would come across too blasé – as if I didn't give a crap.

"Follow me." The old Greek man beckoned me with his hand, pulling me out of my ill-time tete-a-tete with my subconscious. He gestured towards a small two-seater table, cordoned off by a wooden partition with decorative flowers carved into it.

A woman stood to greet me.

"Amelia?" she asked, proffering her hand for me to shake. I gave mine a discreet wipe against my skirt and entered into the handshake, praying she couldn't feel how clammy with nerves I was.

"Yes," I replied, nodding my head ridiculously like one of those toy dogs you see in the back of cars.

"I'm Vanessa. Please, sit down." She angled her hand towards the round wooden seat in front of me and I did as she said and sat down, reminding myself to breathe as I lowered my ass onto the firm seat. There were two cups of coffee on the table and, assuming one was for me, I took one and flooded my arid mouth with some well-needed moisture – allowing my tongue to unstick itself from my palette.

Vanessa was tall – at least four inches above me – with short jet-black hair dancing in all different directions and a firm I-take-no-shit smile. The feathery lines framing her eyes told me she was either in her late forties or a heavy smoker, and she was dressed professionally in a dark-grey pantsuit.

"So, Amelia…"

It's Amy, my subconscious yelled but I didn't have the balls to correct her.

"Let's start by you telling me what attributes you hold that would be of benefit to our company."

Oh crap. The complete English language seemed to have erased itself from my memory.

"Well, I, um, I'm good at-" Jesus Christ, I'd turned into a stuttering imbecile.

I'm with you… Richard's note flashed in my memory, comforting me, encouraging me. Straightening my back, I took a deep breath and blinked my retardedness away – picturing Richard's glistening green eyes in front of me.

"Passion. That's what I have. I've had passion for literature my whole life. I've been an avid reader for as long as I can remember. Books, stories… they're always something you can fall back on no matter what life is throwing at you. They offer you a place to go when you just need to escape for a little while. That is what inspires me to write. I aspire to be able to share my imagination with others, as so many other wonderful authors have done for me."

Wow, I was on a roll. I watched her face intently as I spoke. She cocked an eyebrow and dragged her lips up into a half-smile. Dare I say, she might've even looked impressed?

"Perfect answer."

Phew…

"As regards to skills, that is something you will learn along the way. We have won several awards for our training program, though that means nothing without the passion you describe."

We chatted rather informally for over an hour and I have to say my subconscious impressed me for once, coming up with more-than-decent answers when my mouth dried out. Without wanting to sound egotistical, I think I even managed to sound quite intellectual at times. The only downside to our conversation was that if I was accepted onto the program I would have to attend college two nights a week. *Ugh*. But I figured I could suck it up for the greater good.

Vanessa broached the subject of me working towards a career as a writer and we discussed it for almost half an hour. I squirmed at first – she only knew about that because of Richard – and also thanks to Richard, she had read what I was capable of. She was unexpectedly encouraging, and told me if I had the drive and determination to write a full piece, she would be more than willing to consider it for publication. I wanted to be excited about that, but my subconscious wouldn't allow it – just in case.

"Well, I think we have covered pretty much everything. Do you have any questions?"

Only thousands…

"No, thank you. You've been very informative." I breathed a sigh of stark relied. I'd done all I could. Now I just had to head home and fidget my fingers off while I waited for an answer.

"In that case, it gives me great pleasure to offer you an internship on behalf of Salt House Publishing."

What the…

"*Really?*" I bounced so fervently in my seat I almost hit the ceiling. "Thank you so much!" I added, thankfully managing to restrain myself from swearing every obscenity known to man.

I didn't expect to find out so quickly and my insides were reeling with sheer exuberance, pride and more than a little apprehension as they pirouetted their way through my veins.

"I'd like you to start Monday, 9 AM, if that's okay with you? Obviously if you have prior plans we can make alternative arrangements."

"Monday's fine," I said, doing the nodding-dog thing again.

"Great. I'll email you your internship pack. It contains a comprehensive history of our company, what you can expect to gain by training with us, and also all of our contact information. Here's my card in case you need me in the meantime." She handed me a glossy black card with her details printed in fancy gold script.

"Thank you," I beamed, excited and nervous as hell.

"Right, we're all done," she said, gathering her papers from the table and filing them neatly into her leather briefcase. "I'll see you Monday." She stood up and offered her hand again. I did the same.

"Yes, Monday. Thank you again." Nodding, she smiled her firm smile, and left.

I stood, frozen and mute, as my eyes followed her out of the restaurant. Then, without warning, my hands involuntarily started clapping together like some kind of trained sea lion, and I let out an ear-piercing squeal, startling both myself and everyone else around me. *Oops!*

After managing to drive Richard's precious Audi home without breaking it and then easing it first time into one of his designated bays in the underground lot beneath his apartment, I took a moment slumped over the driver's wheel to compose myself. I did it. I actually goddamn did it. With that thought, I snatched the keys from the ignition and made my way to the elevator.

Richard was waiting for me in the living room and jumped to his feet the second he saw me. His expression was anxious – his hand resting on his forearm in preparation to start rubbing. A wicked streak that I didn't know I held until now was enjoying watching him squirm – karma for going behind my back perhaps – and I decided to drag out his agony a little longer.

I dropped my head and forced a frown.

"*Well?*" he asked, carefully assessing my subdued disposition. I shrugged my shoulders.

"I got it," I purposely whispered so he would struggle to hear. He moved closer, took hold of my hands and drew them up to his chest.

"Never mind. There's plenty-" He stopped mid-sentence, his gleaming eyes widening. "Wait… did you just say… you *got* it?" I'd planned to keep going for longer but excitement swelled in my veins until I feared they might burst under the pressure.

"Yes!" I shrieked.

"I knew it! I knew you'd do it!" He scooped me in his arms and twirled me around so fast I began to feel dizzy. "I'm so proud of you, baby."

"Thank you," I whispered into his ear, pulling him close when he set me back down. "And I'm sorry too." Richard pulled back a little so he could see my face.

"For what?" he asked, puzzled.

"For being an over-reacting, ungrateful bitch." I buried my face in his neck so he couldn't see the smile threatening to explode on my lips.

"Consider yourself forgiven," he teased and even though I couldn't see his face I could feel his wink. "You did good today. I think you deserve a reward," he said through a salaciously suggestive grin. Then he scooped me right back up and carried me to the bedroom.

****

Sunday afternoon and the mall was bursting at the seams. *Isn't Sunday supposed to be a day of rest?*

Saving Amy

Seemingly not... Richard and his wallet were accompanying me on a getting-kitted-out-for-my-new-job shopping spree. For the first time I was reveling in the experience of spending his money. Probably because it would be the last – I'd have my own money soon.

Richard remained the dutiful boyfriend – following me in and out of endless shops and boutiques, nodding and frowning in all the right places and handing me his credit card when required. After passing him my latest bag of goodies, I led him to the shop next door. Clothes-wise I was all done and tucked away in the bags weighing down Richard's strapping arms were two pencil skirts, two pairs of smart trousers, three white blouses and a blazer.

"Now for the shoes," I said, causing Richard's posture to droop. But like a good boy, he breathed through it and followed me inside, perching himself on the stools by the dressing rooms out of the way.

I tried on six different pairs of shoes – heels, wedges, flats, pointed-toe, peep-toe and strappy. I couldn't feel my toes anymore. Eventually I'd narrowed it down to two pairs and I held one from each in my hands. I literally weighed them up in my palms, raising and lowering them alternately while I tried to pick the right ones. I was torn between the sensible flat – and therefore comfortable – option, or the impressive, confidence inducing heels.

Hmm...

"I can't decide. What do *you* think?" I asked Richard, approaching him with my dilemma. He looked up from his cell that he appeared to be texting or emailing on.

"They're both nice."
How helpful. Not.
"But which are nicest?" I pressed, growing frustrated.

"Get both," he said without looking back up, too busy tapping away on his phone. He could've at least *pretended* to be interested.

The shoes cost three hundred and twenty and two hundred and eighty dollars respectively and if he couldn't be bothered distracting himself from his cell for two minutes to help me make a decision, then on his wallet be it.

"Fine," I snapped, stalking off towards the counter. I slammed my shoes on the counter, causing the girl to jump back a step from the cash register.

"Sorry," I muttered. It wasn't her fault I was in a raging bad mood. *It's his,* my subconscious sneered towards Richard who was lagging behind me, fumbling for his wallet. I sighed, exasperated as he handed over his card to the short, bottle-blonde cashier who of course, was fixated with him.

I knew exactly why I was in a foul mood. It was because even though I had my job now – therefore no secret meetings required – Richard's suspicious phone-call behavior remained. Only now, he was texting all the time too. Believe me, I knew it sounded ridiculous, possessive and irrational... but texting is so informal. Too informal for discussing hospital related stuff, right? And it wasn't like he had a ton of friends – not that I knew of anyway. Only... *her.*

Saving Amy

Maybe it was all in my head. Maybe I was just turning into a crazy, insecure, jealous freak. All I needed now was a rabbit and a hot pan.

"All done?" Richard asked, stuffing his wallet back into his jeans and wrapping his free arm around my waist – turning my insides to guilt-ridden mush. I nodded gratefully at him. "Thank Christ for that. I don't think I can take any more 'girl talk'." He bowed his head towards two homecoming-queen-esque girls by the dress rack. "You know, the blonde is *so* screwing the brunette's boyfriend," he said in his best ditzy-blonde voice. It was actually unnervingly good and I made a mental note to fly off the handle if he ever suggested I get my hair cut short.

After giving myself a strict talking to during the ride home I was finally over myself and my pathetic insecurities. Who the hell was I to say who he could and couldn't text? I wasn't his mother. But then even a mother wouldn't get so antsy over a few text messages for fuck's sake.

I gave Richard a full-on fashion show, parading up and down the great living room one outfit at a time.

"This is my favorite," I announced, sporting my gray flared pants, fitted white shirt with ruched sleeves and killer black, three hundred and twenty dollar heels.

"Hmm," he murmured as if he was unsure.

"You don't like it?" I stared myself down and decided I looked pretty damn hot.

"It's very nice. I just think you'd look better with it off," he said, rubbing his chin suggestively. I bent towards the couch, reaching for a cushion to throw at him, but as I stretched my arm he grabbed it, pulling me onto his lap, making me squeal like such a... *girl.*

Feeling his sweet breath on my face as he kissed me, inhaling the scent of his tea-tree infused hair as I clawed at it with hungry fingers... I struggled to believe I could ever be mad at him. I focused on his ragged breathing, on his intense green eyes blazing with desire, and I could see and *feel* how much he loved me – how much he wanted me. All traces of suspicion and jealousy dissipated into nothing.

Until his cell bleeped, vibrating against the glass of the coffee table...

The stern talking to I gave myself earlier flew straight out of the nearest window and into the path of an oncoming truck. Seizing my opportunity to quash my, hopefully irrational, doubts once and for all, I reached for his phone.

"Leave it," he ordered too abruptly and then instantly tried to backtrack. "I mean... it won't be anything important. Now, where were we?" He tried to pull me back into his kiss but my frustration had returned with a vengeance and I pushed him away.

"What's wrong?"

"Who's texting you?"

"I don't know. I didn't check," he answered defensively. "It's probably work related." He sounded irritated. What I couldn't decide though is, was it because he was hiding something, or because of my unjustified interrogation?

"Is hospital stuff really the kind of thing you should be discussing via text?" I pressed, knowing deep down I should really let it drop.

"Amy, what is this? What are you getting at?"

Hmm, what am *I getting at?* I didn't really know.

Saving Amy

"Amy, answer me!" *Crap*. Bossy Doctor had arrived. There went my plan to ignore him.

"You've just been on your cell a *lot* lately." Yep, it sounded even more pathetic out loud and I wished I'd kept my mouth shut.

"I don't understand. Do you think I'm having an affair or something?" he asked, his voice shaking as if he were trying to suppress laughter.

"I'm glad I amuse you," I deadpanned.

"Baby, look at me," he said, his voice turning abruptly serious. "Look into my eyes and tell me if you think I'm cheating on you."

"No. Of course I don't." And I really didn't. Did I? No, that was absurd. I trusted Richard implicitly. Didn't I? Yes. Yes I did. He was the only person I had ever trusted my whole life. Maybe that was the problem. Maybe I was incapable of trust. Maybe I just didn't know how… Yes. Yes that was it. This whole thing was just another symptom of my fucked-up-ness and was actually nothing to do with Richard at all.

"I'm sorry," I confessed, leaning in for a kiss. "Maybe my period is due or something," I joked in an attempt to trivialize my whole bunny boiler episode.

"I would never, *ever* hurt you like that. You're everything to me," Richard declared, his voice grave and meaningful as he tried to reassure me. Which he did - and now I felt even more stupid – and guilty – for doubting him in the first place.

I nestled back into him, burying my face into his neck and relishing the thrum of his pulse playing gently against my cheek. I love him. And he loves me. I just need to work on the believing it part…

Chapter Thirteen

Oh shit. Breathe. Oh shit. Breathe. Oh sh-

"Amelia," Vanessa greeted, interrupting my inward freaking out session.

"Good morning," I said, taking her proffered hand and shaking it. She led me up a long white corridor, the walls either side lined with windows exposing offices littered with desks, bookshelves and people who looked like they knew what they were doing. Much unlike me.

"You'll be based in here, with me." She opened the door to a huge office with 'V A Heart – Editor' etched onto it. I nodded weakly and took in my surroundings.

Vanessa's office was bright and airy. A long horizontal window spanned the full width of the exterior wall and everything was white or glass, with the exception of her peanut-shaped desk which was a smooth pine.

"Right, let's get the important stuff out of the way first," she said, waving her unnaturally long manicured nails in the air. I couldn't help wonder how in hell she used the bathroom with those things. "So, the coffee machine is two doors down the hall on the right, the copier is just through there," she pointed to a door opposite the one we just walked through, "and the café we use for the lunch run is The Mighty Bite, just across the street." She pointed to the window as if I'd be able to see the café in question from where I was standing.

Saving Amy

Wow. Making coffee, running around after everyone... all my dreams and aspirations were being realized before my eyes.

"I also need you to sign these." She thrust a wad of papers under my nose that by the look of them would take forever and a week to read through. "It's just your contract, terms of salary, college placement acceptance etc."

She tossed me a silver, expensive looking fountain pen that thankfully I managed to catch. It seemed she wanted me to sign them there and then without so much as a skim through. I did as expected of me and jotted my autograph down against the little pre-filled x's. Six times in total and I had no idea what I was committing to. I could've been signing my soul over to her for all I knew.

Good job it's probably not worth much then.

"Thank you," she uttered, taking the signed documents from me. "Okay, let's give you a tour of the place."

Vanessa guided me into each office in turn. Dozens of eyes bored into me along the way, assessing the newbie as I entered each room. I was introduced to what must've been thirty different people and I'd already forgotten their name before I went on to meet the next one. One man stood out however – Robert. He was a fellow intern who looked as lost as I felt, instantly relaxing me a little.

Tour complete, I set about fulfilling my first task of the day – stuffing envelopes with generic rejection letters and addressing them to budding authors about to get their dreams shattered. Vanessa informed me she would be out at meetings until after lunch and said that my envelope-stuffing duties should see me through until then. I figured that was surely impossible and I would end up looking silly with nothing to do after an hour…

Until she planked a pile of letters on the desk, stacked so high they towered above the computer monitor in front of me.

Two hours in and I was about three-quarters the way through the pile and my fingertips were shredded with paper-cuts. I was confident all envelopes would be stuffed and ready to go within half an hour, yet Vanessa wasn't due back for another two. I pondered what I could do next. Nothing too drastic seeing as I didn't technically have a clue what I was doing, but I didn't want to just sit there idly. I needed to show initiative. Maybe this was a test? Maybe she knew I would finish early and wanted to see what I could come up with on my own.

A knock on the door startled me from my laborious stuffing.

"Hey. You wanna grab lunch with me?" It was Robert, the other intern. I recognized him instantly with his smooth sandy hair and blue puppy-dog eyes, and by the smell of cheap cologne mixed with stale tobacco that wafted through the air.

"Sure," I agreed out of politeness, even though I wasn't really sure I wanted to. I'm a natural people person – people make me nervous. The whole point of this job however is to change my life and my fucked-up brain, so I knew I needed to make the effort.

Saving Amy

****

I didn't realize I was hungry until I sat down opposite Robert in The Mighty Bite. The smell of sizzling bacon danced into my nose and made my stomach growl so loud I was almost sure he heard it. He was far too polite to say if he had of course.

"How are you finding Vanessa?" Robert asked with an impish grin as I took a sizeable bite of my bacon and egg sandwich.

"Okay, I guess. I haven't spent enough time with her to form an opinion."

"You should know, she's known as 'The Dragon' down in marketing," he said with a wink. I forced a chuckle because I didn't want to offend him.

"Well she's been fine with me so far."

As the conversation started to flow I made a conscious effort to take smaller, *daintier* bites of my sandwich after noticing Robert had a fair way to go to catch up with me. The past ten minutes had taught me that he was quite the joker – almost to the point of being annoying. His ultimate goal was to become an editor, he still lived at home with his schoolteacher parents and he preferred to go by the name 'Rob'.

I gave nothing away about myself.

"Shit," Rob muttered when a rogue dollop of ketchup seeped from his bread and splattered onto his crisp white shirt which still had the fold creases in from being new in the packet.

"Here." I passed him a baby wet-wipe from my purse and his face slipped into an expression that could only be described as horrified. "A girl should never be without them." I repeated the words that Julie had once told me. It seemed to appease whatever he was thinking and his face softened back into a smile.

Did he think I was a mother? Why the hell should that bother him anyway? *Judgmental prick,* my subconscious seethed, and this time I was forced to agree.

"So you just outta college too?"

Damn. He wants to talk about me.

"No. This is the first thing I've done since school."

"*Really?*" His bright eyes widened as if I'd just told him I'd killed a baby. "How old are you?"

"Nineteen."

"*Wow,*" he muttered under his breath, jolting back against his seat as if I'd just punched him. "You must have one hell of a portfolio," he said, sounding utterly dumbfounded.

Portfolio? I hardly classed my old thrown-together notebook that Richard deviously showed to Vanessa a portfolio.

"I know just how difficult it is to impress The Dragon," he continued. "She usually insists on college graduates – won't even consider any other type for an interview. Guess rich daddy's have a lot of clout though hey?"

What the hell was that supposed to mean?

At the risk of sounding bigheaded, I was pretty sure Rob sounded… jealous.

"My *'daddy's'* got nothing to do with it," I snapped. Rob forced out a laugh/huff/snort sound and I was left feeling incredibly uncomfortable.

Saving Amy

I slumped back in my chair – suddenly feeling inadequate. I was willing to accept Richard's theory that I didn't think highly enough of my capabilities to some extent, but I was adamant my crappy and crumpled notebook wasn't *so* good this supposed fierce, nigh on impossible to impress 'dragon' would abandon her usual criteria and protocols because she simply *had* to have me.

There was just *no* way.

None whatsoever.

I automatically began to wonder just how much Richard *really* had to do with me getting this job. The only rational conclusion was that it was probably a lot and the reality was it had nothing to do with me at all. In that moment, any sense of pride or achievement I'd been feeling until now had just leapt from my body and got ran over by a bus.

What influence could he possibly have over Vanessa? Did he know her personally?

"You're very quiet all of a sudden. Did I touch a nerve or something?"

"Oh, um…. Sorry. I was just thinking about what to do when I get back to the office," I lied. Why was I apologizing? He was being a complete dick to me.

"Well don't touch her stuff. I've heard she hates that."

Why would I?

"Oh wait, you've got…" Rob's hand was coming towards my face. Instinctively, I retreated back as far as the wooden slats of the back of the chair would allow. Then his finger brushed over my chin.

What the…

"Ketchup," he said, and then smiled sleazily.

"Thanks," I muttered, wiping his touch away. His unnecessary familiarity unnerved me and I was suddenly eager to get back to work.

"We'd best head back," I suggested. Rob nodded and threw one last gulp of coffee down his throat.

Hmm. Did I like Rob? I was leaning very far towards probably not right now.

****

It was a relief to be back in the office – to be back on my own. I decided Rob was probably a nice enough guy, just a little too cocky and overfamiliar for my liking.

After finally stuffing the last of the envelopes, I used my initiative and set about tackling the tall six-drawer metal filing cabinet – separating the existing and potential client files and then rearranging them into alphabetical order.

I was finished in just over an hour and everything was nicely organized and easier to navigate – to *me* anyway. I just hoped Vanessa didn't count this as me 'touching her stuff' like Rob warned me about. But then I couldn't help wonder if he was simply trying to sabotage any efforts I might make to impress her, what with his jealousy over me being handed this placement on a big fat silver platter.

"Sorry I'm late. My meeting ran over." Vanessa appeared in the doorway dressed in a black pinstripe pantsuit, carrying lever-arch files up to her chin and apologizing unnecessarily.

Saving Amy

"Let me help," I offered, taking the top two files from the stack in her weighed down arms.

"Thanks. Just pop them on my desk." I did as I was told. "Did you manage to finish the rejection pile?"

"Yes," I said, rather proud of myself. "It didn't take as long as I expected so I've rearranged the filing system." I nodded my head towards the filing cabinet. "I hope you don't mind."

"Not at all," she said with an expression that could only be described as impressed. "I've been meaning to get round to that for months." Looking to her silver bracelet watch she added, "It's getting on a bit, you should go for lunch."

"Oh, um, I went for lunch earlier." Itchy heat crawled up my neck and invaded my cheeks. It felt like I'd been caught skipping school.

"Really? I mean that's fine of course. You've done *all* this and still had time for lunch? I'm impressed."

"Well Rob from marketing asked me to join him and I'd almost finished with the envelopes, so…" I trailed off, feeling the need to justify my need to eat.

"*Ugh*. You should be careful around him," she warned, wrinkling her nose in disgust. I was a little taken aback by her unusual informality. Was I missing something? I made a mental note to probe Rob next time we were alone.

"He's the only person who's really spoken to me today," I muttered, feeling some unknown need to defend him. He wasn't *that* bad.

No screw that. He was totally that bad.

"That'll be because everyone else is busy doing what they're being paid to do," she snapped in an acidic tone. "In future, if everyone else is busy, I'd suggest you eat alone."

Wow. She *actually* hated him. Now I was *really* intrigued.

"What would you like me to do next?" I asked eagerly, purposely changing the subject.

"I was actually thinking of heading off early today. You might as well do the same. I'm in all day tomorrow so I can walk you through everything a lot more."

"Sounds good to me. Thank you," I said, already reaching for my black blazer that hung on the back of my swivel chair. "I'll see you in the morning."

"Yes. See you. And thank you for all your hard work today. I think we're going to get along just fine." I flushed, *of course*, and smiled gratefully at her. Inside my heart was dancing a victory rhythm. I'd done it. I'd completed my first day as a working woman and I was still alive.

Go me!

****

Two weeks in and I was at last beginning to get my head around this working business. It felt invigorating to just be... *normal.* To be a normal girl doing normal things. Having normal conversations about normal topics – knowing no one else was aware of my fucked-up past and self-destructive tendencies. To everyone else at Salt House, I was just... normal.

Saving Amy

Vanessa had awarded me free reign of the slush pile, promising to reconsider anything that caught my eye. In my head I classed it as a promotion, but in reality Vanessa was probably just giving me something to pass the time – seeing as though I'd nearly always finished up with anything she threw at me by lunchtime. That impressed her. I could tell by the cocked eyebrow she flashed me every time I completed whatever task I'd been set.

Overall, everything in the slush pile deserved to be there. I came across this one novel today however, which – in my inexperienced mind – showed promise. It was about a young girl who killed her abusive father. The whole concept struck a chord with my tortured soul, and seeing as though murder wasn't a viable option for me in the real world, perhaps reading about a warped, sadistic bastard getting his comeuppance was the next best thing. Anyway, I popped the manuscript in my bag and planned to read it through at home.

Being in the office, surrounded by books and manuscripts made me realize how much I missed reading. I'd barely read anything at all since moving in with Richard. I hadn't needed to – I'd been too busy living my own happy ever after. There and then I made a silent promise to make the effort, vowing to read not because I *needed* to, but because I *wanted* to.

Actually scrap that… I guess I *did* need to. I now worked in a publishing house for Christ's sake!

Vanessa's fingers were ferociously tapping away at her computer and I was typing up what Vanessa called 'potential letters' – thanking would be authors for the submission of their first three chapters and requesting full manuscripts from them. Seeing as though we only mailed three or four 'potential letters' a week, compared to the hundred or so rejections, I guessed I'd be finished up within twenty minutes and then I'd arranged to meet Rob.

Lunch with Rob had inadvertently become routine. I didn't really mind, despite his sleaze-ball qualities becoming more apparent by the day. The complete and utter jerk side of him I witnessed on my first day had wavered more with each day and most of the time he was actually pretty funny. I didn't know what his problem was that day and I didn't care to ask – maybe his dog had just died or something.

I guess I was just grateful for the company. Everyone else in the building was part of their own little clique and going off the fact not one of the miserable bastards had talked to me yet, I assumed they weren't open to new members.

I hadn't felt like I knew Rob well enough yet to press him about the him-and-Vanessa-hating-each-other-thing, but after witnessing her give him a long, intense, *revolted* stare this morning, maybe today was the day.

The phone on Vanessa's desk rang, startling her and causing her to almost choke on her mouthful of coffee. She spluttered and wiped her mouth with the cuff of her blazer – very unprofessional… very un-Vanessa.

"Heart," she snapped down the line and in all honesty I could see why people called her The Dragon. She was curt to the point of being rude with everybody – everybody except me that is. I still hadn't figured out what made me so obviously different – more deserving of her time and patience.

"Ah, Richard," she acknowledged in a tone that didn't suit her – a *happy* tone. For a brief second my heart began to flutter but then quickly resumed normal rhythm – it couldn't be *my* Richard.

"She is indeed… Yes… You were spot on." A brief pause followed and the unimaginable happened – Vanessa *laughed*. Out loud, head thrown back and everything. "Hold on, I'll just pass you over.

Who? Me? My eyes instinctively scanned the room. *Yep. Still just the two of us.*

"Take care, sweetie."

Sweetie?

"It's for you, Amy."

Amy? Vanessa had never called me Amy… not once.

I hesitantly tapped the button for line three, unsure of what use *I* could be to anyone. Surely Vanessa wasn't trusting me to deal with an important client? I was nowhere near ready for that.

"Good morning, Amy Hope speaking," I said, striving to sound confident and assertive but the damn crack in my voice betrayed me.

"Very professional, baby," a velvety voice teased. It *was* 'my' Richard.

They *did* know each other. I knew it! My subconscious had been too preoccupied taking on board the ins and outs of being an intern to confront Richard with my suspicions. I guess they weren't suspicions anymore.

"Oh, it's you," I answered, a little offhand and I think it was down to a concoction of surprise, disappointment and betrayal. I'd speculated since my first day here – back when Rob made it clear Vanessa wouldn't usually touch someone like me with a barge pole – that Richard and Vanessa knew one another - like *properly* knew one another - and that I didn't earn this position through my own merit at all.

"Sorry to disappoint," he griped, but I could hear the smile filtering through his comforting voice.

"Sorry, I just wasn't expecting it to be you. You've never called me here, is everything okay?"

"Everything's fine. I just forgot to tell you we're having dinner with my parents tonight. It's my mom's birthday."

"Talk about last minute! What gift have you got for her? Please don't tell me you forgot that too."

"Don't worry, I'll pick up a gift card on the way or something," he said, ever so blasé.

"Richard!" I scolded. "She's your mother – you can't turn up with a gift card. You need to put some thought into it."

"Well what do you buy the woman who has everything?"

"That's not the point." A long bout of silence followed while I contemplated what Vivienne might like.

Got it!

"Perfume," I announced feeling especially proud of myself for remembering that Vivienne smelt like Julie's mom – of Chanel no. 5.

"*Perfume?*" Richard repeated as if it were a word he'd never heard before. "How the hell would *I* know what perfume she likes?"

"Just trust me. I'll pick some up on my lunch break."

Saving Amy

"Well maybe I should pick up a gift card too. Just in case."

"Richard!" I scolded *again*. I couldn't believe he didn't have faith in my gift buying abilities!

"Fine! No gift card." I could imagine him surrendering his palms on the other end of the line.

"Okay well I have to go now," I said when I noticed Rob waiting for me through the window of the office door. "I'll see you later."

"You sure will, baby. I love you."

"Love you too," I muttered under my breath because it felt awkward being soppy in front of Vanessa. And yes, I might well love the ass off him, but I was also still pissed at him. The more I thought about it – which was a *lot* – the more convinced I became that Richard was the reason I was sitting here, and not my notebook full of crap.

"Am I okay to take my lunch now?" I asked Vanessa. She looked up from her computer and slid her reading glasses up onto her head.

"Sure, Amy."

That was another thing. Why had she started calling me Amy all of a sudden? I'd never once corrected her. Had Richard? He must have, seeing as they were bosom buddies and all.

"Thanks," I replied politely but with a clenched fist hidden behind my back. Deep down I knew I should just suck it up and be grateful. I always knew I'd blown my chances of earning myself a dream job, so when I did – or *thought* I did – I was so proud of myself. And for once, the idea that I held some genuine talent didn't seem so absurd.

But now…

"Hey, good lookin," Rob greeted with a cheeky wink. I smiled awkwardly. "I was thinkin' maybe we should hit the drive-thru today. I'm kinda sick of bacon." He had a point – The Mighty Bite was becoming a little monotonous. But then I just wasn't sure how comfortable I'd feel being trapped in such a confined space as a car with Mr. Touchy Feely.

"Sure," I reluctantly agreed. On the plus side, maybe some privacy would aid my plan to interrogate him about Vanessa.

Rob snaked his arm around my waist and walked me to the elevator. It unsettled me but as much as I wanted to squirm out of his embrace, I focused hard on letting it go. He was just being friendly, I kept telling myself. A 'normal' person wouldn't react like I wanted to. They wouldn't feel itchy with the desire to run away. They would just smile. Nudge his shoulder maybe. Be grateful that they had someone willing to be their friend.

So, as much as it made my insides tighten, I acted 'normal' and let Rob lead me to the car.

"Holy shit! This car is the bomb!" Rob screeched as he stroked the glossy black paintwork of Richard's Audi up and down. We decided to take my car – well Richard's – because I needed to shop for perfume and I didn't want to use him as my own personal taxi service, even though I knew he wouldn't mind.

"It's just a car," I muttered, shrugging.

"That is such a girl thing to say. This ain't just a freakin' car!" he enthused, his eyes practically bulging from their sockets. "I swear I would sell my own grandmother for this baby."

Saving Amy

I couldn't even begin to understand his enthusiasm for what was fundamentally a lump of moving metal, so I ignored him and climbed in the driver's side. Rob took an extra minute fondling the car's exterior before joining me. Then he progressed to caressing every visible inch of the interior too. I had to admit it was pretty amusing. I almost felt like a spare part in an R-rated movie the way he groaned as he stroked and cupped everything in his reach.

We rode in silence for a few minutes. I was pretty sure it was the longest time Rob had ever gone without speaking and it felt as refreshing as it did awkward.

"So what gives with you and Vanessa?" I asked, easing the car into McDonald's Drive-Thru. I was going for the straightforward and to the point approach – we only had an hour for lunch.

"What makes you ask? Has The Dragon said something about me?" he asked – almost demanded. Jeez, just mentioning her name got him all riled up – just like his did with her.

"Nothing in particular. I just get the feeling you don't like each other mu-"

"That's the understatement of the century," he interrupted before I could finish. He did that a lot and quite frankly it annoyed the hell out of me. I didn't have the balls to say as much of course.

"But you've only worked here a few weeks. How have you managed to piss her off so bad already?"

"Hold up, why do you assume it's *me* doing the pissing off?" he retorted, jolting back in his seat.

You seriously want me to answer that?

"Good afternoon, can I take your order please?" the McDonald's girl asked robotically without looking up from under her cap.

"I'll take a Big Mac and Diet Coke, and…" I turned to Rob and he mouthed 'same'. "And the same again, please."

"No fries?" Robot Girl asked, confounded as if I'd just tried to order a bucket of caviar from her. I shook my head and reached for my purse. Rob tried to offer me some cash but I shooed his hand away.

"I'll get these," I ordered. He opened his mouth to speak and assuming it was to object, I held my hand up, shushing him.

"So anyway, Vanessa…" Rob picked up where he left off as I edged closer to Window 3. "I pissed her off way before I got a job here. That's why the vindictive bitch did everything in her power to try and stop me getting an internship. Wasn't down to her at the end of the day though. I just *love* running into her on the corridor," he said with a smug grin – like he'd won whatever battle they were having.

"So, it *was* you doing the pissing off then?" I teased and Rob choked on a laugh.

"Well, yeah… but nice of you to assume anyway."

"So how do you know each other? What did you do?"

"I dated her daughter last summer."

Vanessa has a daughter? This was surprising news. Vanessa just seemed too… professional, too career driven to be a parent. And if I was completely honest, with her short spikey hair and love of pantsuits, I kind of assumed she was a lesbian.

Saving Amy

"That doesn't sound so bad," I said and then mentally slapped myself for sounding so offensive.

'*So*' bad.

"Tell me about it. I mean things got a little messy when we broke up but these things happen right? But now I'm the devil incarnated in her eyes. I get it – I broke her daughter's heart and all that but what did she expect me to do, *marry* her or something?"

"Jeez," was all I could think to comment. Naturally Vanessa would want to side with her daughter but a typical teenage break-up didn't seem to justify just how passionately she seemed to loathe him. Rob said things got messy – I decided to take that as he cheated on her and now Vanessa thought he was a douchebag.

"Sorry for the wait," another robotic McDonald's employee apologized insincerely as she handed me our bag of food. My mind had been so engrossed in the whole Rob versus Vanessa saga I hadn't even noticed we'd been waiting at Window 3 for almost ten minutes.

I took the drinks and paper bag and then handed them to Rob while I found somewhere to park. I circled the lot three times before spotting a tight space by a grass verge and reversing into it in one shot, impressing myself - *and* Rob by the astounded raised eyebrow taking over his surfer-boy face.

We talked about work mainly while we ate, and Rob filled me in about what to expect from my evening classes at college. He started two weeks ago and my first class was next Thursday. I was more nervous about the environment than struggling with the academic side of things. I could only pray it was nothing like school. That it wouldn't be as tedious and oppressive and there wouldn't be an evil Mrs. Clarke clone lurking in the halls.

After crushing our wrappers and leftovers into the overflowing drive-past trashcan I headed towards the perfumery just around the corner from Salt House.

"Look, Aims, before you go in. I just wanted to apologize for being such a jackass to you in the beginning," Rob said sincerely, curling his fingers around my forearm. I had to try extremely hard not to flinch.

"You weren't *that* bad," I replied honestly, smiling as I did so.

"Yeah I was. I'd tried so hard to get an editing internship and Salt House was my last hope. When I found out Vanessa was senior editor, I knew I'd have no chance and ended up stuck in marketing. I guess I thought you were some spoiled rich kid who'd bought your way in. I was… jealous. And that's no excuse for being a dick to you. So, I'm sorry."

Wow. Seriously wasn't expecting that conversation today and any doubts I held about Rob's friendship abilities were quashed in an instant.

"Well maybe you can make it up to me by heading up to Vanessa's office and telling her I'll be five minutes?" I asked, realizing I was already two minutes late but knowing I would be literally two more minutes in the perfumery seeing as I knew exactly what I was looking for. "Oh wait, never mind. I'll just get it after work I don't want things to be awkward." I quickly added when I remembered the fact they hated each other's guts.

Saving Amy

"It's no problem, Aims. Any excuse to remind the bitch that she failed in her mission to fuck me over, remember?" he assured with a wicked grin. I rolled my eyes playfully at him.

"Well don't rile her. I'm the one who's got to work with her all afternoon."

"Who me?" he teased, clutching his hand to his chest as if he was truly offended. "I wouldn't dare," he added, winking devilishly. He was impossible. Yet I'd decided during that single hour with him, that I really liked him.

Rob high-fived me when we got out of the car and then we went our separate ways. I was in an out of the perfumery within five minutes – a little longer than I anticipated but I decided to take advantage of their gift-wrap service and save myself a job later on. Before heading back into work I tucked the shiny gold package into the glove compartment of the Audi and re-fixed my hair into a high ponytail.

When I neared the office building something cold and harsh flexed around my wrist, dragging me backwards. My first instinct was that it was Rob playing around and when I spun around to face him, my heart stopped dead in my chest.

"I need some money, Amelia," my dad said. I gasped when I saw him. He looked so... disheveled. His normally pruned moustache had merged into a full-on unkempt beard. His cheeks were red with hundreds of tiny thread-veins and his eyes were swollen and glassy.

"I- I haven't got any," I choked out as he pulled me around the corner out of view of the street.

"Bullshit. I've ran a background check on that doctor of yours. So don't tell me you've got no fucking money."

He forced my back into the brick wall and pinned me down with his strong hands over my heart, which was hammering against my ribs. For once, it wasn't the stench of Old Spice making my stomach churn, it was whiskey – and lots of it.

"My purse. Let me check my purse," I stuttered, trying to maneuver one hand through the contents because my other was trapped by the weight of his body. I blindly reached into the concealed zipper and pulled out the crumpled notes I had stuffed in there. "Here," I said shakily.

"There's like fifty-dollars here. What the fuck do you expect me to do with that?" I didn't respond. I couldn't. "I've not forgotten all the times you've helped yourself to my wallet. You owe me," he growled and my breathing became rapid.

"H-how much d-do you want?" I gasped, his fingers now encircling the base of my throat. I tried to swallow but the pressure was too great. My pulse began to throb in my ears and my eyes felt swollen, like they were about to burst straight out of their sockets.

"Twenty-five." If I'd been able to breathe I would've let out a sigh of relief. I could go ask Rob to lend me that amount until tomorrow. "Thousand."

Fuck.

"I don't have that kind of money," I wheezed. I tried to shout but it came out as more of a whimper. Instinctively my fingers started clawing at the sleeves of his jacket, in a futile effort to remove the choking pressure around my neck. He laughed villainously and then lowered his head to mine until our noses were almost touching. He reeked of stale whiskey and cigars and I gagged on the urge to retch.

"You'll get me that fucking money and you'll get it me by tomorrow!" he roared, finally letting go of my throat and grabbing my wrists, forcing them up against the coarse bricks. I coughed and spluttered, and as the blood rushed furiously from my face I started to feel dizzy.

"Dad, please…"

"It's SIR!" he yelled in my face, giving my body a jolt so hard the back of my head smacked into the wall.

"I-I… I'll try. I'll have to ask-"

"GET THE FUCK OFF HER!" yelled the voice of my savior. Within seconds Rob had pulled my dad off me and shoved him so forcefully he smacked down onto the sidewalk. "Jesus, are you okay?" he asked in a panic, pulling his cell from his pocket.

"No. No police. *Please…*" I begged, assuming that was his next intention.

"What the fuck, Aims? That dude had you pinned against the fucking wall! Do you know him or something?" He looked to the floor where he'd left my dad's folded body, but he was gone. I could breathe again.

"No, no. He was just some drunk looking for money. Got a bit out of control but I'm fine." I played it down, trying desperately to assure him. I couldn't afford to have the police involved. God only knew what he'd do to me…

Rob eyed me up warily.

"Honestly, Rob. I'm good, I swear."

Huffing, Rob wrapped his arm around my waist and led me into the building.

Chapter Fourteen

I managed to pacify Rob just long enough to get up to Vanessa's office. Then he tried to hug me outside the glass doors and noticed the backs of my arms were grazed.

"Fuck, Aims, he hurt you!" I brought my elbows up and examined the weeping scratches. They were clogged with dirt from the brick. "These need cleaning up."

"It's nothing. Really-"

"What's happened, Amy?" Vanessa asked, appearing from nowhere and throwing a look of true disdain towards Rob – almost like she thought *he* was responsible for the tears burning my eyes.

"Some asshole jumped her outside. Had her pinned against the wall when I got there."

"Oh my god, are you alright?" she fussed, taking hold of my hand and guiding me into the office like I was an invalid. "Has someone called the police?" she added before letting me reply.

"She won't let me," Rob muttered, disapproval saturating his voice.

"Amy?" she pressed disbelievingly, prodding me for an explanation.

"There's no point. He's gone now and I'm fine, really."

"Richard. I'll call Richard," she muttered, seemingly to herself.

I mentally huffed at yet another confirmation of how little I had to do with earning my place here. I didn't disagree with her, even though I felt bad for dragging Richard out of work. I wanted to go home and I didn't know if I felt capable of driving myself. I didn't know how I was managing to hold myself together. I was falling apart inside but the fear of what would happen if the police got involved was enough to keep me functioning normally.

Vanessa and Rob fussed and cooed over me until Richard arrived – Vanessa's voice hitching to a tone only interpretable under the sea when she noticed spots of blood dripping down the back of my neck. I didn't feel the pain until she spotted the wound hidden in my hair and now it was throbbing like a motherfucker – though I played it down.

Rob practically carried me over to my swivel chair and lowered me down as if I was about to break in half.

"Here," Vanessa said as she passed me a cup of steaming coffee. I took a sip and almost choked to death as it cut into my throat like razor blades. "I added a dash of gin. It'll help with the shaking."

A *dash?*

Shit. Looking to my hands I really was shaking. I clamped my free hand down onto my knee in an effort to stem the trembling. They couldn't see me crumble. It would only make them more determined to call the cops.

I took another eager sip of the disgusting coffee – willing it to calm my jittering nerves. It tasted revolting… bitter. Who ever decided coffee and gin made a good combination? Apart from my mother of course.

That thought caused a strange pang to twist around my heart. I hadn't thought about her for so

Saving Amy

long and as much as I hated her, I couldn't seem to stop myself wondering how she was – how much she was suffering now my dad only had her to take things out on.

"Is that helping?" Rob asked, nodding towards my mug when Vanessa left the room to fetch a first aid kit.

No.

"It tastes like shit," I spat, setting the mug on the desk beside me. Rob laughed softly and then swept a rogue strand of hair away as he tried to gain a better view of the cut to my head.

"So this Richard dude," he muttered somberly, "he your boyfriend?"

He seemed a little wounded, disappointed maybe, and then I realized I'd never mentioned Richard to him before. I nodded with an apologetic smile. Christ knows why but I felt this bizarre sense of guilt taking over me. I replayed all the innocent touches, and times he'd walked by me with a hand around my waist…

Rob had a crush on me.

Shit.

"Damn. Guess I missed my chance," he conceded, smiling playfully at me.

In that moment, saving me, the office door flew open, slamming into the wall and startling the crap out of me. Richard sped towards me so fast his panic stricken face merged into a blur. I instinctively jumped to my feet and flung myself into his eggplant colored shirt.

"Jesus, baby, are you okay?" He held me at arms length, examining me up and down with his eyes. I nodded – my mouth too dry to speak – and he pulled me back into him, cocooning me inside his protective arms.

"And you have no idea who it was?" he asked, concern spilling from his every pore. I shook my head, essentially lying to him.

"I'm sorry you were pulled out of work. I hope it didn't cause any problems for you."

"Screw work. Amy, *you* are the most important thing here."

I tried to get him to take me straight home but he wouldn't leave before checking out my wounds and hearing my explanation for not calling the police. I knew lying to Richard would be difficult and I was sure he knew as much while I tried to remember the lies I'd told. Especially when he stopped me a few minutes in, and said I could tell him the rest at home.

"I'm taking her home now," Richard said to Vanessa – *telling* her, not asking, after deciding the cut on my head needed nothing more than some antiseptic and painkillers.

"Of course. Take as much time off as you need, Amy."

"Thanks," I muttered, that pissed off feeling resurfacing as my mind wouldn't quit figuring out how she knew Richard. Rob gave me a knowing nod – one which told me he was there if I needed him for anything. I tried to smile but my face wouldn't work so instead I just nodded before following Richard out of the building.

My stomach crawled up to my heart, chewing away at it as we rode home in silence. When we eventually reached the apartment Richard scooped me into his arms and kissed the top of my head repeatedly.

"It was your father, wasn't it?"

"Yes," I whispered, seeing no point in continuing to lie – he knew me too well. "He wanted money."

"Money?"

"Twenty-five thousand," I stated, nodding weakly. "He looked a mess. Obviously got himself in some kind of trouble." Richard stayed silent as a contemplative look swept over his face. "I don't know how far he'll go to get it," I admitted shakily, the fear I'd forced myself to suppress resurfacing all at once.

"Amy we really need to think about-"

"No!" I interrupted. "No police, Richard. You know as well as I do, he'll get himself out of it and then what'll happen? I can't push him that far. I'm scared. I'm so fucking scared," I admitted for the first time in my life. I thought I'd finally moved on… escaped.

How naïve was I?

"You're safe now," he whispered, drawing my head into his chest. "He won't hurt you again, baby. *Nobody* will hurt you again. I'll make sure of it," he growled, holding me so close his grip smarted a little.

How? No one could make sure of that. I knew he was trying to comfort me and for now, he did. But the minute I inevitably had to step out of the safety of his presence…

****

I sat on the cold, hard granite with my knees drawn into my chest, feeling itchy with dirt as I waited for the bath to fill. I could feel my dad's touch all over my body, as if his slimy fingers had left some kind of revolting residue in their wake. My fingers unconsciously started scratching at my skin, desperate to remove it.

I could still smell him - the vile smell of stale alcohol lingered in my nose and no amount of blowing or rubbing would remove it. I'd brushed my teeth three times but I could still taste his sickening, cigar-infused breath that crawled into my mouth as he yelled at me. His bulging eyes, alive with menace were etched onto my eyelids, making me afraid to close my eyes.

He was still with me and I'd never be able to get rid of him.

"Amy, stop!" Snapping me from the trance I seemed to have slipped into, Richard kneeled beside me, prizing my fingernails off the skin on my arms. "Oh, baby."

I caught sight of my abraded arms as Richard pulled my naked body into his chest. I had unwittingly scratched them to the point of breaking the skin and tiny bubbles of blood were beginning to seep from the harsh grazes.

"Everything's okay. I'm here and I love you," he whispered into my hair, making my weary body surrender, collapsing into the safety of his arms. Bursting under the pressure, tears erupted from their banks and spilled rapidly down my cheeks as I wailed loudly, struggling to breathe.

Richard supported my weight, cradling me with one arm around my waist and one behind my head,

Saving Amy

stroking my hair. And then I felt a tear that wasn't mine drip onto my forehead and he squeezed me tighter. He was crying. I was crying. We sat huddled together, rocking back and forth until the bath water lapped over the edge of the large, oval tub and splashed onto the floor. We both sat up sharply at the sound, but neither one of us jumped to pull the plug.

"We should really sort that out," Richard said with a trace of a smile – his gaze landing on the bath. But we didn't. Not straight away anyhow.

First, Richard wiped the drying tears from my cheeks with his gentle fingers and then I did the same to him – our haunted eyes never leaving each other. Then he gave me a final hug – a hard one, clutching me firmly against him as if it were the last chance he'd ever get to do it – before springing lithely to his feet and diving for the overflowing bathtub.

As I stepped into the steaming lavender water, I noticed Richard undressing. I smiled warmly, realizing he was getting in too. I didn't want to be alone – I didn't trust myself right now in a room full of so many sharp objects.

"Ah, shit…" I winced as the water slapped my scuffed arms, stinging the crap out of them. Then I stared at the mess I'd made of myself and sighed, overcome with crushing feelings of shame and frustration. *Stupid bitch,* my subconscious growled.

Richard tested the water with a dip of his big toe and I parted my legs to make room for him when he stepped over the edge, climbing in opposite me so we were face to face.

"It's not as bad as it looks. They'll soon heal over," he said reassuringly, raising my chin with his forefinger to drag my gaze away from my arms.

"I feel so stupid," I admitted, too embarrassed to look him in the eye.

"Don't you dare," he said sternly, taking my face in his hands and forcing me to look at him. "Don't you dare blame yourself for any of this. Today was *not* your fault. Do you hear me?"

"Maybe not. But my reaction is. Look at what I've done to myself!" I snapped unintentionally. "Sorry. I didn't mean to yell. I'm just... tired. I hate the way I can never seem to cope like normal people. I hate-"

"Stop that. Right now," he ordered. "'Stop it with this desire to be 'normal'. What the hell is 'normal' anyway?" he continued, using air quotes to excess. "'Normal' people as you put it couldn't even begin to *imagine* the things you've been through, let alone survive them. Yet here you are, still fighting, striving. You're right, Amy... you're not normal. You are so much more."

Sighing resignedly, I closed my eyes and absorbed the comfort brought by Richard's hands on each of my thighs as he smoothed shower soap over my wet skin. The warmth of his touch against my flesh was more comforting, more intense, than any blade, and I completely lost myself in the sensation.

We bathed in silence for a while and I just stared at Richard, captivated by the sight of his naked beauty as he washed me down with a soft, white sponge dipped in jojoba crème. The love I felt for him physically throbbed deep in my chest. He was so beautiful in every sense of the word – inside

Saving Amy

and out. I found myself blinking as if trying to pull myself out of a dream.

Is he really mine?

"I'll call my mom – cancel dinner," Richard said as he used his hands to lap the water over my skin and rinse the lather away.

I contemplated his words for a moment. The idea of drying off and heading to bed to hibernate under the super-king sized quilt was awfully tempting.

"No," I decided defiantly. I *wouldn't* let my dad send me back to that place. "I want to go. I just want everything to go back to normal."

"Baby, you've been through so much tod-"

"Please, Richard," I talked over him. "I just want to try and forget it ever happened." If that was even possible.

"Okay. Well, we won't stay long. You need to rest." Ah, Bossy Doctor had arrived and in a strange way I found it bizarrely comforting. It made me feel cared for, protected.

Richard never left my side as I toweled myself dry and threw on my clothes – watching intently the whole time as if I was made of china. I opted for my long-sleeved dusty-pink turtleneck to cover the redness around my throat and my scrawbed arms and wrists that had finger-shaped mottled bruises beginning to appear. I paired it with black flared pants and peep-toe heels, then I roughly curled my hair and applied a smattering of make-up which didn't even begin to conceal my drab, gray skin.

Richard dragged on some black jeans and a tight-fitting white v-neck – going from gloriously naked to Vogue cover material in thirty seconds flat.

"You look perfect," Richard breathed, bending to kiss my forehead.

Liar.

After one final glance in the mirror I caked on a little more blush in an attempt to make my skin look a little less *dead,* and drew in a deep, composing breath before following Richard towards the door.

"Dammit! The perfume." I suddenly remembered that it was stashed away in the Audi that was still parked outside work.

"I've got it right here," Richard said with a wink, teasing the shiny gold package out of his brown leather jacket.

"How did you-" My head involuntarily tilted to one side and my eyebrow was doing Richard's baffled crawling-towards-the-scalp thing.

"I had David collect the car. It's parked downstairs in the lot." That explained it. I had briefly wondered how Richard was managing to cope so well knowing one of his babies was lying alone and abandoned down an isolated street. Then again, it must have been equally difficult for him to allow David to drive his car. Despite being twenty-three years old – therefore a whole four years older than me – Richard sees David as his 'baby' brother.

"I'm still not sure about the perfume thing. My mom is very particular with things like that," he added, and I wanted to slap his perfect face.

"Firstly, will you start trusting me? I'm a woman – we know these things. I'm telling you she'll love it."

Saving Amy

"Fine. Whatever you say," he said playfully, surrendering his palms in the air. "And second?"

"Secondly, she wouldn't say even if she didn't. Your mom's way too nice for that."

Richard let out an exaggerated laugh.

"You really don't know my mom at all. Believe me, she has no problem offending anyone." An impish grin crawled across his face. I didn't believe him though. I couldn't accept that Vivienne was anything less than graceful.

****

Climbing the white stone steps up to the front door of Richard's parents' house, I was looking forward to seeing Vivienne again and hearing more of Richard's childhood antics. I'd met her three times now, twice accompanied by Richard's sister Bethany, and she was such *easy* company. So gracious and attentive.

Vivienne greeted me with a warm, tender hug. It didn't feel as awkward as it used to and I hugged her back with equal affection.

"Happy birthday," I said as she released me. She smiled lovingly at me.

"Happy birthday, Mom," Richard repeated before leaning in for his own hug. He handed her the shiny gold present and she eyed it up curiously. It was evident from the look on her face that she was surprised – clearly not used to getting anything that didn't fit inside a card.

Easing her finger into a gap in the paper, she carefully peeled it open without tearing a single bit.

Her eyes widened, smoothing out the feathery creases, and a surprised smile emerged on her lips.

"My favorite! Thank you, darling," she said to Richard and then winked in my direction. He turned to me, flashing a how-the-hell-did-you-know look and then mouthed 'thank you'.

"You're welcome, Mom," he said, taking all the credit. "Where's Dad?"

"He's taking a call upstairs," Vivienne replied, rolling her eyes. Sometimes it seemed Alexander didn't work to live – he lived to work. But standing in this humongous house, he'd most certainly reaped the rewards of such dedication. "He should be down soon. Come through to the living room. Bethany can't wait to see you."

We retreated to the living room – a different one than last time, confirming my notion that there was a whole host of these rooms dotted around the house. This room was equally huge, *naturally*, with rich brown walls, wooden tables and cream fabric, upholstered furniture.

Bethany was sat on the armchair in the corner with her eyes closed – her head bopping up and down to the beat coming from her earphones which I could hear from across the room. Richard headed over and gave her a playful kick in the shin. Her eyes shot open and she hurdled from her seat, throwing herself onto her brother.

After a minute or so of swaying him from side to side she turned her attention to me, running up and throwing her arms around me. I had to try very hard not to wince when she inadvertently brushed along my delicate forearms.

Saving Amy

"Hey, Bethany," I greeted, returning her hug. I was getting good at the whole being affectionate thing. Richard watched us with a contented glint in his eye. He looked so happy, so at home – surrounded by his beautiful family. It made me smile.

"The guest of honor has arrived. Let's get this party started!" a mischievous voice which could've only belonged to David, bellowed as he came barreling in from the hall, rubbing his hands together. Everyone seemed to take it in turns to roll their eyes before giggling at him.

David had the power to brighten even the dullest of situations in an instant and I'd really grown to love him. He was funny, laidback to the point of being permanently horizontal, and immature in the most loveable of ways. He also brought out a younger, more carefree side of Richard and I often found my jaw aching with laughter when they were together – usually tossing playful insults each other's way.

I watched as he gave Vivienne a birthday kiss on the cheek before handing her a card. She teased it open and thanked him genuinely for the gift-card that fell out into her hands.

Boys.

Alexander joined us just as dinner was served. He offered me my usual peck on the cheek and Richard his formal handshake, and then we all sat down to eat.

"So, darling, it must be almost time for the Little Wishes ball?" Vivienne addressed Richard. I had no idea what she was talking about and I paused mid-mouthful to hear his answer.

"I'm not attending this year," he answered flatly.

What's eating him?

"Why on earth not? Amy would love to go!"

Would I?

"What's the Little Wishes ball?" I asked inquisitively, confused by Richard's sudden change in temperament.

"Little Wishes is a charity endorsed by the hospital. They raise money for terminally ill kids. The hospital hosts a ball once a year with all proceeds going straight to the charity."

"Richard usually gives a speech," Vivienne interrupted proudly. "Have they not asked you to speak this year?"

"No. I'm not going, I told you." Wow, he was *actually* pissed. I didn't get it. Unless it was because he didn't want to take *me?* Shit, that was it… he was ashamed of me.

Richard's snappishness had made it crystal clear that the ball was an unwelcome subject and the conversation was quickly abandoned. For now at least – I planned to bring it up again when we were alone.

Dinner was exquisite as usual. Our starter was spiced tomato soup with croutons and a selection of warm breads, followed by slow-roasted rosemary lamb, roast potatoes and green vegetables, and we finished off with a caramel soufflé – washing it all down with some kind of fruity and no doubt ridiculously expensive white wine.

After taking away our dessert dishes, Gracie soon returned with a spectacular three-tiered iced

Saving Amy

fruit cake – festooned with gold leaf, piped cream flowers and gold candles. Richard flitted from his chair and over to the light switch when he saw it approaching, dimming the bright bulb and letting the delicate candlelight take over.

The candles illuminated Vivienne's bashful expression when Gracie rested the cake on the table in front of her. Richard began the chorus of 'Happy Birthday' and we all joined in… even Alexander! When our terrible singing died down the sound was replaced with cheers and clapping hands as Vivienne blew out her candles.

"For she's a jolly good fellow, for she's a jolly good fellow…" Richard warbled and Bethany and I joined in, clapping along to the beat.

Everyone was so happy – bouncing with birthday joy. The whole atmosphere was a pleasure to be a part of and I had almost forgotten the afternoon that preceded it – until I just reminded myself that was. My mood was slipping, my weary bones returning. Cementing a smile on my face I prayed that Richard couldn't see through my pretense.

"If this is too much we can leave?" Richard whispered into my ear, clearly seeing straight through my fake smile.

"I'm fine. Honestly," I whispered back with a slight shake of my head. I wasn't lying exactly, maybe just stretching the truth a little.

"If you're sure," he said, raising an unconvinced eyebrow at me. I nodded and he squeezed my knee under the table.

"Is everything okay between you two?" Vivienne asked suspiciously, obviously curious by the whispers we thought people were too busy to notice.

"Everything's fine, Mom," Richard assured her with an awkward smile before tucking his arm around my waist. She raised an incredulous eyebrow and it made me smile. Now I knew where he got *that* particular trait from.

"Yeah, Mom, he probably just forgot to put the toilet seat down or somethin'. You know how crazy you women get over shit like that." Vivienne silenced David with nothing more than a chastising glance whereas Richard went for the kicking him under the table option. As usual David had once again lightened an atmosphere that was threatening to darken.

The table topic shifted to Bethany's art assignment that was due in school next week. She was absolutely bursting with enthusiasm and practically bounced Tigger-style out of the room to fetch it. Silence descended in her absence but was soon interrupted by the bleep of Richard's cell.

He ignored it, which instantly confirmed he didn't think it was work related. But then it beeped again, making him fumble around in his jacket pocket while he tried to switch it to silent without actually removing it. Vivienne was observing him suspiciously, but I couldn't work out if that was because she sensed his dubious phone-behavior too, or she could just tell how tense and pissed off it was making me.

"Amy, will you join me upstairs? I'd like some help choosing an outfit for the Finding Hope charity ball next week."

Saving Amy

Seriously? Girly fashion-talk with the mother-in-law… lucky me.

"Of course," I said politely because I didn't want to offend her. Richard pursed his eyebrows at his mom, as if he smelt something fishy. I got up and followed Vivienne without saying a word to him. Justified or not, I couldn't help feeling agitated over his mysterious text-buddy. Bizarrely, and wholly irrationally, I think I felt a little jealous.

Chapter Fifteen

Vivienne and I made our way up the grand spiral staircase and I perched on the edge of a white leather chaise longue in a closet that was easily as big as a bedroom. It had a polished white tiled floor, lilac walls and rows upon rows of shelves and rails.

"You look exhausted," Vivienne noted, casting a probing glance over my face. "Are you sure everything's okay between you two?"

"Richard and me are fine," I said with a little too much unevenness in my voice as my ridiculous text jealousy reared its ugly head. "I've just had a tough day at work," I added, although it was a complete and utter understatement.

"Ah, yes… your internship. How are you finding it?"

Tears stung the backs of my eyes as I explained what it was like working at Salt House. Every word reminded me of my dad as I described the building. I could no longer visualize the building without remembering how it felt to be pinned against it.

Vivienne nodded along, remaining politely interested in everything I had to say. Every so often she'd hold up a dress for my opinion and given the fact I had zero fashion sense, all I kept saying was 'that one looks lovely'. In all honesty, Vivienne didn't seem to be paying that much attention to the outfits (or my opinion of them) and I started to wonder if she'd really invited me up here for some other reason.

Saving Amy

"So, are you going to tell me what's going on with you and Richard now?"

What! I sat up sharply - stunned by her invasive, direct question. Then it dawned on me why she really brought me upstairs.

"I don't know what you mean," I tried to lie, but my treacherous cheeks betrayed me and flushed ruby-red.

"You seem edgy towards him. Come on, what's he done?" she asked in a sympathetic tone that I didn't have the balls (or the heart) to ignore.

"He's done nothing. It's me," I admitted, and then dropped my head in embarrassment. "He's been talking to someone, a *lot*, lately, and I feel like he's purposely keeping whoever it is from me."

Vivienne hung the purple dress she'd been holding back on the rail and then came to sit beside me on the chaise longue.

"I know it sounds ridiculous."

"It absolutely doesn't," Vivienne said, placing a warm, comforting hand on my knee. "Men are very tricky creatures, Amy. You just need to learn how to interpret them." I breathed a small giggle. "You know he's not having an affair though, don't you? I know my son – he would never hurt you like that." I smiled as the love she felt for Richard warmed the air around us.

"I know that. I know he loves me... he's the only person who ever has," I said and then instantly regretted it. I'd forgotten that Vivienne didn't know the full extent of my fucked-up-ness and I hoped she didn't press me to elaborate.

Thankfully she didn't, choosing instead to pull me into a one-armed hug. Her unexpected closeness took me aback and my body stiffened under her hold. I still wasn't one-hundred percent used to it – not when it came out of the blue... Richard was the only person who'd ever held me like that.

I think she sensed my discomfort and pulled away, tucking a rogue strand of her honey-blonde hair behind her ear.

"You know, it's probably just *Joanna*." *Wow*, she said her name with the same distaste as I did. "He knows you two don't get along and is probably just trying to avoid fuelling the fire." It was like a 100watt light bulb springing to life in my mind. I hadn't even considered... *her*. Not for a couple of weeks anyway. It made so much sense.

"I don't know what it is with her. I'll never understand why he can't see her for what she really is," Vivienne said acidly, shaking her head and wrinkling her nose in disgust.

Why? What is she?

"A lying, scheming trollop..." she tacked on and I was stunned into a jaw-dropping silence. Not that I disagreed of course. I had just convinced myself that it was all in my head.

I flashed Vivienne an I-couldn't-agree-with-you-more look. My subconscious was itching for more information but I didn't think I was brave enough to ask.

"What did she do?" I blurted out before I had time to talk myself out of it. I clasped my hands across my knee and eagerly awaited the dirt.

"She broke his heart," she said soberly and I think she just broke mine. I felt it shatter into a billion pieces inside my chest, knowing that Joanna even *had* Richard's heart to break.

Saving Amy

"But he said *he* broke up with *her*," I uttered, my voice rich with confusion… and heartbreak. "Did he lie to me?"

"Oh, he did. And then when she couldn't accept it, she told him she was pregnant."

What. The. Fuck. I scanned the floor of the room disguised as a closet – certain my heart had leapt out of my chest and landed on it somewhere.

"She wasn't of course!" The words sped from Vivienne's throat. "Sorry, I really should have said that sooner."

No shit! I took a deep, rattling breath and realized it was the first one I'd taken since I heard the word 'pregnant'.

"So, she *lied*?" I asked, assuming I must have misunderstood. Surely even *she* couldn't stoop so low. More importantly, surely Richard couldn't forgive something like that.

"Yes, she did. She let my son believe he was going to be a father for three whole months. The lie wasn't sustainable of course. I think she planned to tell him she'd miscarried, but her web of deceit had started to spin far beyond her control. I don't quite know how Richard found out – he's never told me. All I know is that wretched woman destroyed my son that day and I will *never* forgive her for that."

Holy mother fucking hell… How do you possibly respond to this kind of revelation?

"I hadn't seen him flash a single smile since that day. Not until the day he came home and told me about you," she admitted with a warm smile. She grasped my hand and squeezed it gently, almost as if she was *thanking* me. "Of course, we'd just lost Kate too. It was all too much for him. He simply couldn't cope." She bowed her head at the memory. Possibly so I couldn't see the tears burning her eyes. "We barely saw him for the next few years. He cut himself off from us completely."

I felt like I was going to cry. The thought of Richard being unhappy stabbed into my heart like a knife, draining it completely of life. I inhaled deeply, blinking the threat of tears away. *Oh, Richard...*

"From everybody except *her* of course," she added, crinkling her nose again.

"Why would he still talk to her after that? *How* could he?" I asked, genuine bewilderment tainting my voice.

"I honestly have no idea. All I've ever been told is that they 'worked through it'," she said, using her fingers as quotation marks. "He knows what I think of her but he refuses to take me on. He closes down at the mention of her name and I'm too afraid to push it."

Vivienne, afraid? Afraid of Richard? Surely not...

"I couldn't bare it if I lost him again."

So that's what she's afraid of. We had more in common that I realized.

"I'm sure that won't happen. Richard loves you very much," was the only thing I could think of to say. She smiled gratefully at me but I couldn't fathom why – I only offered her the truth.

"He loves you too, you know? I've never seen him so happy."

"I struggle to believe that," I admitted honestly. Vivienne cocked her head to the side and pursed her perfectly pruned eyebrows, looking puzzled. "About making him happy, I mean."

"Oh, Amy, why would you think such a thing? He *adores* you!" I was so tempted to reel off my list of flaws but that would take us into next week.

"I don't have half as much to offer him as he does me," I said, shrugging my shoulders.

"You make him laugh – it'd been so long since he'd laughed. You make him smile… and you love him. He doesn't need anything else." Traitorous heat flooded my cheeks and I raised my palm over my face in an effort to hide my embarrassment.

"I sometimes think that I come with so much baggage though. Far more than he deserves to have to deal with," I blurted without thinking, running the risk of exposing my fucked-up-ness again.

"And now you know about his past with Joanna, and the fact that – as much as it pains me to say it – she still means something to him… do you think any less of him? Do you think he's not worthy of you?"

"No! Of course not," I pronounced a little too loudly and then threw my hand over my mouth, hoping I didn't draw attention from anyone downstairs. Though on reflection, that was probably impossible in a house this size.

"Exactly. You can't choose who you fall in love with, Amy. It's written in the stars." I smiled warmly at her, cherishing the delicate dance my heart was doing over her beautifully simple outlook on life.

"That's such a nice way of viewing things. How do you stay so positive? I mean, you've been through so much. You all have…" My question might seem bizarre to normal people, but it was one that'd been burning a hole in the back of my mind for as long as

I could remember. Positivity was such an alien concept – one I was certain I hadn't been born with.

"Believe me that isn't always the case," she answered, smiling her warm motherly smile. "But I've discovered, if you're ever feeling bad, or lost, or hurt… help someone and it goes away. My charity keeps me strong in that respect. It's extremely difficult to feel down knowing you have helped somebody else transform their life." I smiled half-heartedly at Vivienne. If that was the answer to positivity, I was screwed. What help could I be to anybody?

"And whether you believe it or not, you *have* helped my son." I forced a smile but my subconscious was crying with laughter at the ridiculous notion. "You didn't see him for all those years after Kate… after Joanna. He was like a robot – moving and talking when prompted, but there was no life inside him. *You* brought my boy back to life. *You* put the sparkle back into those gorgeous green eyes of his. *You*. Nothing will ever convince me otherwise."

My heart was fluttering at one thousand beats per minute and I was suddenly desperate to get back to Richard. I wanted to hold him, squeeze him and never let him go. I wanted – *needed* – to tell him how much I loved him, and thank him for loving *me*.

"Therefore nothing else matters to me," she continued. "Your past, your age… it's irrelevant. You'll always be the girl who saved my son and for that I'll never be able to repay you."

"Thank you, Vivienne," I said and then I did something I had *never* done to anyone except Richard before… I reached out and hugged her first. She reciprocated, embracing me ever so gently. Her arms were as light and graceful as a sheet of silk enfolding around me. I wondered if this was what having a mother was like. A *real* mother anyway. One who gave a crap whether you lived or died.

Richard was so lucky to have such a beautiful, compassionate woman in his life…and now, so was I.

"We'd best make our way downstairs before Richard sends out a search party for you," Vivienne pronounced as if she knew all too well just how protective Richard was of me. I smiled and nodded my head.

"And remember, about those phone calls… just ask him. He won't lie to you. I know he won't."

Hmm, ask *him?* The principle seemed ever so rational and straightforward coming from Vivienne's mouth. Maybe that was because Vivienne *was* rational. In my screwed up mind however, I had built the whole situation up into a huge un-climbable mountain – assuming Richard would take it as me being a pathetic, jealous control freak.

Which I totally am.

I role-played the scenario in my head. Richard's phone would bleep. He'd pick it up and look at the screen. 'Hey, who's that from?' I would ask innocently. 'Oh, it's just–*insert name here-*'.

Hmm, sounded simple enough.

"Wait, we didn't choose a dress," I suddenly remembered as we turned to the door.

"Would you be annoyed if I told you that's not really why I asked you up here?" Vivienne replied with her hands outstretched in the praying position. I giggled and shook my head.

"I actually thought as much," I admitted with a coy smile and then she took my hand and led me towards the grand, spiral staircase.

****

Back in the car on our way home Richard eyed me up curiously, flipping his gaze between me and the road. I pretended not to notice and rested my head against the window, admiring the night sky closing in on us.

"What did my mom want you for?" he asked skeptically.

Shit… a direct question.

"To choose a dress, remember?" I lied, keeping my eyes on the stars illuminating the black sky and trying to keep my dishonest voice even. Even though I wasn't looking at him I could almost feel his incredulous eyebrow rising.

"Amy, my mother *never* chooses her own clothes. She pays a young stylist named Gino a small fortune for that privilege."

Damn.

"*So*, come on… what did she want with you?"

Ah, shit… Bossy Doctor had arrived which basically meant I was screwed.

"She wanted to talk about… *you*," I admitted, the word 'you' sticking to my lips.

"Oh *really*? And what about *me*?"

"Not just you… us. She's just looking out for her little boy, that's all."

"What do you mean?" He sounded angry. "She didn't upset you did she?"

Saving Amy

"Of course not! Richard, your mother is adorable. I doubt she could ever upset me," I assured and meant every word. "In fact, she thinks I'm the best thing that's ever happened to you," I said smugly, teasingly, even though I didn't believe it.

"That's because you are," he answered seriously, not a trace of the playful tone I used on him.

I purposely omitted the whole 'Joanna' part of our conversation, deciding that was something I just didn't have the emotional strength to discuss tonight. Besides, in reality there was probably no point – I doubted Richard would have a single word said against the psycho bitch.

"How are the arms?" Richard asked carefully. For a brief second I wondered what the hell he was on about, but then the whole lot came crashing down on top of me and I felt like I was trapped inside a building being demolished – my dad, the fear, scrabbling my arms to shreds…

"They're okay. A little sore I guess." I ran my finger under my sleeve, tracing the coarse, dried-up lesions. I made the mistake of wincing and of course Richard noticed.

"I'll check them over when we get home."

"Okay," I said, too tired to tell him he was worrying unnecessarily. Not that he'd have taken a blind bit of notice if I had.

Back at the apartment I was sitting on the corner suite with my arms caked in some kind of foul smelling ointment with a long complicated medical name. Richard was in the kitchen making hot chocolate and my eyes reveled in the sight of his delicious half-naked body (dressed only in gray sweat pants and Armani cologne) gliding gracefully between the stove and the cupboards.

A few clinks and tinkles later Richard walked towards me with two steady hands holding tall white mugs in front of him. He handed me my mug and lowered himself down beside me. I smiled warmly when I noticed he'd decorated it with marshmallows arranged into the shape of a heart. The mug burned my fingers, letting me know it was too hot to drink right away so I set it down on the coffee table to cool down. Richard copied, and then stretched his arms out, cocking his head for me to lean into them.

I eagerly shuffled closer to him so the edges of our thighs were pressed tightly together, then I nestled my cheek against his warm, bare chest and he wrapped his arm behind my back, stroking it gently. My heavy eyes couldn't seem to stop themselves from closing (not that I tried very hard) and I found myself drifting off to the harmonious thrum of his heart beating beneath my ear.

Then it came… an ill-timed beep crashing unwelcome into the silent air. The high-pitched ding physically crawled under my skin, itching as it skittered its way around my nervous system. I was seriously beginning to doubt my sanity. A cell phone notification tone should *not* have been able to rile me that much.

I decided to put my cunning master plan into action – it was now or never. Richard shifted in his seat and peered down to see if I was asleep. I smiled at him (although it was a little forced) and then sat up. He didn't reach for his cell straight away and I wondered if this was intentional – to throw me off the scent so to speak. He caved (curiosity getting the better of him) after eighty-three seconds. Yes, the whole thing had sent me so crazy I actually counted.

Right, here goes nothing…

"Who's that?" I asked, aiming for nonchalance and hoping I pulled it off. My heart was racing in anticipation. Vivienne's words echoed in my mind, 'he won't lie to you'. I guessed I was about to find out.

An expression that could only be interpreted as 'oh shit' descended on his beautiful face.

"It's just Joanna," he muttered under his breath as if he was hoping I wouldn't hear.

Don't overreact. Don't overreact. Don't overreact.

"She's my *friend*, Amy," Richard rationalized with a don't-start-Amy glint in his eye.

"What? I didn't say anything!"

"You were thinking it."

How the hell does he know?

"No I wasn't!" I protested (*lied*) through pouting lips. He ambled back over to me and reclaimed his seat on the couch.

"*Amy*," he said in a condescending tone before brushing a finger over my lips. "These beautiful, sulking lips come out to play whenever my cell rings lately."

Shit… he's noticed.

"I'm not blind, you know. But, Joanna and I have always spoken a lot, that's just how we are. We're friends." He shrugged his shoulders as he tried to justify their outlandish 'friendship'.

"Even after what she did to you?"

Oh fuck, the words left my mouth before my brain had chance to process them.

"Oh, I see now." *Crap*. He was pissed. He was rubbing his forearm as he stood from his seat like he couldn't bear to be near me. "I bet my mother couldn't wait to fill you in." He turned away from me and my heart flopped out of my mouth.

"It wasn't like that. Richard, I'm sorry. I shouldn't have mentioned it." He turned back around, his expression softening. "I can't help it. I guess I'm just… *jealous*." Yep, I'd just admitted what a possessive crazy bitch I was out loud. An amused smile started to play around the edges of Richard's plump, velvety lips.

"Are you laughing at me?" I mock scolded, the tense atmosphere dissipating by the second.

"I wouldn't dare," he said in a low, masculine voice – trying but failing to sound serious. We both caved and gave in to the fits of laughter bubbling up through our throats. Then Richard perched next to me, taking my face in his hands and turning the atmosphere from carefree to staid just by looking at me.

"I know what she did to me-"

"Richard, you don't have to explain," I said, talking over him. He placed a finger over my lips, cutting me off.

"Yes, I do. Because you are the one person who deserves to know *everything* about me. I'll never forget what she did, but I *had* to forgive her. Living with so much hate inside of you is just… soul destroying." He dropped his hands from my face and took my hands, entwining our fingers together.

"We're just friends, Amy. You on the other hand are *everything* to me. Understand?" I blushed crimson and smiled apologetically.

Saving Amy

"I'm sorry," I muttered, too embarrassed to make eye contact.

"What for?" he asked, seeming genuinely confounded.

"For being a bunny boiling psycho of a girlfriend," I breathed, biting my tongue to stop a smile escaping. He maneuvered his face in front of mine so we were nose-to-nose and I had no choice but to fall into his hypnotic green eyes.

"Well, you're my bunny boiling psycho. Got it?" And then he smiled his breath-taking smile – the one that turned my insides to mush.

I leaned forward and squeezed him close to me, but then I scuffed my grazed arm on the edge of the couch and the day's events came flooding back to me… drowning me. I started to cry.

"You're exhausted. You have coped amazingly well today. I'm so proud of you," he whispered into my hair, stroking my back and trying to shush the tears away. "But you've been through so much. Let's get you to bed. You need to rest," Bossy Doctor ordered and I willingly obeyed and followed him to the bedroom.

Chapter Sixteen

Vanessa insisted I take a week's leave to 'recover' from my ordeal. I agreed immediately. Whenever I pictured the office I couldn't seem to shake the image of my dad standing in the shadows with his sinister blue eyes, waiting to get me alone. I flinched at the thought. I knew I couldn't hide forever of course. Today was Friday, which meant I only had the weekend to try and rid myself of this sickening fear bubbling away inside me, ripping through my dreams and cursing my every waking thought.

The pain, the anxiety, was worse when I was alone. Richard possessed an almost supernatural ability to distract my mind, to make me feel safe. The hours passed impossibly slowly while he was at the hospital and as yet I'd not been able to summon enough courage to leave the apartment, consumed with some irrational fear that my dad will be waiting for me on the other side.

I picked up my cell in an effort to distract myself from thinking. Bejeweled Blitz was always a guaranteed escape. There was a text waiting for me when I unlocked the screen.

```
Rob: How's it going Aims? Hope ur
ok. The Dragon must ask me 50
times a day how ur doin so hurry
up n get ur ass back here so I
```

```
don't hav to deal with her!
Missing u at lunch times.
```

I smiled while I pondered my reply. Rob had sent me a handful of similar texts over the course of the week, reaffirming my opinion that he was a great guy and a great friend.

```
    Me: I'm good. B Back Monday
- Big Mac's on me! Xoxo
```

I caught every ten minutes pass on the pendulum clock. It was now only three hours and eighteen minutes until Richard was due home. Then I could breathe again. I felt as excited as a child on Christmas knowing he would be by my side for a whole day tomorrow. Or at least, how I *imagined* a child was supposed to feel on Christmas Eve. For me, it had always been 'just another day'.

My heart started to flutter as I allowed myself to wonder what *this* Christmas would be like. My first Christmas with Richard. My first Christmas without the threat of arguments or beatings. My first Christmas with an actual Christmas tree. In effect… my first Christmas.

Of course we had Thanksgiving first. It was only five weeks away and Vivienne had everything planned right down to the color of the napkins. According to Richard, Thanksgiving was a *huge* affair for the Lewis clan with Vivienne and Alistair opening their home to friends and family far and near, colleagues and even Finding Hope beneficiaries with nowhere else to go. I sighed heavily as I struggled to summon the enthusiasm I knew I should be feeling for my first festive season. I decided to put it out of my mind for now. Who knew how I'd feel in five weeks time.

Miserable as ever… Oh, fuck off.

Still in my pink satin pajamas I lay down on the four-seater, curled myself into the fetal position and buried my head in the soft leather. I closed my eyes which were puffy from too much sleep and even more crying. Sleep made time pass more quickly you see and so hopefully, if I could sleep away another two hours and forty-three minutes, then Richard would be home.

I'd barely closed my eyes when the sound of the door latch springing open startled them open. I was momentarily paralyzed – frozen to the leather. My dad's malevolent eyes were etched onto my eyelids, making my eyes sting because I was too afraid to blink. The door slammed closed and my heart leapt up into my throat, choking me.

No! I screamed inwardly and leapt defiantly off the couch, refusing to lie there scared and helpless, allowing him to finish what he started. I ran on my tiptoes to the kitchen, picking up a crystal vase along the way, although I wasn't sure what I intended to do with it. Then I crouched down behind the glossy white island and waited for my attacker.

Thumping footsteps grew louder and louder, closing in on me. The vibration of each thud rattled through my petrified body as a tall, menacing silhouette glided eerily slowly across the wall until it stopped in front of me. Taking a deep breath I squeezed my eyes shut, catapulted to my feet and blindly threw the vase in the direction of the shadow.

Saving Amy

A jarring smash followed and I screamed all traces of air out of my lungs.

"Get away from me!" Strong hands weighed my shoulders down and I flung my arms in the air preparing to beat the living crap out of my assailant.

"Shh, shh, Amy, it's me. It's just me." My eyes sprang open and I had never been so happy to see those glistening green eyes in front of me.

"Oh, Richard!" He held me at arms length, examining me with his eyes. "You're not supposed to be back yet. I thought - I thought you were… *him*."

Overwhelmed and completely and utterly exhausted, I collapsed to the floor.

When I came round I was lying back on the four-seater with my head sunk into a plump feather pillow and my body tucked into a red fleece blanket. Richard was by my side in seconds, kneeling on the floor and stroking my hair, his eyes assessing mine.

"I'm sorry about your vase," was the first thing that popped into my mind.

"*Really?*" he asked with a mischievous glint in his eye.

"Of course! Why wouldn't I be?" I asked, furrowing my eyebrows, befuddled by his response.

"Maybe because it was a gift from Joanna." A wicked smile illuminated his face and I noticed he was biting his bottom lip to stop a laugh exploding straight through it.

"Oh. Well, maybe I'm not *that* sorry."

Ugh. Will I ever get through one *day without hearing or thinking of her name?*

"In fact, if I *had* known, I probably would've smashed it sooner." Richard threw his head back, exposing his smooth, muscular neck, no longer able to contain his laughter.

I couldn't help but smile at the sight of him - head back, Adam's apple bobbing up and down, tears of laughter sparkling in the corners of his striking green eyes... He looked so carefree this way, so young, so... beautiful.

"I'm sorry I scared you. I just wanted to surprise you."

"No, *I'm* sorry. I just don't know how much longer I can go on like this."

"Baby, you don't have to go on like this. You can't," he said, brushing his thumb over my cheekbone and nearing his face to mine. "You can't let him destroy your life. If you do, he's won." I shook my head, trying to form some kind of reply out of the words tumbling around inside. "Amy, you have been through so much in your life and come out the other side. You *can* do this."

Confusion swept over my face. He was right, of course. My father had caused me pain far worse than this and yet somehow I still managed to function (be happy even) knowing he was still roaming the streets. So why did this feel so much harder? So much more impossible?

Maybe because now I had so much to lose. There was a time I had nothing for him to ruin. I didn't care what he took from me. I wouldn't have cared if he'd ended me completely.

But I couldn't lose Richard...

"Amy, you *can* do this." Richard repeated himself. "We can do it *together*."

Saving Amy

I nodded meekly. *I can do this. We can do this.* I repeated the mantra in my mind, fighting desperately to believe it.

"We *can* do this," I said and then took up residence in his outstretched arms. *I can do this. We can do this...* My subconscious remained skeptical but I was determined to give it my best shot regardless. My life had only just begun and I wanted it back. I *would* get it back.

****

"Chop chop! Time to get up!" Richard chirped as he twisted the blinds open. Dazzling sunlight pierced my eyes and I huffed and groaned before throwing a pillow over my face. Of course the annoying bastard removed it.

"No time for that. Now get your lazy ass out of bed," he teased with that mischievous wink which made being mad an impossibility. I rolled onto my side, closing my eyes and ignoring him.

"Don't make me pour water on you!" he threatened. It may sound ridiculous but he had in fact done that to me before. A full pitcher of cold water (*with* ice) straight over my face because he wanted to get to the grocery store before it got busy. Seriously...

"Fine!" I sat up, resting my back against the headboard. "Where are we going?" I asked through a yawn, noticing he was all set for the day. He was dressed in dark blue jeans with a black belt and a black turtleneck sweater, and his auburn hair was freshly washed and styled to its usual disheveled perfection. *Yummy...*

"We're going on a day out," he announced with a wicked grin that told me he was giving away nothing.

"A day out where?" I asked pointlessly. He tapped his forefinger against his nose.

"Somewhere fun!" Yep, he was disclosing nothing.

Worth a try...

"Fun?"

"Fun. Now get dressed," he ordered playfully and then turned to leave the bedroom. "Oh, and wrap up warm," he added over his shoulder.

Warm? So, wherever we were going was outdoors I could only assume.

****

We'd been driving for fifty-five minutes and Richard had remained cunningly silent the whole time.

"Close your eyes," Richard said as he pulled off the interchange.

"For how long?" I asked in a how-long-are-you-going-to-keep-this-up tone.

"Just do it," he replied, feigning exasperation. I rolled my eyes and then did as I was told.

"How much longer?" I pressed. At least five minutes must have passed and my eyelids were aching from forcing them closed against their will.

"Nearly there. No peeking." The urge to ignore him and steal a sneaky glance was more than a little tempting but I decided against it, unsure of how convincing my fake 'surprised' face would be.

Saving Amy

Moments later the purr of the car ceased as Richard killed the engine. Curiosity flooded my veins and I found myself clapping like a deranged sea lion in anticipation.

"Open your eyes."

"What the…"

I looked ahead at a set of enormous arched red entrance gates with a bright blue and red steel sign which read 'Welcome to Twisted Towers Amusement Park' attached to it. Beyond the gates was a mass of multi-colored steel twisting and dipping in every direction. Rollercoasters, carousels, and sky-high steel bars throwing carriages down its vertical drop into a huge black hole…

My eyes widened in astonishment, excitement and a fair sized dollop of fear.

"You ready?" Richard asked with a wicked glint in his eyes as he clicked off his seatbelt.

"I-I-" I wanted to say 'no, I've never been on a rollercoaster in my life and I'm absolutely shitting my pants' but the words kept getting lost in the bile rising up my throat.

"Come on," he ordered enthusiastically, cocking his head for me to follow him. Hesitantly, I unbuckled myself and stepped out of the car.

Richard was already by my side with his hand out for me to take. The cold air slapped me in the face and I was glad I followed his advice and dressed in a vest top, t-shirt *and* cream chenille sweater with skinny-jeans and knee high boots for the occasion.

He guided me through the red gates and into the maze of death trap steel spirals. A short thin girl with purple hair slipped a blue wristband onto Richard's wrist (her cheeks beaming as she eyed up the ridiculously handsome man in front of her) and then turned to me to do the same, not bothering to look at me at all.

"Let's ease you in gently," Richard teased with an impish wink as we approached the swirling merry-go-round.

I giggled like an idiot as he pulled me up the three brass trimmed steps and then lifted me onto a pink and white wooden horse with a painted golden mane. Richard took up position of chief rider at the front (typical boy) and I snaked my arms around his waist. A rumble and a judder followed and then we were spinning - twirling into the icy breeze, up, down, round and round with a playful piano tune dancing into our cold red ears.

Next, we hit the teacups and my stomach churned as Richard spun us around faster and faster, thrusting all his weight into turning the wheel as hard as he could. My cheeks stung against the cold air and laughter (such, intense, unstoppable laughter) burned my throat. Richard was in his element, his green eyes wide and glistening with child-like excitement. It was like he was reliving his childhood and it was such a precious sight.

After hitting the dodgems and the haunted house we took a much needed break (for me anyway) and settled ourselves down on a wooden picnic table under the seclusion of a circle of bare oak trees that led onto the nature trail. Richard handed me a Styrofoam cup of hot chocolate and a stick of pink cotton candy bigger than my head.

"Hmm, it's stickier than I thought it would be," I said, smacking my lips together at the unfamiliar taste.

Saving Amy

"Are you saying you've never had cotton candy before?" he asked, widening his eyes and snapping his back upright in his seat like I'd just told him I was born with a ten inch dick.

"Nope, never." And why would I? He must have forgotten that up until the day he saved my life in every way possible, I spent most of my life hiding away in my bedroom.

"And I can't say I've missed out. It's actually pretty disgusting," I decided, feeling queasy as the crystals of pure sugar dissolved on my tongue.

"You're probably right. But you can't visit a theme park without cotton candy. It's the law," he teased through a soft, irresistible laugh.

I rinsed the sickening stickiness from my mouth with a sip of my hot chocolate, which as it happened tasted jack shit like chocolate. I wrinkled my nose and put the cup back on the bench.

"Something wrong?"

"It tastes like piss."

"You've tasted piss? Any good?" he tried to say seriously but his smile betrayed him. If only I'd had a pillow to throw at him right now. I curled my frozen fingers around the cup of hot piss disguised as chocolate and the warmth brought some much needed life back into them. At least it came in useful for something.

"Right, time to take things up a notch." Richard rubbed his hands together like an evil villain whose plan was about to come to fruition. I followed his gaze towards a gigantic rollercoaster that spread across the majority of the park and twisted and looped in every direction.

Oh shit...

"Richard I don't think-" He cut me off with an ice-cold finger over my lips, which were turning a deathly shade of blue.

"Trust me," he said with a devilish wink.

"I do trust *you*. It's that pile of rusty steel I don't trust." Richard threw his head back and laughed. I swear if my hands hadn't been so cold I would've ripped them straight out of my pockets and punched that smile straight off his face.

"Jesus Christ! Did that thing just go upside down?" A wicked smile was the only response I got.

My jaw smacked into the concrete on the ground beneath my feet as I watched The Tremor (although in my opinion it should've been called The Ride of Impending Death) drawing to a close. Our turn came around too soon and my heart slammed against my ribs as the strong (hopefully strong) padded bars lowered themselves down over my head and locked (hopefully locked) into place around my chest. I was absolutely shitting myself, clenching my ass cheeks together to stop me *literally* shitting myself, and the damn thing hadn't even started moving.

I could feel Richard's smile boring in to the side of my face but I couldn't look at him for fear I might lean over and kill him. At that moment in time I was livid with him. I was about to loop the loop to my death and it was all his fault.

Stupid, irresponsible, gorgeous bastard.

The red light above the carriages flipped to green and I decided this was the time to close my eyes. We set off with a thunderous clatter that stopped my heart from beating. Then we moved slowly at first – going upwards, I *think*. Before stopping completely. I waited anxiously for it to start moving again but it didn't, causing sickening fear to pulse through me.

It's broken. I knew it. Oh, sweet Jesus we're all going to die!

Struggling to come to terms with my imminent death, I did something that could only be described as stupid and utterly reckless… I opened my eyes.

"*Holy fuck!*" I yelled out loud. We were teetering on the edge of an almost vertical drop. The trees that towered above us on the picnic table looked like they belonged in a doll's house. And then…

"Aaaaaaargh!" My stomach catapulted out of my body and I could feel my brain beating crap out of the walls of my skull. Before I squeezed my petrified eyes closed again I caught a glimpse of Richard's arms raised high in the air. *How the hell? My* hands were welded to the metal bar in front of me, certain that if I let go I would plummet to my death.

It was a good job my stomach was already splattered on the ground below because it would without a doubt have been spilling it's contents right now, as I was flown upside down twice in succession. Soon after, I was lulled into another false sense of security when we stopped for yet another dramatic pause. And then…bam! We were diving towards the ground so fast my teeth smacked into my tongue. *Ow!*

"Amy, you can open your eyes. We've stopped." Richard nudged my arm but I didn't open my eyes. Knowing what a thrill he seemed to get out of my suffering I pondered whether he was lying, and if really we were hovering in the middle of the sky again waiting for another violent dose of brain-shake.

In fact, I only reacquainted myself with the gift of sight when I heard the hiss of the bars being airlifted back above my head. I flashed a how-the-hell-could-you-do-that-to-me look at Richard and the bastard couldn't contain his laughter.

"You're green!" he said, his voice rich with unwelcome amusement. My stomach seemed to have found its way back inside my body and wouldn't give in reminding me that one wrong move and it would spill everything it'd ever eaten.

Ugh.

"Okay, we'll stick to the *baby* rides from now on," Richard mocked, biting his bottom lip to suppress the laughter he so obviously wanted to let out.

"I need to sit down," was all I could muster as I searched for my equilibrium.

"We've just *been* sitting down."

"*Richard!*" I scolded because I was *so* not in the mood to be laughed at right now. Trying to breathe, walk in a straight line and swallow back vomit all at the same time was enough to deal with.

After ten minutes of deep breathing with my head between my legs I was finally able to take Richard's ridicule without the overpowering urge to smack him in the face. A further ten minutes down the line and I even managed to laugh myself. I can honestly say a rollercoaster was the single most terrifying moving thing I had ever had the misfortune to sit in. Though, the sheer elation from making it out alive kind of made up for it.

Saving Amy

The ride home was a good one. The atmosphere in the car was feathery light, tranquil…happy. Out of the blue, an overwhelming rush of inexplicable emotion struck me and an unexpected tear trickled miserably down my face. Naturally, Richard and his inbuilt tear radar noticed immediately.

"What's wrong?" he pressed gently, his eyes intermittently flitting between me and the road. I shrugged because I was as puzzled as him. Beginning to sense his alarm however, I forced out an answer.

"I'm just really happy. You make me really happy."

But for how long?

And there was my answer. *That* right there was why I was crying. I stared out towards the blur of naked trees as the irony of the death defying rollercoaster swiped me across the face. Suddenly, I was very aware of the definite pattern my life seemed to have developed in recent months. Like that rollercoaster, I was either flying high – soaring amongst the most exhilarating feelings of happiness, or I was crashing back down – being dragged into the black hole, into the depths of despair. There was no in-between. There was no *normal*.

At that very moment (that happy, beautiful moment) life was damn near perfect. I had the dream job I once believed to be utterly unattainable, I had a place in a family – a real life family who seemed to genuinely care for me, and most important of all…I had Richard. I was happy. So why couldn't I shift the feeling that sooner or later it would all get pulled from under me, knocking me flat on my face? Sometimes I wondered if living was easier when all I had to expect was the worst. At least I knew where I stood.

"I'm happy too," Richard said with a warm smile, eyes set firmly on the road.

****

Back in the apartment (more importantly, back in the warm) we perched on the edge of the corner suite, tucking into the six different tubs and boxes of Chinese takeout we grabbed on the way home.

"I've had so much fun today," I said before biting a sizeable chunk off a spring roll.

"Me too. But then I always have fun with you." He winked at me and it sent bashful waves of heat through my cheeks.

How does he still do that?

I was lying across Richard's lap, stuffed to the brim with Chinese food. There was an old black and white movie playing on the sixty-inch flat screen though neither of us were really watching it – our eyes are too busy with each other. Richard was beautiful as usual, his vibrant green eyes twinkling under the ceiling lights and his auburn hair set into a windswept position from our theme park adventure.

"I love you," I felt compelled to tell him. His lips turned up into a heartfelt smile, stealing a beat from my heart.

"I love you too."

Richard lowered his face to mine, his sweet breath caressing my face as he brushed my lips with his, sending delicious tingles all the way through my body. Then… his cell phone rang, shattering the moment into a billion pieces. Richard rolled his eyes and then continued to kiss me. My insides were doing a victory dance. *Amy one... cell phone nil!*

He twisted his fingers into my hair, clutching me closer to him. Then he shifted his body, sliding out from underneath me before rolling me onto my back and positioning himself on top – his lips never breaking contact with mine. Then another unwelcome ring flooded the air...

"Oh for fuck's sake," he breathed as he reluctantly pulled his lips away. "I'll be right back," he muttered through a sigh and then he was on his feet, heading towards the fireplace where his cell was vibrating relentlessly.

"Richard Lewis," he barked down the line. At least it wasn't *her*. He'd have recognized her number. "I can't... I'm busy... well, who's tonight's on call? What about John, can he not do it..." His tone was curt (Bossy Doctor style) and he ran his fingers through his messy hair - presumably because his forearm was preoccupied raising the phone to his ear. "Well, it seems I don't have much choice... yes... okay... tell him I want to see him in my office first thing Monday... I'll be there as soon as I can."

He snapped the phone shut and I sighed as he walked cautiously towards me because I knew what was coming.

"I've got to go into work for a couple of hours," said warily, like a child owning up to raiding the cookie jar. "I'm really sorry. The on call's only gone and turned up pissed as a newt. There's no one else to cover." I bit my lip to stifle an immature giggle that was rippling its way up through my throat. "I'll try not to be too long," he said as he bent down to kiss my forehead. And then he was gone. Without running a comb through his fucked-up hair I might add.

Seeing as though my blissful evening snuggled up with the most beautiful man in the universe had been ruined I decided to be productive. I took myself through to the study and removed the manuscripts I'd rescued from the slush pile out of my workbag. As I started to sift through them I was interrupted by a text from Julie.

```
Julie: O.M.G. I have just been
asked out by the sexiest living
creature on the planet! How's my
girl? Miss U xoxo
```

Well, it didn't take her long to get over the love of her life. It'd only been eight days since he 'broke her heart'. I rolled my eyes and tapped my reply.

```
Me: I'm great. Loving the job.
Can't wait to fill u in. I'll call
u tomorrow. Love u 2 xo
```

Julie didn't know about the latest episode with my father. Probably because I hadn't told her and I didn't intend to. I didn't want such a heavy conversation with Julie. Sometimes I think it was her wardrobe dilemmas and rants about guys that kept me sane. Okay so sane probably wasn't applicable to me, but she kept me smiling nonetheless.

Tucking my cell into the cup of my bra (I'd changed into my purple butterfly pajamas with no pockets) I picked up the manuscripts. I put the one

Saving Amy

about the girl murdering her father to one side - afraid it might cast a cloud of depression over my perfect day - and started reading the synopsis for what appeared to be a Young Adult love story.

So far the only fault I could find was that the pages weren't numbered. A simple human error but that was privy to how strict Vanessa was. On my second day she condemned a submission to the slush pile just because the envelope was addressed to Vanessa 'Hart' instead of 'Heart. She didn't even open it.

Three pages in and I was disturbed by the intercom buzzer. I noticed on my way in here that Richard had left his keys and wallet behind on the half-moon table and hearing the buzzer, a brief flash of hope surged through me, making my pulse quicken. But then I noted the time and realized it couldn't be him. Though it seemed like much longer, he'd only been gone half an hour.

"Hello," I answered after making my way to the receiver in the hall.

"It's Joanna. Can I come up?"

Not again… My body tensed and my hands balled into fists at the unwanted memory of the last time we were alone together.

"Sure," I said reluctantly and then tapped the button to open the main doors.

I literally shook myself off in an effort to dispel some of the anger that was already suffocating me. Then it came… the knock, *her* knock. *Ugh*. Grudgingly, I eased the door open, blinking like crazy to prepare my eyes for the sight of the vile creature they were about to land on.

"Richard's not here," I snapped, flinching at the realization this was exactly how our last little encounter began.

"Oh, shoot."

Shoot? Seriously? Sorry, how old are you?

"I just wanted to tell him I'll be running an hour behind next Saturday so we'll have to meet at eight instead."

What!

"Saturday?"

"Yes. I'm his date for the Little Wishes ball. Hasn't he told you?" A Grinch-like grin radiated from her smug face as she took great pleasure in revealing this information. I assumed she was talking about the ball Richard supposedly wasn't attending - the one he was too ashamed to take me to.

"No, not yet," I muttered under my breath. I planned to say 'yes of course he has, we tell each other everything' but she'd know I was lying due to the fact my jaw had just smacked into my feet.

"*Oops!*"

"Is that all?" I bit, urging her to fuck the hell off.

"Yes. Don't worry about passing the message on, I'll call him through the week." Unable to tolerate the sight or sound of her any longer, I slammed the door in her nasty, spiteful, vindictive, condescending, evil, twisted, fuck-ugly face.

Shrinking back from the door I slid to the floor and wiped away my tears, setting the rollercoaster that was my life in motion. *Why would he lie to me?* Well, technically he hadn't... yet. As far as I was aware he would be at home with me next Saturday. Maybe Joanna lied? It wouldn't be the first time after all. But...why would she? She must've known I'd talk to Richard about it.

A blinding light bulb clicked on in my mind. *That's exactly what she wants!* She *wanted* me to talk to him, *argue* with him, go all psycho jealous girlfriend on his ass - all in the knowledge that he'd probably go running straight to her. In that moment I decided to keep schtum, refusing to give her the satisfaction of causing yet another rift between us. Vivienne's words echoed in my mind again, 'he won't lie to you'. Yes. If it *was* true (*please God don't let it be true*) Richard would tell me. *Wouldn't he?*

I picked myself up off the floor and scurried back to the study to pack away my manuscripts. Then I took myself back to the safest place for me when my mind was in turmoil – bed, under the restraints of my quilt.

****

"Goodnight, beautiful," I heard Richard whisper into my ear as the mattress sank beside me. It roused me instantly, awakening the fire of betrayal that crackled in my heart until I fell asleep.

"I think Joanna might have called before. Did she manage to get hold of you?" I murmured, being purposely ambiguous.

"Um, no. Joanna knew I was at work. She was still there when I first arrived."

The conniving, devious little bitch... It would seem she came straight here knowing full well I was alone. Just like she probably knew I had no idea about their cozy little *date*. In fact, I was almost certain the reason she came was an attempt to reignite my fucked-up-ness in the hope I'd freak out and have a razor blade party, or hook up a bag of gear – proving to Richard what a pathetic mess I was.

The whole situation kept me awake all night. One burning question ricocheting through my mind as I tossed and turned.

Was Richard lying to me? Or was she?

Chapter Seventeen

Even with everything I had endured in my short life, this had got to be one of the most difficult weeks I'd ever lived through. Lying to Richard (or withholding information) ripped through my heart every time we were together. I often wondered if it was doing the same to him.

Work had been a welcome distraction and thankfully Vanessa's diary had been pretty crammed with out of house business meetings. Don't get me wrong I liked Vanessa, but ever since… *that* day, she looked at me like I was about to snap in half. She delegated hardly any work my way and must've asked how I was at least four times a minute. Life was just easier when I was alone.

It always had been…

Richard was peeling potatoes for dinner when the revelation (*LIE*) I'd been dreading spilled out of his mouth.

"I have to work Saturday. Mark's gone sick and there's no one to cover." And just like that he'd finally gone and done it. The one and only person I'd ever found the courage to trust had finally lied to me - just like everyone else. And so effortlessly too. His voice didn't falter - he didn't break eye contact.

I felt sick…

"Are you okay? You've been kind of… *off* all week," Richard asked tenderly, stroking my cheek. I shrank back from his touch.

You're lying to me! How could you?

"I think I'm getting a migraine," I said, shielding my face with my hand to hide my glassy, on the brink of crying eyes. "I think I'm going to head to bed." I was gone before he could reply.

Lying on my side in the huge, lonely bed, I drew my knees up to my chest and sobbed into my pillow. The only thing that was stopping my heart shattering into a million shards of shattered trust right now was hope. Hope that Richard would be honest with me… eventually.

****

Well it arrived. It was Saturday. As it stood, Richard was still 'working' this evening. A dense, uncomfortable atmosphere invaded the air between Richard and I, choking me and making me feel physically sick. He knew something was troubling me (he always did) but he didn't press me. I think he was putting it down to the after effects of the whole 'dad' situation. But in reality, the pain of Richard lying to me felt so much worse than that.

Part of me still thought (*hoped*) Joanna was the liar but I only had a few hours left to prove that was the case. If I didn't, this overwhelming sense of betrayal was going to eat me alive. It was going to hammer away inside my brain until all that was left was a pile of incomprehensible mush.

"Dammit! We're out of milk," Richard cussed as he stared into his black coffee. Richard couldn't stomach black coffee. It tasted too 'coffee-y' apparently. "I'm nipping to the store. You want to

Saving Amy

come?" he asked, reaching across the frosted glass fruit bowl by the microwave for his keys.

"No," I answered curtly, shaking my head.

"Back soon," he whispered into my ear, the collar of his navy blue shirt skimming my cheek as he kissed my hair. I nodded weakly and pulled away from him. My unease forced his eyebrows together and his face crumpled like his heart was being crushed. I hated myself for making him feel this way, but I hated the feeling of being lied to more.

I heard the thud of the door closing and put my plan into action – a plan which I only devised thirty seconds ago. I headed to the study first, ransacking the drawers and filing cabinet for any correspondence relating to the charity ball. After finding nothing I turned my attention to his laptop, sifting through a mountain of emails and pausing to read any from *her*. Again I emerged empty handed – everything was work related as far as my untrained eye could tell.

I closed down Richard's email program and gave the room one last glance to make sure I'd covered my tracks. Then I scurried to the bedroom. A rummage through the dark wood dresser and then under the bed brought up nothing so I turned my focus to the closet.

Bingo.

Richard's usually limp and empty rucksack was sitting bloated in the bottom of the closet beneath the hanging clothes. I dropped to my knees and paused as my fingers clasped the zipper, struggling to come to terms with the fact our relationship had come to *this*. Unzipping the bag went against everything I hoped our life together would stand for.

Sharing, trust, loyalty… but those torturous suspicion-fuelled emotions were destroying me from the inside out so I dismissed my qualms and ripped it open.

A choking lump swelled in my throat when I peered inside and saw Richard's smartest black tux folded pristinely inside. I fell back on my heels and threw my face in my hands.

Oh, Richard. How could you?

Although I wasn't naïve enough to think it wouldn't hurt, I could've at least understood to some degree if he was too ashamed to take me to this godforsaken ball (given my age, fucked-up-ness and the fact that I was an ex patient) but of all the people in the world he could take… why *her*?

Something had changed inside me, just now. Just like that. Suddenly, it felt wrong being here in his apartment. It felt wrong pretending everything was okay when I felt like I was slowly dying inside. It felt wrong that I was ever foolish enough to trust somebody.

Oh, Richard.

The slam of the door startled me and I quickly zipped up the rucksack and shoved it back where I found it. Then I climbed into bed, threw the covers over me and squeezed my tearstained eyes shut, pretending to sleep. Richard's boots clicked against the wood floor, getting louder as he came to find me. The sound came to a halt by the bed.

"Amy." He nudged my shoulder but I stayed 'asleep'. "Amy," he said a little louder.

Damn. He's not going to give up. Grudgingly, I peeled my eyes open.

"What?" I asked, standoffish.

Saving Amy

"Have you been crying?" he asked, concern saturating his voice.

"I've just got a headache," I mumbled and then rolled onto my other side so I couldn't see him. He perched himself on the edge of the mattress and trailed a finger up my spine. His touch was comforting and painful at the same time and slow, mournful tears started to trickle down my flushed cheeks.

"We need to get you checked out. You've been having them a lot lately. I'll make you an appointment with Doctor Pilling." I shrugged at him. "Can I get you anything? Tylenol? Water?"

"No," I snapped briskly, wishing he'd leave. Hearing the worry, the sadness in his voice was making everything so much harder.

"I'll leave you to sleep. Shout if you change your mind." He leaned down and kissed the back of my head, zapping my brain with a thousand unbearable emotions – confusion, anger, betrayal, love…

I must've lay hibernating under the quilt for an hour or more and now I really did have a throbbing, crying-induced headache. Gingerly rising to a sitting position, I felt like fifty sacks of shit.

An all-encompassing feeling that there was no going back from here plagued my mind. Being here with him, sharing the same air, was just too painful – far worse than any physical blow I had ever taken to my body.

It was the lies – it was unbearable. I liked to think (although I would have been monumentally pissed) I could have dealt with him going out with *her* if he'd just told me about it. I got it - they were friends. They worked at the same hospital. In some ways it even made sense. But to *lie* to me... I just couldn't handle it. If I didn't trust Richard, what was the point? What was the point of anything anymore?

A decision I always knew on some level I would make knifed into my heart. But it was the only way. I slid a small gray suitcase out from under the bed and quickly threw in an armful of clothes from the closet and my makeup bag from the dresser before Richard had chance to catch me. Then I stuffed it back under the bed while I conjured up a plan.

I sat, sobbing into my knees for almost half an hour and I was still clueless. I had no idea how to break it to him. I wasn't even sure *what it was* I was breaking to him. I had no idea where I would go, who I would stay with or even if I'd ever see him again.

I briefly considered calling Julie but then realized my job was here in Seattle. In turn that led me to think about whether I even had a job anymore. Would I be able to cope with the endless questions and sympathetic glares from Vanessa? Would Richard use Vanessa to get to me? They were friends after all, something else he'd lied to me about. Would he turn up at the office begging me to come home? The more I thought about it, the more convinced I became that my dream job was something I'd probably have to let go as well.

Where would I go? A hotel perhaps? I probably had enough of my paycheck left to buy me a few nights sleep, but then what? Leon's name popped unwillingly into my mind and I literally shook it away again... *for now*. I could always go... *home*. At least I knew what to expect if I returned to that life. At least my emotions would remain on an even keel – regardless of how unpleasant they were, at least they'd be consistent.

Basically, a plan seemed unreachable just now. One day, one hour even, at a time. Yes, that was my plan. One moment at a time.

All I knew for certain was that I didn't plan on making a dramatic exit. Maybe I'd just slip away while he was out dancing with *her*. I knew it was the coward's way out but that's exactly what I was. There was no point in trying to convince myself I didn't love him – because I did, with every beat of my breaking heart. And so I knew if I did it while he was here, if I risked looking into those hypnotic green eyes while I ripped the sparkle out of them… I'd end up staying.

I couldn't allow that to happen. I couldn't spend another moment of my life on this soul-destroying rollercoaster. I wasn't naive enough to think I'd ever be happy again, and I felt surprisingly okay with that. If I didn't allow myself to ride so high again, I would never feel the pain of being dragged back down.

I knew Richard would need to get ready for 'work' soon and I headed to the living room so I didn't have to sit with him while he changed. Part of me was still hoping that he'd come clean, that honestly would prevail and stop my heart from shutting down.

"Feel better?" he asked, sauntering towards me from the kitchen. I nodded and brushed past him to pour myself a glass of water from the faucet. "I need to leave soon. Will you be okay here on your own?"

Would you stay if I said no? The thought was tempting. The thought of collapsing into his arms and letting him hold me there all night. But no… I *needed* him to go. I needed him to see his lie through. I needed to feel my heart shatter into a billion pieces so I could be sure I'd made the right decision. So I simply nodded and carried on getting my water.

"I wish you'd talk to me, baby," he said solemnly, thankfully keeping his distance. A crushing silence followed and then I heard his footsteps leave the room while a forlorn tear dripped into my water.

He really is going through with it, I thought when he entered the living room a while later dressed in his purple pinstripe shirt, lilac tie and black work-pants. He was carrying the rucksack full of lies and my eyes locked onto it, unshed tears burning the hell out of them.

"How do you know Vanessa?" The words were out of my mouth before I even realized I planned to say them.

"*What?* Where did that come from?" he asked, cocking a puzzled eyebrow as I sat, slowly dying on the couch.

"I know you know her. Just tell me," I snapped, figuring I wanted answers to all my unspoken questions before I left. He owed me that much surely…

"Um, we met through work several years ago. She was publishing a book on cardio thoracic medicine written by our MD," he admitted, being honest for once. "Why? What's this about?"

"So my supposed *talent* had nothing to do with me getting that job?"

Saving Amy

"No! I mean, of course it did. Look, our friendship might have been the reason she agreed to see you, but it was *you* who impressed her enough to employ you. You should know by now Vanessa won't entertain anybody she doesn't believe in," he said and he sounded almost sincere. I shrugged, emotionless.

Whatever.

"Is this what's been bothering you all week?"

I wish... He edged cautiously towards me and then reached out to take my hand. I shrank away from him.

"What's in the bag?" I asked, my interrogation in full swing.

"Um, just some stuff for work. A few files..." His lie stabbed into my heart like a knife, tearing and shredding until I couldn't feel it beating anymore.

"You know, the thing that hurts the most is how easy you seem to find it," I accused. He shook his head, hurt and bewilderment swamping his face. "Lying to me, I mean."

"Amy I-I don't understand." He dropped the rucksack of deceit on the floor, his arms appearing too weak to support its weight any longer.

"Richard, don't," I said, looking to the floor because I couldn't bear the pain of looking at him anymore. "Don't keep lying. Please," I begged. "It's breaking my heart."

"How did you find out?" He bowed his head comprehendingly.

"It doesn't matter how," I shrugged, blinking the stinging tears away. "But I can't stay here." My revelation opened the floodgates to my tears and they swiftly dashed for freedom, pouring themselves rapidly down my face.

"What do you mean? You're not leaving me. You *can't*."

"I have to."

"Amy, no! You don't mean that. You can't. Amy you can't leave me!" he pleaded, dropping to his knees.

"I have to." I repeated.

"I should have told you. I know I should. I just didn't want to hurt you!" I still couldn't look at him, but I could *feel* the agony radiating from his body.

"Richard, you couldn't have hurt me any more if you'd tried."

"So you want to hurt me back? I get that… but not like this. Please, not like this." He pressed his hands together as if he was praying and I had to fight against the crippling urge to look at his face – knowing I would crumble.

"I'm not doing this to hurt you. Believe it or not that's the last thing I want. I love you. I love you *so* much…"

"Then stay!" he interrupted.

"But I don't trust you," I continued.

"Jesus Christ, I didn't even want to go! But I was pushed into doing this stupid fucking speech and… Please, Amy. I'm sorry."

"Are you ashamed of me? Is that why you didn't plan on taking me?"

"No! How could you even think that?" he said, sounding almost genuine as he scooted towards me and clamped his hands around my knees. "I suppose… I was worried."

Saving Amy

"*Worried?*" He nodded slowly, regretfully and then dropped his head again, hiding his angst, guilt-ridden face.

"Although I don't *think* I've done anything wrong, broken any rules… I just wasn't sure what the hospital would make of us. You know, seeing me with a former patient? I was worried for my career. I was… *selfish*." His excuse seemed reasonable, and to some extent I understood - felt sorry for him even. But it was just that – an excuse. An excuse I'd have probably never even got to hear if I hadn't questioned him.

"In hindsight, I should never have let Joanna talk me into it. Knowing how you feel about her and all."

So it was all her idea… figures.

"I can't lie," *like you*, "and say that doesn't sting, but this is nothing to do with her. I've never been able to trust anyone my whole life until I met you. And now I know even *you're* capable of being dishonest… I just can't deal with it, Richard."

"Please, Amy. I never meant to hurt you. I didn't think it would make you feel like this."

"That's because you didn't think I'd find out." I made the grave mistake of looking at his face. Desolate tears were streaming down his beautiful face, his eyes were scrunched closed and his whole body was shaking. My heart sank into the depths of my stomach and I snatched my eyes away, the pain too great to endure.

"Richard, we could go on like this all day…"

"Then we will! Stay and we'll go on for as long as it takes," he retorted, still on his knees, begging me, *pleading* with me.

"It's too late," I said, shaking my head. "Look, I'm not laying all of this on you. I'm just as much to blame. We both know how fucked-up I am. Maybe if I wasn't this would never have been an issue… you could have told me about the ball, and Joanna, and I would have accepted it like a *normal* person. But I'm not a normal person, and you know that. You knew how I would react and that's why you didn't tell me."

"No! This isn't down to you. I just-"

"Don't you see," I said, cutting him off. "This was *always* going to happen." I succumbed to the uncontrollable urge to touch him, tracing the side of his face with my finger, catching his tears and knowing this would be the last time I'd ever feel his soft, magnetic skin against mine.

"I'm just not cut out for this. I'm not capable of… of love, and trust and…" I trailed off, the lump in my throat making my voice crack. "I *do* love you, Richard. But it has to be this way. For both our sakes."

"Amy, no, please. Please don't do this. I'm begging you, baby. *Please!*" I rose from the couch and he grabbed my arm, pulling me back. He wrapped his body around me, clinging to me with such intensity, such desperation it became heart wrenching and I almost surrendered.

"Let go," I asked gently, sniffing in my tears and trying not to watch as his fell even faster. Twisting myself free, his body too weak to resist, I brushed past his crumpled body. Then I dragged on my black sneakers and headed to the bedroom to slide my sparsely packed suitcase out from under the bed.

Saving Amy

"Please don't go. I'll do anything. I LOVE YOU DAMMIT!" Richard pleaded, his voice breaking... and my heart.

"I have to. I'm so sorry." I pushed past him in the hallway, knocking into the glass half moon table by the door and almost hitting the now wobbling ceramic bowls. "Please don't follow me.

"Amy, I-"

"*Please.*" And then I was gone, slamming the door and the love of my life behind me.

Chapter Eighteen
(Richard)

"She's gone," I whimpered as my mom opened the front door, launching myself into her loving arms and sobbing like a giant fucking baby.

"Who's gone? Richard what on earth's happened?" she asked in a panic stricken voice.

"Amy. She's gone. I've lost her, Mom."

My mom took me inside with one arm around my waist – just like she would if I grazed my knee as a young boy. Her gentle arm guided me all the way to the corner sofa and the soft cream leather molded to my body as I flopped into it. My mom sat down next to me, sweeping her fine, blonde hair from her eyes as she assessed me up and down.

"Please tell me you didn't drive here in this state?" she admonished, wrinkling her nose at the smell of stale bourbon oozing from my breath. I shrugged, unbothered. What's the worst that could've happened? I could have veered off the road and wrapped myself around a tree – killing me instantly… killing this unbearable pain. *Yeah, that doesn't seem so bad.*

She narrowed her stern eyes at me – making it clear she disapproved.

"What happened, darling? Tell me…"

"I've been a selfish bastard, that's what. And now…" I felt my voice cracking as the words clung to my throat. "She's gone."

Saving Amy

"What did you do?" she asked tenderly, motherly – full of compassion.

"I agreed to accompany Joanna to the Little Wishes ball, and I-"

"You did what!" she interrupted, jolting upright.

"I know. I know I-"

"*Her* again. Why does everything always come back to her?" she blasted, cutting me off again.

"It's not Joanna's fault. Just like it's not Amy's. It's *mine*. I should never have agreed knowing how she feels." I hid my shameful face in my hands. I was such a dick.

"Oh, Richard, stop being so blind. Can you genuinely not see *why* Amy feels that way about her?"

Here we go…

"Please, don't start, Mom," I sighed, exasperated.

"Fine," she said, grudgingly holding her hands up in the air. "So, you told Amy about the ball, and then she left?" she pressed, trying to piece the puzzle together.

"No. I didn't tell her. That's *why* she left." My mom's brow furrowed, confusion veiling her face.

"You *lied* to her?" I nodded, utterly ashamed of myself. "So how did she find out?"

"I don't know." I shrugged. "She wouldn't say."

"And you don't think maybe *Joanna* told her?" she insinuated. She said Joanna's name with such disdain, as if the word was burning a hole in her tongue.

"No way. Joanna wouldn't do that," I replied confidently. *Would she?* No. She wouldn't. I was sure. *I think.* My mom almost choked on a sarcastic laugh but I ignored her, throwing off the ridiculous idea that Joanna would do such a thing.

"Did you go after her?"

"No," I admitted, sounding every bit like the douchebag I was. "She asked me not to," I explained – like that made it all okay.

"And you *listened* to her?" she asked incredulously, practically accusing me of being a first class fucking idiot. Which I was of course.

"I thought she'd come back. I thought she just needed some space, some time. But that was a week ago – I haven't heard from her since." I stared down at my hands, concentrating on my fingers as they knotted themselves together.

"A *week?* Why on earth didn't you tell me sooner?" Her tone was sympathetic now and she clasped my hand within hers.

"Because I was embarrassed. And, hopeful that she'd come back." A long silence followed. The only sound was that of my heavy breathing and the sniffs of my pathetic tears. "I tried to call her, but then I found her cell in the bedroom. I tried work, but then Vanessa told me she'd cleared her desk and handed in her notice the very next day. I don't know where she is. Or if she's in trouble, if she's scared… I love her, Mom, and I'm never going to see her again."

The thought of never seeing her again, never holding her, never kissing her, never running my fingers through her soft blond hair which smelt of vanilla… it pierced into my tear ducts like a salt-tipped knife, and suddenly I was blubbing like a moron again.

"You will. She loves you, Richard."

Saving Amy

"But she doesn't trust me. I lied to her. I let her down. After everything she's been through in her life…" I threw my head in my trembling hands. "I'll never forgive myself if anything happens to her."

I spent the next couple of hours filling my mom in about Amy's past in excruciating detail and she simply listened – completely supportive and un-judging. She gasped in parts, shook her head in others… but at least now she had a better understanding of why Amy reacted the way she did, why trust was such a difficult process for her.

"So, this friend in Florida… have you checked to see if she's there?"

"Kind of." I nodded.

"*Kind of?*"

"I didn't ask her directly. I sort of made out like I'd dialed her by mistake, figuring I'd be able to sense if she was aware of what'd happened. I didn't want to worry her unnecessarily." *Or to have to explain what an insensitive jackass I am.* "It worked. She was all chirpy and full of herself, and kept asking how Amy was doing."

My mom ran her finger across her chin contemplatively.

"And her parents? You've checked with them?"

"No. She would never go back there," I said adamantly. "That bastard has already nearly killed her once before, remember?" I unintentionally snapped as I thought of her sadistic father – my mind wondering back to when I paid a visit to the slimy son of a bitch after he cornered Amy outside work.

I caught up with him outside his house. He looked like a fucking tramp and smelt even worse – it was eleven in the morning and he was wasted. He was old and weak – frail. Seemed life was doing a good enough job of paying him back for some of the shit he'd put Amy through but I still felt better giving him a little taste of his own medicine.

I pinned him against the wall of the house in the same position he'd had Amy in God knew how many times. He tried to spout some bull about how influential he was and that he could have me struck off in a heartbeat. But weighing him up – the way he stank like a urinal, the way he slurred his words, the way his crumpled, vomit stained clothes draped from his emaciated body… we both knew he couldn't influence a fucking fly…

That was why he took it. Why he just stood there while I rammed my fist into his prominent ribs. Why he barely raised a hand when I grabbed his throat and slammed his head into the brick. Why he didn't mutter a word when I told him I would fucking kill him if he ever went near Amy again…

He was too weak to fight back and he knew it. Or maybe I was just the wrong gender.

"Richard, it's all she knows. She might feel like she had no other choice," my mom suggested as insightful as ever. I shook my head, refusing to believe she would willingly return to the suffering that'd plagued her whole life. Refusing to think of her cowering on the floor just inches away from the evil fucker's fist. No. I *couldn't* believe that, because if I did, if I even considered the possibility that I'd pushed her back into that torturous existence, I would never be able to live with myself.

"We'll think of something. We *will* find her," my mom tried to reassure but the irresolute tone to her voice suggested she too had reached an impasse.

Saving Amy

Under strict mother's orders I spent the rest of the afternoon lying down in the guest room to sleep off some of the bourbon before my shift at the hospital tonight. I didn't sleep however. I couldn't even close my eyes because Amy's beautiful, porcelain face – crumpled and hurting, swamped with the pain of my betrayal was etched onto my eyelids and I couldn't bear it.

I swore I would never make her feel so bad again after almost losing her once before back in Florida. I swore I'd never be such a god damn selfish, insensitive, thoughtless, inconsiderate, stupid fucking cunt ever again. Yet somehow, I managed it.

My mom was drowning me with a near constant supply of black coffee (I can't fucking stand black coffee), bringing in the next before I'd even finished the first, each one accompanied by a lecture on the dangers of drink driving. It did the job though. Each sip clearing my distorted vision a little more, calming my trembling hands… The only problem with that was, I was slowly starting to *feel* again, and the pain was excruciating.

Where are you, beautiful?

****

"Jesus, Richard, you look terrible! Are you sure you're well enough to come back?" were the words Joanna greeted me with the second I stepped foot on the pastel blue floor of the ward. I hadn't told her yet. I hadn't told anyone except my mom. As far as Joanna and everyone else was concerned, I'd been sick with the stomach flu this past week – starting the night I lost Amy, hence my bailing out on the ball.

"I'll be fine," I said curtly, reluctant to divulge the fact that I was dying inside, that the heart I once barely knew existed was now broken, scarred and bursting with pain.

"You're lying. I know you too well. Something's wrong, tell me."

Ah, shit, I thought, feeling backed into a corner. Joanna was one hell of a determined, tenacious woman and I knew from experience the only way to shut her up was to tell the truth.

"Amy's left me." My voice wavered like I was hitting puberty and I didn't blink for fear the pressure would tip my tears over the edge and leave me crying like a fucking girl. Joanna's pupils dilated so fast and so wide there was hardly any visible irises left.

"Wow, I didn't see that one coming," she vilified with an almost delighted glint in her hazel eyes.

"You're fucking pleased aren't you?" I snapped fiercely at her. She bit her lower lip and I was sure she was trying to suppress a smile. "Do you think this is funny? Because I'm telling you, Joanna, I'm in pieces here. I've never felt pain like this before." Her expression instantaneously turned serious, wounded even, and I knew she was wondering why I never felt like this with her.

"No, Richard, I don't think it's funny. It hurts me so much to see you this way," she said, realizing she'd overstepped the mark. "But you know how I feel about the whole thing. It never would've worked."

Saving Amy

Whatever happened to sympathy for fuck's sake?
"Why wouldn't it?" I found myself scowling at her.
"For starters she's too young."
"Don't give me that bullshit. She's more mature than half the people my age – she's had to be. When someone's lived through what she has, age is just a number. An irrelevant fucking number." I fixed my eyes on the nurses station, focusing on the pale wood desk, on the stainless steel plate with 'Nurses Station' etched onto it, on the strip lamp, the computer… on anything that wasn't Joanna's face.
"That's another thing… she has *so* much baggage, Richard. I get it's not her fault, but it sure as hell isn't yours either. And don't you see? It's always going to be there. Controlling her… controlling *you*. You will never be able to fully relax, be *happy*…"
"You're out of order here. I won't listen to anymore of this shit," I said, raising my palm to my face to block out the sight of her.
"Oh, Richard, enough now! Come on, you're not a stupid man. You have to see this is for the best. It went on too long as it was. I mean, Christ, the bitch couldn't even handle you going out for the evening with your oldest friend!"
What the fuck! I dragged in a deep breath - so deep and forceful my lungs throbbed under the pressure - to try and calm this pool of bright red rage that was ripping its way through my body.
It was *her…*
"How the fuck did you know about that?" I yelled, drawing attention from passing staff and patients alike, innocently making their way down the sunflower yellow corridor.

Could they really have been right about her all along? My mom, Amy…

"Richard, I-I-" she stuttered, 'busted' written all over her contrived face. I took a step back, my fingers bound so tightly into fists that my fingernails almost pierced my flesh. I took another step back, for the first time in my life fearing I might actually hit a woman.

"How could you do that to me? Was this all part of some master plan to split us up? Is this why you pushed me into going in the first place?" I fired question after question at her. "I thought you were my friend."

Peering around I noticed we seemed to have gathered quite an audience. Patients had dragged themselves and their IV stands from their beds and were littering the corridor gaining front row seats to our little spectacle. I threw my hands in the air and stomped off to my office four doors down. Joanna followed me - I could hear her heels clicking against the hard floor as her short legs ran to keep up with my long strides.

"I thought we were friends," I repeated desolately as I sank into my high-back leather swivel armchair.

"We are!" she screeched, her voice like nails on a chalkboard. "Richard you know how much I love you. That's-" I held my hand up, cutting her off.

"Wait a minute, is that what all this is about? You can't have me so no one else can?"

"Oh don't be so obtuse," she said but I struggled to find the sincerity in her voice. "Look, I know I've probably come across quite cold about all this…"

Saving Amy

"*Cold?* Try minus fucking five hundred!" She rolled her eyes at me.

"Please, Richard, let me finish." I offered up my hand telling her to go ahead. Though I doubted she had anything to say that I wanted to hear. "Dealing with people like Amelia-"

"*Dealing?* Shouldn't that be *helping?*"

"Oh, just stop picking apart everything I say. You said you'd let me speak!" I shrugged my shoulders like a stroppy teenager. "Well, anyway, that is my job. I deal, *help*, people like her everyday of my life – so I know how to distance myself. That's where you went wrong. You broke the golden rule of our profession… you let yourself get attached. That means you're incapable of seeing the bigger picture. Granted, kids like that straighten themselves out sometimes, but you know as well as I do they'll always be that little bit…" She circled a straightened finger at the side of her head.

My jaw dropped open in disbelief. I had spent hours upon hours of my life in the company of this woman and I had never once witnessed just how cruel, insensitive and downright fucking nasty she could be. Until now…

"You need to remind yourself she's not Kate," she said so condescendingly… so cock sure of herself. My love for Amy had *nothing* to do with my sister. It never did.

"What a croc of shit!" Joanna bolted upright - taken aback by the fact I didn't take a swim in the sea of bullshit that just flowed from her acidic mouth.

"So let's see, you've played the 'thinking of my interests' card, the 'age' card, the 'how screwed up she is card', and now you're trying the Kate tactic? I've heard enough, Joanna. Now get the fuck out of my office." I swiveled my chair towards the vertical window, my eyes wandering over the hospital grounds that were frosted over by the frigid November air.

"Richard, please! Let's start again!"

What, the conversation? Or us?

"Get out!" I barked, spinning to face her so fast I almost catapulted out of my chair.

"As you wish," she complied, her voice rich with anguish. But I didn't give a damn how sad she was feeling. The scheming bitch could go take a jump under a speeding bus for all I cared.

The door closed behind her and I punched the wall, denting the plasterboard as it slammed into my fist. Fuck, it hurt. Not my hand - my heart. I was almost sure it was beating a little slower with each day that passed. I feared eventually the pain would grow so bad it would stop beating altogether. And the nausea… gut wrenching, not-able-to-eat-a-thing nausea. I'd barely eaten more than a few slices of toast all week and yet I felt so full… so burdened.

I wondered if Amy felt the same. I wondered if she was alone, if she was scared or hurting, if she thought of me… I folded my arms over my desk and let my head fall into them, the sleeves of my navy blue shirt soaking up my pathetic tears.

Where are you, beautiful?

****

After snapping my laptop closed a little too firmly I peeked inside again to make sure I'd not

Saving Amy

smashed the screen. Thankfully, it was crack free and I nodded, closing it with a little more respect. I remembered how Amy once said she'd not seen her grandmother since she was nine but didn't have any definitive proof that she was actually dead. I thought maybe Amy had looked her up, discovered her alive and well on some sunny beach resort and had gone to live with her. But of course, that would be too easy.

I stayed behind at work for a couple of hours two nights ago, scanning the system for any elderly 'Hope's' that died around the time Amy last remembers seeing her. I came away with a Carol Hope – died aged eighty-two from unknown causes, a Victoria Hope – died aged sixty-nine from carbon monoxide poisoning, a Beatrice Hope – died aged seventy-three from respiratory failure and an Evelyn Hope – died aged seventy from a CVA.

Armed with my list of names I headed down to King County Court House to search the BMD records. I was then faced with a list of nineteen Carol Hope's, Twenty-seven Victoria Hope's, eleven Beatrice Hope's and seventeen Evelyn Hope's. Over half of them were dead and I had no way of knowing which one was Amy's grandmother – if any of them.

I'd just about given up when I came across the birth certificate for a James Arthur Hope – mother… Evelyn Marie Hope. A little more digging turned up a marriage certificate for one James Arthur Hope and one Mary Anne Monroe dated three years after Amy was born. The fact that Amy had already been born when her parents married (assuming I had found the right parents of course) warranted a little more searching to make sure I was onto the right grandmother.

But Amy was proving impossible to find. I thought I'd cracked it when I came across an Amelia Anne born to a Mary Anne Monroe on the date of Amy's birth but then slammed my fists into the shabby wooden table (almost getting my ass kicked out in the process) when I noted the Amelia in question was also a Monroe, and the father was listed as Jack Edmund Monroe.

I ploughed on for another hour or so, switching from the digitalized records to a hefty wad of dust-covered papers, but there were no Amelia Anne Hope's born June 19th 1993 at any Seattle hospital so I moved onto bordering cities. After scanning the records for hospitals in Bellevue, Mercer Island, Kingsgate and then Redmond and drawing on nothing, I gave up.

I shrank back in my chair and like the big fat pussy I'd turned into since Amy left me… I cried.

Where are you, beautiful?

****

I took some leave from the hospital. Basically by lying through my teeth and saying my grandmother was really sick – praying the whole time that Martin (the MD) didn't already know that she'd been dead for twelve years. I just couldn't focus – Amy's beautiful face crumpling at my betrayal haunted my every waking thought. I couldn't stop thinking about the first time we met. The look in her rich caramel eyes peering out from under a veil of golden hair the night I found her lying in the street –

the pain, the fear. They were silently begging for someone to save her, to love her – for *me* to love her. They drew me in that night and I'd been hooked ever since.

Yesterday I almost killed myself with a defibrillator and prescribed two sets of the wrong meds. Thankfully Jenny (a red-haired rhesus -nurse) noticed before the poor bastards had them administered. That was when I knew it was time to take some time off – before I inadvertently ending up killing someone.

Since getting home I'd done nothing but wallow on the sofa in nothing but my three-day old boxer briefs, with Against All Odds playing on the loop. It honestly felt like Phil Collins had crept inside my body while I was sleeping and stole the lyrics straight from my heart. We had shared so much laughter, just as much pain. Amy *was* the only one who really knew me at all. There really wasn't anything left, but the memory of her face… it wasn't until she'd gone I realized I didn't even have a photo of her.

And there really was so much I needed to say to her – so many reasons why.

Where are you, beautiful?

My mom suggested that Amy wasn't doing this because I'd been such a selfish, dumbass bastard. She thought Amy was trying to *save* me. She said, that time when she took her upstairs to 'find a dress', she'd mentioned how she didn't feel worthy of me. Of *me!* All that told me was that I'd failed in my mission to make her feel like the most important person in the world… because that's exactly what she is.

I wish she could've seen me before I met her. She thought I had everything… but I had *nothing*. Yes, I had a career, money, a family I barely spoke to… Well, I never lost touch with David – he'd been my own personal gofer since he was four years old - but I always asked him not to tell anyone he'd seen me. On reflection that was unfair but he never went against me. I could trust him; I still can.

For years I literally just worked, ate and slept. I wouldn't entertain a relationship that lasted longer than one night and a social life was just something 'other' people did – people who deserved to be happy. I was so lonely. Consumed with impervious guilt and the idea that I didn't deserve to be loved after what I did to Kate. Sometimes, I still feel like that. Sometimes, I feel Amy leaving me is exactly what I deserve.

But I was too selfish to accept it. I *needed* to find her.

I went to see Kate yesterday. I sat by her headstone in the pouring rain until my clothes were more water than fabric. I talked to her for almost two hours. Sometimes I swear I could hear her answer me. In fact I was pretty sure she told me what a prick I'd been on more than one occasion. I asked her what I should do, and I heard her sweet voice as clear as anything in my mind. 'Fight,' she said. Instantly I knew what she meant and what I should do. 'I miss you, Kate,' I whispered into the burnished stone, and then I jumped to my feet and headed home to change.

After wrestling out of my sodden clothes and changing into some dry ones I set straight back out again. I trawled the streets of Seattle until 4 AM in search of Amy. I drove, I walked, I waited… I headed everywhere I knew she'd ever been – anywhere she'd ever mentioned even in passing. And I would keep going. I would search until I found her no matter how long it took. I would only come home to shower and sleep. Or rather, lie awake with my eyes closed for a couple of hours.

I will find her.

After shrouding my body in three layers of clothes in preparation for the uncharacteristic heavy snowfall Seattle was apparently expecting tonight, I snatched the keys for the Audi from the ceramic bowl in the hall and headed out again without knowing where to look next. The Audi was now the only car I drove. It was the one Amy drove most often and the smell of her perfume still lingered in the fabric. I closed my eyes and inhaled her scent and it was as if she was sat right next to me.

And then it hit again – the stabbing pain in my heavy heart. It was excruciating.

I drove for a while, completing a full 360 of the city. I drove past Salt House, the little Italian I took her to one Saturday night when neither of us could be bothered cooking, the grocery store, the park, the cemetery…

Nothing.

My mom's words about Amy's parents echoed unwelcome in my mind. I still didn't believe she would put herself in such danger, allowing herself to live through that harrowing existence all over again. I couldn't believe it. I wouldn't.

Still, I found myself making a U-turn and heading east towards their house. I didn't want to, but it was like my feet had become independent from my body, pushing harder and faster on the gas despite my brain telling them it was a ridiculous idea. I parked the car inconspicuously at the end of the street between two overgrown thorny bushes. Then I set off on foot.

Christ, it was cold. The frigid air froze my breath into a cloud in front of me and sporadic flakes of glistening snow started to fall, melting into nothing as they landed gracefully on the ground. I felt a sharp pang in my chest, like a glass bomb detonating in my heart. What if she was out here somewhere, freezing to death with nowhere to go?

Where are you, beautiful?

I walked down the street and pulled my black hood over my head. An elderly woman crossed the street when she saw me. With my sullen eyes and black hoody she clearly feared for her purse's life. The snow was picking up its pace, the flakes swelling to twice their size and starting to stick, blanketing the darkening street with a fine layer of shimmering white. I spotted the house - the sight of it sending a chilling shiver down my spine - and perched myself on a small brick wall guarding somebody's lawn adjacent.

I adjusted my body so I was sitting at an angle. That way I could see the Hope house but anyone inside wouldn't be able to see me. Then I kicked the dusting of snow off my boots and waited…

I waited for almost an hour. I waited until I was camouflaged by the thick snow soaking through my clothes and burning my dithering skin. There was no sign of life – no shadows lurking behind the windows, no lights being flipped on despite the evening darkness setting in. Resigned to failing yet

Saving Amy

again, I stood up and the snow crunched beneath my feet as I prepared to leave.

Then, I saw her…

Chapter Nineteen

"Amy!" I heard my name reverberating across the street. My already weak heart stopped dead, instantly recognizing the velvety voice behind it.

Shit.

I was momentarily paralyzed – frozen like the snow. *What do I do?* Did I run? Run in the opposite direction and never look back? Or run into his arms and let his touch make everything okay?

His body slammed into me, sending me skidding into the snow. His strong, protective arms were beneath me before I hit the floor and he pulled me into him so tightly I struggled to breathe. For a minute I didn't move. I just let him hold me… let him take the pain away. But it couldn't last. I realized I was only postponing the inevitable and I wriggled free from his embrace.

"You're freezing," was all I could think of to say.

"Yeah. Snow does that to you," he said with a soft laugh and for a brief moment it was like the last two weeks never happened.

"Amy, come with me. *Please*," Richard begged, picking straight up from where we left off two weeks ago. His voice was hoarse, gruff like he'd been crying for days – just like me.

"I can't." The words ripped chunks out of my throat as they fought to stay buried.

"No. No, no, Amy, *please!* I'm begging you. I've only just found you!" His grip tightened around me

Saving Amy

like a boa constrictor, crushing me, refusing to let me go. "Please, Amy. I only want to talk."

"I can't!" I repeated, prizing my body free and refusing to allow myself to even consider the idea. He couldn't see it now but I was doing this for him. I was giving him his life back. A life where he could do whatever made him happy without fear of my reaction. And that's what it all boiled down to, what *everything* boiled down to – I just wanted Richard to be happy. And as much as it hurt (and holy fuck it hurt) I knew he couldn't have that with me.

So, I pulled myself into him, twisting his hair between my fingers while I kissed him. I inhaled his soothing tea-tree and Armani cologne scent, tasted his sweet coffee and mints lips one last time… then I jumped to my feet and ran like I'd never ran before.

My feet hammered the ground and I sprinted until my breath ran out, the icy wind stabbing into my cheeks like shards of glass as I raced through it. I didn't know how far I'd come when I veered into an alley down the side of a seedy strip joint. The night sky was drawing in. The moon was a shimmering orb illuminating the sky as the flakes of snow danced in the breeze. Exhausted and weak, I dropped to the ground, sliding against a tall, reeking dumpster.

I was alone and scared. My wet clothes had fused to my skin and my freezing body was shivering violently in protest. I stole a generous swig of vodka from the bottle I'd had stashed away in my bag, just in case. The neat liquor burned and scratched at my throat but I kept glugging, knowing it would alleviate my fear. I didn't really know what exactly I was afraid of. Losing Richard? The fact I had another bruised rib with compliments from my father? The fact I had a glass bottle in my hand that would easily smash into a handful of razor-sharp implements?

A different face was imprinted on my eyelids with each blink. My father's, Joanna's, Richard's… They all brought pain, unbearable pain that writhed through my entire body, for a whole host of different reasons. I couldn't stand it. I shook my head but the faces wouldn't go away. I wanted them to go away. I *needed* them to go away.

I needed it all to go away…

I glugged the vodka eagerly, one gulp after another in quick, reckless succession. Gradually it slowed everything down, calming me – my blinking, my breathing, my thoughts… I kept going until my brain was too fuzzy to think at all. Maybe that's why my empty bottle was now a carpet of shattered blades, and why my fingers felt compelled to pick one up.

Blood seeped through the jagged tears in my black pants, marbling the snow, tainting it. I didn't bother to roll up my pant legs, that would require a thought process and thinking was something I was either incapable of, or not allowing myself to do right now. I sliced and shredded heedlessly, ripping straight through the black cotton and rending gaping wounds into my flesh with not a hint of the meticulousness I would normally use. There was no savoring the moment. No relief.

I wanted it out. The pain. The torment.

I need it out!

My right hand became independent from my body, clutching the red-stained glass and rapidly carving the flesh of my thigh in all different directions until it unknowingly started its relentless assault on my left forearm, ripping out all the hurt and hatred. I couldn't feel it. I couldn't feel anything. The glacial snow had numbed my skin and the vodka had numbed my thoughts and my nerves. In fact, I don't think I'd ever felt so calm, so sated, so peaceful…

My eyes grew heavy, my limbs weak. I didn't feel my arm drop but I heard a playful, melodic clink as the shard of glass fell onto the others that were nestled in the red snow. Darkness invaded my vision but I couldn't feel whether my eyes were closed. I couldn't feel anything. I couldn't see anything. I couldn't hear anything. I was falling into the most welcoming, heavenly sleep…

"Amy! Amy!" said a celestial, velvety voice as it danced into my ears. "Oh, dear God, beautiful, what have you done?" The sound was magnificent. I tried to reach out for it but my body wasn't working. *Is this heaven?* I decided it must be as the divine voice continued.

"Jesus Christ, Amy!" Confusion swamped my foggy mind. Why was the voice so deluged with panic? Was I not supposed to be here? Was I supposed to be… *in hell?*

I thought I felt myself being pulled and dragged until I was lying on the icy ground. I thought I felt my arms and legs being bound and prodded. I thought I felt warm, ragged breaths sweep over my face. But I wasn't sure. I wasn't sure I even had a body anymore.

The heavenly voice changed from distraught and anxious to calm and authoritative in an instant, as if a switch had been flipped. I didn't hear what it was saying and soon it started to fade altogether, until it was nothing but an incoherent echo in the distance. I was falling again, my mind succumbing to the darkness.

I was going to hell…

****

My eyes flickered as I tried to wake up, refusing to open the whole way. Eventually I managed to push through it, summoning enough energy into my heavy eyelids to prize them apart. My pupils were met by a bright, blinding light but I fought against the urge to close them again, forcing them to adjust.

For a brief moment, gazing into the stream of yellow light, I wondered if I was in heaven. But then I looked down and realized I was in the hospital. My arms and legs were cloaked in blood stained bandages, tubes were springing from the backs of my hands and a metal incarcerating rail surrounded the edges of my bed.

Then my heart skipped a beat, or several. A body was slouched over the edge of my bed. He was dressed in a white long sleeved sweater that looked like it hadn't been washed in days. The guardrails were digging into his armpits, and his head – adorned with the most striking shade of auburn/copper hair – was slumped onto the mattress just inches away from my hand.

Richard…

My fingers itched to touch him and - perhaps foolishly - I let them. His head bolted upright, exposing a set of unusually dull green eyes that were red and swollen around the edges.

Saving Amy

"She's awake! Charlie, get in here, she's awake!" he yelled while slamming his fist repeatedly into a round, red button on the wall by my bed.

Almost immediately a tall dark-haired man - late forties by the look of him - dressed in a crisp blue shirt, black pants and white overcoat came charging into the room.

"Amy can you hear me?" Richard pressed in a fluster, positioning his face so our noses were almost touching. I nodded, trying to speak but all that escaped was a croak.

The tall doctor (Charlie, I assumed) was by my side in seconds, fiddling with the wires protruding from my hands.

"Can I-can I-" I tried to ask for some water but the words were lodged in my throat which was as coarse and dry as sandpaper. "Water," I mouthed.

Richard shot to the foot of the bed so fast it was like he possessed supernatural powers. Then he poured some water into a paper cup from the transparent plastic jug and turned back to me – his return much slower as he steadied the cup in his hand. He put one hand behind my head, supporting it as I leaned my mouth towards the cup that he was tipping tentatively towards it. The water was cold and refreshing. It served its purpose, hydrating me, lubricating my arid mouth and extricating the words that were stuck in my throat.

"What happened to me?" I asked, dazed and confused. Richard dropped his distraught face, refusing eye contact with me like he didn't want to have to tell me.

"You got drunk…" He paused, sucking in a deep breath as he prepared himself. "And then you did... *this* to yourself," he said solemnly, cracks invading his velvety voice. He gestured his hand towards the blood-stained bandages and then brought it over his face, hiding the pain he was in. "Right after you ran away from me."

My brow furrowed as I delved into my memories. And then it slammed into my brain like a bullet. I remembered. I remembered the love I felt for him, the safety of his arms, the guilt, the fear, the vodka... I remembered *everything*, and I wished with all my heart that I didn't.

"I'm sorry," I mumbled, shame rendering me unable to look at him. As usual he was having none of that though, and he tipped my chin with his finger then angled his face just inches from mine.

"Not as sorry as me," he said, closing his swollen eyes as if he was trying to blink away all the hurt he was feeling. "Baby, please stay with me. *Please*," he begged. His voice broke on the last word and a rogue tear laced with pure suffering escaped from the corner of his red-rimmed eye.

"Richard, can I talk to you outside for a moment?" the tall doctor interrupted. I'd completely forgotten he was here.

"Richard, I-" He silenced me with a trembling finger over my lips as if he was too afraid to hear what I had to say.

"I won't be long." He squeezed the sorrow from his eyes again and left with the tall doctor – to talk about me, I suspected.

I'm so fucked up, I thought as I weighed up my mummified limbs. My arm... I couldn't believe I went for my arm. Thighs were so much simpler – so much easier to hide. I guessed it was year round long sleeves for me now. *I'm so fucked up.*

I hated what I'd done to myself. I hated what I'd done to Richard. The torment clouding his beautiful green eyes was all because of me and I knew I should stick to my guns and free him from all the pain I would inevitably cause if I stayed with him. I knew I should up and leave. Head to Florida maybe? Or even another country so he had no choice but to forget about me and move on with his life. I knew I should let him go…

But the thing that was scaring the hell out of me right now was that I also knew I was too selfish to go through with it.

There was a definite pattern emerging. This was the third time in less than a year I had ended up wounded and unconscious – each and every time at a point where Richard was missing from my life. Yet, miraculously, he'd always been the one who saved me. Just like when we were together - granted I was living on a rollercoaster – the turbulence throwing my emotions up, down and around – but I always landed in the safety of his arms before I had chance to hit the concrete. Nothing seemed insolvable when his body was wrapped around mine. My life remained worth living. Whatever feeling was ripping my insides apart, one particular always prevailed – my love for the beautiful man on the other side of the door, and my *need* for him to love me back.

The heavy yellow door swung back open and Richard strolled in unaccompanied. His body was hunched, his eyes strained. He looked so… *destroyed*.

"Hey," I said with a heavy heart.

"Hey." He tottered cautiously towards me and perched next to me on the bed, taking my hand in his.

"Richard I-" He cut me off, raising a palm in the air.

"I want to go first," he said, his voice trembling. "I know how much I hurt you, Amy. I lied to you and-" I opened my mouth to tell him this wasn't necessary, refusing to allow him to take all the blame. But he raised his hand again and started to talk over me. "I need you to know these have been the worst two weeks of my life. I never knew it was possible to feel such pain… such intense, all consuming *sadness*. That's how I know I will never, *ever* hurt you again. I will never risk losing you again, Amy. I can't live without you."

Oh Sweet Jesus, the guilt was overwhelming. My cheeks were on fire as it pulsed through my body, incinerating me from the inside out.

"Please say you'll come home with me?" I contemplated his words for a few dramatically long seconds, thinking of all the different ways I could say yes. In the end I settled for a weak nod. Relief washed over his face, visibly smoothing all the burdened creases around his tired eyes.

"Thank you. Oh, baby, thank you." Tentatively, he reached across my body to kiss my eager lips. But as he did, his chest clashed gently with my ribs and the slight pressure made me cry out.

"Ow!" I winced at the stabbing pain rippling through my chest. Richard flew off me with the superhuman speed he'd developed while I'd been gone.

Saving Amy

"I'm so sorry!" he blurted, surrendering his hands. "What is it? What did I do?"

My mind flashed back to when I was lying on the kitchen floor with my dad's boot ramming into my side last Thursday. He came home and caught me smoking in the house. It was my first smoke in forever and as I lit it I wondered if I was doing it intentionally. I almost wanted him to catch me... to *finish* me.

I started to wonder how Richard didn't know. Did he not see the damage when he brought me in here?

"I had a run in with my dad," I admitted, nodding my head towards my throbbing ribs. "I thought you would have seen it and assumed as much."

He must *have seen,* I thought, realizing I must have been naked at some point while they dressed me in the faded blue gown I was wearing.

"I wasn't allowed in while they worked on you," he said with a shrug. I think that must have pissed him off.

"Jesus, Amy!" he cried as he slid my gown up to my chest. "I'm so sorry."

"Richard, this isn't your fault. I *chose* to go home." He shook his head, dismissing me as his wide eyes bulged with guilt. "Could you fetch me some painkillers, please?" I asked, forcing a subject change. As soon as I asked for them my arms and legs start burning like crazy. It felt like my raw skin was trying to crawl away from my body.

Stupid, fucked-up bitch.

"Sure. I'll be right back."

When Richard exited the room I was left alone with my guilt. It was just a tiny bit easier to breathe with only one person's remorse flooding the atmosphere. *How are we supposed to get past this?* Did we talk… pouring the contents of our heavy hearts out before they burst under the pressure? Did we draw a line and pretend the last two weeks never happened, vow never to mention it again? Or did we start from the beginning, as if we knew nothing about each other?

Richard came back with two little pink tablets in a transparent dispensing cup. He tipped them into my hand and passed me the paper cup of water from the wheeled table at the foot of my bed.

"You should go home and get some sleep," I suggested as he tried to conceal an impressive yawn with the back of his hand.

"I'm not leaving you. I'm never leaving you again." His voice was rich with determination and I smiled gratefully. I knew in reality he couldn't stay by my side forever, but he was here now and in that moment, that was all that mattered.

He settled in beside me on the bed, scooting higher so I could nestle my head in his chest. Christ, I'd missed him. His smell, his warmth, his heartbeat beneath my ear...

"I'm sure there are rules about patients letting hot men climb into bed with them," I teased.

"Well, as Katharine Hepburn once said, 'if you obey all the rules, you miss all the fun'." I couldn't see his face but I just knew he was winking.

"You badass." I felt the vibrations of his laughter beneath my cheek. I closed my eyes and savored the feeling, the sound of his happiness.

Saving Amy

"What day is it?" I asked curiously.

"Tuesday."

"*Tuesday?*"

"You've been out for three days. You lost a *lot* of blood." I flushed redder than my blood-stained bandages and I was pleased he couldn't see the shame spill onto my face.

"That bad, huh?" I asked too flippantly. I regretted it almost immediately, wincing as he described the damage I'd inflicted upon myself.

Apparently I sliced straight through my Rectus Femoris (whatever the hell that is) and required emergency surgery to my left thigh to repair the damage before I bled to death. I had forty-two stitches in my thighs and nineteen in my arm, and as an added bonus I'd had my stomach pumped – seemed like I thought it was good idea to give myself alcohol poisoning too. Oh, and I mustn't forget the two blood transfusions…

I stared down at the bandages wrapped around the extent of my fucked-up-ness. I'd never felt so disgusted with myself, so ugly.

"You're beautiful," Richard whispered into my hair doing that amazing thing which made me wonder if he could hear my thoughts. I smiled bashfully even though I knew he couldn't see my face and squeezed my arm around him a little tighter.

We fell silent but it was a welcome, comfortable calm. We didn't need to talk. We were together – everything else was insignificant. I lay, snuggled into his chest, inhaling his scent and cherishing the hum of his healing heart for an immeasurable length of time. Richard's arm was draped over my shoulder and he circled the small of my back with his thumb until I fell asleep.

****

"Let's get you to bed," Richard said when we arrived at his – *our* – apartment, steering me towards the bedroom with one arm around my waist.

"No. I don't want to lie down," I argued stubbornly, pulling against him in the opposite direction.

"You need to rest."

"Richard, I've been resting for five days," I protested. "Besides, I can rest on the couch," I tacked on when I saw the worry set in on his face.

"What was that?" I asked. A noise resembling the closing of a door startled me. Richard shrugged looking equally baffled and set off to follow the noise.

"What the hell are you doing here?" I heard Richard say in a rage-fuelled tone. Seconds later Joanna stormed into the living room, stopping dead in her tracks and dropping her jaw to the floor when she saw me.

How the fuck did she get in?

"The um, door was left open," she mumbled, signaling over her shoulder and answering my unspoken question. She tripped on her words, clearly stunned, and maybe even disappointed by my presence.

"That's not what I asked," Richard snapped. "I'll say it again... what the hell are you doing here?"

He seemed so angry with her – something I'd only ever witnessed in my dreams. I wondered if he was only doing it for my benefit or if something went down with them while I was... *gone*.

"Maybe we could step outside? I'd like to talk with you in private," she asked while throwing me a look that could freeze hell over.

"No. You can say whatever it is in front of Amy." Joanna shrugged petulantly.

"I came to sort things out. We're best friends, Richard. You can't hate me forever."

What! He hates her? Result!

"Finished? Because I'm kind of busy," he said in full on condescending-bastard mode.

Go on, Richard!

"Looking after *her*? What's she done this time?"

Whoa! Richard's eyes widened and his nostrils flared open. Then he took a step back, as though he was afraid he might strangle her.

"Get out. We're done here," he ordered, wrinkling his nose in disgust.

"Richard, please. I'm sorry okay? I was out of line." She tried to pull it back but I thought – *hoped* – she'd pushed him too far. I idly pondered if it was okay that I was secretly pleased (elated even) with the way this conversation was heading.

Richard ushered Joanna out into the hallway. I expected to hear the door slam behind her at any moment but it didn't come. Instead I heard fraught whispers, though I couldn't make out what they were saying. I scooted further up the couch and cupped my hand around my ear.

They were right down the hall by the door going off how faint their voices were. I picked up a few jumbled words coming from Richard's mouth – 'her father', 'love her', 'responsible' and then in her irritating whiney voice – 'I'm sorry'. I tried to piece the words together to form a conversation but then gave up realizing I'd only make it sound worse in my head.

Then I remembered Richard's conversation in the hospital and how he swore he would never lie to me again. Seeing the anguish obscuring the vibrant green of his eyes, it was impossible not to believe him. Therefore when he returned I put him to the test by asking what the vindictive bitch wanted.

"Let's just say I saw a side of her I didn't like while you were…" He swallowed hard, like he was choking on the word, 'gone'.

About time.

"So, how did you leave it with her, just now? Did you tell her where to go?"

"Not as such. I accepted her apology, gave her a quick rundown on what happened to you and said goodbye."

"Why would you do that?" I asked, sounding more pissed than I intended to.

"Do what? Accept her apology, or tell her about you?"

"Both," I said, fighting to keep my voice even and the green-eyed monster in its cage.

"Because it was easier, and because she asked," he answered honestly, warily. His expression was anxious as if he was waiting for me to flip out. Amazingly, I didn't and I wasn't sure who was more surprised by the restraint I was managing to possess. In fact, I simply said "okay." Maybe our time apart really *had* changed us both.

After lunch (grilled cheese sandwiches) Richard called his mom to tell her I was home. Something

Saving Amy

had changed between them and I couldn't quite put my finger on it. Talking away, he just seemed more relaxed, more forthcoming. I started to wonder what else I had missed. His relationships with everyone he knew seemed to have mutated in my absence.

While he chatted with his mom I called Julie. At first I was pissed that Richard had told her everything while I was unconscious, but then I realized it was because he loved me and *Julie* loved me too… she deserved to know. She offered the obligatory ramblings that I expected – 'why didn't you come to me?' 'I could've helped you.'

But the truth is, depression, fucked-up-ness, whatever you want to call it, is essentially a very selfish illness. When you are on a mission to self-destruct you become determined. It's almost addictive – the urge to find some sense of release, to escape. It consumes you entirely – leaving no room to consider anyone else, and the only person that can help you is yourself.

Next he decided it was time to remove my dressings when he caught me jabbing a ballpoint pen underneath in an effort to relieve the irritating itchiness. For the first time I allowed myself to see the damage lurking underneath. Back in the hospital, if anyone went near my bandages I would either close my eyes or stare at the round white clock above the door. But now, alone with Richard, I felt brave enough to face what I'd done.

I regretted it immediately.

I wrinkled my nose, disgusted with myself as I studied the hideous, raised and weeping scars crisscrossed all over my limbs.

"Don't do that," Richard said, interrupting my inward self-loathing.

"Do what?" I stared myself down. I wasn't doing anything.

"Hate yourself."

Of course, he knows what I'm thinking.

I shrugged, trying but failing to follow his advice.

"Amy," he said seriously – holding my gaze. "New start, remember? Things never have to get this bad again."

"And what if they do?" I said, ever the pessimist – because they *always* did. I always ended up at this point.

"Then we'll deal with it. *Together.*"

He trailed a finger along my cheekbone, sending delicious shivers through my whole body, right down to the tips of my toes.

God, I've missed this feeling.

Next, he grazed the tips of his gentle fingers over the mass of stitches, carefully tugging at ones which looked like they were being lost in the swelling and checking they were secure. Then he rubbed the familiar foul smelling ointment over each scar in turn – apologizing constantly even though it didn't hurt… much.

"Amy," Richard said, his voice oozing uncertainty.

"*Yes?*" I replied nervously.

"Now, don't get mad until I've finished."

Why do I think I'm not going to like this?

"But, well, I'd like you to reconsider counseling."

Saving Amy

I exhaled for the first time since he said 'don't get mad'. I was expecting him to say something terrible.

"What, like Joanna?" I asked sarcastically.

"Yeah, maybe we should try somebody else this time," he said with a heart-stopping wink.

"I'm not sure," I answered hesitantly. Richard's back stiffened and his green eyes - which were beginning to sparkle again - widened.

"Well, that's a start. When I played this conversation over in my head, I got an outright 'no'."

"I nearly did say that," I admitted. "But let's face it, I'm not doing such a good job of sorting my shit out on my own." Silence followed. I think we were both equally stunned that I was actually considering the idea of spilling my guts out to a complete stranger.

"I could make you an appointment with my therapist, if you'd like?" Richard offered, interposing the stillness.

"*Your* therapist?" I repeated, shaking the bewilderment from my face.

"Yes. Her name is Caroline Winters. I've been seeing her since…" he swallowed back a lump in his throat, forcing his Adam's apple up and down, "since Kate died."

"I had no idea. Why have you never mentioned it?" Richard dropped his head, pondering my question.

"Because I was embarrassed, I guess."

I know that feeling well.

"Oh, please. I'm the queen of fucked-up-ness. I'm the last person you need to feel embarrassed with." As hoped, my light-hearted statement lifted the mood and we both ended up laughing. It felt so invigorating... so *normal*. Just a few days ago I doubted I would ever laugh again.

Chapter Twenty

"I'm so proud of you," Richard beamed, twisting a loose tendril of my blond hair behind my ear as we walked out of the therapist's office.

"I couldn't have done it without you. Thank you for coming in with me."

"You know, she's probably going to want to see you on your own at some point. She might feel like my presence is hindering your progress."

"No," I said firmly, shaking my head. "There's nothing I can't say in front of you. In fact, if you weren't there, I doubt I would've said anything at all."

Caroline Winters was small and round with thick gray hair and the dress sense of a hobo. But she seemed nice enough. She was friendly, sympathetic and asked lots of questions which was just what I needed. I'd never been a fan of the 'I'm just here to listen' approach, given that it wasn't in my nature to willingly volunteer information about myself.

I had just spent the best part of two hours sat on a brown leather couch in a bright yellow room with giant poppies painted on the wall, answering an incessant ream of questions about my fucked-up childhood. I spent the first half an hour blushing and stuttering like a moron and staring at an orange wooden bookend in the shape of a cat. But then Richard placed his hand on the small of my back, sending sparks flying through my whole body and bursting the bubbles of trepidation canoeing through my veins along the way. Suddenly and unexpectedly, I couldn't seem to shut myself up.

I began with my earliest memory – the one where my mom was crumpled into a tight ball on the living room floor with my dad hovering over her, hammering a rolling-pin into her back over and over again. When he saw me watching, crying into the little blue teddy my grandma bought for me by the doorjamb, he flew towards me with the rolling pin raised high in the air as he prepared to bring it down on me too.

I gradually worked through my memories, reeling them off in minute detail – as fresh in mind as if they happened just yesterday. Then at 01:58 (according to the stereo sat alone on an empty table at the back of the room) Caroline looked to her watch and said we'd ran out of time for today. I'd been talking nonstop for ninety minutes yet I'd only managed to get as far as my seventh birthday.

I relived the day where my father grabbed my ponytail and rammed my face into the round birthday cake with pink frosting and edible daisies that my grandma made for me, after he caught me crying about not getting any presents. Naturally, he lit the candles first. As I described what happened, I brushed my finger along my cheek, still being able to feel the burn of the candles as they extinguished themselves on my skin. Sometimes, when I was drifting off to sleep, the sulphurous odor of singeing hair still lingered in my nose.

I had a feeling I would be visiting Caroline Winters for a *long* time to come.

Saving Amy

Richard had some files to pick up from work (apparently he needed to 'get back in the zone' before his first shift back tomorrow) so after leaving the therapy session we headed straight to the hospital. Richard was busy concentrating on the road and I was busy concentrating on Richard. He was wearing his cream turtleneck, the one that made him look like he just stepped out of a magazine, and fitted black jeans. I found myself blushing at the pure fuckability of him, and the fact that he was all *mine*.

I switched my focus to the window before I ended up pouncing on him and causing an accident, absorbing the sight of buildings and skyscrapers merging into one another as we whizzed past them. I felt... different. *Better*, I think. Lighter...

I rolled my shoulders and for the first time in my life it felt effortless – as if the encumbering weight that had been bearing down on them since the day I was born had finally packed its bags and fucked the hell off. I was slowly making my way back up the rollercoaster. Hopefully, this time it would malfunction when I reached the top, keeping me there – on top of the world, instead of dragging me back down into the black hole.

"Be right back, beautiful," Richard said before bringing my hand up to his mouth and brushing the fading I.V. marks affectionately with his lips. Then he slid out of the car and scurried towards the automatic glass doors of the hospital, shielding himself from the rain with his black military style jacket slung over his head.

I felt like a fish in a glass bowl. It seemed like every passer-by and his dog felt compelled to pause and stare my way. I imagined (*hoped*) it was Richard's ostentatious Mercedes that was catching their eye but still, I felt awfully self-conscious and started to squirm uncomfortably in my seat.

In an effort to distract myself from the unease I fiddled with the stereo. Richard had all the stations pre-programmed with depressing classical shit so I tapped the little silver button until a song I recognized comes on. 'So What' by Pink blasted from the speakers and I closed my eyes, flopped my head back on the neck rest and sang (or perhaps wailed like a banshee would be more apt) knowing nobody was around to endure it.

The car door slammed closed, scaring the living crap out of me.

"I've literally just shit all over your upholstery," I said to Richard, jolting upright in my seat. I *hadn't* actually shit my pants of course - I was just trying to be funny. Richard couldn't be any less amused however. His arms were rigid as he twisted his fingers around the steering wheel. I reached out and grabbed one before he started the engine.

"Everything okay?" I asked, unnerved by his edgy disposition.

"Sure," he said with a crack in his voice. "Okay, I'm not actually sure," he admitted, taking his hands from the wheel and rubbing his forearm.

"What's wrong?" I pressed, unwittingly rubbing his other forearm for him.

"I don't want you to panic. I mean, she was probably bullshitting… after all, it wouldn't be the first time she's lied to me. I just-"

"Who was? Richard you're scaring me," I interrupted, pushing him to get to the point. His tense fingers drifted from his forearm to his hair, tugging at it so fervently I worried he was going to rip it clean from the follicles.

"*Joanna*. She says she's informed the authorities about your father."

In my head I was screaming 'she did what!' but in reality I couldn't seem to move my lips to let the words pass. I couldn't seem to move anything actually. I was paralyzed… numb.

"Apparently, if things are as bad as you say then…" he trailed off, guilt clouding his emerald eyes. "Amy I'm so sorry. I should never have trusted her."

I told you that at the time, my subconscious snapped. Thankfully I still hadn't regained the ability to speak. The rational part of my brain knew Richard wasn't to blame. This was my father's fault for being a sadistic bastard. Or Joanna's fault for being a vindictive, jealous bitch. Or probably even mine, for not being brave enough to end this all a long time ago – back when Richard wasn't around to watch me suffer the inevitable consequences.

"Amy, say something. *Please*," Richard begged. Tears clogging in the back of his throat made his voice tremor as he cupped my face in his hands.

"I guess we better go home and wait for my dad to show up," I said, feeling remarkably composed. Waiting for a beating from my father was one of the few things I coped pretty well with. Maybe because it was familiar. I knew what to expect – I knew how it would feel both outside and in.

"It won't get that far. *If* Joanna is telling the truth," he said, emphasizing the word 'if', "then he can't get to you from inside a cell." I almost choked on an inappropriate laugh.

"Richard, you know who my father is. He is one of the best defense attorneys in Washington State – there's nothing he can't talk himself out of."

"He's a different man now. You've seen him. He's losing it – he's losing everything. And if by some miracle he does find a loophole, he still won't get anywhere near you. I'll make sure of it." Fear slammed into my chest, forcing my heart into my stomach. Not fear of my dad (though I expected that to creep up on me soon enough) but fear for Richard. The idea of him blocking my father's path, the knowledge that my dad would willingly beat him until he was unrecognizable to get to me… the thought exploded in my mind like shards of glass.

The drive home was quiet, uncomfortably so. Unable to bear the torment drowning Richard's expression I stared out of the window, watching the rain wash away the last traces of snow, dissolving the residual murky slush into muddy puddles. I gnawed at my fingernails until all that remained was inflamed, frayed skin. My life was balancing in the carriage at the top of the rollercoaster, waiting to plummet at any moment.

Walking from the underground parking lot I found myself looking over my shoulder with every couple of steps. Then I caught Richard doing the same. *Is this life from now on?* I couldn't stand it – the unease, the fear, the ups and downs… It was just too much and as soon as we hit the safety of the apartment, I started bawling like a baby.

"Let's not get ahead of ourselves," Richard tried to reassure, smoothing the tears from my cheeks

Saving Amy

with the sleeve of his cream turtleneck. "Let me call the station – see if I can find anything out."

I was on edge – jumpy and nervous. Goosebumps mottled my pale skin even though I wasn't cold and the slightest sound made me flinch. I was pouring a glass of water when Richard entered the kitchen. The sound of his heavy footsteps scared the life out of me and I dropped my glass, gasping as it crashed to the tile floor and shattered into a million pieces. Richard sidestepped the shards of glass, dismissing them, and then placed a hand on each of my huddled shoulders.

"It's true," he breathed. "They brought your father in for questioning this morning."

"Okay," I said, unfathomably calm, without so much as a dip in my heart rate.

"You know, they're going to need to talk to you," he added, as if he was trying to provoke a reaction out of my expressionless face.

"Yes." Richard's crinkled eyes scrutinized my face and he led me over to the couch with an arm around my waist as if he was expecting me to collapse at any moment.

"What are you feeling?" he probed gently with a perplexed glint in his eyes. I shrugged at him.

"I don't feel anything." And it was the truth. I didn't feel scared, angry, nervous… A little numb perhaps, but nothing overwhelming. In fact I almost felt impatient. Part of me wished my dad would burst through the door right now and get whatever he had planned over with so I could move on…
again.

The day dragged in silence. Richard was too nervous to say anything and I was too numb. At 06:30 PM the intercom buzzed, flooding the dense air and startling us both.

This is it...

We both hesitated and my pulse thudded violently in my ears as my body and mind started to regain feeling – like they were preparing for battle. I'd never fought back before, but I'd replayed the possible scenario of my dad's fist landing on Richard's body over and over in my mind and each time it ended with me smashing something blunt and heavy across the twisted fucker's skull.

I noticed Richard flex the muscles in his neck (his own pre-battle ritual I assumed) and then he ambled cautiously, slowly, out into the hall to pick up the receiver.

"You're not welcome here," was the first thing I heard him say.

He's here... My heart fluttered furiously like a butterfly with a broken wing and even though my dad was nineteen floors away, locked behind a set of heavy duty glass doors I could smell the putrid, musty stench of Old Spice.

"I have nothing to say to you..."

Wait, he wants Richard? I wondered as I stared down at my knotted fingers. One-sided conversations were so frustrating.

"Have you any fucking idea what you've done, you stupid bitch?" I let out an involuntary gasp, relief and disappointment coursing through my veins when I realized he was talking to Joanna.

I wanted this over with.

Saving Amy

I heard the receiver slam against the wall and Richard was back by my side soon after.

"Joanna?" I questioned – just to make sure. Richard nodded and we fell back into the well of desolate silence.

Richard sat back in the chair, his posture tense, rigid. I drew my legs up and lay down with my head on his lap, fiddling with a loose thread on his gray sweatpants. My heart started to slow and my body relaxed as he twiddled with strands of my hair between his fingers. Then, I bolted upright at the thunderous sound of someone pounding shit out of the door.

"Wait there," Richard ordered sternly, signaling me to stay with the palm of his hand. I ignored him, refusing to let him take the beating that was meant for me.

I followed him to the door and it felt like we were walking in slow motion. When we reached the end of the hall I heard Richard deep breathing through pursed lips, hovering his hand above the latch but not feeling quite ready to touch it.

"Richard, please, I just want to talk."

"For fuck's sake," we said in unison, hearing Joanna's muffled voice on the other side of the door. She must have lurked downstairs until someone else buzzed the entrance.

"I'm not leaving until you speak to me," she ranted when she got no response. Richard flashed me a look as if asking me for permission to open the door. I shrugged at him.

"Whatever." *Just get rid of her.*

I turned away as he unclasped the latch, sure she had nothing to say that I wanted to hear. I heard her talking as I turned into the living room but my brain shut off to the words. Heading into the kitchen I noticed the floor was still peppered with broken glass so I set about sweeping it up with a flowery pink dustpan from under the sink. I eyed it up curiously, wondering why I'd never seen it before. I decided Vivienne must've brought it round while I was... *away,* although I couldn't think why.

Hovering my hand over the stainless steel trashcan (still amazed at how it opened all by itself) I angled my other hand ready to tip the fragments of glass inside. But then I heard a loud thud, followed by a smash that made me drop the dustpan, re-scattering the glass all over the floor.

"I said you'll stay the fuck away from her!" I heard Richard yell, stopping my heart dead in my chest.

This really is it.

Knowing Richard was in danger I immediately darted towards the noise. My dad had Richard pinned against the wall by his throat. There were shards of shattered ceramic littering the hardwood floor and the half moon glass table had a hefty crack down its center. Richard's eyes were bulging and bloodshot as he struggled to breathe and the sleeves of my dad's light blue shirt were rolled up, exposing his protuberant veins.

"Do something!" Joanna yelped, drawing my attention to her cowering in the corner, sniveling into the black sleeve of her jacket. My dad's neck quickly snapped in my direction.

"There you are," he breathed in that horrifyingly calm voice of his – the voice that let me know he was enjoying it.

Saving Amy

He gave Richard's neck one last thrust into the wall and then let go, turning his focus to me. My heart constricted as I watched Richard's eyes roll into the back of his head and he slid down the white wall. I wanted to run to him, hold him, let him hold me, but I was trapped – my dad was just inches away and closing in on me. Instinctively I walked backwards but my every step was matched by my father's until I was cornered in the living room. That familiar look of hatred tinged with pleasure shone bright in his blue eyes and I hunched my body, preparing myself.

"You are one stupid bitch. I always knew you wouldn't be able to keep that grubby little mouth of yours shut. Have you any fucking idea of the shame you've brought upon me today?" I shook my head, recoiling back into the pathetic little coward who just wanted to say the right thing – to please him.

"You think your hot-shot doctor friend can save you? Is that it? Because I'm telling you now I could have him struck off before sunrise if I wanted to." And I knew he was telling the truth. My dad had that kind of power over things. Like I'd said a thousand times to Richard – he *knew* people.

"SPEAK GODDAMMIT!" he roared, and then I was blinded by a swift, harsh blow to the face, knocking me back on my heels. I opened my eyes and the room spun around me.

"I'm sorry," I whimpered through quivering lips. "Please, Daddy, it hurts." I don't know what happened to me. I'd retreated back to the frightened seven-year-old little girl who felt bad for making her daddy angry as he yanked on her ponytail.

"DON'T. CALL. ME. THAT!"

My vision was blurred like heat rising from a fire but I saw the rippling outline of a fist speed towards me. I heard a crack as his knuckles rammed into his favorite spot - my ribs. My body doubled over as I cried out, falling to the floor.

Bells rang in my ears – after effects of the first punch – but I could hear faint wailing in the background. I could tell from the screeching nails-down-chalkboard tone that it was coming from Joanna. I tried to hear past her, desperately searching for a sound that belonged to Richard… I got nothing.

Please, God don't let him be dead.

Needing to get to him, I clawed my fingers into the grooves of the wood floor and tried to hitch myself along like a slug. But then I let out an ear splitting scream, rolling onto my back in agony as a heavy black boot stomped onto the back of my hand.

"Please, sir. Please, no more," I pleaded, for the first time ever *begging* him to stop, even though I knew it would make no difference. The lumbering boot lifted from my hand and through flickering eyes I caught it swinging backwards, preparing to kick.

"ARGH!" I screamed as the boot collided with my stomach. I curled up into a tight ball, cradling my stomach as I watched the boot lift back again. I closed my eyes, anticipating the pain… but nothing happened.

A deafening crash startled my eyes wide open and I gasped at the sight of my dad lay crumpled over the coffee table.

"Don't just stand there, call the fucking police!" Richard blasted, briefly turning his gaze to Joanna

Saving Amy

who was still trembling in the hall and then flipping it back to my dad. All my pain and fear melted away at the sound of his voice. *He's alive...*

I tried to move, desperate to get to Richard, to save him, but the mere movement it took to breathe sent crippling pain all the way through my body. So I lay, frozen and helpless as I witnessed my dad uncurl himself and rise to his feet. He pierced Richard with the most terrifying look I'd ever seen him possess.

He's going to kill him.

My dad lunged for Richard, letting out a deep growl like some kind of jungle animal. Richard ducked, throwing my dad off balance and then when he reached for Richard's throat, Richard grabbed his arm, twisting it behind his back and forcing his body up against the wall by the fireplace.

"Amy? *Amy?*" Richard called out to me, tightening his grip around my dad's arm. "Amy, talk to me. Are you okay?"

I nodded weakly, noticing the hurt and frustration clouding his face because he couldn't rush to my side. He couldn't risk letting go of the sadistic animal he had pinned to the wall, and I wouldn't want him to. Suddenly, my dad let out a piercing shriek and fell limp in Richard's constraints.

"What the fuck?" Richard breathed while struggling to support my father's weight. I was convinced it was a hoax – a rouse to get Richard to release him. And so when he did, I squeezed my eyes closed and waited for the sound of the next punch.

It didn't come.

I dared a peek and my dad was lay flat on his back with Richard kneeling over his lifeless body.

"Joanna!" Richard beckoned. "Get an ambulance with that police car. Tell them he's gone into cardiac arrest!"

Holy shit, is he… dying? Has Richard… killed him?

Still paralyzed with pain and fear, I had no option but to lie and watch as Richard pounded into my dad's chest, fighting to save the life of a man who moments ago would have willingly taken his away.

"I'm so sorry. I just didn't realize. I just didn't think…" Joanna whined in the doorway.

"Quit the self pity and call a fucking ambulance!" Richard roared at her as he hammered away, his back jolting up and down to the rhythm.

I heard Joanna rambling on her cell phone in the background but I didn't listen to what she was saying. Instead I kept my flickering eyes fixed on my father lay helpless and dying in front of me.

"Come on, you son of a bitch!" Richard roared through clenched teeth as he pressed his ear against my dad's mouth. Part of me wondered why he was bothering.

Just leave him to rot, my subconscious seethed.

In that moment a heavy rasp evolved from my dad's throat. It sounded like he was choking.

"He's breathing," Richard appeared to mutter to himself, wiping the sweat from his brow with his fingers. He looked… relieved. *Why?* "Where the hell is that ambulance?"

Just then, as if they heard him, an ambulance crew consisting of two female paramedics and a dark-haired man who I vaguely recognized burst into the room. Richard and the doctor shook hands briefly and I listened to them exchange incomprehensible jargon as Richard explained what'd happened.

I didn't realize my eyes had closed until a warm pair of Armani Cologne scented hands cupped my face, startling them open.

"Richard," I breathed. In my head I was smiling but I couldn't be sure if it actually reached my face.

"You're going to be okay. Everything's going to be okay."

"What about my dad?" I croaked, still winded from my blow to the stomach. I think I sounded more concerned than I intended to.

"He's breathing... for now."

For now?

I genuinely didn't know which way I was hoping it would swing. Part of me wanted him dead. Gone. Out of my life for good. But a stronger part of me thought wishing for such a thing would make me no better than him.

"Can you stand?"

"Um, I'm not sure."

I didn't admit that I hadn't even thought to try – that selfishly, I'd just been lying there, too consumed by the pain to bother. Richard snaked an arm around my waist, hoisting me upwards. I cried out from the shooting pain reverberating through my insides. It stole my breath away and my body buckled – straight into Richard's arms. Once standing, I felt better – physically at least. The pain was... bearable.

Richard guided me to the corner couch and settled me down while he examined my swollen purple hand. I tried to focus on him but my eyes kept wandering back to where I didn't want them to be. I watched as the familiar man and paramedics attached various tubes and wires to my dad's body and then slid him onto a long white board.

"We'll meet you there," Richard said to the man who was clearly his friend as the paramedics began the process of my wheeling my dad out the door on the gurney they strapped the white board to.

"It's not safe for you to drive until you've been checked over." Richard started to protest his friend talked over him. "I've called in the QRV to pick you both up. I've also redirected the police to the hospital." Richard nodded and everyone left, leaving just me, Richard and a quivering Joanna.

I started to wonder if I'd ever see my dad again. I felt an inexplicable pang of sadness that I might not and I couldn't even begin to understand why.

"Amy, look at me," Richard said softly. And so I did. It was only then that I witnessed blood congealing around the base of his nose, and the finger shaped bruises marking his neck. I realized that was because this was the first time I'd actually looked at him. Before now, my eyes refused to shift from my dying father.

"Oh, Richard," I whimpered as I traced my finger along the marbled bruises, "I'm so sorry."

A fire of guilt ignited in my stomach. I felt so responsible. He was *my* father after all, and it was *me* he wanted – not Richard.

"Don't you *dare* apologize for him!" Richard ordered sternly, making me shrink back a little. "I'm fine. It's nothing a splash of cold water won't sort out," he assured – his voice hoarse but tender.

"Can you wiggle your fingers?" he asked, switching his attention back to my ballooning hand.

"Ow!" I shook my head when I realized that I couldn't.

"I think it's broken…"

"Richard I-" Joanna's sniveling voice surprised us both and our necks jerked towards her at the same time. "I had no idea things were this bad." She bowed her head, her cheeks burning with shame.

"Funny that, because I remember telling you *exactly* how bad things were," Richard snapped, shooting Joanna with a look of pure revulsion.

"I thought… I thought you were just making excuses for *her*."

I bit my top lip to stifle an inopportune giggle at just how fucking pathetic she was. Richard glowered at her but I couldn't quite decipher the expression on his face. Anger? Hurt? Both?

"I'm sorry," Joanna tacked on. It was worth shit to me, but then I doubted it was me she was saying it to.

"Just leave, Joanna. There's nothing left for you to destroy here."

Tears welled up around Joanna's hazel eyes, making them glimmer like glass. She nodded once, defeated and ashamed, then picked up her black leather bag from the floor and turned to leave.

"For what it's worth, I really *am* sorry," she declared as she reached the other side of the doorjamb. As much as I didn't want to, I believed her.

She's still a total bitch, my subconscious sneered and I didn't hesitate to agree.

As Joanna left, two paramedics entered – they must have crossed in the hallway. *How the fuck are all these people managing to just waltz up here without being buzzed in?* I dismissed the thought as quick as it appeared, realizing not only did I not have the capacity in my brain for it, but that I didn't actually care either.

The paramedics – one short man with more hair on his chin than his head, and one woman with bright red hair scraped into a bun – checked me and Richard over in turn. When they'd finished their prodding and poking, Richard helped me to my feet – the pain rendering me breathless again – and we followed them out to the red and white SUV.

Chapter Twenty-One

Although neither of us were admitted, by the time Richard and I had finished being patched up it was almost morning. I had my first broken hand and second cracked rib – all gifts from my father, and I was now the proud owner of a strapped hand – bound tightly with tan bandages and two wooden splints securing my fingers together.

A box of chocolates really would have sufficed, I thought – trying to make light of the situation. Because if I didn't, I would cry – and I wasn't sure I would ever be able to stop.

"I have some news about your father," Richard said cautiously upon his return from getting his nose fixed. It was starting to turn blue and he had two little white strips hugging the bridge. "Do you want to hear it?"

I swallowed back the choking lump swelling in my throat and nodded slowly, unsure I was making the right decision but knowing I would have to find out sooner or later.

"He has a pulmonary embolism, and given the fact he's been suffering from coronary heart disease for the last few years, his heart is too weak to endure surgery."

What? My dad's been sick for years? I was surprised I didn't know this. Then I was surprised that I was surprised. *Why would I know?* I didn't know anything about my father.

"Preliminary what? What does that mean? Is he... *dying?*" The word stung more than I thought it would. More than it *should*.

"Sorry... *Pulmonary* embolism – it means a blood clot has formed in his veins and migrated to his lung, blocking the main artery there. Amy, he doesn't have long." Richard cupped my face, assessing it with his concerned eyes. "Are you alright? You're as white as a sheet."

"I-I don't know." I thought I felt sad, but I couldn't determine if that was because I really was sad, or I just thought I should be. "Is he awake? I'd like to see him." Richard furrowed his eyebrows and stared at me intently – as if I'd lost my marbles. "It's not like he can hurt me is it?"

I couldn't blame him for being anxious or confused. Even *I* didn't really know why I wanted to see him. I'd hated him for as long as I could remember and possibly even before that. But as crazy as it sounds, he was my dad... and he was *dying*.

"Well, he's drifting in and out of consciousness. I can't guarantee he'll be able to hear you."

"That's okay. I'm not planning on talking to him."

"Then, *why?*" he asked incredulously. I shrugged.

"I don't know. Maybe because I know I'll never get another chance." Richard nodded, trying and failing to understand. Then he pulled me into his chest and kissed my hair.

"I love you," he whispered.

"I love you too."

Saving Amy

Two strong black coffees and a few crumbs of burnt toast later, I was ready to see my dad for the last time. Richard led me up three floors in an elevator and then down two corridors to the Critical Care Unit.

"After you," he said, holding open the heavy green door to my dad's bay.

"I'd rather do this alone, if you don't mind," I said sensitively, certain I wouldn't be able to hold myself together with Richard in such close proximity. Richard's forearm was being graced with a good old rubbing and I knew he was about to disapprove.

"I don't know, Amy. I'm just not comfortable with you being alone with him."

"Richard, he's unconscious… he can't hurt me," I reassured, placing a hand on each of his shoulders and stepping up on my tiptoes so our eyes were almost level.

"Okay," he shrugged in defeat, tracing the fresh bruise under my eye with his fingers. "I'll be right here if you need me." I nodded gently and then brushed his lips with mine, giving him a meaningful kiss bursting with a thousand different emotions – love, gratitude, fear, hope…

Using the weight of my entire tiny body to push open the heavy door I didn't realize I was holding my breath until the door slammed loudly behind me, startling my lungs back into action. I closed my eyes before I looked at him, breathing deeply, forcefully, through pursed lips as I tried to psyche myself up. Knowing that time was against me and unable to procrastinate any longer, I peeled my eyes open.

He looked so small, so frail – like his body had literally shrunk as it prepared to die. It was almost comforting to see him so vulnerable – stripped of all his menace and power. His skin was a deathly shade of gray. It was rugged and withered, as if all the moisture was evaporating along with his life. He was hooked up with tubes and wires to a whole host of different machines, all purring and beeping in sync with each other like they were in a band.

I edged closer to the bed and stared at his chest, watching as it struggled to rise and fall. I wasn't sure what I felt. I wasn't sure what I *should* feel. I started to wonder what he was like as a child. What could have happened to make him who he was? Maybe he was just born that way. Could people be born evil?

Accepting that I would probably never find my answers my thoughts moved on to what *my* life could have been like if he'd have been different – if he'd loved me. Would I be sitting on the edge of his bed right now, crying as I clutched his hand and praying to some higher being for just a little more time with him?

Numb. That's what I felt. Empty.

I didn't know why but I felt an overwhelming urge to touch him. It was mainly curiosity I think - wondering what it would feel like for his skin to *touch* mine, rather than slamming into it, or grabbing it, or twisting it…

Cautiously, I grazed the skin over his knuckles with my thumb. It felt so much softer than I thought it would. I recalled how that same skin felt when it rammed into my face, my ribs or my stomach… It felt so much firmer, so much rougher when it struck you with such speed. My whole body shivered at the unwanted memories and when I felt tears clawing at the back of my eyes I turned to leave, having accomplished nothing.

"Amelia? Is that you?"

Fuck. Fuck. Fuck. My heart stopped. My feet melted into the floor. My stomach churned. *Fuck.*

"Amelia?" His voice was a hoarse, rasping whisper. Hesitantly, I turned to face him.

"Yes. It's me." Fear pooled in my stomach even though I knew he couldn't hurt me – physically at least.

I waited anxiously for a reply but after a single weak nod I got nothing more. It infuriated me. *What does he want? Should I ask him? Should I leave?* And then, completely unplanned and out of the blue, my mouth opened in preparation to speak words my brain hadn't even thought of yet.

"Dad, did you *ever* love me?"

An intense silence followed and the faint bleeps of the machines pounded like thunder in my ears. I didn't know if it was because he was thinking or he was dying but his response seemed to take hours.

"I don't know *how* to love, Amelia," he croaked, never opening his eyes.

The words scraped at my heart, ripping it to shreds. For the first time in my life I didn't feel responsible. It wasn't me – I didn't push him too far or not try hard enough to be a good girl. I wasn't such a bad kid that I made it impossible for him to love me… It was him. It was always him. He was broken…

I closed my burning eyes in an effort to stem the river of tears. But as I did the machines surrounding my dad roared to life, flashing and buzzing to their own raucous melody. Seconds later a swarm of white coats and blue scrubs burst into the room, shouting unintelligible medical terminology and flocking towards my dad's bed like flies on shit.

A man in a blue scrubs pulled a lever which instantly flattened my dad's bed with an almighty crash and then he tipped my dad's head back and prized his mouth open.

"You need to wait outside," a woman who I didn't bother to look at said to me, nudging me towards the door. I did as I was told, pausing at the door to take one last look at my dad as his wretched life slipped away from him– knowing it would be the last time I ever did. Then I heaved open the double doors and flew into Richard's arms.

We didn't speak. Richard brought me into his chest and cradled my head against his shoulder. I could feel his heartbeat fluttering against my chest, just as fast and erratic as mine. There were muffled voices and machines singing behind the door of my dad's room… and then it fell silent.

This is it. He's dead. My father is dead.

The heavy green door squealed in protest as it scraped open against the floor. I eased myself out of Richard's grasp and shot my gaze towards a man in a white overcoat who had just stepped out.

"Simon?" Richard said, speaking the doctor's name like it was a question. The doctor – Simon – shook his head, bowing it slightly, respectfully.

I let out an involuntary gasp and threw my hand over my mouth.

"I'm very sorry," Simon said automatically and then disappeared down the corridor.

Saving Amy

I felt... *devastated*. And I hated myself for it. Tears sprung from my eyes, washing over the fresh bruises inflicted by the man I was mourning for. I rubbed frantically at my cheeks, trying to wipe away the tears before they even fell.

"It's okay, Amy. Everything's okay," Richard whispered as he attempted to wrap his arms around me. I batted them away with my tear soaked hands.

"It's not okay!" I snapped. "That man has destroyed my life. He stole my childhood. He tortured me until I didn't want to live anymore. And now he's dead and I'm upset! I'm actually fucking sad because he's dead! How is that okay?"

I was full on hysterical. My chest was tight. My pulse racing. I couldn't breathe...

"I should be happy for Christ's sake! Why am I not pleased? Why can't I hate him? Richard, I *need* to hate him!" I yelled, draining my lungs of their last drop of air. I heaved my chest up and down but I couldn't drag in enough oxygen. I felt like I was drowning.

"Shh, shh, baby, you need to calm down. Breathe, Amy. Just breathe." Richard had his hands on my shoulders. He was speaking but I couldn't hear him. I couldn't breathe. I was choking.

"FUCKING BREATHE, AMY!" he roared straight into my face, shaking hell out of my shoulders. My body jolted upright and I clutched my pounding chest as air finally crashed into my lungs. "Good girl."

He snaked one arm around my waist and one around my neck, cradling me. I didn't resist this time. I let my weak, weary body collapse into his arms and as much as I despised my tears, I set them free –

letting them soak into Richard's shirt until there were none left to shed.

****

The human mind is an amazing thing. Just when you think it's ran out of room, when you start to worry it might physically burst under the pressure, it surprises you by squeezing in just a little more. A little more pain, a little more fear, a little more heartache, confusion, love, hatred… Or maybe that's just *my* mind.

My head was fucked. My body wasn't too far off either. It was covered in bumpy, hideous scars, scratches and bruises. It was disgusting. *I* was disgusting. That was down to me as much as my father. We'd both hacked and punched away at my body in equal measures until it became what it is today. Maybe that was why I was struggling to hate him – because deep down, I knew I was no better.

Richard was lying next to me in bed. He shifted onto his side, propping himself up on one elbow and trailing his thumb along my cheek.

"You're crying," he noted.

Am I?

"Sorry. I didn't mean to wake you." I squinted my eyes towards the bedside clock. It was 03:47 in the morning. I hadn't been to sleep yet.

"I wish I could help you."

He buried his head in my shoulder. His expression was painful to witness. He was so worried about me – it broke my heart. I wanted something to be able to help me too. I wanted something to slice into my brain and cut away all the badness, all the hurt, all the anger… But nothing could help me. The only thing that'd ever been able to help me was… lying right next to me. The realization struck me like lightning.

Richard… I needed Richard.

I rolled myself onto my side and hitched one leg over Richard's hips, pulling myself up on his shoulders so I was straddling him. I took his angst-ridden face in my hands and brushed his lips with mine. Prizing his lips apart with my tongue, I deepened the kiss… exploring him, tasting him, kissing our pain away.

I worked my way down his body, kissing his cheeks, his neck, his torso – his involuntary groans intensifying my desire to be with him.

"Amy, stop," he breathed, lifting my head from his chest. "What are you doing? I can't make love to you like this. You're exhausted. You're hurting. You're-" I silenced him by placing a finger over his lips.

"*Please*, Richard. I need this. I need *you*," I whispered as I returned my lips to his bare chest.

I need you to take it all away…

I trailed my hand down his chest, along the defined muscles hugging his hips and then into the waistband of his sweatpants. He didn't resist as I reached inside and felt him growing between my fingers. He wanted this. He wanted *me*.

Richard grabbed me by the waist and flipped me onto my back, slipping his fingers under the hem of my purple satin nightdress. Instinctively I raised my arms above my head and he slid it off me, following its path with kisses – frantic, passionate, demanding kisses. His touch made my entire body quiver and every hair stood to attention. My heart was racing so fast it was only just not frightening.

I arched my back, pressing myself into him as he kissed along my neck, his deep craving groans vibrating against my skin. His hands wandered to my breasts, cupping them, stroking them, and then he brought his head down letting his tongue take their place. I gasped as his fingers trailed across my overly sensitized skin and down into my panties. Slowly, tantalizingly, he peeled them off, sliding them down my legs and tossing them onto the floor behind him. Then he paused at the foot of the bed to remove his own pants and my body was left alone and helpless, writhing with desire and need.

As he slid himself back up onto the bed my hips started to thrust against him – wanton and desperate, craving the feel of him. Lowering himself on top of me, he tucked one hand behind the base of my neck, lifting my head to meet his lips. He kissed me fervently, his tongue delving into my mouth and entwining with mine. His fingers were teasing me, twisting and circling my nipples. Then he glided his smooth fingers down my body, being extra gentle as he caressed my bruised ribs.

I moaned when he slipped two fingers inside me, sliding them in and out, circling them, teasing me, *torturing* me… Then he ripped them abruptly out of me, making my breath hitch and my body shiver. But before I had chance to plead for more he nestled himself between my legs and slammed into me. My back arched and my hips matched his slow, tantalizing rhythm.

Saving Amy

"You're amazing, Amy," he whispered through gritted teeth, his hungry green eyes penetrating mine. "So strong. So beautiful."

My fingers clawed at the back of his neck, kneading beads of his sweat into his skin. As he picked up his pace he kissed me hard – my lips, my cheeks, my breasts… His body moved faster. His kisses grew harder. My body began to tighten around him – pleasure, heat, *need,* building up inside me, intensifying with every delicious thrust.

"I love you," Richard breathed and his words tipped me over the edge. I cried out loudly, screaming his name as my legs tightened their grip around his waist. With one last thrust, one hard, determined thrust, he breathed my name and poured himself into me – his body juddering until it stilled altogether. "So much," he whispered as he let his body collapse onto mine.

And as if by magic, all the anguish, the hurt, the need to hate… melted away. For now at least.

****

It'd been a week since my dad died. Today was his funeral and I decided to attend literally five minutes ago. I felt like I needed to see it through to the end. I needed… closure. I hadn't told Richard and I didn't plan to either – at least not until it was over. It took me three days to persuade him to go back to work, to convince him that I could cope. So I wasn't about to call him and tell him that I couldn't.

I was just about ready to leave. I was hardly dressed for the occasion in my black jeans and

Richard's gray hoody, but that didn't matter because I wasn't planning on letting anyone see me. After heading to the bathroom and scraping my wayward hair back into a ponytail, I slipped on my black pumps, grabbed the keys to the Audi and left.

I pulled up outside the church, trying but failing to remember a single time my dad visited church while he was alive. Then, after a few long minutes arguing with my subconscious about whether to turn around, I stuck to my guns and stepped out onto the gravel. I pulled my hair down to conceal my face as I weaved through a fairly large gathering of people dressed in black from head to toe.

The possibilities were slim seeing as my dad never introduced me to anyone but still I kept my head down in an effort to go unrecognized. I wasn't sure I'd be able to listen to anyone offer their condolences without screaming what a violent monster he was. When I reached a cluster of evergreen shrubs I tucked myself behind them while I waited for everyone to head inside. The sick bastard had received quite an impressive turnout. It made my stomach churn.

I watched the mourners curiously, studying their serious faces, their tears, their sadness. I didn't recognize anyone therefore I doubted they'd recognize me, so I hesitantly edged my way nearer to the crowd grieving for the man they thought they knew. My ears pricked up at the sound of tires crunching the gravel and the mourners slowly dispersed to the edges of the church grounds.

"He's here. Jimmy boy's here," I heard someone say.

Saving Amy

I looked behind me and saw the scattering people making room for the hearse. I threw my hand against my mouth, fearing that I might throw up when it drove unnervingly slowly past me. Sprays of white lilies shrouded the dark wood coffin and flowers arranged into the name 'JIM' lined the horizontal window. I started to wonder who arranged all this – who would care enough? My mom perhaps? But then I remembered she'd not been in a state fit enough to tie her own shoelaces for as long as I could remember. Instinctively my eyes scanned the swarm of people closing in on the hearse in search of her, even though I knew in reality she wouldn't be able to drag herself away from her bottle of gin long enough to come.

The crowd merged into a line and slowly followed the four pallbearers dressed in black top hats and tailcoats who were carrying my dad's casket into the arched, medieval looking doors. I didn't join the line. I didn't come here to listen to prayers and speeches about what a wonderful man he was. I came to watch him being lowered into the ground, to watch him be buried beneath the earth where he couldn't hurt me anymore.

While the service was in motion I headed back to the car and began the short journey to Lake View Cemetery. When I arrived I took myself off to mine and Julie's bench, scraping the dirt beneath my feet and reminiscing about all our skipping school antics. I only ever remembered being happy when I was sat here, secluded from the cruel world that lingered on the other side of the trees. But now he'd taken that from me too. I would never be happy here again knowing my dad was rotting just a few yards away.

I jumped to my feet when I saw a hearse approaching in the distance. It stopped smoothly beside the war memorial and before long the swarm of mourners were slowly closing in on it. The short balding priest came into view first, followed by the pallbearers and my dad, with the sea of black trailing dolefully behind them. I waited for them to reach the mound of freshly dug dirt a few headstones away before moving forward. Gradually I inched myself nearer to them, periodically pausing and pretending to read the headstones as I tried not to draw attention to myself.

I was soon standing behind a sniffling woman dabbing her heavily mascaraed eyes with a pink tissue. I swear it took all my inner strength not to slap the truth into her. I noticed thick black velvet ropes resting underneath the coffin… resting under *him*. The four pallbearers bent in unison to pick up an end each and then they lifted him effortlessly, suspending him above the deep hole lined with green felt before gracefully lowering him into it – all the while the priest talked away with his hands offered up to the sky.

"I'm surprised his wife isn't here," I heard a tall man with snow white hair whispered into a plump, brown-haired mans ear in front of me.

"Well, from what I've heard she likes a drink or twenty, if you get what I mean," he whispered back, molding his hand into the shape of a glass and gesturing it towards his mouth.

"Wow. Poor bastard going home to that every night, huh? No wonder he started going downhill. I heard he'd taken to gambling. Lost everything." They nodded at one another and I almost choked trying to stifle a humorless laugh. "That must be where his daughter's at... taking care of her."

The ignorant man's words struck a chord inside my heart and I stumbled backwards. *Should I be taking care of her?* There was sure as hell no one else who would. She'd not stepped beyond the front door in years and I started to wonder - worry even - if she'd managed to buy food since he died – if she'd eaten, if she'd showered... Then I started to wonder why I even cared.

The priest gave a little speech that I didn't listen to, made the sign of the cross and then passed a box of dirt into the crowd of mourners. One by one people scooped a handful of earth from the little wooden box and tossed it on top of my father before making their own sign of the cross.

'Good riddance' I muttered under my breath but I wasn't convinced I actually meant it.

****

I couldn't stop thinking about my mom during the drive home. I didn't want to think about her. I didn't want to care about her. But I did... and it was confusing the hell out of me. The idea of paying her a visit turned over and over in my mind. Eventually I decided that I absolutely, definitely would *not* go and see her.

Then I change my mind...

I convinced myself I didn't have to help her or form any kind of relationship. But maybe I could finally get some answers now she didn't have to worry about the ramifications from my dad. I'd had questions burning holes in the back of my head for so long I'd persuaded myself I didn't need the answers — that they were irrelevant. They wouldn't change anything after all. But maybe I'd never be able to move on without them. Maybe I'd always be fucked-up if I didn't ask them.

I wanted to know how she felt when she found out she was pregnant. Was she happy or was I a mistake from the start? Did she ever love me? Why did she allow me to suffer at the hands of my father? Why didn't she at least *try* to stop him? Or whisk me away somewhere he could never find us? Did she hate me *that* much?

After swiping access to the underground lot I noticed the Mercedes was parked up in bay seven. Richard was home. I wasn't expecting him for another hour so I spent the short walk and elevator ride to the apartment conjuring up an excuse for my whereabouts. I did plan on telling him but there was really nothing to tell and he'd only worry — something I'd already caused him to do too much of.

"Hey, beautiful," Richard greeted, kissing my lips as soon as I walked in the door.

"Hey." I hugged him, hard. We'd only been apart for a few hours but I'd missed him incredibly.

"Are you okay? Where have you been?" he asked curiously. "You look upset."

"I'm fine. I just nipped out for groceries," I lied, burying my head in his shoulder so he couldn't see my face. Somehow my expression always gave me away.

"So, where are they?" he quizzed, holding me at arms length so he could study my big fat lying face.

Shit. Great excuse there, Amy.

"Oh. I, um…"

Saving Amy

"Amy..." He tilted my chin up with his finger, trying to break me with his intense gaze. "No more lies, remember?"

Busted. I exhaled in defeat.

"I went to my dad's funeral," I admitted quietly, hoping he didn't hear.

"What! Why didn't you tell me? I would've come with you." His furrowed brow oozed concern. He tucked a loose strand of hair behind my ear and kissed my forehead.

"I decided last minute. I just wanted to make sure he was finally gone, I guess. It's no big deal. I was fine on my own."

"You still should've told me. I can't support you if you shut me out, Amy." Great. Now I felt guilty on top of everything else. I had planned to visit my mom alone too, but suddenly that didn't seem like such a good idea. He was right – secrets only ever led to pain.

"I know. I'm sorry," I said, and then took a deep breath in preparation for my next revelation. "I want to go and see my mom. Will you come with me?"

"Of course I will," he said, tenderly brushing along my cheekbone with his forefinger. "When do you want to go?" I hadn't thought that far ahead. In fact I thought (maybe even hoped) he'd try and talk me out of it.

"Um... I don't know. Tonight?"

Might as well get it over and done with.

"And you're sure you want to do this?"

"Yes. I need to know what she's got to say for herself."

"Okay. Well, we'll have dinner first. I was thinking lasagna?" I really wasn't expecting him to be so accepting of my plan.

"Sounds good." Richard pulled me in for one last hug and then turned to head into the kitchen. "Richard…" I called after him and he turned back around. "Thank you." He raised one of those delicious confused eyebrows of his. "For being you," I clarified.

"For being perfect you mean?" he teased with a wink. "Oh, and not forgetting sexy as hell?" I rolled my eyes and laughed at him. If I had a pillow to hand he'd have *so* been getting it right now.

Chapter Twenty-Two

I barely touched my lasagna and the little I did manage was eaten out of guilt. I hated leaving it when Richard had gone to the trouble of preparing it from scratch but all I could think about was my impending visit to my mom and it was making me nauseous. Right now, sitting on the driveway trying to summon the courage to actually get out of the car, I was regretting the two mouthfuls I did eat. I was almost certain they wouldn't be in my stomach for much longer.

"Ready?" Richard asked, squeezing my knee encouragingly.

"Yes," I lied, because whether I was ready or not didn't actually matter. I *had* to do it.

Hand in hand we approached the arched russet door. I told Richard to prepare himself for a lengthy wait seeing as though my mom hadn't answered the door in years. I began with a gentle knock and wasn't surprised when five minutes later we were still stood outside. I knocked harder… still nothing.

"Mom! Are you in there?" I shouted while opting for the tactic of beating crap out of the door.

Richard ambled over to the bay window, stepping over the dead shriveled up flowers lining the lawn. He cupped his eyes with his hands like binoculars to block out any unnecessary light and then pressed his head against the glass.

"Ah shit! Amy, call an ambulance!" The words were like an electric shock to my heart.

"What! Why?"

"Just do it!" he yelled, hurrying over to me. "Step back."

He backed me away from the door with his forearm and then tensed his whole body as he rammed his shoulder into the wood. Nothing happened so he did it again and I covered my ears as the sound of wood crashing into his body sent me into a panic.

The stubborn door started to buckle as it peeled away from its hinges. With his arms outstretched to the sides Richard raised his leg and with one forceful karate-style kick it collapsed to the floor. He flew into the house, disappearing down the hallway and into the living room. For a moment I thought I was following him but then I realized I hadn't moved an inch.

"The ambulance, Amy!" Richard bellowed, his voice fading as it travelled through the hall. It snapped me out of the trance I'd slipped into and I pulled my cell from my pocket and dialed 911. After requesting an ambulance I was asked for the address – easy, I knew that off by heart. But then the lady on the other end asked me what the problem was and I had no idea. I also didn't think I waned to find out.

"Are you still there, ma'am?" the lady's voice asked down the line and I realized I stopped talking after giving the zip code.

"Um, yes, I'm here."

"There's an ambulance on its way to you now. Is the casualty breathing, ma'am?"

"I don't know!" *I hope so.* Don't I? *She has to be.* This couldn't be happening again. "I'll go and see."

Saving Amy

Hesitantly, I clambered over the demolished door and made my way down the hall. I paused briefly, deep breathing, blinking away impromptu tears and psyching myself up. There were no sounds coming from the living room – none whatsoever. My heart voluntarily crawled into my stomach to hide as I stepped around the doorjamb.

I immediately stumbled back, steadying myself on the door. My hand flew over my gaping mouth and my cell slipped from my ear, bouncing off the floor and splitting the casing in two. Richard was on his knees by my mom but jumped to his feet when he saw me, throwing his arms around me, shielding the horror from my vision with his body.

"No! Why aren't you helping her until the ambulance gets here?" I snapped at him, shoving him away from me. He leaned forward, cupping my face in his hands but I didn't look at him. My eyes wouldn't leave my mom.

"It's too late, Amy. Your mom is dead."

No...

I wanted to argue with him, tell him he was wrong... but looking at the lifeless body on the beige carpet, I knew there was no point.

Blood. It was everywhere. It was pooled around her wrists, seeping into the fibers of the carpet. It was soaked into the sleeves of her white gown. It was smeared across her face. It was dripping from the knife blade by her feet. It was matted in her hair, splashed up the legs of the oak coffee table, smattered onto the empty med bottles behind her head, stained onto the empty gin bottle... it was *everywhere*. And when I looked at Richard, it was all over him too.

"I can't breathe," I choked before running back outside, doubling over and spewing my guts out onto the sidewalk. I heaved and retched until my throat burned and my stomach ran dry and when I'd finished, I felt absolutely no better. Richard had been holding back my hair and when I stood up he wiped the corners of my mouth with the sleeve of his baby-blue shirt and pulled me into him.

"Cry, beautiful. Let it out," he whispered into my hair. And so I did. I cried so violently my whole body started to shake. I cried and screamed and flung my arms into his chest until my body was too weak to support me. And then I slid to the floor… dazed, confused and utterly heartbroken.

Instead of catching me, Richard slid down with me until we were sitting on the cold, damp asphalt rocking back and forth in each other's arms. Flashing lights temporarily blinded my eyes and blaring sirens deafened my ears. A police cruiser screeched to an abrupt halt in front of us, followed almost immediately by an ambulance. Richard drew me in for one last squeeze, kissed my forehead and stood up to meet the crew.

He approached the female curly-haired paramedic and instantly all traces of urgency had vanished from their footsteps. *He's told them.* He'd told them my mom was dead. My mom *and* my dad… are *dead*.

I drew my knees into my chest and sank my head into my hands. I closed my eyes and was haunted by the image of my mom, lifeless and covered in blood. So I opened them again, fixing my gaze onto the little white mailbox across the street. I could hear voices, feet shuffling against the gravel, radio-receivers, doors opening and closing… But I didn't know where it was all coming from because I refused to shift my focus from the pretty white mailbox with a little wooden bluebird perched on its roof.

It was shaped like a small wooden house with an apex roof and a brown door that opened for the mail. There was even red windows painted on the side, complete with painted yellow curtains. I wondered if the man who lived there (Mr. Dawson I think he's called) made it himself or if you could buy ready made house-shaped mailboxes with bluebirds on top. I think the bluebird had a yellow beak but it was too dark to be sure. It was so pretty. How did I never notice it before?

"Amy, let's get you home," Richard said God knows how long later, squatting beside me and enclosing me in his arms.

"I've never noticed how pretty it is before. Ours is so dull in comparison."

"What is? Amy, what are you talking about?" he asked worriedly, trying to follow my gaze.

"Would you say its beak is yellow, or is that just the street lamps?" Richard shifted his body so he was directly in front of me, holding my shoulders and blocking my view.

"Move! I can't see it! I need to see it!" I yelled at him, swinging my neck from side to side to try and see past him.

"Amy, stop," he ordered firmly, taking my face in his hands so I had no choice but to meet his gaze. "You need to get up. They're about to bring out your mom's…*body*."

"No," I said, shaking my head against his hands. "I'm not moving. I need to stay here. I need to know what color its beak is goddammit!"

"Amy, look at me!" he snapped but without a hint of anger. My eyes reluctantly found their way to his. "I'm going to lift you up now. We need to make room for the undertakers. Hold on to my neck."

Undertakers? I looked to my right and saw a glossy black van parked beside the ambulance. *When did that get here?*

Richard raised my arms and wrapped them around his neck. Instinctively I grabbed on when I felt my body being lifted off the ground. He carried me across the lawn, cradling me to his chest like a baby. Then we reached the car and he broke one arm free to open the passenger door before lithely lowering me inside.

Moments later I heard the wheels of the gurney scratching their way through the gravel. I told my eyes not to look but they betrayed me and forced me to watch the balding men in black suits wheel the black, zipped body bag into the back of their van.

My mom is in that bag. My mom is dead and she's wrapped in that bag. My mom is dead. My dad is dead. My mom and my dad are dead...

"Amy, I have something to show you. It was tucked inside your mom's hand when I found her."

I stared warily at Richard, confused and curious as he reached into the top pocket of his padded black jacket and pulled out a scrunched up, blood stained envelope.

"If you're not ready, I can keep hold of it," he said, hovering the envelope over his pocket.

Saving Amy

"No. I want to see it," I claimed, but judging by the fact I wasn't breathing, I think that might have been a lie. Uncertainly, I took the envelope, smoothing out the creases between my thumbs.

'Amelia Hope' was printed on the front in my mom's shaky handwriting. I slid my finger under the edge of the flap that hadn't been stuck down properly and gently teased open the letter. A single tear dropped onto the paper, soaking straight through it and blotching the black ink. I dried my cheeks with the sleeve of my gray sweater (well, Richard's gray sweater), took a deep breath and started to read.

My dearest Amelia,
If you're reading this, that means you opened the envelope. So for that, thank you. I wouldn't have blamed you for tossing it straight in the trash.

I would like to start by saying I am sorry. I am sorry that I allowed you to suffer. I am sorry I was too afraid to stop him. I am sorry I was too wasted to stop him. I am sorry for putting myself first. I am sorry for pretending nothing was happening. I am sorry for drinking myself numb.

I am sorry for never teaching you to smile. To laugh. Or even to cry – I'm sorry you had to learn to cry all by yourself. I am sorry for not cuddling you, kissing you, comforting you. I am sorry for not braiding your hair, singing you to sleep, holding you when you had nightmares.

I am sorry for not telling you how pretty you are – and my word you are beautiful – I hope someone else has told you. You deserve to be told every single day. I am sorry for not taking you clothes shopping for your sixteenth birthday, for not 'talking boys', for not taking you on a spa weekend. I am sorry for never telling you your skirt was too short, or grounding you, or telling you 'not to see that boy again'.

I am sorry for not telling you that I loved you. So, here it is... I love you, Amelia – my beautiful baby girl. I am sorry for everything. I am sorry for not giving you the life I had planned for you when I felt your first tiny kick in my womb. I am sorry for being too weak to protect you.

I need you to know, you were the most wanted baby girl in the world. I can't describe how happy I was to discover I was carrying you. You won't understand just now, but when you do, know that that's why I wanted to keep you with me. I loved you too much to let you go and that makes me the most selfish person in the world. I have never forgiven myself for keeping you, Amy. I thought I could keep you safe, I promised to keep you safe.

I failed.

But my biggest regret, the thing I am most sorry for, is not telling you the truth about your father. His name is Jack Monroe and everything you need to know about him is buried in the back yard under the apple tree by the shed. He is a good man, Amelia. Whatever you do, don't blame him.

It's nearly time for me to go now. There is nothing left. Jim took you from me, he took me from you, he's gambled everything we own away and I'm not strong enough to learn to live again. I'm too weak. Too tired. But I want you to know that if you can't forgive me, that's okay. That's not

Saving Amy

what this letter is about. I don't expect forgiveness, nor do I want it. I just needed to say goodbye before I set you free. Jim and I have ruined your past – DON'T LET US RUIN YOUR FUTURE.

Whatever you do in life, be happy, baby girl. Live the life I always dreamed you would. Love people and let them love you back. Believe in the impossible. Dare to dream. And smile, baby girl. Laugh until your insides ache. Live the life that was meant for that perfect little girl I first cradled in my arms at 03:42 AM on June 19th 1993. But most importantly, Amelia… don't trust anybody. That doesn't mean you can't love, just don't let love control you, baby girl - always keep a little piece of your heart locked away. My father had a saying that I never understood until it was too late…

'Love Many, Trust Few, and Always Paddle Your Own Canoe'

I love you, Amelia, and I am so, so sorry.
Mom

P.S. I know I have no right to ask anything of you, but nevertheless I hope you can find it in your heart to honor this request. Please don't let them bury me next to Jim. I would like to be cremated – gone for good. I don't care what you do with my ashes, as long as they're far, far away from Lake View. Again, I understand if you want no part in this, but I had to ask…

I'm sorry

"Amy, you're shaking," Richard said, trying to stem the quivers by rubbing my arms.

"I-I-" I could barely breathe. "He's not my father? How the fuck can he not be my father? Why the hell would she make me live with him, suffer by him… if he's not even my fucking father!"

"May I?" Richard asked, pinching the top of the tear and blood stained letter. I shoved it further into his hands – I sure as hell didn't want it anymore. Richard set his eyes down on the blotchy ink, furrowing his brow, concentrating.

"Why didn't *he* save me? If he's that much of a fucking good man why didn't he take me away? Why would he allow *them* to take care of me? Am I that goddamn fucking unlovable?"

"Amy, you're hysterical." He shifted in his seat to face me and took my hands in his.

No shit!

"You need to calm down. Breathe for me, baby."

Ignoring Richard completely, I tugged my hands free, swung my door open and jumped out of the car without bothering to close it behind me.

"Amy, you can't go in there until the police…" Richard called after me until I'd ran so far ahead I couldn't hear him anymore.

"Amy!" His voice was faint in the distance but I could tell by the tone he was shouting.

I leapt over the broken door, raced down the hall, straight past the blood-drenched living room and to the back door. Thankfully the key was nestled in the lock already so I didn't have to pause before yanking it open and bounding over the patio steps, running to the apple tree by the shed.

Saving Amy

The dirt was hard and frosted over. I dropped to my knees and started to claw away at it with my bare fingers.

"Amy, stop. We'll come back tomorrow when the ground's thawed." Richard had appeared behind me. I ignored him and carried on scratching at the earth. The frost burned my skin and my fingernails split as they scraped through gravel and shards of rock but I kept going.

"Here, let me do it." Richard prized my hands away from the dirt. I tried to fight him off until I saw he'd taken the more sensible, practical approach of busting the lock off the shed and fetching a shovel.

I fell back on my heels and watched as Richard pounded the ground with the shovel. His chest muscles flexed beneath his shirt as he forced it into the ground over and over again, using his tensed foot as leverage. He stopped when something clanked against the metal.

I flipped back onto my knees and bent forward to peer into the hole. Sure enough there was something glinting under the bright orb of the moon. Richard gave it a tap with the tip of the shovel. It sounded like metal. A tin perhaps? I brushed away the top layer of dirt with my hands and wedged my fingers between the tin and the earth, rocking it from side to side and loosening the dirt until it slid free.

It was an old square cracker tin – dented and rusty with a faded Christmas fern pattern printed all over it. Immediately I pressed my fingers into the seam and attempted to prize it open but the lid wouldn't budge. I kept trying – refusing to let myself think about the pain radiating from my frozen fingers as they started to bleed under my nails.

"We'll do it at home. Please, Amy, let me take you home now." Richard gently took the tin from me and I started to resist but then realized I was too weak to fight him. He was right - as usual. I was cold, damp, bleeding and exhausted. I needed to go home.

****

Richard ushered me straight into the bathroom when we got back and together we took an hour-long bath. It helped... a little. I was free from dirt and blood and my skin had returned to a comfortable temperature. I wished my mind could be washed clean so easily. It was so full of torment, and I was starting to think it always would be.

After wrapping myself in the fluffy pink gown that Vivienne bought for me while I was in the hospital, I headed to the living room. Richard was setting two mugs of hot chocolate and marshmallows on the coffee table, either side of the rusty cracker tin. Suddenly, it was the only thing I could see. The rest of the room and everything in it had morphed into an insignificant blur.

Richard settled himself on the edge of the couch and patted the space next to him for me to join him. I did, and for the next few minutes we both stared in silence at the conspicuous tin.

"Do you think she was telling the truth? Do you really think he wasn't my dad?" I asked Richard, my eyes refusing to leave the tin - almost as if they were afraid it would disappear.

Saving Amy

"There's only one way to find out," he said. "Open it."

I lifted the tin onto my lap, noticing that Richard had cleaned it. Then I closed my eyes and counted to ten in my head, sucking in a deep breath with each number. When I opened my eyes I ran what was left of my fingernails along the groove, and now that the dirt had been rinsed away it flipped effortlessly back on its hinges.

Inside there were papers, letters, photographs and… my birth certificate. Or was it mine? The birth date was correct but it said my name was Amelia Anne Monroe. I slumped back in my seat before I fell back involuntarily.

"*Amy?*" Richard pressed, concern clouding his beautiful eyes. "What is it?"

"I'm not sure. I think it's my birth certificate." I cast it one last glance, noting my mother's name – Mary Anne Monroe – and the father was listed (just like the letter said) as Jack Edmund Monroe.

They were married? I thought as I handed the tatty certificate to Richard.

"I've seen my birth certificate though. I'm sure I have. When I applied for my drivers license for instance…"

"Well, your father – or *Jim*- was a lawyer. I'm sure it wouldn't have posed that big of a problem to get a fake one drawn up."

Of course. Duh.

Richard was biting his lip, his eyebrows heavy as he intently studied the birth certificate.

"What is it?" I asked, lightly grabbing his forearm.

"It's just, um, I've seen this before," he admitted casually like it was last month's copy of Cosmo.

"What! When did you – how did you - did you know all along?"

"No!" he protested, flipping his body to face me and taking my hands. "When you were gone, I wondered if you'd tried to look for your grandmother, that maybe you were there. And while-"

"But she's dead," I interrupted, the words panging in my heart.

"I know. But, I *didn't* know - neither did you, remember? Could you really take your fath- *Jim's* word for it?"

"So, she's alive? Richard, are you telling me she's alive!" I bounced up and down on my seat, smiling in anticipation. But then the lugubrious expression taking over Richard's face made my smile fade.

"No, Amy. She's not. I'm sorry." My heart had twisted into a reef knot and it was like I'd just lost her all over again.

"But you see, to help me find her I had to look for you, but it was like you didn't exist. The closest I came was this exact same certificate – the date tallied, as did your mother's name and your forenames, but then the father… I just assumed it wasn't you and discarded it as a dead end."

"When did she die? What killed her? Would she have suffered?" I fired at him, my mind still grieving the fresh loss of my grandma. This was the third time I had lost her. First when I was nine or ten, then when I discovered Jim wasn't my father

Saving Amy

therefore she wasn't technically my grandmother, and then now… I kept my eyelids forced open, knowing if I blinked I would cry and not be able to stop.

"She died in 2008…"

"2008!" I yelled as though it was Richard's fault. "Sorry. I just… I can't believe Jim lied to me about something like that." As soon as I spoke the words I realized they were ridiculous. Of course he was capable of such a thing. "So, did she suffer?" I repeated.

"No. She died of a massive stroke. It would have been very quick. She wouldn't have felt any pain," he stated very matter-of-fact, assessing me with his eyes.

"My whole life just seems like one big fat lie," I said, deflated.

"Not your *whole* life. If there's one truth you can count on, it's that I love you," he said as he cupped my face in his hands and kissed my forehead. I smiled, I *think*, before flicking my eyes back to the tin of dishonesty.

I sifted through the photographs, straightening the worn, bent edges between my fingers. At first glance I didn't recognize anyone in them, but then I noticed how much the woman resembled my mom. She looked young – early twenties at a guess. Her black hair was curled all the way down to her lower back and she was full figured in all the right places. Her skin was pale, flawless like porcelain and… she was *smiling*. I'd never seen her smile before. She looked… *beautiful*.

The woman who I was almost sure was my mom was holding a young girl – two years old, three maybe – with straight glossy blonde hair settling on her shoulders, big golden eyes and an adorable smile. She was looking up at my mom with such fondness in her eyes. It was only a picture but you could see how much they adored each other. A man stood next to my mom and the girl with his arms stretched around them both. He was tall with the same gold eyes and blonde hair as the little girl and a very out dated moustache.

"This must have been taken before I was born," I said, passing the photo to Richard. "Do you think that's him? Do you think that's my father?"

Richard shrugged his shoulders, studying the picture while I picked another one up from the tin. This one had the same man crouching beside the same little girl – though she looked a little younger. They were hugging and looked to be in some kind of zoo.

"Um, Amy, have you seen this?" Richard passed the photo back to me. It was flipped over with something written on the back in my mom's handwriting.

Me, Jack and Amy. September 12th '95.

"That *can't* be me," I breathed, feeling winded. "I'd remember."

"Amy, you'd have been, what? Two?"

I flipped the photo back over and stared at the little girl. There was no denying she looked like me, but it couldn't be… she was too happy. And she *loved* my mom. I shuffled faster through the photographs. They were all of the same three people. Each one full of smiles and laughter and love. I couldn't let myself believe that little girl was me – it only made the idea that I could have been spared my horrific

Saving Amy

upbringing, the idea that I used to be *normal*, so much harder to bear.

I set the photos down in a neat pile on the coffee table and unfolded a letter. It was written with black ink in handwriting I didn't recognize on yellow paper (although I think it used to be white).

Dear, Mary,
Please don't do this to me. Please don't take my baby girl from me. Access – that's all I want. Twice a week, once a week, once a goddamn month - I'll take anything! Please don't keep her from me Mary. I'm begging you with all my heart. I've accepted that you're moving on, that you don't love me anymore – but do you really hate me this much? This is killing me Mary. I love her. I NEED her! Please let me see my little Amy. PLEASE.
Jack

Going off the letter it sounded like he actually gave a shit. But I knew that couldn't be true because according to the sloppily written address in the corner he only lived in Boise, Idaho. That was what, a seven hour drive maybe? An hour on a flight? Obviously too far out of his way to come and save me. I rolled my eyes, handed the letter to Richard and picked up the next one.

Mary,
What the hell kind of lawyer is he? I can't find a single attorney willing to help me take him on, but then I'm sure you're well aware of that. I WANT ACCESS TO MY DAUGHTER! Just call me, PLEASE. Use a payphone if you don't want me

knowing your number – I don't care. Just call! We can sort this out. It's gone too far. We used to love each other didn't we? I was a good husband and a great father. This isn't fair and you know it. I need my girl back Mary. I'm begging you.
Jack

The envelopes were missing so with no postmark I had no idea when the letters were sent. I started to wonder how long I knew him for, how long I *loved* him for, how long I belonged to a *real* family for.

How long it took him to give up on me?

There was one letter left. The ink was blotchy as if it'd been cried over. I wondered whose tears they were, his or hers.

Mary,
I promise this is the last time. You've won. HE'S won. I just need you to promise me one thing – please don't let him hurt our baby. Whatever he's done to me, whatever he's STILL doing to you – promise you'll keep her safe. She's our little girl Mary. Our little Amy. She's almost five now and as much as it breaks my heart, I know she probably doesn't remember me anymore. But I also want you to promise that if you ever get the chance, please tell her how much I love her, and that I'll never EVER stop thinking about her.

How did things get here Mary? How did life become so unbearable?
Jack

Fresh tear stained splodges marked the paper as I read it. I dropped it onto my lap and willingly

Saving Amy

allowed my tears to flow. He gave up. He stopped trying. He abandoned me. He left me to suffer.

"I don't know who I am anymore," I said with a hollow heart. I felt lost, empty… everything and everyone I ever knew had been a lie.

"You're Amy," Richard said, enfolding me in his arms, "*My* Amy. My beautiful, strong, brave, fucked-up little Amy." I could feel the muscles in his cheeks turn up into a smile against my forehead. "And I love you more than life itself."

I buried my face into his chest, sobbing into his black, fleecy gown. We stayed like this for what could've been forever. He stroked my hair and shushed me until my tears ran dry and I fell into an exhausted, overwhelmed sleep.

****

It was Thanksgiving - my first Thanksgiving where I actually had something to be thankful for. This year, for the first time ever, I was thankful to be alive. I was thankful for knowing the meaning of happiness, of love, of friendship, of courage… and I was most thankful for the person who made all of those things possible – I was thankful for Richard. And, I never thought I'd say it, but I was also thankful for Richard's pre-existing friendship with Vanessa. Hence the reason I was also thankful I had my job back. Last but not least, I was thankful that this godforsaken, itchy and sweaty as hell cast was coming off my hand in three days.

After quite a lengthy battle with my subconscious, I eventually decided not to look for my real father. I'd not ruled it out forever, but right now I was just too bitter, too hurt. If he loved me as much as he said her did, he would have saved me, right? No matter what the cost or consequences.

I didn't reach my decision until the day of my mom's funeral. I attended her cremation as an official mourner instead of skulking behind bushes. In fact, Richard and I were the *only* people to attend. She said in her letter she was setting me free and although I couldn't deny her suicide and my dad's (well, *Jim's*) death hit me hard – harder than it should, harder than *they* deserved it too– I did in fact feel free, exonerated even. I felt lighter, calmer, *hopeful…*

And so, I decided I needed a break from parents. So far all three had let me down, allowed me to suffer, scarred me in every way imaginable – and so (possibly selfishly) I don't want to find my father. I don't *need* a father. I don't need anyone except the man who saved my life – Richard.

Richard took me to visit my grandmother's grave at Lake View yesterday. I must have walked by it dozens of times in the past without a clue. All those times I missed her or wanted to talk to her, and she was right there. I'll never forgive Jim for keeping me away from her. The pain of knowing I missed out on four extra years with the only woman who ever loved me – or at least *showed* it - hurt far more than any beating he had to offer me.

Her headstone was so small and impersonal. It was a tiny gray oblong stone, which stood no higher than my calves. On it was my grandmother's name, date of birth and date of death – that's it. No 'Loving Mother', no 'Rest in Peace'… *nothing*. Richard suggested we get it replaced to which I immediately

Saving Amy

agreed, and so we were planning a visit to the monumental mason's after the holidays.

Julie was back home for the holidays and she only admitted yesterday that she would be staying here in Seattle indefinitely after being kicked out of college. I wasn't as surprised as I should've been. Every conversation between us centered around parties and boys – not once did I hear her talk about classes or studying.

She told me the news during my lunch break at work yesterday. This was also when she met Rob for the first time and decided that he was gorgeous in an Alex Pettyfer kind of way and she wanted to have his babies. Poor Rob. He was totally doomed.

Joanna had shown her first shred of decency since I'd known her and stayed the hell away from me. Richard wasn't so lucky of course - he still had to work with her. But as far as I knew (and as far as I *wanted* to know) their relationship was strictly professional.

Everything just seems to have slotted into place like a jigsaw puzzle. I am living a life I never deemed possible – a life filled with even more hope and happiness than in the endings of my favorite books. Will it last? I have no idea. But if there is one thing this year has taught me, it's that I'm strong enough to get through whatever shit life tries to throw at me. And you know what, I've finally accepted that I do deserve to be happy. I've taken my fair share of crap and then some – it's about time life cut me some slack.

"I've been thinking," I said to Richard when he strolled into the living room all half-naked and wet after his shower. *Yummy…* "I want to change my name."

"*Why?* I like the name Amy," he said seriously, wrestling with his lips to stop them turning up into a smile.

"My surname, douchebag."

"*Douchebag?* Seriously? Sorry, what grade are we in again?" I pouted, fighting against my own smile and then threw a cream, feather cushion at him.

"So that's how you wanna play, huh?"

Uh oh…

Richard charged towards me and I stepped from side to side, trying to outsmart him. I blocked his path by running behind the coffee table but then in a move I was totally not expecting, he leapt straight over it and wrestled me to the ground – losing his towel along the way.

"Hmm, naked wrestling? I kinda like it," I teased with a wink.

"Only problem is, only one of us is naked," he teased back, unbuttoning my shirt and kissing the exposed skin underneath.

I decided to tell him to stop in a minute, mindful that we were due at his parent's dining table in an hour. He'd undone all but one button when I decided to give him just *one* more minute. Damn, now my bra was unfastened. *Maybe, two more…* Crap, he'd only gone and slid my skirt straight off my legs. *Okay, just one more… ah, fuck it.*

****

"We really need to think about getting our asses into gear. We're already running late," I said breathlessly, studying his hypnotic green eyes and fiddling with his hair as we lay spent and naked side by side on the living room floor.

"Do we have to?" he uttered in his best sulky teenager impression.

"You know we do. Your mom's going to a lot of effort.

"Oh, please, my mom's never made an effort in her life as far as catering's concerned. The hardest part of her day will be telling Gracie whether she wants boiled or roasted carrots."

"Oh, Richard!" I swiped him with a cushion again. Thankfully, he didn't retaliate.

"So, your name? What do you want to change it to?" Richard asked inquisitively. I suspected he was just stalling – he hated Thanksgiving dinner, what with his mom inviting half the world and their plus one. Apparently he got 'face ache' from all the fake smiling.

"I'm not sure. I don't even know how I'd go about it. 'Hope' just feels… *wrong* somehow. Especially when my life has held anything *but*. And of course, technically that's not my real name anyway. That name was forced upon me."

"So, you're thinking about using the name you were born with? Monroe?"

"No," I said flatly, shaking my head. "That doesn't feel right either. I remember nothing of that life. That's not who I am. Besides, I don't think I want anything that's passed down through my line of fucked-up parents. I want something new. Something…"

"How about HotAss? Yeah, Amy HotAss. I like it!"

"Seriously, you want another piece of this?" I teased, holding up the same cushion responsible for landing us here – lying cold and naked on a hardwood floor.

"Don't tempt me, beautiful." He winked at me and I rolled my eyes – purposely avoiding eye contact with him, because I knew if I allowed myself to look at him, I wouldn't be able to resist pouncing on him.

"Wait there. I have an idea." Richard jumped to his feet before I had chance to ascertain the expression on his mighty fine face.

I sat up and grabbed his damp towel that was still draped over the coffee table before wrapping it around myself. He returned almost immediately with one hand tucked mysteriously behind his back.

"How about Lewis?" he asked with a suggestive grin.

What? I was pretty sure my expression conveyed my confusion.

"I was going to wait until after Thanksgiving dinner… but it seems I am very much lacking in the self-control department." He smiled at me, but it was a nervous smile I had never seen before. Then he dropped down on one knee in front of me and brought his arm, mottled with goosebumps, out of hiding. He was holding a small gray velvet box in his hands.

Holy shit.

"Amy, I love you. I have loved you since the day you woke up in my guest room, and I will love you beyond forever. I promise to always take care of you, protect you, and make you happy. Will you do me the great honor of changing your surname to Lewis, and becoming my wife?"

Ho. Ly. Fu. Ck.

My jaw slammed into my chest as a thousand different thoughts and emotions exploded inside my head. A thousand thoughts which all revolved around how to say... yes.

I watched Richard intently as he pressed his finger into the seam of the velvet box and slowly teased open the lid. Inside, resting on a bed of silver satin, lay a single dazzling diamond nestled into the center of a stunning white gold ring.

Wow.

"Yes!" I squealed and I was almost sure it was a noise that could only be understood in the animal kingdom. I threw myself onto him, knocking him to the floor. "Yes! Yes! Yes!"

"I love you, Amy. You have just made me the proudest man alive!" He took my face in his hands and kissed me with a whole new intensity.

"I love you too."

Wow. I was engaged. I was to marry the man who saved my life in every way possible. The man who saved me from my past and rescued my future.

And... he was gloriously naked!

Epilogue

Six Years Later…

"DON'T TOUCH ME!" I roared when Richard tried to take hold of my hand. Why the hell did I let him do this to me again?

"It's okay, baby. You're doing great. Remember to breathe."

"*You* fucking breathe!" I blasted.

The pain was excruciating – like an industrial vice tightening around my belly. I cried and whimpered and screamed and swore and thumped Richard as hard as I could whenever he came within touching distance.

"You're doing really well, Amy. I can see the head… Next time you feel a contraction coming, I need you to push right down into your bottom for me," my midwife, Andrea, told me.

It came on cue – the torturous pain that ripped my insides apart. Everyone seemed to prattle on at me about the importance of breathing, but how could I breathe when it felt like a giant pumpkin was trying to force its way out of my ass? So I did it my own way and held my breath. Then I pushed… hard. I pushed until the veins in my neck felt like they were about to explode under the pressure. I pushed until my legs started to tremble. I pushed until it felt like a glass bomb had detonated inside my ass…

"Jesus, baby… he's almost here!" Richard wailed, sounding utterly awestruck.

Saving Amy

"ARRRGGGGGGH!" I pushed again, my entire body juddering violently – the pressure between my legs unbearable.

And then it was gone… the pain, the pressure, the stinging…

In the time it took me to breathe one breath, my whole world had changed and I was a mom for the second time.

"Oh my God," Richard breathed. "You did it! You did it, baby!"

My newborn son was laid gently onto my bare chest – the lumpy, purplish cord still connecting us. My mouth dropped open as I took in the sight of him. His chubby cheeks smeared with blood and gore, his tiny blue eyes blinking as they struggled to accustom themselves to the light, his cone-shaped head adorned with Richard's rich auburn hair, his perfect little fingers wrapped around my pinky…

He was beautiful.

Perfect.

I loved him so much my heart physically ached.

I saw Andrea cut my baby's cord from the corner of my eye as Richard perched himself on the edge of my hospital bed and wrapped his arm around my shoulder – his eyes never leaving his son.

"Welcome to the world, little man. I'm your daddy," Richard murmured, pure adoration dripping from his voice. In that moment I noticed a solitary tear trickle slowly down his cheek and taking one hand off our son, I wiped it away, smiling lovingly at my husband.

"Thank you," he whispered. "Thank you for my children. I'm so proud of you."

My eyes grazed over the scars on my arm while I stared up and down the length of my perfect child. I wear them with pride now. They are a reminder of how far I've come. A symbol of what I've been through, what I've achieved. They're a part of me, who I've been and who I am now. They give me strength, peace. Looking at them I no longer feel disgust, or guilt. Instead I feel content, grateful. Safe in the knowledge I never have to suffer what brought me to inflict them on myself ever again.

And that's exactly what I tell the young people I work with at Vivienne's Finding Hope charity. I started by sitting in on group sessions until I found the courage to speak out about my own experiences with everything from abuse, to drugs to self-injury. The more time that passed the stronger I became... the more I learned about myself and my issues. Now I run my own sessions two days a week and each and every attendee knows they can contact me directly whenever they need support or guidance from someone who truly understands them.

It's important they have someone to reach out to that isn't too close – someone unemotionally involved. There's no guilt that way. Talking to someone detached and unbiased is so much easier. There's no fear of them judging or pitying you. No fear of *hurting* them with your honesty. And that's why I still see my therapist once a week without fail, and probably always will.

I may not cut anymore, but I'll always be a cutter.

When I'm not busy with the charity, my full time job remains at Salt House as Junior Editor, under Vanessa Heart. It is without a doubt my dream role and I am absolutely loving it. When I'm not busy reading or promoting other people's work I am writing my own, and now have four successfully published novels under my belt. Apart from my wedding day and the birth of my precious children, the day I made the New York Times Bestsellers List was the proudest of my life.

Life is beyond wonderful. Who'd have thought it?

We sat in silence for what could have been hours, our eyes never leaving those of baby Jack. We relished those first moments of being just us, before the rest of the world wanted a piece of the perfect little bundle sleeping soundly against my breast.

"Daddy!" Kate beamed as she skipped into the room to meet her baby brother for the first time. An entourage followed, with Vivienne, Alexander, David and Bethany trailing behind my daughter's feet.

"There you are, princess. I've got someone who wants to say hi to you," Richard said, bending down and scooping Kate in his arms. He spun her around a couple of times before carrying her over to the crib where baby Jack lay sleeping beside me. She stared at him for a few seconds, looking rather unimpressed.

"He no say anything," she muttered, seeming irritated. Richard laughed softly as he swept her blond hair from her eyes.

"He's thinking it, princess. He's thinking what a beautiful, smart big sister he's got. He just needs someone to teach him how to talk. You think you can help him with that?"

"Sure, daddy. Me good at being teacher," she stated proudly, flashing every one of her tiny, brilliant white teeth. She is adorable. Perfect. My children are perfect. My *family* is perfect.

Getting bored with the fact her baby brother didn't do anything interesting, Kate settled in beside me on the bed. I wrapped my arms around her and held her close, telling her what a big girl she was for sharing her mommy and daddy with Jack.

"He's beautiful," Vivienne cooed, tears welling up in her eyes as she peered over the crib. "Can I?" she asked, holding out her hands to pick him up.

"Of course," I nodded.

"Me next!" Bethany sang, smiling and whispering high-pitched gibberish to her nephew. Alexander sauntered over, peering over at the baby in his wife's arms.

"Well done, son," he said firmly, followed by a masculine cough. Alexander wasn't one for expressing his emotions very well, but the glassy glint in his eyes said more than words ever could. He loved his family without question, and with a single glance in Richard's direction, it was clear just how proud he was of him.

"Why's his head shaped all funny? He looks weird," David commented bluntly, causing Vivienne to tut and roll her eyes and me and Richard to laugh. Richard flipped into doctor mode and started explaining in great detail about baby's skulls being malleable to allow them to pass through the birth canal more easily.

"Dammit, Dicky Boy, too much information!" he said, wrinkling his face with unease from hearing the word vagina. I wonder if David will ever reach puberty sometimes…

Saving Amy

There was a knock on the door followed by Julie's head popping into the room. When she saw me she rushed in excitedly, clapping her hands together and smiling so hard her lips almost cracked. After kissing my cheek briefly and patting the top of Kate's head, she scurried straight to Vivienne – holding out her arms as the game of Pass The Baby began.

Rob trailed behind her, looking altogether terrified as he watched his fiancée fuss over my tiny baby. Julie got her wicked way with Rob just three weeks after moving back to Seattle and they've been together ever since. Julie's tenacity coupled with Rob's warped sense of humor makes for a rather interesting, and at times downright entertaining couple.

"He's gorgeous. I want one!" Julie enthused, her eyes unable to leave Jack – just like everyone else. Rob's face was comical. I could literally see the blood drain from his cheeks, leaving him paler than the white wall he was leaning against.

"Whoa, whoa, whoa… we said we'd start with a dog," he interjected – panic causing his body to stiffen. Everyone in the room giggled at his nervousness. Everyone except Julie who gave him a firm wait-till-I-get-you-home glare.

Pass The Baby continued and little Jack ended up in Bethany's arms. She sang and whispered to him, staring at him like he was the most precious thing in the world. Which he is… he and his big sister are the most important people ever to breathe.

I still find myself staring at Bethany some days, unable to comprehend how she grew up so fast without me noticing. She only has a year to go before she gets her teaching degree, she's been steadily dating a nice young guy called Darren for over a year and they are even looking for a house together.

"Your dad just called. He's on his way," Julie said, plopping down into a visitor chair Rob had just dragged in from the corridor. I smiled, excited to introduce my dad to his new grandson.

I decided to look for Jack when I found out I was carrying Kate. I suddenly felt this absurd desire to know who I was, where I came from – where Kate came from. I didn't expect it to turn out how it did though. I never believed I could really forgive him for abandoning me - that was if he even *wanted* my forgiveness. It was always etched in the back of my mind that he might not even want me anymore.

He was easy to find. He'd never moved from the address in the letters I found buried in the back yard. He said that was intentional, that he always prayed I'd try and find him one day. He'd never remarried or had more children. He said it felt like a betrayal to even consider it, which left me feeling sad and possibly a little guilty. He'd wasted so many years, alone and heart broken, because he couldn't move on from the wife and daughter who were so cruelly snatched away from him.

It didn't take me long to forgive him. The first time he wrapped his arms around me I fell automatically into them. Bizarrely it felt like home – like I *knew* him, like he was a part of me.

To this day I don't think he forgives himself however. By the time Jim had finished with him he spent three months in traction with half his body's bones shattered. And then, as an extra gesture… Jim had fabricated a whole case against him, saying that my mom was forced to leave him after he repeatedly beat and raped her. With Jim's connections it wouldn't have been difficult to conjure up some fake evidence, and of course my mom would do or say anything he told her to out of fear.

The way I see it, Jack was left with no choice. He could lose me, or lose his whole life and reputation… *still* without me in it. He couldn't win either way. Jim was too powerful a man to take on. But Jack has spent the last twenty years believing he was weak and selfish. That the fact he was afraid meant he was a poor excuse for a man, even less a father. That he should've fought harder – took whatever was coming to him if it meant I didn't grow up thinking he didn't care.

Maybe I did think that for a while… but not now. I have suffered too much pain, and loss, guilt and hatred in my life to hold on to anything negative. He is here now. He is a wonderful, natural grandfather and he is trying his utmost to be a good dad too. That is all that matters to me.

After two more rounds of Pass The Baby our visitor's left us alone. My dad called to say he was running late after getting stuck in traffic so it was just me, Richard and our two beautiful children while we waited for him.

Richard was propped up behind me on the bed, Kate had fallen asleep curled up in my lap and Jack was trying to get his head around taking a bottle in my arms.

"You make me the proudest man alive you know that?" Richard breathed straight into my ear. "I will never get tired of loving you."

My heart swelled, literally aching with the love I felt for these precious people surrounding me.

"Thank you," I replied, arching my neck so I could brush his lips with mine. "For saving me."

The End.

Acknowledgements

As always, I would like to thank my wonderful family for all their love and support. Especially my parents for providing me with such creative genes!

Thank you to my husband Michael for always believing in me and telling me daily I can do anything I set my mind to. For looking after our wonderful children whilst I'm hiding out in my own world with my fictional friends and for putting up with me whilst I ramble on about my constantly changing dreams and ideas.

Thank you to my beautiful children for being perfect (most of the time!) and for being excited about the fact that "Mum is an author!" Thank you for leaving me alone and taking your squabbles to your dad whilst I'm tapping away on the computer and thank you for the kisses and cuddles when I am done for the day.

Thank you to all the amazing bloggers out there who continue to support me every single day. I love and appreciate you all so much.

Thank you to James at Cover Designs by humblenations.com for my beautiful cover.

Thank you to my sister in law and best friend in the whole world, Keeley Wall. Thank you for being as fun and immature as I am! Thank you for your encouragement, advice and for all the hours spent dreaming about our book boyfriends together. Love you to the moon and back!

Nicola Haken

Finally, thank you to all my readers. You guys continue to amaze me every single day by reading my books and I love and appreciate each and every one of you!

About the Author

I know technically this should be in third person but writing about myself like that feels kind of stupid so I'll just tell you a bit about myself instead!

I was born in Rochdale, England and have lived there my entire life – therefore I hope my use of English spelling doesn't put off all my fabulous readers from across the pond! A true home bird I still live there, just a few doors down from my parents and a few up from my sister and her family, with my wonderful husband. I am a full time mum to my four delightful (sometimes!) children and our Heinz 57 puppies, Pippa and Gio (named after one of my favourite vampires, Giovanni Vecchio from The Elemental Mysteries series by Elizabeth Hunter.)

When I'm not busy being a mum/housewife/all round slave or studying towards my degree in English Literature I can usually be found with either a laptop or kindle stuck in front of my face. Sometimes – if I'm feeling particularly wild – I might even have a real-life paperback there instead!

All in all I'm just your ordinary mum spending my days doing ordinary mum things. Unless I'm reading or writing of course and then I can be whoever I want to be! And that's usually someone young, slim and gorgeous with a hot muscly man on her arm ;-)

Nicola Haken

Other Titles by Nicola Haken

Missing Pieces
Take My Hand
Hold On Tight (Take My Hand #2)
Lean On Me (Take My Hand #3)

Thank you for reading. You are amazing!

Fancy knowing what's going down in the world of Nicola? Stalk me on Facebook and Twitter, or visit my website!

www.facebook.com/nicolahaken

Twitter I.D. @NicolaHaken

www.nicolahaken.net

Printed in Great Britain
by Amazon.co.uk, Ltd.,
Marston Gate.